STATE OF MIND

JOHN KATZENBACH

STATE OF MIND

BALLANTINE BOOKS
NEW YORK

http://www.randomhouse.com

Library of Congress Cataloging-in-Publication Data
Katzenbach, John.
State of mind / John Katzenbach.—1st ed.
p.   cm.
ISBN 0-345-38631-0
I. Title
[PS3561.A7778S73   1997]
813′.54—dc21   97-1415

Text design by Ann Gold

Manufactured in the United States of America

First Edition: August 1997

10 9 8 7 6 5 4 3 2 1

"I wanted the ideal animal to hunt," explained the general. "So I said: 'what are the attributes of an ideal quarry?' And the answer was, of course: 'it must have courage, cunning, and above all, it must be able to reason.' "

"But no animal can reason," objected Rainsford.

"My dear fellow," said the general, "there is one that can."

—Richard Connell, "The Most Dangerous Game"

PROLOGUE:
THE WOMAN OF PUZZLES

Her mother, who was dying, slept fitfully in an adjacent room. It was nearly midnight, and the air around her was stirred slowly by a ceiling fan that seemed only to rearrange the day's leftover heat.

The old-fashioned jalousie window was cracked open to the licorice night. A moth beat itself desperately against the window screen, seemingly determined to kill itself. She watched it for a moment, wondering whether it was attracted by the light, as the poets and romantics thought, or whether, in truth, it hated the light, and had launched itself in a hopeless attack against the source of its frustration.

She could feel a thin rivulet of sweat creeping between her breasts, and she mopped at it with her T-shirt, all the time refusing to remove her eyes from the single sheet of paper resting on the desktop in front of her.

It was cheap white paper. The words were written in simple block print.

THE FIRST PERSON POSSESSES THAT
WHICH THE SECOND PERSON HID.

She leaned back in her desk chair, tapping a ballpoint pen against the tabletop like a drummer trying to find a rhythm. It was not uncommon for her to receive notes and poems in the mail, all written in wildly varying codes and cryptograms, all concealing some sort of message. Usually these

1

were testimonials of love, or desire, or merely an effort to force a meeting. Sometimes they were obscene. Occasionally they were challenges, a message designed to be so complicated, so obscure, that she was stumped. This was, after all, what she did for a living, and so she did not think it totally unfair when one of her readers turned the tables on her.

But what made this particular message unsettling was that it had not been sent to her mailbox at the magazine. Nor had it come over the electronic mail slot on her office computer. The letter had been stuck that day into the sun-beaten, rusty box at the end of their driveway so that she'd find it as she arrived home from work in the evening. And, unlike almost all the other messages she was used to decoding, there was no signature, no return address. The envelope hadn't been stamped.

She did not like the idea that someone knew where she lived.

Most of the people who played the games she invented were harmless. Computer programmers. Academics. Accountants. The occasional policeman, lawyer, or physician. She had come to recognize many of them through the distinctive ways their minds worked when they solved her puzzles, which often had the same uniqueness as a fingerprint. She'd even come to the point where she could guess which of the regulars would be successful with certain kinds of games; some were expert at cryptograms and anagrams. Others excelled in discerning literary mysteries, identifying obscure quotations, or fitting lesser known authors with historical events. They were the sorts who did their Sunday crossword puzzles in pen.

Of course, there were a few of the others as well.

She was always alert for the people who found their paranoia in every hidden message. Or who discovered hatred and anger in every mind maze she created.

No one is truly harmless, she told herself. Not anymore.

And on weekends she took a semiautomatic pistol back into a mangrove swamp not far from the run-down, single-story, two-bedroom, cinder-block house she had shared for most of her life with her mother, and made herself into an expert.

She looked down at the hand-delivered note and felt an unpleasant tightening in her stomach. She opened her desktop drawer and removed a short-barreled .357 Magnum revolver from its case, placing it on the desk beside her computer screen. It was one of a half-dozen weapons she owned, a collection that included a fully automatic assault rifle, loaded, hung from a peg in the back of her clothes closet.

Out loud, she said: "I do not like that you know who I am and where I live. That is not part of the game."

She grimaced, thinking she'd been careless, and told herself that she would find where the leak had occurred—what secretary or editorial assistant had given out her home address—and take whatever steps necessary to plug it. She was devoted to her secrecy and considered it not merely a necessary part of her job, but of her life as well.

She looked at the words in the note. Though pretty certain it was not a numerical code, she did some quick calculations, fixing alphabet numbers to each letter, then subtracting and adding, probing variations, to see if she could make any sense of the note. This was almost instantly fruitless. Everything she tried was gibberish.

She clicked on her computer and slid in a diskette containing famous quotations, but found nothing even remotely similar.

She decided she needed a glass of water, and rose from her seat and went into the small kitchen. There was a clean glass drying next to the sink, and she filled it with ice and tap water, which had a slightly briny taste. She scrunched up her nose and thought that it was one of the smaller prices one paid for living in the Upper Keys. The larger prices were paid out in isolation and loneliness.

She paused in the doorway, staring across the room at the sheet of paper, and wondered why this particular note was making her lose sleep. She heard her mother groan and turn in her bed, and knew immediately that the older woman was awake even before she heard the words: "Susan? Are you there?"

"Yes, Mother," she said slowly.

She hurried into her mother's bedroom. Once, there had been color there; her mother liked to paint, and for years had kept stacks of her paintings piled up against the walls. Paints and exotic, flowing, colorful dresses and scarves, tossed about haphazardly, hanging from an easel. But these had been shoved aside by trays of medications and an oxygen machine, shunted into closets, replaced by signs of infirmity. She thought the room no longer even smelled like her mother; now it simply smelled antiseptic. Scrubbed. A clean, whitewashed, dully disinfected place to die.

"Does it hurt?" the daughter asked. She always asked this, and she knew the answer and knew that her mother would not reply truthfully.

Her mother struggled to sit upright. "Just a little bit. It's not too bad."

"Do you want a pill?"

"No. I'll be okay. I was thinking about your brother."

"Do you want me to call him for you?"

"No. It will just worry him. I'm sure he's too busy, and he needs his rest."

"I don't think so. He'd probably rather talk with you."

"Well, perhaps tomorrow. I was just dreaming about him. And you, too, dear. Dreaming about my children. Let's let him sleep. You, too. Why are you up?"

"I was working."

"Were you inventing another contest? What will it be this time? Quotes? Anagrams? What sort of clues do you have in mind?"

"No, not one of my own. I was working on something someone sent me."

"You have so many fans."

"It's not me they like, Mother. It's the puzzles."

"It needn't be. You should take more credit. You shouldn't have to hide."

"There are plenty of reasons for using a pseudonym, Mother. And you know them all."

The older woman leaned back against her pillow. It was not so much that she was old, as it was that she'd been ravaged by the disease. Her skin was flaccid, hanging around her neck, and her hair was loose, tumbling chaotically across the white sheets behind her. She still had auburn hair; her daughter helped her color it once a week, an hour they both looked forward to. The older woman did not have much vanity left; cancer had robbed her of most of that. But she would not give up her hair coloring, and her daughter was glad she wouldn't.

"I like the name you chose. It's sexy."

The daughter laughed. "A lot sexier than I am."

"Mata Hari. The spy."

"Yeah, but not the best, you know. They caught her and she got shot."

Her mother snorted, and her daughter smiled, thinking if only she could find more ways of making her mother laugh, then the disease would not spread so quickly.

The older woman rolled her eyes skyward, as if she could find a memory in the ceiling, and then spoke eagerly:

"There was a story, you know—I read it in a book, when I was still little myself—that just before the French officer gave the firing squad the command to fire, Mata Hari tore open her blouse, baring her breasts, as if daring the soldiers to ruin such perfection. . . ."

The mother closed her eyes briefly, as if recalling the memory took an effort, and the daughter sat on the side of the bed and picked up her hand.

"But they still shot. How sad. Just like men, I guess."

The two women grinned together for just a moment.

"It's just a name, Mother. And a good one for the person who creates magazine puzzles."

The mother nodded. "I think I will take that pill," she said. "And tomorrow, we'll call your brother. We'll make him tell us about killers. Maybe he knows why those French soldiers obeyed the command to fire. I'm sure he'll have some theory. That will be entertaining." The mother coughed a small laugh.

"That would be fine." The daughter reached over to a tray and opened a vial of capsules.

"Maybe two," her mother said.

The daughter hesitated, then poured the two pills into her hand. Her mother opened her mouth, and the daughter gently placed the pills on her tongue. Then she propped her mother up and held her own cup of water to the older woman's lips.

"Tastes terrible," the mother said. "When I was young, did you know, we could drink straight from the streams in the Adirondacks? Just reach down and scoop the clearest, coolest water right from your feet up to your lips. The water was thick and heavy; it was like eating when you swallowed it. It was cold. Lovely, clear, and very cold."

"Yes. You've told me—many times," the daughter gently responded. "It isn't that way anymore. Nothing is. Now, try to get some sleep. You need to rest."

"Everything here is so hot. It's always hot. Sometimes I can't tell the difference, you know, between how hot my body is and the air around us."

She paused, then added: "Just one more time, you know, I'd love to taste that water again."

The daughter lowered her mother's head to the pillow and waited while the woman's eyes fluttered, then closed. She snapped off the bedside lamp and returned to her own room. For a moment she looked around, wishing there was something in it that wasn't utilitarian and ordinary, or as heartless as the pistol waiting on her computer table. Something that spoke to who she was, or who she wanted to be.

But she could find nothing. Instead, the note stared back at her.

THE FIRST PERSON POSSESSES THAT
WHICH THE SECOND PERSON HID.

You're just tired, she thought. You've been working hard, and it's been too hot for this late in the hurricane season. Far too hot. And there are still large storms swirling around in the Atlantic, drifting away from the coast of Africa, sucking up strength from the ocean waters, searching for a landfall in the Caribbean, or worse, in Florida. She thought: Maybe one will hit here. A late-season storm. A malevolent storm. The old-timers in the Keys always say those are the worst, but it truly makes no difference. A storm is a storm. Again she stared at the note. She insisted to herself: There is no reason to be unsettled by an anonymous note, even one as cryptic as this.

For a few moments she devoted some energy to believing that lie, then sat back down at her desk, grabbing a pad of yellow legal paper.

"The first person . . ."

That could be Adam. Perhaps this is biblical.

She began to think more obliquely.

The first *family*—well, that was the president; but she didn't see how that would work. Then she remembered the famous eulogy for George Washington—"First in war, first in peace . . ."—and worked along those lines for a while, only to get quickly frustrated. She could not think of anyone she knew named George. Or Washington, for that matter.

She sighed deeply, and wished that the air-conditioning in the house worked. She told herself that her expertise in puzzles was founded in patience, and if she were simply methodical, she would be successful. So she dipped her fingers into the ice water, rubbed a line of cool water across her forehead and then down her throat, and told herself that no one would send her a coded message that they didn't want her to solve. Otherwise it made no sense to send it.

Every so often one of the regular puzzle solvers among the magazine's readership mailed in notes, but always to her pseudonym, at the office. And these were invariably accompanied by a return address—often coded itself—because the people she attracted were more often dying for her acknowledgment of their brilliance rather than the actual opportunity to meet her. There had actually been a few, over the years, who had stumped her, but these defeats were always followed up by successes.

She stared again at the words.

She remembered something she'd once read, a proverb, a small bit of wisdom passed along in a family. *If you are running, and you hear hoofbeats pursuing you, it is wiser to assume that it is a horse and not a zebra.*

Not a zebra.

Be simple, she told herself. Look to the easy answer.

All right. The first person. First person singular.

That would be *I*.

"The first person possesses . . ."

First person possessive?

I have . . .

She bent over her pad and nodded to herself. "Making some progress here," she said quietly.

". . . which the second person hid."

The second person. That would be *you*.

She wrote: *I have blank you.*

She looked at the word *hid*.

For a moment she thought the heat had made her dizzy, and she inhaled long and hard and reached for the glass of water.

The opposite of *hide* would be *find*.

She looked down at the note and said out loud:

"I have found you. . . ."

The moth at the window screen finally quit its frantic suicidal efforts, tumbling to the sill, where it fluttered in death, leaving her all alone, gasping in an unfamiliar, abrupt fear, in the midst of a superheated silence.

THE PROFESSOR
OF DEATH

It was nearing the end of his thirteenth period class, and he was uncertain if anyone was listening. He glanced toward the wall where there had once been a window, but it was boarded up now and filled in. He wondered for a moment if the sky was clear, then guessed that it was not. He envisioned a great, gray overcast world just beyond the green cinder-block walls of the lecture hall. He turned back to the assembly.

"Haven't you ever wondered what human flesh actually tastes like?" he asked suddenly.

Jeffrey Clayton, a young man wearing the sort of studied indifference to fashion that gave him an unprepossessing, anonymous appearance, was lecturing on the curious propensity of certain types of repetitive killers to develop cannibalistic tastes, when out of the corner of his eye he noticed the silent alarm on the underside of his desk blink a red warning. He caught the sudden surge of anxiety as it rose through his throat, and, with only a small interruption in his speech, maneuvered away from the center of the small stage, moving behind the desk. He slowly slid into his seat.

"And so"—he pretended to shuffle some notes in front of him—"we can easily see how the phenomena of devouring one's victim has antecedents in many primitive cultures, where it was thought that by, say, eating one's enemy's heart, one could acquire that person's strength or bravery, or by eating their brains, their intelligence. A strikingly similar conversion occurs to the murderer who becomes obsessed with the attributes of his prey. He is seeking to become one with his target. . . ."

As he talked he carefully slipped his hand beneath the desk. He warily began to survey the hundred or so students shifting about in their seats in the dimly lit lecture hall before him, moving his gaze across their shadowy faces like a sailor alone peering through the ocean darkness for a familiar buoy.

But all he could see was the usual fog: boredom, distraction, an occasional eruption of interest. He searched for hatred. Anger.

Where are you? he wondered. Which one of you wants to kill me?

He did not ask himself why. The why of so many deaths had grown irrelevant, unimportant, almost obscured by frequency and commonality.

The red light beneath his desktop continued to flash. With his index finger, he pushed the security alert button a half-dozen times. An alarm was supposed to go off at campus police, and they would automatically send their special weapons and tactics squad. But that was assuming the alarm system was functioning, which he doubted. None of the toilets in the men's room had been working earlier that morning, and he imagined it was unlikely that the university could actually get a tenuous electronic thread to operate when it couldn't even keep the plumbing running.

He told himself: You can handle this—you have before.

His eyes continued to sweep across the lecture hall. He knew that the built-in metal detector enclosing the rear entry to the classroom had a nasty habit of malfunctioning, but he was also aware that earlier in the semester another professor had ignored the same warning and was shot twice in the chest as a result. The man had bled to death in the corridor, mumbling about the next day's written assignment, while a deranged graduate student screamed obscenities over the dying teacher's body. A failing mark on a midterm examination had been the ostensible reason for the explosion—which was as understandable an explanation as any.

Clayton no longer gave out any grades below C precisely to avoid that sort of confrontation. Flunking a sophomore wasn't worth dying over. Those students he thought clearly on the verge of some murderous psychosis were automatically given a C plus/B minus for their work—regardless of whether they handed any in. The registrar in the Psychology Department knew that any student receiving that particular grade from Professor Clayton was considered a threat, and campus security was contacted.

There had been three such grades the previous semester, all from his Introduction to Aberrant Behavior course. The students had nicknamed the course "Killing for Fun, One-oh-one," which, he thought, if not totally accurate, was at least creatively alliterative.

" . . . becoming one with his victim is, when all is said and done, the purpose of the killer's actions. There is an odd sort of hatred and desire involved. Often they want what they hate and hate what they want. A fascination and curiosity as well. A marriage that becomes a volcano of different emotions. This, in turn, creates perversion, and its handmaiden, murder. . . ."

Is that what's happening to you? he inwardly demanded of the invisible threat.

His hand, searching beneath the desktop, wrapped itself around the grip of the semiautomatic pistol he kept holstered there. His finger touched the trigger while his thumb released the safety. Slowly, he withdrew the weapon. He remained slightly hunched over, like a monk hard at work on a manuscript, trying to produce a smaller target. He felt a twinge of anger; the bill providing funds to purchase faculty bulletproof vests was still hung up in legislative committee, and the governor, citing budget restraints, had recently vetoed an appropriation to modernize the video monitoring cameras in classrooms and lecture halls. On the other hand, the football team was to get new uniforms that fall, and the basketball coach had received yet another raise in salary—but the teachers, as usual, were being ignored.

The desk was reinforced steel. The campus Buildings and Grounds Department had assured him it could only be penetrated by high-powered, Teflon-coated ammunition. But, of course, he and every other member of the faculty knew that those bullets were available at any number of sporting goods stores within easy walking distance of the university. Explosive bullets as well, and dumdums for those willing to pay the inflated, near-campus premium prices.

Jeffrey Clayton was a younger man, still on the optimist's side of middle age and not yet introduced to the inevitable stomach paunch, the rheumy, disillusioned eyes and nervous, frightened tones that afflicted so many of the older faculty. His own expectations of life—which had been minimal to start with—had only recently begun to shrink, withering like a plant stuck away from the light in some darkened corner. He still had a rabbitlike quickness in the wiry muscles of his arms and legs, and an alertness that was concealed by an occasional tic at the corner of his right eyelid and the old-fashioned, wire-rimmed glasses he wore. He had an athlete's gait and a runner's bearing—which is what he'd been since his high school days. He was prized by some faculty for his sardonic sense of humor, an antidote, he claimed, to his relentless study of violence causality.

He thought: If I dive to my left, that would bring the weapon up into a shooting position and my body will be shielded by the desk. The angle for returning fire will be wrong, but not unmanageable.

He forced his voice into a steady drone: ". . . There are theories among anthropologists that several primitive cultures not only frequently produced individuals who in today's society would be likely to devolve into serial killers, but instead, honored these men and gave them positions of social prominence."

He continued to let his gaze investigate the assembly. There was a young woman in the fourth row, to the right, nervously fidgeting. Her hands twitched in her lap. Amphetamine withdrawal? he wondered. Cocaine-induced psychosis? His eyes continued to scan, and he picked out a tall boy in the dead center of the auditorium wearing sunglasses, despite the dark, dim atmosphere created in the lecture hall by limp, yellow overhead fluorescent lamps. The boy was sitting rigidly, muscles tense, almost as if he was strapped into his chair by ropes of paranoia. His hands were clenched together in front of him. But empty, Jeffrey Clayton saw instantly. Empty hands. Find the hands that are concealing the weapon.

He listened to himself lecture, as if his voice were emanating from some ghost that had separated from his body: ". . . Presumably, by way of example, the ancient Aztec priest who was in charge of ripping the living heart out of their human sacrifice, well, he probably enjoyed his job. Socially accepted and supported serial murder. Most likely that priest went happily off to work each morning, after kissing his wife on the cheek and tousling the hair of his little ones, briefcase in hand, copy of the *Wall Street Journal* under his arm to read on the commuter train, looking forward to a good day at the sacrificial altar. . . ."

There was a small tittering in the room. He used the laughter to conceal the metallic clicking sound as he chambered a round in the pistol.

In the distance a klaxon bell rang, signaling the end of the class period. The hundred-plus students in the lecture hall began to shuffle in their seats, collecting their jackets and backpacks, squirming about in the last seconds of class.

This is the most dangerous moment, he thought.

Again he spoke out loud. "Please remember: blue-book examination next week. And you should all have completed reading the transcripts of Charles Manson's prison interviews. They are available in the reserved section of the library. There *will* be material from those interviews on the test. . . ."

Students rose from their chairs, and he gripped the pistol on his lap. A few students started to approach the front, but he waved them away with his free hand.

"Office hours are posted outside. No conferences now . . ."

He saw a young woman hesitate. A boy-man was beside her. A weight-lifter's arms and raging acne, probably from steroid abuse. They both wore jeans and sweatshirts that had the arms sliced off. The boy's hair was cropped short, like a condemned prisoner's. He was grinning. The professor wondered if the same dull scissors that had performed the surgery on his sweatshirt had also been used on his hair. Under most circumstances, he probably would have asked. The two of them stepped forward.

"Use the rear exit," Clayton said loudly. Again he gestured. The couple paused.

"I want to talk about the final exam," the girl said, pouting.

"Make an appointment with the department secretary. I'll see you in my office."

"It will just take a minute," she wheedled.

"No," he replied. "Sorry." He was looking past her, and at her and the boy alternately, afraid someone else might be pushing through the tide of students, weapon in hand.

"Come on, Teach, give her a minute," the boyfriend said. He wore menace as easily as he did a grin made lopsided by a metal stud piercing his upper lip. "She wants to talk now."

"I'm busy," Clayton replied.

The boy stepped forward. "I don't think you're so fucking busy that—"

But the girlfriend put out her hand and touched him on the arm, which was all that was needed to restrain him.

"I can come back," she said. She smiled coquettishly at Clayton, displaying discolored teeth. "It's okay. I need a good grade, and I can see you in your office." She quietly ran a hand through hair that was shaved close to her skull on half her head and allowed to grow, falling in luxurious curls, on the other half. "Privately," she added.

The boy pivoted toward her, and away from the professor. "What the fuck do you mean by that?" he asked.

"Nothing," she said, still smiling. "I'll make an appointment."

She endowed this last word with an excess of promise, and gave Clayton a small, encouraging smile, accompanied by a gentle lift to her eyebrows. Then she grabbed her backpack and turned to leave. The weightlifter snarled in his direction once, then hurried after the young woman. Clayton could hear a torrent of "What the fuck was that all about" as the couple exited, moving up the stairs toward the rear of the lecture hall, disappearing into the darkened back of the room.

There isn't enough light, he thought. The bulbs are always burning out in the last rows, and aren't replaced. There should be light in every corner. Bright light. He peered into the shadows near the exit, wondering whether someone was hiding there. His eyes swept over the now-empty rows of seats, searching for someone hunkered down in ambush.

The silent alarm continued to flash red. He wondered where the SWAT team was, then realized they wouldn't be coming.

He insisted to himself: I am alone.

And then, in the next instant, he realized he wasn't.

The figure was slouched down, in a seat far to the rear, on the edge of the darkness, waiting. He couldn't see the man's eyes, but saw that he was large, even crouched over.

Clayton raised the pistol and brought it to bear on the figure. "I will kill you," he said, speaking in a flat, harsh tone.

In reply he heard a laugh slide from the shadows.

"I will kill you without hesitation."

The laugh drained away, replaced by a voice. "Professor Clayton, I'm surprised. Do you greet all your students with a weapon in your hand?"

"When I must," Clayton replied.

The figure rose from his seat, and Clayton saw that the voice belonged to a large, somewhat older man in an ill-fitting three-piece suit. He held a small portfolio in one hand, which Clayton noted as the man spread his arms out wide in a gesture of friendliness.

"I'm not a student . . ."

"Clearly."

". . . although I enjoyed that part about becoming one with the victim. Is that true, Professor? Can you document that? I'd like to see the studies that support that contention. Or was it merely your intuition speaking?"

"Intuition," he said, "and experience. There are no successful clinical studies. There never have been. I doubt there ever will be."

The man smiled. "Surely you've read Ross and his pioneering work on deformed chromosomes? And what about Finch and Alexander and the Michigan study on the genetic makeup of compulsive killers?"

"I'm familiar with those," Clayton responded.

"Of course you are. You were a research assistant for Ross. The first person he hired when he got that federal grant. And I'm told that you actually wrote the other, didn't you? Their names but your work, right? Before you got your doctorate."

"You're well-informed."

The man began to approach him, moving slowly down the lecture hall steps. Clayton sighted down the pistol barrel, steadying it with both hands, keeping himself in a shooter's stance. He noted that the man was older than he, probably in his mid- to late fifties, with gray-streaked, closely cropped, military-style hair. Though large, he seemed agile, almost light-footed. Clayton assessed him as he would another runner; not a man for distances, but dangerous in a sprint, probably capable of a substantial burst of speed.

"Move more slowly," Clayton said. "Keep your hands where I can see them."

"I promise you, Professor. I'm not a threat."

"I doubt that. You set off the metal detector when you entered."

"Really, Professor, I'm not the problem."

"I doubt that as well," Jeffrey Clayton responded sharply. "There are all sorts of threats and all sorts of problems in this world, and, I suspect, you embody a good number of both. Open your coat. Without sharp movements, please."

The man had stopped and was standing about fifteen feet away. "Education has changed since I was in school," he said.

"You're stating the obvious. Show me your weapon."

The man displayed a shoulder harness, which contained a pistol similar to the one Clayton was holding. "May I also show you my credentials?" he asked.

"In a moment. There will be a backup, won't there? On the ankle, perhaps? Or in the belt at the small of your back? Where is it?"

Again the man smiled. "Small of the back." He slowly lifted his suit coat and turned around, displaying a second, smaller automatic pistol holstered behind him. "Satisfied?" he asked. "Really, Professor, I'm here on official business. . . ."

"Official business is a wonderful euphemism for any number of dangerous activities. Now lift the pants legs. Slowly."

The man sighed. "Come on, Professor. Let me show you my identification."

Clayton merely twitched the barrel of his own pistol. The man shrugged and lifted first the pants cuff on the left leg, then the right. The second revealed a third holster, this time sheathing a flat-bladed killing knife.

Again the man smiled. "Can't have too much protection in my line of business."

"And what might that be?" Clayton asked.

"Why, the same as you, Professor. The same as you."

He hesitated, allowing another small grin to slide across his face like a cloud passing in front of the moon.

"Death."

Jeffrey Clayton gestured with the pistol toward a seat in the front row. "I'll see that ID now," he said.

The visitor to the lecture hall gingerly slid his hand into his suit pocket and withdrew a synthetic leather folder. He held it out to the professor.

"Just toss it up here, then sit down. Place your hands behind your head."

For the first time, the man let exasperation flicker in the corners of his eyes, then covered it, almost instantly, with the same mocking, easygoing smile. "I think you're being excessive, Professor Clayton. But if it makes you more comfortable . . ."

The man assumed the position in the front row, and Clayton bent over and picked up the identification wallet. He kept the weapon pointed at the man's chest.

"Excessive?" he responded. "I see. A man who is not a student but is armed with at least three different weapons enters my lecture hall through the back door, without an appointment, without an introduction, seems to know at least a little something about who I am, immediately promises he's not a threat, and urges that I not use caution? Do you know how many faculty have been assaulted this semester? How many student-involved shootings there have been? Do you know that we're currently under a court order to cease pre-enrollment psychological screening, thanks to the ACLU? Invasion of privacy and all that. Delightful. Now we can't even weed out the crazies before they arrive here with their assault weapons."

Clayton smiled for the first time. "Caution," he said, "is an integral part of life."

The man in the suit nodded. "Where I work, that's not a problem."

The professor continued to smile. "That statement, I suspect, is a lie. Or else you wouldn't be here."

The man opened his wallet, and Clayton saw a gold-embossed eagle above the words: DIVISION OF STATE SECURITY. The eagle and the title were superimposed over the unmistakable square shape of the new Western Territory. Beneath that, in distinctive red numerals, was 51. On the opposite page was the man's name, Robert Martin, his signature and his title, which was given as Special Agent.

Jeffrey Clayton had not seen credentials from the proposed Fifty-first State in the Union before. He stared at them for some time before saying slowly, "So, Mr. Martin, or should I say Agent Martin, if that is your real name, you're with the S.S.?"

The man scowled briefly. "Out there, we prefer to call it State Security, Professor, and not to abbreviate it, as I'm sure you're aware. The initials have some nasty historical connotations, though, myself, I can't really see the problem. But others are, shall we say, more sensitive to these things. And the identification and the name are real. If you would prefer, we can find a telephone, and I can give you a number to call for verification. If that would make you more comfortable."

"Nothing about the Fifty-first State makes me comfortable. If I could, I'd vote against it receiving statehood."

"Luckily, you're in a distinct minority. And have you ever been inside,

Professor? Have you ever felt that sense of safety and security that exists there? There are many who believe it represents the real America. An America that's been lost in this modern world."

"And just as many who believe you're all cryptofascists."

The agent once again grinned, a self-satisfied smile that replaced the shadow of anger that had ridden his face a moment earlier.

"Surely you can do better than that shopworn cliché?" Agent Martin asked.

Clayton didn't at first respond. He flipped the identification packet back to the agent. He saw that the agent's hand was scarred by burned skin tissue, and that his fingers were clublike and powerful. The professor imagined that the agent's fist was quite a weapon in and of itself, and he wondered whether the scars covered other parts of his body. In the weak light, he could just make out a reddish streak on the man's neck, and was curious about the story behind it, but knew that whatever it was, it had likely created some rage that echoed inside the agent's head. This was elementary aberrant psychology. Still, Clayton had done extensive work on violence causality and physical deformity, and so he told himself to make note of it.

Clayton lowered his weapon very slowly, but left it on the desktop in front of him, his fingers drumming a brief tattoo against the metal. "Whatever you're about to ask, I won't do it," he said after a moment's hesitation. "Whatever you need, I haven't got. Whatever brought you here, I don't care."

Agent Martin reached down and grasped the leather portfolio that he'd placed at his feet. He tossed it up onto the stage, where it made a slapping sound as it fell, echoing in the lecture hall. It finally scraped to a stop at the corner of his desk. "Just take a look, Professor."

Clayton started to reach down, then stopped. "And if I won't?"

Martin shrugged, but the same Cheshire cat grin that he'd worn earlier creased the corners of his mouth. "Oh, you will, Professor. You will. It would take much greater willpower than you have, to just reach out and nudge that case back to me without inspecting what's inside. No, I don't think so, not at all. Already your curiosity has been pricked. Even if it's only an *academic* interest. You're sitting there wondering what's brought me away from the safe world I live in, out to where just about anything can happen, aren't you?"

"I don't care why you're here. And I will not help you."

The agent paused, not in reflection of the professor's refusal, but as if considering a different approach. "You were a student of literature once, weren't you, Professor? As an undergraduate, I seem to remember."

"You seem extremely well informed. Yes."

"Distance runner and obscure books. Very romantic. But very lonely as well, no?"

Clayton merely stared at the agent.

"Part professor, part hermit, correct? Ah, I preferred more physical sports myself. Hockey team. I like my violence controlled, organized, and appropriately sanctioned. Anyway, do you recall the scene at the start of the late Monsieur Camus's great novel, *La Peste*? Delicious moment, right there in that sun-baked North African city, when the doctor who has done nothing but good for society looks out and sees that rat stagger from the shadows and die in the midst of all that heat and light. And he realizes, doesn't he, Professor, that something terrible is about to happen? Because never, not ever, does a rat emerge from the sewers and alleys and dark places to die. Do you remember that scene, Professor?"

"Yes," Clayton replied. As an undergraduate, taking a course on apocalyptic literature of the mid-twentieth century, he'd used that precise image in the conclusion to his final paper. He knew immediately that the agent sitting before him had read that paper, and he felt the same quick start of fear as when he'd first spotted the red alarm light beneath his desk.

"It's sort of the same thing right now, isn't it? You know that something terrible must be resting at your feet, because otherwise why would I give up my own personal safety to come to your classroom, where even that semi-automatic pistol might prove inadequate someday?"

"You do not sound like a policeman, Agent Martin."

"But I am, Professor. A policeman for our times and our conditions." He made a sweeping gesture toward the lecture hall alarm system. There were old-fashioned video cameras mounted in the corners by the ceiling. "Those don't work, do they? They look to be at least a decade old. Maybe older."

"Correct on both counts."

"But they leave them up, don't they, because they might just throw an element of doubt into someone's head, right?"

"That's probably the rationale."

"I find that interesting," Martin said. "Doubt might create hesitation. And that would give you the time you need to . . . what? Escape? Draw your weapon and protect yourself?"

Clayton considered several responses, then discarded them all. Instead, he looked down at the briefcase. "I've helped the government on several occasions before. It has never been a profitable relationship."

The agent stifled a small laugh. "For you, perhaps not. On the other hand, the government was pleased. You come highly recommended. Tell me, Professor, did the wound in your leg heal properly?"

Clayton nodded. "You would know about that," he said.

"The man who put it there—whatever happened to him?"

"I suspect you know the answer to that question."

"Indeed I do. He's on Death Row down in Texas, isn't he?"

"Yes."

"No more appeals left, correct?"

"I doubt it."

"Then he should be scheduled for lethal injection any day now, don't you think?"

"I don't think."

"Will you be invited, Professor? I would think you'd be an honored guest at that particular soiree. They wouldn't have caught him if not for your work, correct? And how many people did he kill? Was it sixteen?"

"No, seventeen. Prostitutes in Galveston. And a police detective."

"Ah, that's right. Seventeen. You might have been the eighteenth if you hadn't been so quick on your feet. With a knife, right?"

"Yes. He used a knife. Many different knives. At first, a large Italian switchblade with a six-inch cutting edge. Then he switched to a hunting knife with a serrated blade, followed by a surgeon's scalpel, and finally an old-fashioned straight razor. And in one or two instances he used a hand-sharpened butter knife, all of which caused the police considerable confusion. But I don't think I'll be attending that execution, no."

The agent nodded, as if understanding something that had been unsaid but implied. "I know about all your cases, Professor," he said cryptically. "There haven't been many, have there? And always reluctant. That's in your FBI file as well. Professor Clayton is always reluctant to lend his expertise to whatever the problem is. I wonder, Professor, what is it that convinces you to leave these oh so elegant and delightfully hallowed halls of ivy and actually help out society? When you *are* persuaded, is it money? No. You don't seem to care much for material things. Fame? Obviously not. You seem to avoid notoriety, unlike the other academics in your profession. Fascination? Perhaps. That seems more plausible—well, when you do emerge, you do seem to have some singular successes."

"I have been lucky once or twice. That's all. It's mostly just educated guesswork. You know that."

The agent took a deep breath and lowered his voice. "You sell yourself short, Professor. I know all about those successes. And I would guess that despite your protests, you're probably better than the half-dozen other academic experts and specialists the government sometimes relies on. I know about the man in Texas, and how you trapped him, and about the woman in Georgia working in the old-age home. I know about the two teenagers in Minnesota with their little murder club, and about the drifter you found down in Springfield, only a little ways from here. Nasty little city, that place, but even there they didn't deserve what that man was delivering to them.

Fifty, was it? At least those are the ones you got him to confess to. But there were more, weren't there, Professor?"

"Yes. There were more. Fifty was where we stopped."

"Little boys, right? Fifty little abandoned boys, hanging out around the youth center, living, and then dying, on the streets. No one cared much about them, did they?"

"You're correct," Clayton said flatly. "No one cared much about them. Either before they were killed or after."

"I know about him. Ex–social worker, right?"

"You say you know, then you shouldn't be asking me."

"No one wants to know why someone commits a crime, do they, Professor? They just want to know who and how, correct?"

"Since they passed the No Excuses Amendment to the Constitution, you're right. But you're a policeman and you should know all that."

"And you're the professor with the antique interest in the emotional background of criminals. The outdated but sometimes unfortunately necessary psychology of crime."

Martin took a deep breath.

"The profilest," he said. "Isn't that what I should call you?"

"I will not help you," Clayton said again.

"The man who can tell me why, right, Professor?"

"Not this time."

The agent smiled once more. "I know about every scar that those cases have given you."

"I doubt it," Clayton replied.

"Oh, but I do."

Clayton nodded toward the briefcase. "And this one?"

"This one is special, Professor."

Jeffrey Clayton burst out with a single shot of sarcastic laughter that echoed throughout the empty lecture hall. "Special! Every time I've been approached—and it's always the same thing, you know—a man in a not particularly expensive blue or brown suit with a leather briefcase and a crime that demands some unique expertise—every time, you say precisely the same thing. Whether it's a suit from the FBI or the Secret Service or the local police in some big city or some small out-of-the-way jurisdiction, it's always *special*. Well, you know what, Agent Martin of the S.S.? They aren't special. Not in the slightest. The cases are just awful. That's all. They're ugly and depraved and sickening. They're always death at its most repugnant and disgusting. People molested and sliced and diced and eviscerated or chopped up in any number of inventive and repugnant ways. But you know what they're not? That's special. No, sir. What they are is the same. The same thing wrapped up in slightly different clothing. Special? No. Not at all. What they are is commonplace. Serial killing is as ordinary in our society as the common cold. It's as routine as the sun rising and setting each day. It's a diversion. A pastime. An entertainment. Hell, we ought to run box scores in the sports section of the newspaper, right next to the standings. So, perhaps this time, no matter how baffled and bewildered you are, no matter how frustrated you've become, this time I think I'll pass."

The agent shifted in his seat. "No," he said quietly. "No, I don't believe so."

Clayton watched as Agent Martin slowly rose from his chair. For the first time, he saw an edge in the man's eyes, which had narrowed sharply and were fixed on him with the same intensity a sharpshooter brings to bear on his target in the milliseconds before squeezing off a round. His voice had a rigid, stilettolike sound to it, each word he spoke like the jab of a knife.

"Keep the briefcase. Examine what's inside. There's a number for a local hotel where you can reach me later. I'll expect your call this evening."

"And if I say no?" Clayton asked. "If I don't call?"

The agent continued to stare at him. He took a deep breath before speaking.

"Jeffrey Clayton. Professor of Abnormal Psychology, University of Massachusetts. Appointed shortly after the turn of the century. Full professorship, three years later by majority vote. No wife. No children. A couple of off-and-on girlfriends that wish you'd make up your mind and settle down, but you don't do that, do you? Not because you're a closet homosexual, but for some other reason, right? Maybe we'll talk about that sometime. What else? Ah, yes. You like to bicycle in the hills and play pickup basketball games at the gym, in addition to running a daily seven, eight miles. A modest academic writing output. You're the author of several interesting studies on homicidal behavior, none of which obtained much widespread interest, but which did attract the attention of police authorities around the nation, who tend to respect your expertise much more than your colleagues in academia. Occasional lecturer at the FBI's Behavioral Studies division at Quantico, before it was closed down. Damn budget cuts. Visiting lecturer at the John Jay College of Criminal Justice in New York . . ."

The agent paused, catching his breath.

"So you have my résumé," Clayton interrupted.

"Committed to memory," the agent replied harshly.

"You could have obtained it from the university's public relations department."

Agent Martin nodded. "A sister living in Islamorada, Florida, who's never married, has she? Like you on that score. Now, isn't that an intriguing coincidence? She takes care of your elderly mother. Invalid mother. And she works for a magazine down there. Writing puzzles. Once a week. Interesting job, that. Does she have the same drinking problem you do? Or is she into some other sort of substance abuse?"

Clayton sat up, rigidly. "I do not have a drinking problem. Nor does my sister."

"No? Good. Glad to hear it. Now, I wonder how that little detail arrived in my research. . . ."

"I wouldn't know."

"No. I guess not."

The policeman laughed again.

"I know everything about you," he said. "And much about your family as well. You're a man of a few accomplishments. A man of interesting notoriety in the field of murder."

"What do you mean?"

"I mean, you've been called in on cases with success, but you show no interest in following up on those achievements. You've worked with the top people in your field, but seem to be happy with your own anonymity."

"This," Clayton said briskly, "is my business."

"Perhaps. Perhaps not. Do you know that behind your back the students call you the Professor of Death?"

"Yes. I've heard that."

"So, Professor of Death, why do you choose to continue to labor here, at a large, underfunded, and frequently decrepit state university, in relative secrecy?"

"That, too, would be my business. I like it here."

"But now it's become my business as well, Professor."

Clayton did not respond. His fingers slid across the steel of the pistol on the desk in front of him.

The agent spoke harshly, almost as if hoarse. "You will pick up the briefcase, Professor. You will examine what's inside. Then you will call me and you will help me to solve my problem."

"You are sure?" Clayton said, with more defiance than he thought he truly had.

"Yes," Agent Martin answered. "Yes. I'm certain. Because, Professor, not only do I know all that curriculum vitae stuff, the who's who biography crap and the public relations filler, and not only because I've read the FBI dossier they keep on you, but because I know something else, something more important, something those other agencies and universities and newspapers and students and faculty and everyone else doesn't know. I have become a student myself, Professor. A student of a killer. And then, by accident, a student of you. And that's led me to some interesting discoveries."

Clayton had difficulty masking the tremor in his voice. "And what would those be?" he demanded.

Agent Martin smiled. "You see, Professor, I know who you really are."

Clayton said nothing, but felt a withering cold plunge through him.

The agent whispered: "Hopewell, New Jersey. Where you spent the first nine years of your life . . . until one October night a quarter century ago, and then you left, and never returned. That's where it all started. Correct, Professor?"

"What started?" Clayton shot back.

The agent nodded his head, like a child in a playground sharing a secret. "You know what I mean."

Agent Martin paused, watching the impact the words had on Clayton's face, as if not expecting an answer to his question. He allowed the silence that grew in the empty space between them to sweep over the professor like so much early morning mist on a cool fall day.

Then he nodded. "I look forward to hearing from you this evening, Professor. There's much work to do and, I'm afraid, not much time to accomplish it. It's best we get started quickly."

"Are you threatening me with something, Agent Martin? If so, perhaps you'd better be more explicit, because I don't have a clue what you're talking about." Clayton spoke rapidly, far too rapidly to be convincing, which he knew as soon as the words tumbled from his mouth.

The agent shook himself slightly, like a dog awakening from a nap. "Oh," he replied passively, "oh, yes, I think you do." He hesitated just momentarily. "You thought you could hide, didn't you?"

Clayton didn't reply.

"You thought you could hide forever?"

The agent made a last gesture toward the briefcase resting against the corner of the desk, then turned and, without looking back, briskly climbed the stairs, moving swiftly, forcefully. He seemed to be swallowed up in the darkness in the back of the room. There was a flash of light as the door at the rear opened to the well-lit corridor, the agent's broad back outlined in the exit. The door closed with a thudding sound, leaving the professor finally alone on the stage.

Jeffrey Clayton sat still, as if melded to his seat.

For an instant he looked wildly about him, gasping for breath. He suddenly couldn't stand it that there were no windows in the lecture hall. It was as if there were no air inside the room. Out of the corner of his eye he saw the red warning light continuing to blink with unanswered urgency.

He placed his hand on his forehead and understood. *My life is over.*

A PROBLEM THAT WILL NOT
EASILY GO AWAY

He walked slowly across the campus, ignoring the knots of students that jammed the pathways, distracted by cold thoughts and black ice anxiety that seemed to come from some unfamiliar location within him.

Nighttime lurked at the edges of the autumn afternoon, sliding darkness through the naked branches of the few remaining oak trees that dotted the university landscape. A brief gust of cool wind sliced through Jeffrey Clayton's wool overcoat, and he shivered. He raised his head momentarily, gazing west, where a slash of purple-red horizon creased distant hilltops. The sky itself seemed to be fading toward a dozen different shades of weak gray, each laying claim to the winter that was steadily approaching. He thought of this as the worst time in New England, after the vibrancy of the fall colors had fled, and before the first snows arrived. The world seemed to be gathering in, unsteady like an old man tired of life, stumbling around on ancient, brittle bones that gave pain with each step, going through the obligations of the hour, knowing that the first frost of death was nearby.

Some fifty yards away, outside Kennedy Hall, one of the many dull, poured-cement buildings that had replaced the antique bricks and ivy, a scuffle erupted, angry voices carried alongside the cold breeze. Jeffrey ducked down and lurched behind a tree. No sense in getting stung by a stray shot, he told himself. He listened but could not tell what the argument was about; all he could hear were torrents of obscenities flung back and forth like so many dead leaves caught in a swirl of wind.

He saw a pair of campus policemen rushing toward the fight. They wore heavy steel-toed boots and full body armor, their feet sounding like hooves striking the macadam pavement. He could not see their eyes behind the opaque face shields on their helmets. From another direction he saw a second pair of policemen fast approaching. As they ran past, a street lamp flashed on, throwing yellow light that glinted off their drawn weapons. The campus police only patrolled in pairs now, he understood, ever since the incident the previous winter term, when several members of a frat house had captured one man, working alone in an undercover narcotics operation, and set him afire in their basement after stripping him naked and performing a number of indignities on his unconscious body. Too much liquor, too many drugs, some kerosene, and a complete lack of conscience.

The officer had been killed and the frat house burned down. The three students responsible were never charged with the crime, most of the evidence disappearing in the blaze, although it was fairly common knowledge around campus who they were. Now, only one of the three was left. One had died before graduation in an odd occurrence in one of the high-rise student dormitories. He'd either fallen or been pushed twenty-two stories down a vacant elevator shaft. The other was killed in a car wreck on an August night on Cape Cod, when he drove his sports car into a cranberry bog and subsequently drowned.

There had been some evidence, Jeffrey had been told, that another vehicle was involved, and that there was a late-night, high-speed pursuit. But the state police in that jurisdiction had officially declared it to be a one-car accident. Of course, campus security was a branch of the state police.

The third student reportedly had returned for his senior year, but never left his room and was said to be either going steadily insane or slowly starving to death, barricaded inside the dormitory.

Now, he saw the four policemen wade into the crowd. One was swinging a graphite truncheon in a wide arc. To his left there was a sound of shattering glass and a high-pitched squeal of pain. Moving out from behind the tree trunk, he saw that the crowd had spread out, losing intensity, and that several students were already walking swiftly away. The four policemen were standing over a pair of young men, handcuffed and shoved to the cold ground. One of the teenagers arched his body and spat at the cops, only to receive a sharp kick delivered to his rib cage. The boy cried out, the sound echoing off the campus buildings.

The professor noticed, then, a clutch of young women watching the confrontation from a second-story window in the School of Racial Management building. They seemed to find the incident amusing, pointing and laughing, safe behind the bulletproof glass of the window. His eyes traveled to the first story of the classroom building, which was dark. This was standard for almost all the departments on campus. It was considered too difficult and too expensive to keep the ground-floor offices and classrooms open. Too many break-ins, too much vandalism. So the ground floors had been abandoned to graffiti and broken glass. Security stations were established on the stairwells leading to the upper floors, which helped keep most of the weapons out of the classes. The problem that had lately emerged, however, was the propensity of some students to set fires in the empty rooms beneath rooms where they were scheduled to take tests. Now, during exam periods, campus security was experimenting with releasing guard dogs in the vacant areas. The dogs tended to howl a great deal, which made concentrating during the exam hard, but otherwise the plan seemed to be working.

The policemen had lifted the two arrested students and were walking toward him. He saw they maintained a wariness, their heads pivoting, watching the rooftops.

Snipers, he thought. He listened for the sound of a helicopter, which would provide additional cover.

He half expected to hear gunshots, but there were none. This surprised him; it was believed that more than half of the 25,000 students at the university carried arms much of the time, and taking the occasional potshot at campus police was as much a rite of passage as going to a pep rally had been a century earlier. On a Saturday night, Student Health Services customarily handled a half-dozen random shootings, in addition to the usual steady stream of knifings, beatings, and rapes. But all in all, he knew, the numbers weren't horrific, just consistent. He was reminded how fortunate the university was to be located in a small, still mainly rural college town. The statistics at the large, urban universities were far worse. Life in those worlds was truly dangerous.

He stepped out onto the pathway, and one of the policemen turned to him.

"Hey, Professor, how yah doing?"

"I'm okay. Any trouble?"

"These two? Nah. Business school majors. Think they already own the world. Just gonna lock 'em up for the night. Cool 'em off. Maybe slap a little learning into them." The policeman tugged sharply at the teenager's twisted arms, and the young man cursed in pain. Few campus security officers had ever taken a college-level course. For the most part they were the products of the nation's new system of vocational high schools, and generally had contempt for the university students they lived amidst.

"Good. Nobody hurt?"

"Not this time. Hey, Professor, you alone?"

Jeffrey nodded.

The policeman hesitated. He and his partner had one of the combatants gripped between them, half dragging him down the walkway. The policeman shook his head.

"Shouldn't travel alone, especially when night's falling, Professor. You know that. Ought to call Escort Services. They'll provide a guard to get you over to the parking lots. You armed?"

Jeffrey patted his semiautomatic pistol, which he kept stuck in his belt.

"Okay," the policeman said slowly. "But look, Professor, you got your jacket buttoned and zipped. You need to be able to get to that weapon quick-like, not be needing to half undress before you can get a shot off. Hell, by the time you get that weapon out, some snotty freshman with an assault rifle and a grudge and strung out on uppers is gonna turn you into Swiss cheese. . . ."

Both policemen laughed, and Jeffrey nodded, smiling.

"That'd be a tough way to go. Turned into a psych sandwich, I guess," he said. "A little ham. A little mustard and Swiss. Sounds okay."

The cops continued to laugh. "Okay, Professor. You be careful. Don't want to be zipping you up in no body bag. Make sure you vary your route, too."

"Guys," Jeffrey replied, arms held wide in a open gesture, "I'm not that dumb. Of course."

The policemen nodded, although he suspected they believed anyone who taught at the university was, in actuality, that dumb. With another jerk on the arms of their prisoner, they continued down the path. The teenager yelled something about having his father sue them for brutality, but his cries and complaints were scattered by the early night wind.

Jeffrey watched them disappear across the quadrangle. Their path was lit by the yellow-tinged street lamps, which carved out circles of light from the fast-dropping darkness. Then he continued rapidly on his way. He ignored a firebombed car that was burning out of control in one of the unsecured parking lots. A few moments later a student prostitute emerged from one shadow, offering sex in exchange for tuition credits, but he declined quickly and kept moving, his thoughts once again devoted to the briefcase he carried and the man who seemed to know who he was.

His condominium was located several blocks from the campus, on a relatively quiet side street that had once held what was termed faculty housing. These were older, whitewashed, wooden-framed clapboard homes, with some slight Victorian touches—wide porches and beveled glass windows. A decade earlier they had been in demand, in part because of their nostalgic quality and their centuries-old heritage. But like almost anything of age in the community, practicality had lessened their value; they were prone to break-ins—their isolation, set back from the sidewalks, shaded by trees and shrubs, rendered them vulnerable, along with old-fashioned wiring that made them unsuitable for the more modern heat-sensing alarm systems. His own apartment depended on an older video-scanning device.

By habit, this was the first thing he checked when he arrived home. A fast playback of the video showed him that the only visitors to his place were the local postman—who was, as always, accompanied by his attack dog—and, shortly after the postman departed, two young women wearing ski masks over their faces so they could not be recognized. They had tried his door handle—looking, he realized, for an easy score—but were put off by the electric shock system he'd installed himself. Not enough to kill someone, but enough to make anyone grabbing the handle feel as if something had smashed their arm with a brick. He saw one of the women knocked to the floor, howling in anger and pain on the video playback, and felt a surge of satisfaction. The design was his own and relied upon human nature. Anyone trying to break in anywhere is bound to try the door handle first, just to ascertain that it was indeed locked. His, of course, was not. Instead, it was charged with 750 volts of electricity. He reset the video recorder.

He knew he should be hungry at the end of the day, but he was not. Exhaling slowly and loudly, like a man exhausted, he moved to his small kitchen and found a bottle of Finnish vodka in the freezer. He poured himself a glass and sipped an inch from the top, letting the bitter, cold liquid mimic his spirit as it plunged through him. Then he went to his living room and tossed himself into a leather armchair. He could see there was a message on his telephone answering machine, and knew as well that he would ignore it. He reached forward, then stopped himself. Instead, he took another pull from the glass and leaned his head back.

Hopewell.

I was only nine years old.

No, there was more.

I was nine years old and terrified.

What do you know when you're nine? he suddenly demanded of himself. Again he breathed out slowly, and knew the answer. *You know nothing and everything all at once.*

Jeffrey Clayton felt as if someone were driving a pin into his forehead. Even the liquor couldn't hide the throbbing pain.

It was a night like this one, perhaps not quite as cold, and there was rain in the air. He thought: I remember the rain, because when we left, it spat at me as if I'd done something wrong. The rain seemed to hide all the angry words, and he was standing in the doorway, finally quiet after all the shouting, watching us leave.

What did he say?

Jeffrey remembered: "I need you. You and the children . . ."

And her reply: "No you don't. You have yourself."

And he'd responded: "You are all a part of me. . . ."

Then he'd felt his mother's hand, pushing him into the car, thrusting him into his seat. He remembered she was carrying his little sister, who was crying, and all they'd had time to pack was a little knapsack with some extra clothes. He thought: She threw us into the car and said, "Don't look back. Don't look at him," and then we were driving.

He pictured his mother. That was the night she grew old, and the memory frightened him. He told himself he had nothing to be concerned about.

We left home, that's all.

They had a fight. One of many. Worse than the others, but that was because it was the last. I was hiding in my room, trying not to listen to the words. What were they fighting about? I don't know. I never asked. I never learned. But this time it was the end, and I did know that. We got into the car and drove away and we never saw him again. Not once. Not ever.

He took another long drink.

So. A sad story, but not that uncommon. An abusive relationship. Wife and children walk out before permanent damage is done. She was brave. It was the right thing. Leave him behind. In a different world. Grow up in a place where he couldn't hurt any of us. Not atypical. Clearly creates some psychological damage, I know that from my own studies, from my own therapy. But overcome, all overcome.

I wasn't crippled.

He looked around at the apartment. There was a desk in the corner loaded with papers. A computer. Many books shoved haphazardly onto shelves. Utilitarian furniture, nothing that couldn't be forgotten or easily replaced once it was stolen. Some of his awards and diplomas were displayed on one wall. There were a couple of framed reproductions of common twentieth-century modern art classics, including Warhol's soup can and Hockney's flowers. They were there to splash some color into the room. He'd also mounted some movie picture posters, because he liked the sense of action they conveyed, because he thought his life frequently too sedate, and surely too drab, and he was uncertain how to change it.

So, he asked himself, why is it when a stranger mentions the night when as a child you left your home, you are thrown into a panic?

Again he insisted: I did nothing wrong. He remembered now. She said, "We're leaving . . ." and we did. And then there was a new life, one that was far away from Hopewell.

He smiled. We went to South Florida. Just like the refugees that showed up there from Cuba and Haiti. We were refugees from a similar dictatorship. A good place to get lost. We didn't know anyone. No family. No friends. No connections. No job. No school. There were absolutely none of the usual reasons that someone moves to a specific location. No one knew us, and we knew no one.

Again he remembered his mother's words. She said once—was it a month later?—that it was the place he would never look for them. A child of the North, she'd always hated the heat. Hated the summers, especially the thick humidity of the mid-Atlantic states. It made her skin break out in red hives and her asthma kick in so that she'd wheeze with the slightest exertion. And so she had told him and his little sister: "He'll never think I went south. He'll think I went to Canada. I was always talking about Canada. . . ." And that was the explanation.

He thought about Hopewell. A rural town, surrounded by farms—that much he knew and recalled. It was adjacent to Princeton, which had once held a well-known university until the turn-of-the-century Newark race riots had traveled uncontrolled, like a match touched to a stream of gasoline, fifty miles down the highway and the university had been burned and pillaged. And the town was well-known because, years before he was born, it had been the site of a famous kidnapping.

But we left, he reminded himself. And never went back.

He finished the glass of vodka with a gulp, throwing the last of the liquor down his throat. He was suddenly filled with a defiant rage. *We never went back,* he repeated to himself three or four times. *So screw you, Agent Martin.*

He wanted another drink, but thought it would be wrong, and then thought, Why not? But this time he only poured himself half a glass, which he forced himself to sip slowly. He reached down, found the telephone on the floor, and swiftly dialed his sister's number in Florida.

The phone rang once and he hung up. He did not like to call them unless he had something to say, and he recognized that he had nothing except questions so far.

Leaning back, he closed his eyes and pictured the little house where they had all once lived. The tide is falling, he thought. I'm sure of it. The tide is falling and you can walk out from shore a hundred, no, two hundred yards, and listen for the sound of a leopard ray leaping free in one of the channels, landing back in the azure water with a resounding slap. That would be nice. To be back in the Upper Keys, wading in the shallows. Maybe he could spot a bonefish tail popping up, reflecting the failing afternoon light. Or a shark fin as it cruised the edge of a flat, searching for an easy meal.

Susan would know where to go, and we would be certain to hook up.

When they were young, brother and sister had spent hours fishing together. Now, he realized, she went alone.

He allowed himself to recall the gentle pull of the warm ocean against his legs, but when he opened his eyes, all he saw was the agent's leather briefcase, tossed haphazardly on the floor in front of him.

He picked the briefcase up and was about to throw it across the room, but stopped even as he drew his arm back to launch the case.

He thought: *All you hold is another nightmare. And I have allowed my life to be filled with nightmares, so one more will mean nothing.*

Jeffrey Clayton leaned back in the chair, sighed once, and opened the cheap metal clasp that held the case together.

There were three tan manila dossiers inside the briefcase. He glanced quickly into all three and saw that each contained more or less the same things, and more or less what he'd expected; crime scene photographs, truncated police reports, and an autopsy protocol for each of three victims. He thought: This is the way it always starts. A policeman with some photographs who supposes that somehow, magically, I'll be able to look at them and tell him instantly who the killer is. He sighed loudly, opened each dossier, and spread the contents on the floor in front of him.

He saw, as soon as the photographs caught the light, why Agent Martin was concerned. Three different dead girls, all, he guessed, in their early teens, all with similar slashing wounds to their naked bodies, all arranged postmortem in similar poses. Straight razor? he immediately thought. A hunting knife? They were each placed faceup on the earth, naked, their arms stretched out to the sides. It was the position that children playing in newly fallen snow tumble into when they make the impression of a snow angel. He could remember making those same figures as a child, before they moved south. He shook his head. Obvious religious symbolism, he noted. It was as if they'd been crucified—which, he supposed, in an odd way, they had been. He took another quick glance at the photographs and saw that each victim had their right-hand index finger severed. He suspected they were also missing some other body part, or a lock of hair as well. "You must like to take a souvenir," he said out loud to the killer inexorably beginning to take shape in his imagination, almost like a person slowly forming out of the air and sitting on a seat across from him.

He took a quick glance at the areas where the bodies were located. One seemed to be a forest, the young girl spread out on a flat rock surface. The second was considerably swampier, an area of thick, muck mud and looped vines and tendrils. Someplace near a river, he thought. The third was difficult for him to assess; it appeared to be, once again, a rural area, but the crime had obviously taken place in early winter; there were patches of clean snow around the body, which had only partially decomposed. He examined the areas a little more closely, looking for signs of blood, but saw few. "So, you put them in your car and drove them to these places, after you killed them, huh?" He shook his head. This, he knew, would be a problem. It was always easier to assess a crime scene if it was the actual spot of the killing. Bodies that traveled created a particular difficulty for authorities.

He rose from his seat, thinking hard, and went back to the kitchen, where he poured himself another glass of vodka. Again he took a long swig, and nodded to himself, pleased with the light-headedness it was delivering. Abruptly, he noticed that his headache had dissipated, and returned to the documents spread out on the floor of his small living room.

He continued to speak to himself, out loud, in a singsong voice, like a child at play alone in a room, amusing himself with a game: "Autopsy, autopsy, autopsy. Bet you twenty bucks all the gals were raped postmortem and that you didn't ejaculate, my man, did you?"

He found the three reports and, running a finger swiftly through the narrative of each, located the pathologist's entry that he was searching for.

"I win," he said, again out loud. "Twenty bucks. A double sawbuck. Twenty smackeroos. Really, a no-brainer. Right again, as usual."

He took another drink.

"If you did ejaculate, it was when you killed them, wasn't it, fella? Because that's where the real intensity is, right? That's the moment for you. Moment of light? Some great explosion flashing behind your eyes, right into your brain and reaching into your soul? Something so wondrous and mystical that it renders you awestruck?"

He nodded. He looked across the room, gesturing toward an empty chair, and addressed it, as if the killer had just entered the room. "Why don't you have a seat? Take a load off your feet." He began to formulate a portrait in his mind. Not too young, he thought. Sort of nondescript. White. Non-threatening. Maybe a little bit of a nebbish or nerd. Certainly a loner. He laughed as the killer started to meld together across from him, because not only was he describing a completely typical serial murderer, he was also describing himself. He continued to speak to the ghostly visitor in a sarcastic, slightly tired voice.

"You know, buddy, I know you. I know you well. I've seen you a dozen times, a hundred times. I've observed you in your trials. I've interviewed you in your prison cell. I've given you a battery of scientific tests and measured your height, weight, and appetite. I've administered Rorschach and Minnesota Multiphasics and IQ and blood pressure exams. I've drawn blood from your arm and performed DNA breakdowns. Hell, I've even sat in on your autopsy after your execution, and studied samples taken from your brain under a microscope. I know you inside out. You think you're unique and superpowerful, but sorry, fella, you just ain't. You present the same goddamn tendencies and perversions as a thousand others just like you. The case books are filled with men no different. Hell, so are popular novels. You've been around for centuries in one form or another. And even if you do think that you're something truly unique and demonically wonderful, you're just goddamn wrong. You're a cliché. As commonplace as a cold in wintertime. You wouldn't like to hear that, would you? That might make that angry voice inside you start to spit and sputter with all sorts of demands. Right? You'd want to go out and howl at the full moon and maybe grab another young girl, just to prove me wrong, huh? But you know, fella, in reality, the only special thing about you is that you ain't been caught yet and that the chances are you're gonna be lucky enough to stay uncaught, too, not because you're so goddamn smart, like I'm sure you think, but because nobody's got the damn time, or the inclination, because there are better things to do than chasing around after sickos, although what the hell these better things are, I haven't a clue. Anyway, most of the time that's what happens. You get left alone because no one really cares all that damn much. You just aren't the big fucking deal you think you are. . . ."

He sighed, searched around inside the folder for the number that Agent Martin had said was there, and found it on a yellow piece of scrap paper. He gave the photographs and the documents another quick glance, just to be absolutely certain there wasn't something obvious or telltale that he'd overlooked, and took another pull from the glass of vodka. He chided himself for the sense of apprehension and dread that had overcome him when the policeman had so obliquely threatened him.

Who I really am?

He sighed his response: I am who I am.

An expert in awful death.

With the hand that held the glass, he made a small, dismissive gesture toward the three case files on the floor in front of him.

"Predictable," he said out loud. "Totally predictable. And probably impossible at the same time. Just another sick, anonymous killer. You won't want to hear that, will you, Mr. Policeman?"

He smiled and then reached for the telephone.

Agent Martin picked up the phone on the second ring. "Clayton?"

"Yes."

"Good. You didn't waste any time. Have you got a video link on your phone?"

"Yes."

"Well, then plug the damn thing in, so that I can see your face."

Jeffrey Clayton did as he was told, switching on the video monitor, snapping the telephone into the connecting hookup, and then settling back across from it in his chair. "That better?"

On his screen the agent jumped into sharp focus. He was sitting on the corner of a bed in one of the downtown hotels. He still wore his tie, but his jacket was draped over a nearby chair. He also continued to wear his sidearm.

"So, what can you tell me?"

"A little. Probably stuff you already know. I've only taken a cursory look at the photographs and documents."

"What do you see, Professor?"

"Same man, obviously. Pretty obvious religious overtones in the symbolism of the body placements. How about an ex-priest? Maybe a former altar boy. Something along those lines."

"I've considered that."

Jeffrey had another idea. "Perhaps an art historian, or someone connected to religious art in some way. You know, Renaissance painters almost always posed their Christ figures in the same fashion as those bodies. A painter who's hearing voices? That's another possibility."

"Interesting."

"You see, Detective, once you introduce the religious angle, you're bound to head off in some specific directions. But oftentimes a slightly more oblique interpretation is required. Or a combination. The onetime altar boy who grew up to become an art historian. See what I'm saying?"

"Yes. That makes some sense."

An idea struck him, and he blurted out: "A teacher. Maybe a teacher."

"Why?"

"Priests tend to go for young men, and these are young women. An element of familiarity, perhaps. Just jumped into my head."

"Interesting," the detective said again after a brief pause to digest what he had just heard. "A teacher, you say?"

"That's right. Just an idea. Need to see more to be more definite."

"Go on."

"Other than that, not much else. The lack of evidence of sexual congress, although there's evidence of sexual activity, makes me suspect that religion is the way to go on this. Religion always brings all sorts of guilts along with it, and maybe that's what makes your man there unable to finish. Unless, of course, he finished earlier, which is what I'd guess."

"Our man."

"No, I don't think so."

The agent shook his head. "What else did you see?"

"He's a souvenir hunter. He'll have that jar with the fingers in it somewhere in his possession, close by so that he can relive his triumphs."

"Yes, I suspected that as well."

"What else did he take?"

"What?"

"What else, Agent Martin? Index finger and what else?"

"You're clever. I expected that. I'll tell you later."

Jeffrey sighed. "Don't tell me. I don't want to know." He hesitated, then said, "It was hair, right? A lock from the scalp and some from the pubic region as well, correct?"

Agent Martin grimaced. "That's right. On both counts."

"But he didn't mutilate her, did he? No slashes to the genitals, right? All to the torso, correct?"

"Yes. Again."

"That's an unusual pattern. Not unheard of, but slightly off the beaten path. An odd way of expressing his anger."

"That interests you?" the agent asked.

"No," Jeffrey replied bluntly. "It does not interest me. Anyway, your big problem is that each victim appeared to have been killed somewhere else, then transported to the spot where they were eventually discovered. So, you'll have to find the conveyance. I didn't note any fibers or other evidence in the police reports that would indicate what sort of vehicle they were placed in. Maybe this guy wrapped them in a rubber sheet. Or had plastic coating placed in the trunk of his car. There was a case out in California of a guy who did that. Drove the cops nuts."

"I remember the case. I think you're right. What else?"

"On the surface, the guy presents pretty much like many other killers."

"On the surface."

"Well, you probably have a lot more information you weren't willing to share. I noticed the autopsy protocols and the police reports were pretty skimpy. For example, the lack of obvious defensive wounds indicates that each victim was unconscious when molested and murdered. That's a compelling detail. How did he render them unconscious? There were no signs noted of head trauma. And other things, too. Like, there was no identification of the young women, no dates or locales for the crimes and nothing about follow-up investigations. Not even a list of suspects interviewed."

"No. You're correct. I didn't show you those."

"Well, that's about it. Sorry I couldn't be more help. You came a long way simply to be told a couple of things you already knew."

"You're not asking the right questions, Professor."

"I don't have any questions, Agent Martin. I see you have a problem and that it isn't going to go away very easily. But that's all. Sorry."

"You don't get it, do you, Professor?"

"Don't get what?"

"Let me give you some of that information that's not on the reports you have. The third case, you see the designation on the folder? The red flag?"

"The one found on the rock? Yes."

"Well, that child's body was discovered approximately four weeks ago at a location inside the Western Territory. Do you understand what that means?"

"Inside the Territory? She was a resident of our soon-to-be Fifty-first State?"

"Precisely," the agent replied. His voice was hard-edged and filled with rage.

Jeffrey sat back in his chair, considering what he had just heard. "I thought that wasn't supposed to happen. I thought the Territory was supposed to be crime-free?"

"Yes, goddamn it," the agent said bitterly. "It is."

"But that's not supposed to be," Jeffrey said. "I mean, the whole point of the Fifty-first State is that these things don't happen there. Isn't that right, Detective? A world where there isn't any crime, correct? Especially crime like this."

Again Martin seemed to be having trouble constraining himself. "You are correct," he said. "It is in actuality the sole basis for its existence. It is the reason it's now being considered for statehood. Think of it, Professor: the Fifty-first State. A place where you can be free. Live a normal life, without fear. Just like the way things used to be."

"A place where you give up your freedom in order to be free."

"I wouldn't have put it precisely that way," Agent Martin responded coldly. "But fundamentally correct."

Jeffrey nodded, now beginning to see the depth of the agent's problem.

"So your dilemma is twofold. Criminal and political."

"Now you catch on, Professor."

Jeffrey had a twinge of sympathy for the hulking policeman, a sensation, he recognized, that was probably inspired primarily by the vodka. "Well, I suppose I can understand your urgency. Isn't that vote in Congress scheduled for just before this Election Day? That's barely three weeks. But the fact of the matter is that these types of crimes don't lend themselves to rapid solutions. Not unless someone gets lucky, and maybe you get a witness and a description or something. But usually if they get solved—and that's a pretty damn big if, Detective—it's more or less by accident and months after the fact. So . . ." He took another swig of vodka and paused.

"So what?" Martin asked bitterly.

"So, I'm glad I'm not in your shoes."

The detective's eyes were narrowed, harsh, staring at the professor through the television screen. His voice remained flat, calm, totally without nervousness.

"But you are, Professor." Martin made a gesture toward the screen. "I'll tell you why in person."

"Look, I examined your files," Jeffrey interrupted. "I'm home now. I've done my bit for tonight."

"This isn't a request. Think for a moment what sort of trouble I could make for you, Professor. Maybe with the Internal Revenue Service. With other police agencies. With your goddamn precious university. Let your imagination run with that thought for a minute or two. Got that? Okay. Now, pick out some spot where we can meet that's secure and quiet. I don't know who may be monitoring this transmission. Or who may be listening in on your phone line. Probably some of your more enterprising students have a tap, looking for some inside information on tests or something to blackmail you with. But I want to meet, and meet now. Tonight. Bring those case folders. I keep telling you—we don't have much time."

Jeffrey dressed in dark clothing, moved cautiously from shadow to shadow through the neon reflections of light in the downtown of the small college town. There was the usual crowd outside of Antonio's Pizza, waiting to get inside; he saw the shotgun-wielding guard that kept order over the hungry students. Another line of people snaked out from the box office at the Pleasant Street cinema, which was showing the latest in what the kids called *viporn*, a word that blended the two dominant themes to most current movie plots.

He flattened himself against the brick wall of a video outlet as a knot of feral preteens moved past him. The children marched in military unison, occasionally breaking into a flat, songlike answer and response. There were probably twelve children in the group, in formation behind a lanky, acne-ridden leader who, with a malevolence that promised awful things, eyed anyone with the bad taste to stare at them. They wore identical jackets sporting the logo of a professional basketball team, knit watch caps, and high-tech sneakers. The youngest, probably only nine or ten, brought up the rear of the formation. His short legs struggling to keep up with the leader's pace would have been comical to the professor, if he hadn't known how dangerous the gang could be. Every so often the leader would abruptly turn around, facing the group, and while jogging backward would call out: *"Who are we?"*

Without hesitation, in high-pitched voices, the gang behind would shout back their reply: *"We are the Main Street Dogs!"*

"What do we own?"

"We own the street!"

Then they all clapped their hands together three times, like rifle shots echoing off the downtown businesses.

Even the students at Antonio's gave the children plenty of space, parting like the banks of a river to let the gang quick-march through. The pizza house guard trained his shotgun on the leader, who merely laughed and made an obscene gesture. Jeffrey saw that a town police car was shadowing the group from a safe distance. Everyone fears the children, he thought. More than anyone else. You can take some simple precautions against serial killers, rapists, thieves, and rabid animals; you can inoculate yourself against smallpox, flu, and typhus—but it is difficult to hide from the scores of abandoned children who have nothing but hatred for the world they have been delivered to. He wondered if the politicians who had repealed all the abortion rights laws ever noticed the gangs of children roaming the streets, and wondered where they'd sprung from.

Jeffrey hurried out of the darkness that had concealed him and cut across the road, behind the police car. He saw one of the officers turn sharply, as if his shape looming behind them was threatening, then they slowly accelerated away. He angled through the streetlights, heading toward the town library.

He thought: What do I know about the Fifty-first State? And then realized that he didn't know much, and what he did know made him uncomfortable, though he would have been hard pressed to say precisely why.

Slightly more than a decade ago, two dozen or more of the largest corporations in the United States had started buying large tracts of federally owned land in a half-dozen western states. They had also purchased property from the states themselves—the states, in effect, ceding the corporations the land. The idea was simple, an extrapolation of a concept the Disney Corporation had first started in central Florida in the 1990s—to start over, building cities and towns, housing, schools, and communities anew, while at the same time reinvoking images of an America long past. Initially, the corporate worlds were designed to house the people who worked for these businesses, and house them in safety and security. But the attraction of the world being created was powerful. On more than one occasion Jeffrey Clayton had sat through television advertisements for the Fifty-first State. It was seen as a place of warmth, safety, and old-fashioned values.

A half-dozen years earlier the area had been designated a territory, the Western Territory. And, as with Alaska and Hawaii more than fifty years earlier, the process of becoming a new state of the Union was begun. New, and very different.

He'd been surprised when so many of the contiguous states had given up their land—but then, money and opportunity were powerful inducements, and borders weren't really a part of any person's tradition.

So, the map of the United States had changed.

There were billboards on some roads, advertising life in the new state. Internet web sites, with information. The computer would also give you a tour of the soon-to-become state, complete with a three-dimensional ride through its urban areas and wild places.

Of course, not without some cost.

Many poorer families were uprooted—although experiencing a financial windfall when they found their property was located within the boundaries of a new subdivision. There had been a few reluctant types as well, like the militia, back-to-the-earth deep woods crazies—but even they had been twisted out, by local ordinance and the power of bribery. Many of these folks had retreated to northern Idaho and Montana, where they had space and political power.

The Fifty-first State had become a sanctuary of a different sort.

There were prices to pay; high taxes, inflated building costs.

And, more critically, there were laws inside the Fifty-first State that controlled privacy, access and egress, and certain fundamental rights. It wasn't so much that the First Amendment had been done away with—as much as it was constrained. Voluntarily. The Fourth and Sixth amendments had also been given new meaning.

Not the place for me, Jeffrey decided. But he wasn't exactly sure why he felt this way.

He hunched his jacket up around his shoulders and hurried down the street. You don't know much about the New World, he thought. Then he realized: You're about to learn much more.

He wondered for a moment what sort of person would make the trade the Territory demanded: freedom for protection.

But what one really received in return was a seductive promise: safety. Guaranteed safety. Absolute safety.

Norman Rockwell America.

Eisenhower 1950s America.

An America long forgotten.

And there, he thought, was Agent Martin's dilemma.

He clutched the briefcase with the three separate crimes under his arm and thought: This is an old problem. The oldest problem. What happens when the fox gets loose in the henhouse?

He smiled to himself. Trouble like no one's ever seen.

There were several homeless people living in the vestibule to the library. They recognized him as he came through the door and called out greetings.

"Hey, Professor? Come to visit?" a woman asked. She had a gap where her front teeth should have been. She followed her question with a wild laugh.

"Nope. Just doing some research."

"Won't need to do any research soon enough. Be dead, just like all the people you study. Then you'll know, firsthand, right, Prof?" She laughed again, and nudged an elderly man next to her, who shook himself, making his tattered and dirt-encrusted clothing rustle as he shifted about.

"Professor doesn't study dead people, you old hag," the man said. "He studies the people who do the killing. Right?"

"That's right," Jeffrey said.

"Oh," the woman said, breaking into a wide grin. "So he doesn't have to be dead himself. Just be a killer maybe once or twice. That what you need to study, Professor? How to kill."

Jeffrey thought the old woman's logic as unsteady as her voice. Instead of replying, he fished a twenty-dollar bill out of his pocket.

"Here," he said. "Line outside Antonio's wasn't too bad. Get yourselves a pizza." He dropped the bill onto her lap. She snatched it quickly with a clawlike hand.

"This'll only get us a small pizza," she said with sudden anger. "With only one topping. I like sausage, and he likes mushrooms." She nudged her companion sharply.

"Sorry," Jeffrey replied. "Best I can do."

The old woman abruptly broke into a half giggle, half shriek. "No mushrooms, then," she cackled.

"I like mushrooms," the man said piteously. His eyes abruptly filled with tears.

Jeffrey turned away and pushed through a set of steel double doors to the library's entry checkpoint, a bulletproof glass partition. From behind it, the librarian gave him a smile and a wave, and he checked his weapon with her. She gestured toward a side room and said, "Your friend's waiting for you in there." Her voice, coming through a metallic intercom, sounded distant and foreign. "Your well-armed friend," she said, grinning. "He didn't like too much giving up his arsenal."

"He's a policeman," Jeffrey said.

"Well, he's an unarmed policeman now. No guns in the library. Just books." She was older than Clayton, and he suspected she spent her free time back in the stacks reading romantically about the past. "Once upon a time there were more books than guns," she said, mainly to herself. She looked up. "Isn't that right, Professor?"

"Once upon a time," he replied.

The woman shook her head. "Ideas are still more dangerous than guns. Just not as immediate."

He smiled and nodded. The woman turned back to simultaneously monitoring her security video screens and electronically logging books into a computer. Jeffrey passed through the portal of the metal detector and entered the library's periodicals room.

The agent was alone in the room, sitting uncomfortably in an overstuffed leather chair, and he struggled momentarily as he thrust himself from the seat, rising to approach Clayton.

"I don't like giving up my weapons, even if we are surrounded by learning," he said, a wry look sliding onto his face.

"That's what the lady at the door said."

"She's got an Uzi slung over her shoulder. She can say whatever she likes."

"There's some truth in that," Jeffrey said. Then he pushed the leather case with the three files within it toward Agent Martin. "Here's your dossiers. As I said, short of your handing over all the information on each killing, I'm not sure how I can help you."

The agent didn't respond to this, but instead said: "I spoke earlier with the dean of the Psych Department. He's okayed an emergency leave of absence for you. I wrote down the names of the professors who'll be taking over your course schedule. I thought you might want to speak with them before we get going."

Jeffrey's mouth opened in astonishment. He stammered briefly as he replied. "Bullshit. I'm not going anywhere. You have no right to contact anyone or arrange any damn thing. I told you I wasn't going to help and I meant that."

The agent continued, ignoring what Jeffrey had said: "I wasn't certain how to handle those girlfriends. Figured you'd want to talk to them first. Make up some sort of convenient lie, because I sure as hell don't want you telling anyone what you're working on or where you're going. Your department chair thinks you're heading to Old Washington. Let's just leave him thinking that, okay?"

"Screw you," Jeffrey interrupted angrily. "I'm out of here."

Agent Martin smiled wanly. "I don't think we're going to be friends," he said. "I think you will come to admire, or at least appreciate, some of my more singular qualities—but no, not on the basis of what's gone on so far. No, I don't think we'll become friends. But, of course, that's not really important, is it, Professor? That's not what this is all about."

Jeffrey shook his head. "Take your damn files. Good luck."

He started to turn, only to feel the agent grip his arm. Martin was a powerful man, and the pressure he exerted was like a promise constricting the muscles, as if to say he was capable of much more, but that the pain he was delivering now was adequate for the situation. Jeffrey tried to snatch his arm back, and couldn't. Agent Martin pulled him closer, whispering heatedly into his face.

"No more debates, Professor. No more arguments. You're just going to do what I say because I think you're the only man in this fucking country that can do what I need done. So I'm no longer asking, now I'm telling. And for the moment, you're just listening. Got that, Professor?"

Menace crawled over Jeffrey's skin like a burn on a hot summer day. He fought hard to contain himself and remain calm.

"All right," he said slowly. "Tell me what you think I need to know."

The agent stepped back and gestured to a reading table next to his leather chair. Jeffrey stepped ahead of him and pulled out a seat. He sat down and said crisply: "Get started."

Martin slid into a stiff-backed wooden chair across from him, opened the briefcase, and withdrew the three files. He scowled briefly at Jeffrey and threw the first file onto the table in front of the professor.

"That's the current case," he said bitterly. "Walking home at night after visiting a neighbor's house, where she'd been baby-sitting. Body discovered two weeks later."

"Keep going."

"No, set that aside. See this girl?" He pushed the second file at Jeffrey. "Look familiar, Professor?"

Jeffrey stared at the young woman. Why should I know her? he wondered. "No," he said.

"Maybe the name would help." The agent was breathing hard, as if trying to control some harsh anger within him. He took a pencil and scrawled *Martha Thomas* on the dossier cover. "Ring a bell, Professor? Seven years ago. Your first year here at this hallowed institution of higher education. Remember now?"

Jeffrey nodded. He felt a singular coldness within him. "Yes. Of course I do, when you tell me her name. She was a freshman in one of my introductory lecture courses. One of two hundred fifty. Winter term. She was in the class for one week before she disappeared. She attended one lecture. I don't recall that I ever even met her. Certainly never had a conversation. That's all. Found three weeks later in the state forest not far from here. She'd been an avid hiker, I remember. Police believed she'd been abducted on an outing. No arrests. I don't recall even being questioned."

"And you didn't offer to help out when one of your own students was killed?"

"I did. The local police politely declined my offer. I just didn't have quite the same reputation then that I do now. I never saw the crime scene materials. I didn't realize that she was a victim of a repetitive killer."

"Neither did the local idiots," Martin replied bitterly. "Girl eviscerated and laid out on the ground like some religious token, finger missing and . . . and these fools didn't have a clue what they were dealing with."

"Too many people get killed these days. A homicide detective performs a sort of intellectual triage, deciding which cases to pursue, which might be solvable."

"I know that, Professor. Still doesn't mean they weren't idiots."

Jeffrey leaned back. "So, a young woman who was once just barely a student of mine, seven years ago, is murdered in the same fashion as your current case. I still don't see why that demands my presence on the case."

Agent Martin slid the third file across the table, where it bumped into Jeffrey's right hand.

"This case is old," Martin said slowly. "Very old and cold. Ancient fucking history, Professor."

"What are you trying to say?"

"The FBI keeps good records on these homicides," Martin continued. "In their Violent Criminals Apprehension Program. VICAP. They cross-reference the unsolved killings in all sorts of interesting ways. The body position, for example. And the index fingers. That's the sort of thing a computer drone filing cases has an easy time isolating, wouldn't you say? Of course, it usually doesn't do the FBI or anyone else a damn bit of good, all the computer referencing, but occasionally it creates some interesting combinations. But you know all about that, don't you, Professor?"

"I'm familiar with the serial crime identification process. It's been around for a couple of decades. You know that."

Agent Martin had risen from his chair and paced briefly around the room, finally throwing himself back into the large leather reading chair and looking across the table at Jeffrey Clayton.

"That's how I put them together. This last one, you know when it took place? More than twenty-five fucking years ago. I mean, back in the Stone Age, right, Professor?"

"Three killings in a quarter century is an unusual pattern."

The agent sat back hard, staring up at the ceiling for a moment before lowering his eyes and fixing them on Clayton.

"No fucking kidding," he said. "But, Prof, that last one, that's real interesting."

"Why is that?"

"Because of where and when it took place and one of the people the state police questioned. Never arrested the bastard—he was just one of a half-dozen prime suspects questioned—but his name and the interview was in the old file. Sure was hell to find it, but I did."

"So, what was so interesting?" Jeffrey asked.

Agent Martin started to stand up, then seemed to think better of it. Abruptly, he dropped forward, leaning his bulk across his knees, bending forward like a man describing a conspiracy, his voice low, harsh, and filled with an angry, malevolent ferocity.

"Interesting? I'll tell you what was interesting, Professor. Because that young woman's body was discovered in Mercer County, New Jersey, just outside a little town named Hopewell about three days after you and your mother and your little sister left home forever . . . and because the man the police so unsuccessfully questioned a few days after this girl disappeared, and you and your family hightailed it out of there, was your goddamn father."

Jeffrey didn't reply. He felt hot, as if the room had suddenly burst into flames around him. His throat was immediately dry and his head spun dizzily. He gripped the table to steady himself, and thought: *You knew, didn't you? You knew all along, all these years. You knew someday someone was going to come up to you and say what you just heard.*

He imagined he couldn't breathe, as if the words themselves were choking him.

Agent Martin saw all this and narrowed his eyes, staring hard at the Professor of Death.

"So now," he said quietly, "we're ready to begin. I told you, there's not much time."

"Why?" Jeffrey choked out.

"Because less than forty-eight hours ago another girl inside the Western Territory disappeared. Right now, in an office where it's supposed to be safe and comfortable and where life is supposed to be normal, goddamn it, there's a man and a woman and a little brother and an older sister all sitting around trying to understand that which is incomprehensible. Getting an explanation of the inexplicable. Being told that the one thing they were absolutely guaranteed would never happen to them has happened."

Agent Martin scowled, as if the thought was sickening him.

"You, Professor. You're going to help me find your father."

UNREASONABLE
QUESTIONS

Jeffrey Clayton's head reeled momentarily and his cheeks stung, as if he'd been slapped hard.

"Ridiculous," he replied quickly. "You're out of your mind."

"Am I?" Agent Martin asked. "Do I look crazy? Do I sound crazy?"

Jeffrey took a long, slow breath, pausing as he released it, so that the wind from his lungs hissed as it passed through his teeth. "My father," he said with a deliberateness that tried to impose order on all the careening thoughts within him, "my father died more than twenty years ago. A suicide."

"Uh-huh. You're sure of that?"

"Yes."

"Did you see his body?"

"No."

"Did you go to the funeral?"

"No."

"Did you read any police report, or a coroner's statement?"

"No."

"Then why is it that you're so certain?"

Jeffrey shook his head. "I'm saying only what was told to me and what I believed. That he died. Back near our home in New Jersey. But exactly how, or where, I don't remember. I've never wanted to know the precise circumstances."

"That makes lots of sense," Martin said quietly, rolling his eyes sardonically.

The agent smiled, but once again it was a humorless grin, one that spoke more of threat and anger than anything else. Jeffrey started to open his mouth to say something else, then decided to remain silent.

After a few seconds Martin arched his eyebrows and said: "I see. You don't recall where your father died, or exactly when. Or precisely how. I mean, a suicide could mean almost anything. Did he shoot himself? Hang himself? Step in front of a speeding train? Jump from a bridge? Did he leave a written note? Or maybe a videotaped last message? How about a will? You don't know, huh? But you're certain that he did die and it was somewhere different but not that different from where he once upon a time lived. Would that be scientifically certain?" he asked sarcastically.

The professor let the question hang in the air between them for an instant before answering.

"What I know, I know simply from a single conversation with my mother. She told me that she'd been informed that he'd killed himself, and she said she didn't know the reason why. I don't recall that she told me how she'd been informed of his death, and I don't recall ever asking her how she knew. Regardless, there was no reason for her to lie to me, or mislead me in any way. We did not often speak about my father, so I had no additional reason to pursue any details. I just went on doing what it was that I was doing. Studying. Teaching. Getting my degrees. He was no longer a relevant factor in my life. Hadn't been since I was a small child. I did not know him. Nor did I know anything much about him. He was my father solely due to a single act of copulation and not because he and I had any relationship. When he died, it didn't affect me one way or the other. It was like being told of some distant, peripheral event of little consequence. Something that happened in a far corner of the world. He was a cipher. Nonexistent. A vague memory from a long-past childhood. I don't even carry his name."

Agent Martin sat back in the large leather lounge chair, which seemed to envelope even his considerable bulk easily. He struggled for a moment to get comfortable, shifting about. "Hell," he muttered, "you could live in this chair. There's room for a kitchen." He looked over at Jeffrey.

"Nothing you just said is even remotely close to the truth, is it, Professor?" he asked offhandedly.

Jeffrey stared hard at the man sitting across from him, trying to see him more clearly, like a surveyor no longer confident in the measurements received from his instruments and equipment, who sights down a line with his naked eye to reassure himself. He was only barely aware of Martin's dimensions, he realized, and thought it might be wise to refigure his assessment. He noticed that the burn scars that marred the detective's hands and neck seemed to glow with a muted red when Martin controlled some anger within him, as if inadvertently signaling his emotions.

"Well," Martin continued softly, "maybe one thing. I believe your mother did tell you he'd died, and probably she said a suicide, at that. That part's probably true. That she said it, that is." He coughed, as if trying to be polite, but it was more of a mocking sound. "But that's about the only thing, huh?"

Jeffrey shook his head, which only made Martin grin again. Apparently, the angrier the detective got, the more frequently he smiled.

"It happens all the time, doesn't it, Professor? Mr. Expert on Death. Serial killers are frequently so overcome with remorse at the depravity of their murders that they can no longer tolerate their own pathetic, diabolical existences and they kill themselves, thereby saving society the trouble and expense of actually ferreting them out and bringing them to trial. Correct, Professor? That's a commonplace scenario, no?"

"It happens," Jeffrey said harshly. "But it's unusual. Most of the repetitive killers we've studied have no claim to remorse. None whatsoever. Not all, of course. But most."

"Then they would have some other reason for committing one of these infrequent suicides?"

"What they have is an accommodation with death. Their own—or someone else's—they seem comfortable with any."

The agent nodded, pleased with the impact his sarcastic question seemed to have had.

"How is it," Jeffrey asked slowly, "that you've come here? How is it that you've connected me to this man who may or may not have committed a crime or some crimes twenty-odd years ago? How is it that you think my father, who is actually dead, has somehow come back to this earth and is your suspected killer?"

Agent Martin leaned his head back. "Not unreasonable questions," he said.

"I'm not an unreasonable man."

"I think you are, Professor. Eminently unreasonable. Prominently unreasonable. Wildly and fantastically unreasonable. Just like me, on that score. It's the only way to get through each and every day, isn't it? Being unreasonable. Every breath you take in this nice little academic world of yours is unreasonable, Professor. Because, if you were *reasonable*, then you wouldn't be who you are. You'd be the man you're afraid lives inside you. Just like me, like I said. But still, I'll try to answer some of your questions."

Once again Jeffrey thought he should respond, that he should angrily deny everything the detective had just said, get up, walk out, leave him behind. But he did none of these things.

"Please," he said coldly.

Martin shifted in his seat and reached down for his leather portfolio. He shuffled some papers about inside, removing a stapled sheaf of reports. He flipped through these quickly until he found what he was searching for, then plucked a pair of horn-rimmed, half-moon reading spectacles from an inside jacket pocket. These he placed on his nose, peering up just once at the professor before turning his glance down to the writing before him.

"Make me look old, don't they? And just a little bit distinguished, no?" The detective laughed to himself, as if to underscore the incongruity of his appearance. "This is a transcript of an interview between a New Jersey State Police detective and a Mr. J. P. Mitchell. You know that name?"

"Yes, of course. That was my father's name. My late father."

Agent Martin smiled. "Sure. Okay, the detective goes through all the standard stuff, on the record, and says what case he's dealing with, and gives the date and a location and a time of day . . . everything nice and official, right down to every element of the Miranda warning. And he gets telephone numbers and Social Security numbers and addresses and all sorts of stuff from your old man, who doesn't seem to hold anything back. . . ."

"Maybe he didn't have grounds to."

Again the agent grinned. "Sure. Okay, then the detective goes into some details about the girl's murder and gets a nice bunch of denials from your dear old dad."

"Right. End of story."

"Not exactly."

Martin flipped through the sheaf of papers, finally pulled three from the center of the file, and slid these across to Jeffrey. The professor saw immediately that they were numbered in the upper nineties. He made a quick calculation—two pages per minute—so, he recognized the police were already close to an hour into the interview with his father. He let his eyes flow over the words. The interview had obviously been transcribed from a tape by a stenographer; there was no embellishment beyond the questions and the answers, no description of the two men speaking with each other, no details about inflection or nervousness. He wondered: Was the policeman on his feet? Did he move about, circling like a bird of prey? Was there a line of sweat on my father's forehead, and did he lick his lips with every response? Did the detective slam the table? Did he hover over my father, threatening? Or was he cold, collected, quietly thrusting questions like needles at him? And my father, did he sit back, grinning slightly, parrying every thrust with a fencer's footwork, enjoying the game as it accelerated around him?

Jeffrey envisioned a small room, with probably a single overhead light. A small, bare room, with empty walls, modern soundproofing, and a haze of cigarette smoke hanging over a utilitarian, square table. Two simple steel chairs. No handcuffs, because he wouldn't be under arrest. A tape machine on the table, quietly collecting the words, capstans turning as if patiently awaiting a confession that would never arrive.

What else? A mirror on the wall that was really an observation window, but he would have recognized that and ignored it.

Jeffrey stopped himself abruptly. How would you know that? he demanded of himself. How would you know anything about how your father looked, or acted, or sounded one night, all those years ago?

He noticed a slight tremor in his hand as he began to read the pages from the transcript. The first thing he noticed was that the policeman wasn't identified by name.

Q. Mr. Mitchell, you say that on the night of Emily Andrews's disappearance, you were at home with your family. Correct?

A. That is correct.

Q. Can they confirm that for us?

A. Yes. If you can find them.

Q. They are no longer living with you?

A. Correct. My wife has left me.

Q. Why is that? Where have they gone?

A. I do not know where they've gone. As for why, well, I presume you'd have to ask my wife. That, of course, might be difficult. I suspect she's gone north. Perhaps New England. She has always maintained that she enjoys the colder climates. Odd, don't you think?

Q. So there's no one available to confirm your alibi?

A. Alibi is a word that assumes a certain connotation in this context, doesn't it, Detective? And I'm uncertain why I need an alibi. Alibis are for suspects. Am I a suspect, Officer? Correct me if I'm mistaken, but the sole connection you have made between myself and this unfortunate young woman is that she was a student in my third-period history class. On the night in question, I was at home.

Q. She was seen getting into your car.

A. I believe on the night she disappeared it was raining and dark. Are you certain it was my car? No, I didn't think so. And anyway, what would be wrong with giving a student a lift on a cold, stormy night?

Q. So you're saying she did get into your car the last night she was seen alive?

A. No, I'm not saying that. I'm saying that it would not be unusual for any teacher to give a student a lift. On that particular night. Or any night.

Q. Your wife just all of a sudden left you?

A. We're backtracking, are we? Nothing like that happens all of a sudden, Detective. We'd been estranged for some time. We argued. She left. Sadly common. Perhaps we're ill-suited for each other. Who knows?

Q. And your children?

A. There are two. Susan is seven, and my namesake Jeffrey is nine. She will come back, Detective. She always has. And, if not, well, then I'll find her. I always have. And then we'll all be together again. You know, sometimes you have that sensation, a feeling of inevitability, perhaps, that no matter how difficult or discouraging life together is, you're absolutely destined to stay together. Forever. Linked.

Q. She's left you before?

A. We've had troubles before. An occasional, temporary separation or two. I'll find her. It's nice of you to show so much concern for my family situation.

Q. How will you find her, Mr. Mitchell?

A. Her family. Her friends. How does anyone go about finding someone, Detective? No one really, truly, wants to disappear. No one really wants to vanish. At least, no one who isn't a criminal. They just want to go somewhere new and do something different. And so, sooner or later they pick up some thread connecting them to their old life. They write a letter. They make a phone call. Something. You just merely have to be holding the other end and feel that little tug when it occurs. But that's something you know, isn't it, Detective?

Q. Your wife's maiden name?

A. Wilkes. Her family comes from Mystic, Connecticut. Let me write down her Social Security number for you. Are you interested in doing my job for me?

Q. Why is it that I found a pair of handcuffs in your automobile?

A. I see. Now we're jumping ahead. You found them because you illegally searched my car without a warrant. You need a warrant for a search.

Q. What were they for?

A. I'm a mystery and crime buff. Collecting police paraphernalia is a hobby.

Q. How many history teachers keep handcuffs with them?

A. I don't know. Some? Many? A few? Is it against the law to own handcuffs?

Q. Emily Andrews's body had marks consistent with handcuffs around her wrists.

A. Consistent is a weak word, isn't it, Detective? A sort of flimsy, weak-kneed, pathetic word that really doesn't mean much. She may have had marks, but not from my handcuffs.

Q. I don't believe you. I think you're lying to me.

A. Then feel free to prove me wrong. But you can't do that, can you, Detective? Because if you could, we wouldn't be wasting all this time, would we?

The detective's response wasn't recorded on the pages Jeffrey held. For a moment he did not look up, although he could sense Martin watching him. He reread some of his father's statements and realized that he could hear the words spoken in his father's voice across all the years, and that in his mind's eye he could see his father sitting across from the detective as he'd once sat across from him at the dinner table in their house, almost as if he was watching some scratchy, herky-jerky antique home movie. This startled him, and he abruptly looked up and thrust the transcript pages back at Agent Martin.

Jeffrey shrugged, confused like a poor actor caught in a spotlight meant for a different performer on some other part of the stage.

"This doesn't tell me much. . . ." he lied.

"I think it does."

"There's more?"

"Considerably, but it's much the same. Argumentative and evasive, but rarely confrontational. Your father is a clever man."

"Was."

The agent shook his head. "He was clearly the best suspect. The victim was seen maybe getting into his—or a similar—car, and there was some blood matter uncovered beneath the passenger seat. Then there were those handcuffs."

"And?"

"That was pretty much it. That detective was going to arrest him—was dying to arrest him—until the blood testing came back from the lab. No dice. The blood residue didn't match the victim's. The cuffs had been cleansed of any tissue. Steam-cleaned, I think. Your house was searched with interesting but negative results. Getting a confession was their best chance. That would be standard procedure back then. And the detective gave it a good try. Kept him there for almost twenty-four hours. But in the end he seemed fresher and more alert than the cop did. . . ."

"What do you mean 'interesting but negative' search of the house?"

"I mean pornography. Of a particularly virulent, violent nature. Sexual devices usually associated with bondage and torture. An extensive library on murder, sexual aberration, and death. A regular home-style, do-it-yourself kit for a sexual predator."

Clayton swallowed hard, his throat dry. "None of that means he was a killer."

Agent Martin nodded. "Right you are, Prof. None of it *proves* he committed a crime. All it proves is that he knew *how*. Like those handcuffs. Fascinating. In an odd way, I sort of admired what he did. Obviously he used them on the girl at one point, and just as obviously he had the good sense to dump them into boiling water as soon as he returned home. Not many killers are quite so attentive to detail. Actually, the lack of tissue matter helped him in his discussions with the New Jersey State Police. Their inability to connect them to the crime fueled his self-confidence."

"And the causality? The link to the dead girl?"

Agent Martin shrugged. "None ever developed that amounted to anything. A student in his class, just like he said. Seventeen years old. Couldn't actually prove a thing. It was more in the walks like a duck, quacks like a duck category. You know that, Professor."

Martin drummed his fingers sharply, frustrated, against the leather of the armchair.

"It's obvious the damn cop was overmatched from the start. He did the interrogation from page one right by the book. Just like he'd been taught in every seminar and course. Introduction to Obtaining Confessions." The agent sighed. "That was the problem with the old days. Miranda warnings. Criminals' rights. And the police. Christ! The New Jersey State Police were this quasimilitary, spit and polish, button-down, shoe-shined bunch. Even their plainclothes and undercover guys looked like they belonged in those tight-ass uniforms. Put your ordinary, run-of-the-mill killer in there with them—you know, the guy who blows away his wife when he discovers she's been cheating on him, or the punk who shoots someone in a convenience store robbery—and it's all over. The words just tumble on out, like turning on a spigot. Yes sir, no sir, whatever you say, sir. Easy. But that wasn't the case here. That poor jerk cop didn't have a chance against your old man. At least, not intellectually. Not a chance. He went in thinking your old man was just gonna sit back and tell them how he did it and why he did it and where he did it and just any damn thing they wanted to know, just like every other damn stupid killer he'd ever collared. Right. Instead, they just went round and round. Do-si-do. Like a little two-step waltz."

"It seems that way," Jeffrey replied.

"And that tells us something, correct?"

"You keep saying cryptic things, Agent Martin, implying that you think I have knowledge and powers and intuition that I've never claimed. I'm just a professor at a university with a specialty in repetitive criminals. That's it. Nothing more. Nothing less."

"Well, it tells us he was indefatigable, doesn't it, Professor? He was able to outlast a detective who desperately wanted to solve the case. And it tells us that he was clever, and that he wasn't afraid, which is most intriguing, because a criminal who isn't afraid when confronted with authority is always interesting, isn't he? But mostly what it says to me is something different, something that has me truly worried."

"What is that?"

"You know those satellite weather photographs that the television weathermen are so fond of? The ones where you can see a storm cell gathering intensity, forming, strengthening, feeding off the moisture and the winds, gathering itself before it breaks loose?"

"Yes," Jeffrey replied, surprised at the force of the man's imagery.

"People are like those storm cells. Not many. But some. And I think your father was one of those. Feeding off the excitement of the moment. Every question, every minute that went by in that interview room, made him stronger and more dangerous. That cop was trying to get him to confess . . ." Martin paused, taking a deep breath. ". . . but he was learning."

Jeffrey found himself nodding. I should be panic-stricken, he thought. But instead he felt a singular coldness within. Again he took a deep breath. "You seem to know a great deal about that confession that never happened."

Agent Martin nodded. "Oh, absolutely. Because I was the damn stupid rookie detective trying to get your old man to talk."

Jeffrey sat back quickly, recoiling.

Martin watched him, seemingly thinking about what he'd just said. Then he leaned forward, pushing his face close to Clayton's, so that his words carried the force of a shout: "You become what you absorb as a child. We all know that, Professor. It's why I am who I am, and it's why you are who you are. You may have successfully denied this up to now, but no longer. I'm going to see to that."

Jeffrey rocked back. "How did you find me?" he asked once again.

The agent relaxed. "A little old-fashioned detective work. I remembered all that stuff about names your father was talking about. You know, people hate giving up their names. Names are special. Ancestry. Connection to the past, that sort of thing. Names give people a sense of location in the world. And your father gave me the clue when he mentioned your mother's maiden name. I knew she'd be clever enough not to return to that—he would have found her too easily. But names, well, like I say, people don't like to give them up that quick. You know where Clayton comes from?"

"Yes," the professor replied.

"So do I. After your father mentioned your mother's maiden name, I thought to myself, well, that would be too easy and too obvious, but people hate to give up family, even if they are trying to hide from someone they think just may be a monster. So, just on a whim, I checked and found your mother's mother's maiden name. Clayton. Not quite so obvious, that, huh? And clickity click, I put them together—'My namesake, Jeffrey . . .' Well, I didn't think any mother would change her children's first names, no matter how prudent it might have been—and lo and behold I arrived at Jeffrey Clayton. And that set off the buzzer, didn't it? The not exactly famous, but not exactly unknown to professional policemen, Professor of Death. And don't you think that connection intrigued me, when I learned that another one of our spread-eagled, crucified, finger-missing victims just happened to be a student of *yours* once. Your mother's mother's maiden name. That was neat. You think your daddy made that connection, too?"

"No. At least, we never saw him again. Never heard from him. I told you. He was no longer a part of our lives after we left him behind in New Jersey."

"You sure about that?"

"Yes."

"Well, I think you should be less sure. I think you should be unsure about everything when it comes to your old man. Because, if I could see my way through that nifty little deception, maybe he could, too."

The detective reached out, grasped the photograph of Clayton's murdered student, and spun it across the table, where it fluttered to a halt in front of the professor.

"I think you did hear from him."

Jeffrey shook his head. "He's dead."

Agent Martin looked up. "I love your certainty, Professor. It must be nice to always be so sure of absolutely everything." He sighed before continuing, "All right. Well, if you can prove that to me, you'll have my apology and a nice check for your time from the Western Territory governor's office and a limousine ride home in safety, comfort, and quiet."

Madness, Jeffrey thought.

And then he asked himself: Is it?

He found himself staring past the agent, into the central room of the library. There were a few people quietly reading; mostly older people, half buried beneath the words they held open in front of them. There was a quaintness to the scene, he thought, an antique quality. It almost made him think the world outside was safe. He let his eyes wander across the stacks of books, lined up, patiently awaiting the moment when they would be taken from a shelf and opened up, releasing whatever information they held to the eyes of some inquisitor. He wondered whether some of the books would remain closed forever, the words contained within their covers somehow rendered obsolete, useless by the passage of time. Or perhaps, he thought, ignored, because the knowledge they harbored didn't come on a disk, wasn't instantaneously available with a few strokes from a computer keyboard. Wasn't modern.

He pictured his father again, with his child's eyes.

Then he thought: It's not new ideas that are truly dangerous. It's the old ones that have been around for centuries and thrive in any environment. Vampire ideas.

Murder as a virus, immune to any antibiotic.

He shook his head and saw that Agent Martin was once again smiling, as he watched him struggle. After a moment, Martin stretched, grabbed the arms of the leather chair, and thrust himself to his feet.

"Get your things. It's late."

Martin gathered the reports and photographs, stuffing them into his briefcase, and strode swiftly toward the exit. Clayton hurried after him. At the metal detectors, they both nodded to the librarian, who returned the detective's weapons to him, although she kept a hand hovering over an alarm button as he strapped the sidearms beneath his coat.

"Come on, Clayton," Martin said grimly as he stepped through the doors into the jet-black night of the small New England town at the edge of winter. "It's late. I'm tired. We have far to travel tomorrow, and someone I need to kill is waiting for us."

MATA HARI

Susan Clayton watched a thin column of smoke rise in the distance, framed by the setting sun, a swirling black line penciled against the fading blue of the daytime sky. That something was burning out of control barely registered within her; instead she was struck by the insult the smoke cast against the perfect horizon. She listened, but could not hear any siren's insistence penetrating the windows of her office. She did not think this all that unusual; in some parts of the city it was far more common, and considerably more reasonable, not to mention cost effective, to simply let whatever building was torched burn to the ground, rather than risk the lives of firemen and police officers.

She swiveled about in her seat, her eyes sweeping over the end-of-day bustle in the magazine offices. A security guard with an assault rifle slung over his shoulder was preparing to make an escort trip to the parking lot, gathering the employees into a tight little group. For an instant Susan pictured a school of small fish, packing themselves into a tight mass of protection against a predator. She knew: It's the slow fish, the loner, the fish who darts out on its own, that gets picked off and eaten.

This thought made her smile inwardly, and she spoke to herself: Better swim fast.

One of her coworkers, the editor of the celebrity pages, stuck his head inside the opening to her small work cubicle and said: "Come on, Susan, pick yourself up. It's time to go."

She shook her head. "Just want to finish a couple of things," she replied.

"What seems necessary to finish tonight can always be something to start with tomorrow. There's a bit of wisdom for our current conditions. Words to live by."

Susan grinned, but made a small dismissive gesture with her hand. "I'm just going to be a little bit longer."

"But you'll be left alone," he said. "Which is never good. Better make sure that Security knows you're here. And lock the doors and put on the alarms."

"I know the drill," she replied.

The editor hesitated. He was an older man, with streaks of gray hair and a salt and pepper beard. He was an accomplished professional, she knew, and had once been prominent at the *Miami Herald* until a drug addiction had cost him his job and relegated him to writing snippets of gossip and benign lies about the city's upper classes for the weekly magazine they both worked on. This was a job he did with sturdy detail, devoid of passion, although not lacking in a sardonic humor that was prized, collecting a paycheck that was immediately and dutifully split into equal shares—so much for his ex-wife and so much for his children, the rest for cocaine. She knew that he was currently supposed to be sober, but she had more than once seen wisps of white powder littering the hairs of his mustache as he emerged from the men's room. She ignored this, as she would have for anyone, knowing that to say anything was to inject herself into his life, even if minimally, which she would not allow herself to do.

"Don't you worry about the danger?" he asked.

Susan smiled, as if to say it was nothing, which of course both knew was a lie.

"Whatever happens, happens," she said. "Sometimes I think we spend so much time taking precautions to prevent so many terrible possibilities that we're left with not much that means anything."

The editor shook his head, but with a small laugh.

"Ah, a woman of puzzles and philosophy," he replied. "No, I think you're wrong. Once there was a time when you could leave things pretty much to fate, and more than likely nothing bad would happen to you. But that was years ago. No more."

"Still, I'd rather take my chances," Susan replied. "I can handle myself."

The editor shrugged. "What is it that you have to do?" he asked, annoyed. "What would make you want to stay in here when everyone's gone? What's so goddamn attractive about this place? Surely you're not so entranced by the beneficence of our employer that you would risk your life for the greater glory of *Miami Magazine*?"

"True. When you put it that way . . ." she answered. "But I want to add a special to my latest game, and I'm still working on it."

The editor nodded. "A special? Some message for a new admirer?"

"I guess."

"Who's the special for?"

"I got a coded letter at home," she replied. "And I thought I'd play the person's game."

"Sounds intriguing. But dangerous. Better be careful."

"I'm always careful."

The editor looked past her, out at the smoke still rising, seemingly just beyond reach, just past the glass of the window, as if the scene outside were a still life of urban neglect.

"Sometimes I think I can no longer breathe," he said.

"I beg your pardon?"

"Sometimes I think I won't be able to take a breath of air. That it will be too hot to inhale. Or too smoky, and choke me. Or filled with some wildly virulent disease, and I'll be instantly coughing up blood."

Susan did not reply, but thought: *I know precisely what you are saying.*

The editor continued to look past her. "I wonder how many people will die out there tonight?" he asked, in a forgotten, quiet tone that implied he didn't expect an answer. Then he shook his head back and forth, like an animal trying to shake an annoying insect away. "Don't turn yourself into a statistic," he abruptly warned her, adopting a patrician tone. "Keep to the approved schedules. Use the escorts. Stay alert, Susan. Stay safe."

"I intend to," she replied, wondering whether she actually meant it.

"Anyway, where could we find another puzzle queen? What's it to be this week? Something mathematical? Something literary?"

"Literary," she said. "I've hidden a half-dozen key words from famous Shakespearean speeches inside a concocted dialogue between a pair of lovers. The game is to recognize which words come from the Bard, and identify the speeches."

"Like someone idly saying, 'I just want to be right,' but the key phrase to identify is 'to be,' from 'to be or not to be'?"

"Yes," she said. "Except that particular phrase would be far too easy for my readership."

The editor smiled. " 'Whether to suffer the slings and arrows of out-rageous fortune or' . . . what comes next? I never get them, you know."

"Never?"

"That's right." He continued to smile. "Too dumb. Too uneducated. And much too impatient. Not enough attention span. Probably ought to take something for it. Just can't make myself sit and dope it out the way you can. Just too frustrating."

She didn't know how to respond.

"Ah well," he said, shrugging. "Don't stay too late. No one on the staff has been either raped or murdered yet this year, at least that we know about, and management would like to keep it that way. And when you get finished, send an electronic beeper message with your copy, so the compositors don't screw up again. Last week they missed three separate corrections we sent in late."

"I will, but you know, those guys like me. They've never met me, but they seem to like me. I get mash notes all the time over electronic mail."

"It's the name you use. Mysterious. Middle Eastern exotic. Veiled and elusive. Reminds people of hidden things, lost in the past. Very sexy, Mata Hari."

Susan retrieved a pair of reading glasses from her desk, which she infrequently used but occasionally needed. She slipped them on, perching them on the end of her nose. "There," she said. "More schoolmarm than spy, don't you think?"

The editor laughed, and gave her a small wave as he walked away.

A few moments later the security guard stuck his head in the cubicle. "You're staying late?" he asked, a note of incredulity in his voice.

"Yes. Not for long. I'll call when I need an escort."

"We're off at seven," he said. "Just the night guy on after that. And he's not licensed for escort duties. And anyway, he'll probably just shoot you when you come down the elevator, because he'll be so goddamn scared when he realizes there's someone else besides him in the building."

"I won't stay long. And I'll let him know when I come down."

The man shrugged. "It's your neck," he said, then left her sitting at her desk.

You can't be alone anymore, she thought. It's unsafe.

And solitude is suspicious.

Again she took a look out the window. The evening gridlock was just beginning to form, great snakes of traffic heading away from the downtown. The evening commute reminded her of scenes from old western movies, where the cattle in the midst of their drive north, unwittingly traveling to their own slaughter, would suddenly spook, and the entire sea of slow, lowing beasts would abruptly surge into panic, charging across the landscape as the cowboy heroes in that stylized version of history struggled to bring them back under control. She watched as overhead police helicopters buzzed above the bumper-to-bumper traffic like so many carrion birds, searching for carcasses. There was a ringing sound behind her, which she knew was the elevator doors shutting. She could suddenly feel the silence in the office as if it were a breeze blown in off the ocean. Picking up a yellow scratch pad, she wrote at the top: *I have found you.*

Once again the words gave her a start. She bit down hard on her lower lip and began to formulate a reply, trying to think of the right way to code whatever she chose, because she wanted to begin drawing a picture of her correspondent in her head, and making this person solve a puzzle of her design would help her understand who it was out there who had found her.

Susan Clayton, like her older brother, still carried her athlete's shape. Her own sport of preference had been diving; she'd enjoyed the sensation of abandonment, standing on the end of the three-meter platform, solitary, in danger, gathering herself mentally before thrusting her body out into the air. She realized that much of what she did—including staying late in her office—was much the same. She didn't understand why she was so frequently driven to take risks, but she understood that these moments of high tension were integral to her being able to complete each and every day. When she drove a car, it was almost always in the unrestricted highway lanes at more than a hundred miles per hour. If she went to the beach, she would venture into currents far from shore, testing herself against the tug and pull of the riptides. She had no steady boyfriend, and turned down almost every offer of a date, because she felt an unusual incompleteness about her life, and understood that a stranger, even an eager one, would add a complication she didn't need. She realized that her behavior carried a much greater chance of bringing about her early death than helping her fall in love, but this was an accommodation Susan was oddly comfortable with.

Sometimes, looking in the mirror, she wondered whether the edginess around the corners of her eyes and in the set of her mouth were caused by her parachutist's approach to life, free-falling through the years. The one thing she feared was her mother's death, which she knew was inevitable and closing in on her more rapidly than she knew how to cope with. She sometimes thought that taking care of her mother, which most would have seen as a debilitating millstone of a task, was the only thing that kept her grasping hold of her job, and some meager semblance of normal life.

Susan hated the cancer with intensity. She longed to be able to fight it on some fair ground, face-to-face. She thought it cowardly, and delighted in those moments when she saw her mother battling the disease.

She missed her brother immensely.

Jeffrey created in her a tangle of contradictory emotions. She had relied on his presence so much, growing up together, that it was inevitable she would feel some resentment when he left home. She had become both jealous and proud, and did not fully understand why she had never been able to strike out on her own. She thought her brother's adult expertise and obsession with killers unsettling. It was difficult, she understood, to both be frightened of and attracted to the same thing, and she worried that in some way that she was unfamiliar with, she might actually be like him.

In the last few years, when they'd talked, she discovered herself holding back, unwilling to share her feelings, as if she wanted him to understand her as little as possible. She could not easily answer his questions about her career, her hopes, her life. She kept herself vague, concealed behind a fog of half truths and limited details. Though she considered herself a woman of sharply defined lines and edges, she presented to her brother only a gauzelike vapidity.

And most curiously, she had persuaded her mother to help conceal the full extent of her illness from Jeffrey. Her argument had been something about not disrupting his life with the knowledge, protecting him by not introducing him to the erratic but consistent progression of her death. He would worry too much, she'd said. He'd want to come back to Florida and be with them, and there wasn't room. He'd want to go over all the painful, awful decisions—about medicines and treatments and hospices—that they had already talked out. Her mother listened to all this, and halfheartedly sighed in agreement. Susan thought this rapid acquiescence uncharacteristic. Her mother's death, Susan had decided, was something that she intended to possess. It was as if she thought the dying was somehow threatening, contagious. Susan lied to herself that Jeffrey would thank her someday for protecting him from the awfulness of its progress.

She occasionally thought she was wrong for doing this. Perhaps even foolish as well, and at times briefly despaired over her solitude, and was at a loss as to where it came from, or how to defeat it. Sometimes, she thought that she'd managed to confuse independence with loneliness, and that was the trap she found herself in.

She wondered, too, whether Jeffrey was trapped as well, and believed that the time was rapidly approaching when she would have to ask him.

Susan sat at her desk, doodling with a pen, drawing concentric circles over and over, until the circles filled with ink and became dark spots. Outside, night had by now fully overtaken the city; there were sporadic orange glows where fires had broken out in the inner city, and the sky was frequently sliced by shafts of lights from police helicopters searching out the ever-present crime. These appeared to her as so many pillars of celestial light, streaking toward earth from the darkness above. At the edge of the panorama from her window, she could see bright arcs of glowing neon defining safe areas, and, moving through the city, a continual highway stream of headlights, like water flowing through canyons of night.

She turned back away from the window, toward her pad.

What is it you need to know? she asked of herself.

And then, just as quickly, she answered. *There is only one question.*

She concentrated on that single question, wondering first if she could express it mathematically, but then discarding that idea in favor of a narrative approach. The issue, she thought, is how to express the question both simply, yet with difficulty.

She smiled to herself, warming to the task.

Outside, the nighttime city war continued unabated, but she was now oblivious to the sounds and sights of the routines of violence, sealed away as she was, in the darkened offices, hidden amidst her reference books, encyclopedias, almanacs, and dictionaries. She realized she was having fun, as she tried expressing the question in different forms, then finding it in famous quotations, but not really getting it precisely the way she wanted.

She started to hum to herself, snatches of recognizable tunes that seemed to fray around the edges and disintegrate into droning sounds as she went off on different tangents, all the time trying to construct a puzzle. She thought: It is always the core that's known—the answer. The game is in building the maze around it.

An idea struck her, and she almost knocked her desk lamp over as she reached out for one of the many books she kept surrounding her work space.

She leafed through the pages swiftly until she found what she'd been searching for. Then she leaned back in her seat, rocking with the satisfaction of someone who has feasted well.

I am a librarian of the trivial, she told herself. A historian of the arcane. The sage of the obscure. And I'm the best.

Susan wrote the information onto her yellow pad, and then wondered how best to conceal what she had in front of her. She was caught up in what she was doing when she heard the noise. It took several seconds for it to register that a sound had penetrated the air about her. A scratching sound, like a door being pushed open, or a foot scraping against the floor.

She sat up sharply.

She leaned forward slowly, like an animal, trying to pick the sound out of the silence.

It's nothing, she told herself.

But she slowly reached down and removed a handgun from her purse. Gripping it in her right hand, she swiveled her chair toward the cubicle opening.

She held her breath, continuing to listen hard. But the only noise she could now hear was the abrupt sensation of her own heart thrusting blood through her temples. Nothing else.

Still turned toward the darkness of the office, she carefully reached out and picked up the telephone receiver. Without turning to look at the keypad, she punched in the building security code.

The phone rang once, and it was answered by a guard. "Building Security. Johnson."

She whispered: "This is Susan Clayton. Thirteenth floor. *Miami Magazine* offices. I'm supposed to be alone."

The security guard's voice came over the line briskly. "I got a memo that you were still here. Whassa problem?"

"I heard a noise."

"A noise? Ain't nobody s'posed to be there 'cept you."

"What about cleaning crews?"

"Not till midnight."

"The other offices?"

"All cleared out and gone home. You're alone, lady."

"Can you check your video and heat sensors?"

The guard grunted, as if this was more difficult than merely flicking a few switches on a computer keyboard.

"Ahh, thirteenth-floor video, now I can see you. That an automatic?"

"Keep checking."

"I'm swinging about. Damn, but you all got lots of crap in there. Fellow could be hiding under a desk and I wouldn't see him no way."

"Check the heat sensors."

"I'm doing that now. Let's see. Well, maybe, nah, I doubt it."

"What?"

"Well, I'm reading you fine and your light there. And there's some folks left their computers on, those always give off false positives. Now maybe there's enough heat for another person up there, ma'am. But ain't nothing moving. It's probably just leftover computer heat. Wish folks would remember to turn those suckers off. Screw up the sensors something terrible."

Susan realized that her knuckles were turning white where she gripped the weapon.

"Keep checking."

"Ain't nothing else to check. You're alone, lady. Or else whoever's up there with you is hiding beneath a computer terminal and not moving nothing, like barely breathing, and just waiting there 'cause he knows how our equipment works and he can hear us talking away. That's the way I'd do it," the guard said. "Gotta be real careful-like. Just move from heat source to heat source real quiet-like and then get in my business real quick. You might wanna chamber a round in that weapon, ma'am."

"Can you come up?"

"That ain't my job. Escort does that. I'll see you out, but you got to get down here all by your lonesome. I ain't heading upstairs till cleaning gets here. Those boys carry some serious weapons."

"Damn," Susan whispered.

"What's that?" the guard asked.

"You still see nothing?"

"Nothing on the video, but it don't work so good anyways. And nothing excepting all those false positives on the heat. At least, they seem like false positives. Whyn't you just move nice and slow to the elevator, and I'll keep an eye on you through the camera?"

"I just need to finish one thing."

"Well, suit yourself."

"Keep watching, will you? This will only take a couple of minutes."

"Got an extra hundred on you?"

"What?"

"I'll watch while you finish. Cost you a hundred."

She thought hard for an instant. "All right. Deal."

The guard laughed. "Easy money."

She heard another sound. "What was that?"

"Just me making the remote camera swivel about," the guard said.

Susan slid her pistol onto the desk next to her computer keyboard, removing her fingers from the grip reluctantly. It was even harder for her to turn in her seat, putting her back to the opening to her cubicle and whatever was out there making the sound she'd heard. Maybe a rat, she told herself. Or even just a mouse. Or nothing. She breathed in slowly, controlling her racing pulse, feeling the stickiness of sweat beneath her light shirt. You're alone, she told herself. Alone. She flicked on the computer screen and quickly keyed in the necessary information to send a message to the electronic composing department. She placed her slug, *Mata Hari*, at the top, and swiftly typed in the instructions for the compositors.

Then she wrote:

Special for My New Correspondent:
Rock Tom Seventy-one Second Choo-choo Five.

She paused, staring at the words for a moment, satisfied with what she'd created. Then she shipped the message off electronically. As soon as the computer told her the document had been moved and received, she turned about in her chair, grabbing the automatic pistol in the same motion.

The offices seemed quiet, and she again insisted to herself that she was alone. But she was unable to convince herself of this fact, and she thought that silence, like a warped mirror, can sometimes be an illusion. Looking up at the video monitoring camera that was pointed at her, Susan gave a small wave to the guard she hoped was paying attention, and with her free hand started to collect her things, thrusting them into a satchel, which she then slung over her shoulder. As she rose from her chair, she raised the pistol and gripped it with both hands, in a shooter's stance. She took a deep, calming breath, like a marksman would in the millisecond before firing. Then, moving slowly, keeping her back constantly against whatever wall she could find, she cautiously began her journey home.

ALWAYS

Not a mile away from the house she shared with her mother, Susan Clayton kept her boat moored to an old, ramshackle dock. The dock was swaybacked and unsteady, like a horse on its way to the glue factory, and to all appearances would come flying apart in the next high wind and thunderstorm. She knew, however, that it had survived much worse, which, she thought, was a true qualification in the world of impermanence she lived in. The dock, she believed, was like the Keys themselves, hiding resilience within decrepitude; something that is what it is, but far stronger than it appears. She also hoped that she herself was like this.

The boat was out of date as well, but immaculate; an eighteen-foot flats skiff, low-slung to the water and a glistening, sleek white. She'd purchased it from the widow of a retired fishing guide who'd died far from the waters he worked for decades, in a Miami hospital for the terminally ill, similar to the one she'd refused to consider for her mother.

Beneath her feet, the gravelly sand and bits of whitened shells that made up the pathway crunched with every step. This was a reassuring and familiar sound, which she welcomed. It was a few minutes before dawn. The light appeared yellow, as if tinged with indecision or remorse at giving up its grip on the darkness; a time when what's left of the night seems to spread through the waters, turning them a slick gray-black. She knew it would be another hour until the sun had risen high enough to fill the ocean with light and turn the shallow Keys channels and flats into a changing, opalescent, liquid palate of blues.

Susan hunched her shoulders against the slight damp chill in the air, a false cold that she told herself was due more to the hour and held no promise of relief from the oppressive heat that would arrive with little delay to take over the day. It was always hot in South Florida now, a constancy of humid warmth that spawned larger and more violent storms and made people hide deep within cocoons of manufactured air-conditioning. When she was young, she remembered, she could actually feel the changes of the seasons, not in the way one could up in the Northeast, where she'd been born, or farther north, in the mountains her mother spoke of so longingly as she prepared herself for death, but in a peculiar southern fashion, recognizing only the smallest dip in the intensity of the sun, an insinuation in the breeze, which told her that the world was somehow changing over. But even that modest sense of change seemed to have vanished in recent years, dissolving in never-ending stories of global climactic changes.

The inlet leading out onto the wide expanses of flats was empty. There was a slack tide, the black water at rest, a smooth eight ball of ocean. Her skiff hung at the side of the dock, the bow and stern lines falling in limp coils on the dew-glistening deck. The large two-hundred-horsepower engine seemed to catch the first light reflections, gleaming. She looked at it and thought it not unlike a good fighter's right hand, held in check, motionless, balled up into a tight fist waiting for the command to crash forward.

She approached the skiff as she would a friend.

"I need to fly," she said quietly to the boat. "Today, I want speed."

She rapidly stowed a pair of fishing rods in holders beneath the starboard gunnel. One was a short spinning rod, which she brought for its efficiency and simplicity, the other was a longer, more graceful fly rod, which satisfied her sense of indulgence. She double-checked the long, graphite push pole, fixed to retractable holders on the deck and nearly as long as the eighteen-foot boat itself. Then she went over the quick checklist of safety items, like a pilot in the minutes before takeoff.

Satisfied that all was in order, she unfastened the lines to the dock, shoved off, and pushed down on the electric tilt, lowering the engine transom into the water with a high-pitched whine. Settling into her seat, she automatically touched the transmission to make certain it was in neutral, then started the engine. It rattled once like a can with rocks being shaken hard, then turned over with a satisfying gurgling noise. She let the engine idle the skiff forward down the inlet, slipping through the water like the blade of a scissors cutting through silk. Reaching inside a small compartment, she removed a pair of ear protectors and fixed them on her head.

As the skiff cleared the end of the channel, past the last house perched up on the waterway, she pushed the accelerator forward, raising the bow for an instant as the engine directly behind her throatily sounded its pleasure. Then, almost as quickly as it rose, the bow slid downward, the skiff leapt forward as it planed across the inky waters, and she was abruptly, completely, swallowed by speed. She leaned forward into the wind that puffed out her cheeks as she gulped at the freshness of the morning; the ear protectors muffled the engine noise, so that it was only a dull, seductive tympani behind her.

She thought someday she might be able to outrun the morning.

To her right, in the shallows of a small mangrove island, she saw a pair of starkly white herons stalking pinfish, their ungainly, spindly legs moving with an exaggerated caution, like a pair of dancers unsure of the music. Ahead of her a fish spooked, and she caught a glimpse of a silver back leaping free from the water. She touched the wheel lightly and the skiff raced on, steered away from the shoreline and out into the back country, slicing between wild, tangled green islands.

Susan ran the skiff hard for almost thirty minutes, until she was certain she was far away from anyone who might be venturing out into the heat of the day. She was close to where the Florida Bay curls in toward shore and meets the wide mouth of the Everglades. It is a place of great uncertainty, as if unsure whether it's part of the ocean or the land, a maze of channels and islands. It is an easy place for the unfamiliar to get lost.

Susan thought of the empty spaces where the sky, the mangroves, and the water all met as antique and ancient. There was nothing modern about the world surrounding her, only life settled in its ways over eons.

She throttled back on the engine and the skiff hesitated in the water like a horse suddenly reined in. She cut the ignition and glided forward silently, the water beneath the prow changing as the boat slid onto the edge of a wide expanse of shallows, stretching a mile along the edge of a low green mangrove island. A flight of cormorants rose from the snarled branches of the shoreline, perhaps twenty birds at once, their black shapes outlined by the early-morning light as they wheeled and fled. Susan stood up and removed her ear protection, her eyes scanning the surface of the water, then rising for a glance at the sky. The sun had taken over; an insistent iridescent clarity was almost painful as it slapped the waters surrounding the skiff. She could feel heat like a man's grip on the back of her neck.

She removed a plastic container of sunblock from a compartment beneath the transmission console, and liberally smeared it on her neck. She was wearing a khaki one-piece cotton set of coveralls, a mechanic's outfit. She undid the buttons up the chest and let the suit fall to the deck, standing suddenly naked. Stepping out of the outfit, she let the sun grab at her like an anxious lover, feeling the glare as it settled on her breasts, between her legs and caressing her back. Then she smeared more sunscreen over the entirety of her nakedness, until her body glistened as brightly as the waters of the flat.

She was alone. There was no sound, save the plopping of a light chop against the hull of the skiff.

She laughed out loud.

If there was a way to make love to the morning, she would have done it; instead, she let her insides quicken with excitement, turning herself as the sun covered her.

She stood that way for a few minutes. Inwardly, she spoke to the sun and the heat, saying: You would be worse than any man; you would love me, but then you would take more than your due, you would burn my skin and turn me old before my time. Reluctantly, she reached inside the compartment and found a thin black polypropylene cowl, the sort worn by Arctic adventurers beneath their other layers of clothes. She slipped it over her head, so that only her eyes were exposed, giving her the appearance of a burglar. Rummaging about, she found an old, green and orange University of Miami baseball cap, which she jammed on her head, and then put on a pair of polarized sunglasses. She started to step back into the coveralls, then hesitated.

One fish, she told herself. I'll catch one fish naked.

Realizing she looked a little ridiculous, with her head and face completely covered, but otherwise bare-butt naked, she let out a single loud laugh, took the two rods out of their holders and arranged them where she could reach them, removed the push pole and climbed up onto the poling platform, a small, elevated flat deck above the engine, which gave her additional purchase on the water. Slowly, she worked the long graphite pole, maneuvering the skiff forward across the shallow water.

She expected to see a bonefish or two, tailing up as it dug small shrimp and crabs out of the muddy sand of the flat. That would be nice, she told herself; they were very honorable fish, capable of withering speed. Barracuda were always possible as well; they would hang in the opaque water nearly motionless, with only the occasional quiver from their fins to let her know that they weren't a part of the liquid world. She thought of them as gangsters; they sported dangerous, canine teeth, and fought savagely when hooked. She knew she would see some mid-sized sharks, cruising the shallow edges of the flat like playground bullies, looking for an easy breakfast.

She slid the pole into the water quietly, gliding forward.

"Come on, fish," she said out loud. "Who's here this morning?"

What she saw made her inhale sharply and look twice to be certain.

Fifty yards away, moving in a patient zigzag through barely two and a half feet of water, was the unmistakable torpedo shape of a large tarpon. Six feet long, and perhaps 120 pounds. Far too large for the shallows, and out of season as well; the tarpon migrated in the spring, huge schools making their steady way north. She'd caught her share then, in slightly deeper channels.

But this was a large fish, out of place and out of time, moving right toward her.

She quickly dug the pointed end of the push pole into the sandy bottom and looped a rope over the end, so that it held, like an anchor. Gingerly, she leapt down from the platform and grabbed the fly rod, crossing the boat and jumping to the bow in a single stride. She could still see the massive bulk of the fish as it penetrated the water, its scythelike tail pushing it inexorably forward. Occasionally the silver side of the fish would catch a reflection, like a burst of explosives in the water.

She stripped out line. The rod she carried was more suitable for a fish one-tenth the size of the one working toward her. Nor did she truly think that the tarpon would eat the small crab imitation on the end of the line. But it was all she had that might work, and even if failure was inevitable, she wanted to try.

The fish was a hundred feet away, and for an instant she marveled at the incongruity of it. She could feel her pulse rate beating a tattoo within her.

At eighty feet she told herself: Still too far.

At sixty feet she thought: Now I can reach you. She started to move the light, wandlike rod through the air, filling the sky with a small swishing sound as the fly line cut a long arc above her head. But she made herself wait another few seconds.

The fish was fifty feet away when she released the line, with a small grunt, and watched as it rocketed across the water, stretching out and finally settling down, the crab fly plopping the water surface perhaps three feet in front of the tarpon's nose.

The fish surged forward without hesitation.

The sudden burst astonished her, and she let out a small cry of surprise. The fish did not instantly feel the hook, and she swallowed hard and waited as the line grew tight in her hand. Then, with a great shout, she pulled back on the line, swinging the rod tip backward to her left, sweeping it away from the fish. She could feel the hook take grip.

The water exploded in front of her, a sheet of silver-white.

The fish thrashed once at the insult of the hook; she could see the open maw of the tarpon's mouth. Then it turned and raced away, angling for deeper water. She held the rod above her head, like a priest raising a chalice, and the reel began to shriek with protest as yards of thin, white line streamed out.

Still holding the rod tip high, she maneuvered to the rear of the skiff and unfastened the rope holding the push pole, so that the boat was no longer anchored.

She realized that in another minute the fish would take all the line, and a few seconds later there would be nothing more to take. He would surge forward and either throw the hook, break the leader, or simply steal all 250 yards of line. And then he would swim off, a little sore around the jaw but none the worse for wear, unless she could somehow turn him. She didn't think she could do this, but perhaps if the fish pulled the boat through the water, instead of against the anchor, she might manage for a minute to make him stop and fight.

Susan could feel the tarpon's energy pulsating through the rod, and she held out no hope, but even when the situation is doomed, she thought, it's still worth trying everything you know, so that at least when defeat inevitably arrives, you will have the satisfaction of knowing that you fought as well against it as you could.

The prow of the boat had spun, following the fish.

Still naked, feeling sweat starting to trickle down beneath her arms, she stood back up on the bow. She could see the reel's spool, emptied of line, and thought: Here's where I lose this fight.

And then, to her surprise, the fish did turn its head.

She saw a huge geyser of water in the distance as the tarpon flung itself skyward, hanging in the air, twisting in the sunlight, before landing explosively.

She heard herself cry out again, not in surprise, but in admiration.

The tarpon continued to leap, corkscrewing and somersaulting, throwing its head back and forth as it struggled against the hook.

For a moment she allowed herself the narcotic of hope, then, almost as swiftly, dismissed this thought. Still, she realized: It is a strong fish, and I truly have no right to have kept him on even this long. She leaned back, pulling on the rod, trying to regain some line, praying that the fish would not simply bull ahead and run again, because that would end the fight.

She was not aware how long the two of them remained locked in this position—the naked woman on the deck of the boat grunting with exertion, the silver fish thrashing skyward in explosion after explosion. She fought as if the two of them were alone in the world, battling every distant thrust the fish made until the muscles on her arms screamed at her and she thought her hand might cramp. Sweat stung her eyes; she wondered if fifteen minutes had passed, then reconsidered and told herself no, perhaps an hour, maybe two. Then, in partial exhaustion, she insisted it couldn't have been that long.

She groaned deeply and continued to fight.

Susan felt a shudder run the entire length of the line and through the spine of the rod, and she saw another sheet of white water and silver fish splash in the distance. Then, oddly, she sensed a slackness, and the rod, which had been bent in a quivering C, abruptly straightened. She gasped.

"Damn it!" she said. "He's gone!"

And then, in almost the same second, she realized: *No.*

And alarm. *He's running back toward me.*

Her left hand on the reel seemed wooden with cramps. She smashed it against her thigh three times, trying to get it to bend, and then frantically began reeling in the slack line. Fifty yards came in, then a hundred. She lifted her head and saw the fish racing toward her, then continued her frenzied assault on the reel.

The fish had closed to perhaps seventy-five yards when she finally caught sight of the second shape chasing behind him, and in that same instant understood why the fish had surged back at the boat. She could feel a sense of dreadful quiet within her as she measured a massive dark black splotch in the water, twice the size of her tarpon. It was as if someone had taken black ink and thrown it onto some old master's perfect landscape.

The panic-stricken tarpon went airborne again, hanging in the blue sky, perhaps six feet above the ideal blue of the water.

She stopped reeling and watched, motionless.

The shape closed inexorably, so that for a second the pristine silver of the fish seemed to blend with the blackness of the hammerhead. There was another explosion on the surface, another sheet of water flying into the air, and then a frothing white, which she saw was streaked with red blood.

She lowered the rod, and the line hung from its end.

The water continued to boil, like a pot left on the stove. Then, just as swiftly, it settled, an oily slick calming the surface. She held her hand up to shade her eyes, but only caught the smallest glimpse of the dark shape sliding back into deeper water, blending and disappearing like an evil thought in the midst of a noisy celebration. She continued to stand on the bow, breathing hard. She felt as if she'd witnessed a murder.

Then, slowly, she started the task of retrieving the line. She could feel some weight on the end, dragging through the water, and knew what she would find. The hammerhead had severed the tarpon's body about a foot below the head, which remained attached to the hook. She reeled in the gruesome prize. At the side of the skiff she bent down and started to reach for the hook, still embedded in the tough jaw of the dead fish. But she couldn't bear to touch it. Instead she retreated to the console and found a thin-bladed filleting knife, which she used to slice the leader. For an instant she could see the tarpon's head and torso descending to the bottom, then it was lost.

"I'm sorry, fish," she said out loud. "If I hadn't been so ambitious, you would have lived. I had no right to hook you, and no right to exhaust you. I had no right to fight you in the first place. Why didn't you just throw the damn hook, like you should have, or broken off? You were strong enough. Why didn't you do what you knew to do, instead of turning yourself into prey? I helped you do that, and I'm genuinely sorry, fish, for having caused you to be eaten. It was my fault, and you didn't deserve it."

She thought: I have no luck. I have never had any luck.

Susan abruptly grew afraid, and gasped back a half-finished vision of her own mother. She shook her head hard, then breathed in deeply. Suddenly embarrassed by her nakedness, she stood and searched the empty horizon, thinking there might be someone out there, in the distance, watching her through high-powered binoculars. She told herself she was crazy, that the sun and her exhaustion and the way the fight ended had all conspired to unsettle her. But still, she reached down to the deck where her coveralls had been kicked into a corner and seized them, holding them up against her chest as she swept her eyes across the wide expanse of sea. There are always sharks, she told herself, out there where you cannot see them, and they hone in inexorably on the distressed signals of struggle. They can sense when a fish is wounded and exhausted and no longer strong enough to elude them or fight them. That's when they emerge from the darker, deeper waters and attack. When they're certain of success.

Susan's head spun dizzily with the heat. She felt the sun burning the skin on her shoulders, and so she quickly pulled on her coveralls, buttoning them tightly, up to her neck. She rapidly stowed her gear, then she pointed the skiff toward home, and felt relief as the engine surged to life behind her.

It was less than one week since she'd sent out her special at the bottom of her regular magazine column. She didn't expect to hear from her anonymous subject that quickly. Two weeks, she had thought. Perhaps a month. Maybe never.

But about that, she was wrong.

At first she didn't see the envelope.

Instead, as she stepped into the driveway to her house, she was filled with a sense of quiet, and this made her stop in her tracks. She thought the quiet was caused by the end-of-the-day light, fading from the yard, then wondered whether something was out of place. She shook her head and told herself she was still unsettled from the shark's attack on her fish.

For reassurance, she let her eyes sweep over the approach to the single-story, cinder-block house. It was a typical, unprepossessing Keys house, with nothing remarkable about it, save its occupants. It had no inherent charm or style; it had been built out of the most practical materials in a stolid, cookie-cutter design, a building intended to provide shelter to people whose aspirations were limited and whose resources were modest. A few bedraggled palms swayed on one side of the yard, which was mostly burned down to dirt, with a few patches of stubborn grass and crabgrass, and had never, even when she was a child, been an inviting place to play. Her car was where she'd left it, in a small circle of shade donated by the palms. The house, pink once, an enthusiastic color, had by now been bleached by the sun to a dull, helpless coral. She could hear the air conditioner laboring hard against the heat, and realized the repairman must have finally showed up. At least now it won't be the damn heat that kills Mother, she thought.

She repeated to herself that nothing was out of the ordinary, that everything was where it should be, that nothing was different this day than from a thousand days just like it, and she stepped forward, not really believing this. In that false moment of relief, she saw the envelope propped against the front door.

Susan stopped, as if she'd seen a snake, and felt a surge of fear ripple through her.

She took a deep breath.

"Damn," she said.

She approached the letter cautiously, as if it might explode, or it carried some dangerous disease. Then she gingerly reached down and picked it up. She tore open the envelope and quickly removed the single sheet of paper it contained:

Very clever, Mata Hari. But not quite clever enough. *Rock Tom* made me think. Tried a number of things, as you might imagine. But then, well, who knows where inspiration comes from? It occurred to me that you might be referring to the British rock-and-roll quartet, amongst whose hits so many decades ago was the "opera" *Tommy*. And so, if you were talking about The Who, what was the rest of the message? Well, *Seventy-one* could be a year. *Second Choo-choo Five?* That wasn't too hard, when I looked at the listing of songs on the second side, track number five of the album they released in 1971. And lo and behold, what did I come up with? *"Who Are You?"*

I don't know if I'm quite ready to answer that question. Eventually, of course. But for now, I will add this single statement to our correspondence:

Previous 524135217 coffee emerald thant.

Now, that shouldn't be too hard for a smart gal like yourself. Alice would have been a good name for a puzzle queen, especially a red one, too.

As before, the note was unsigned.

Susan fumbled with the front door dead bolt as she sharply called out: "Mother!"

Diana Clayton was standing by the stove, stirring a small portion of chicken broth in a saucepan. She heard her daughter's voice but did not hear the urgency in the cry, and so replied matter-of-factly, "In here, dear," only to be answered by a second demand, from the front: "Mother!"

And so, louder, "In here," with a small exasperation. To raise her voice did not cause her pain, but it took more effort than she felt she could spare. She husbanded her strength and was resentful of any small, unfair drain of energy, because she knew she needed all her resources at those moments when the pain truly came to visit. She'd been able to reach some compromises with her disease, a sort of internal negotiation, but thought the cancer was forever behaving like some dishonest shyster; it was always trying to cheat and steal more than she was willing to give up. She took a sip from the soup as her daughter pounded through the narrow house to the kitchen. She listened to Susan's footsteps, thinking that she could almost certainly read the entirety of her daughter's mood in the sound they made, so when Susan entered the room, she was ready with her question:

"Susan, dear, what's wrong? You sound upset. Wasn't the fishing good?"

"No," her daughter replied. "Yes, that's not it. Listen, Mother, did you see or hear anything unusual today? Anyone come by the house?"

"Just the air-conditioning man, thank God. I gave him a check. I hope it doesn't bounce."

"Anyone else? Did you hear anything?"

"No. But I took a nap this afternoon. What is it, dear?"

Susan stopped, uncertain whether she should say anything. Into this hesitation, her mother spoke sharply:

"Something is bothering you. Don't treat me like a child. I may be sick, but I'm not an invalid. What is it?"

Susan still hesitated another second before replying. "There was another letter delivered here today. Like the one the other week in the mailbox. No signature. No return address. Left right by the front door. That's what's upsetting me."

"Another?"

"Yes. I sent out a reply to the first in my regular column, but I didn't think the person would figure it out so quickly."

"What did you ask him?"

"I wanted to know who he is."

"And his answer?"

"Here. Read for yourself."

Diana took the sheet of paper that her daughter pushed forward. She stood by the stove and quickly absorbed the words. Then she slowly put the paper down, reached over, and turned off the gas jets that were cooking her broth. The soup simmered, steaming. The older woman took a deep breath.

"And what is it this person is asking this time?" she said coldly.

"I don't know yet. I just looked at it."

"I think," Diana said, her voice level with fear, "that we'd better figure out what the code is. And what he's saying this time. Then we can assess the tone of the entire letter."

"Well, I can probably figure out the number sequence. Those are usually not too difficult."

"Why don't you do that while I cook dinner?"

Diana turned back to the soup and began fussing with utensils. She bit down hard on her lip and told herself to bide her own counsel.

The daughter nodded, and moved to a small table in a corner of the kitchen. For a moment she watched her mother at work, and this cheered her up; any sign of normalcy, she took to be a sign of strength. Anytime life seemed routine, she believed the disease had been pushed back and stymied in its inevitable process. She breathed out deeply, took a pencil and a pad of paper out of a drawer, and started calculating. At the top of the pad she wrote *524135217*. Then she wrote out the alphabet, assigning *A* with the number *1* and ending with *Z* and *26*.

This, of course, would be the simplest interpretation of the number sequence, and she doubted it would be fruitful. But on the other hand, she had the odd impression that her correspondent didn't want her to struggle too hard with his message. The point of the game, she thought, was merely to display how smart he was, along with conveying whatever thought was contained in the note. Some of the people who wrote her used such arcane and crazily con-cocted codes that they would have defied even military code computers. These usually grew out of the sense of paranoia the people held dear. But this writer had a different agenda. The problem was, she didn't know yet what it was.

But, still, she believed, he wanted her to figure it out.

Her first attempt produced *EBDAC* . . . which was where she stopped. Still working on the first five digits, she tried seeing them as 5–24–13 . . . which produced *EXM*. . . . This was impossible, so she continued, until she reached *EXMEB*, then *EXMEUG*.

Her mother brought her a glass of beer, then returned to the food she was now cooking on the stove. Susan took a slow pull at the frothy brown liquid, let the coldness of the beer settle within her, and continued to work.

She rewrote the alphabet, assigning *26* to *A* and working backward. This gave her *UYW* at first, then, looking at the numbers differently, *UBN*. . . .

Susan filled her cheeks with air and puffed out like a blowfish. She doodled a small picture of a fish on the corner of her page, then drew a shark fin cutting through an imaginary ocean. She wondered why she hadn't spotted the hammerhead earlier, then told herself that predators usually show themselves when they're ready to strike, not before.

This thought made her return to the numerical sequence.

It will be hidden, she told herself. But not hidden that well.

Forward, backward, what was next?

Subtraction and addition.

A thought occurred to her, and she picked up the letter.

". . . I will add this single statement . . ."

She decided to rewrite the sequence, adding 1 to each number. This gave her *635246328*. This instantly produced *FCEBDFCBH*, which was no help. She tried the sequence backward, which also produced gobbledygook.

She held her sheet of paper out from her, then bent over it closely. Look at the numbers, she told herself. Try different combinations. She thought: If I rewrite *524135217* as different sequences . . . and she arrived at 5–24–13–5–21–7. She saw that she could also write the last digits as 2–17 as well. Then still adding one, she came up with 6–25–14–6–22–8. This gave her *FYNFWH*, and she began to wish she had a computer programmed for searching out numerical patterns.

Keeping with her steady approach, she reversed the numbers again, coming up with more gibberish. Then she tried changing them again. It's here, she said. You simply have to find the key.

She pulled again at the beer. She fought off the urge to start randomly selecting the numbers, knowing that she would lead herself into a frustrating tangle of letters and digits, forget where she'd begun, and have to retrace her steps. This was to be avoided; like all puzzle experts, she knew that salvation lay in logic.

She looked again at the note. Nothing he says has no meaning, she thought. She was certain he'd intended for her to add 1, but precisely how was the question. She fought off frustration.

Breathing deeply, she tried again, reexamining the sequence. She waved away her mother, who had approached with a plate of food, and bent to her task. She thought: He wants me to add, so that means he subtracted one from each number. That, in and of itself, is too simple. But what's leading me into meaningless letters is the direction they flow. Again she looked at the note.

Alice and then *red queen*. Through the Looking Glass. A little literary reference. She told herself that she should have spotted it earlier.

When you look in a mirror, that which is backward becomes clear.

She took the sequence, reversed the numbers, and added *1*.

822641526.

Was it 8–22–6 . . . or 8–2–26?

She barreled ahead, dividing the digits as 8–2–26–4–15–26. This produced *SYAWLA*.

Her mother stood over her shoulder.

"There it is," Diana said coldly. She snatched a breath from the air, and her daughter saw it as well.

ALWAYS.

Susan looked down at the word on the page and thought: It is a terrible word. She heard her mother's sharp intake of breath, and in that instant determined that a show of strength was called for, even if phony. Her mother would know this, she understood, but still, it would help her remain calm.

"Does it frighten you, Mother?"

"Yes," she replied.

"Why?" the daughter asked. "I don't know why, but it does me, too. But there's no threat. There's nothing even to suggest that it isn't someone just eager to play some intellectual game. That's happened before."

"The first note said what?"

"I have found you."

Diana felt a dark hole sucking away within her, like some great whirlpool threatening to swallow her whole. She fought this sensation off, told herself there was no evidence of anything yet. She reminded herself that for more than twenty-five years she had lived quietly, without being found; that the person she'd hidden herself and her children from was dead. And so, in a swift and probably inadequate assessment of the events that had overtaken her daughter and her, Diana decided that the notes were probably precisely what they appeared to be: the slightly twisted pleadings of one of her daughter's many fans. This, in and of itself, could be dangerous enough. And so she did not mention any other fear, believing that the current fear was enough for the two of them, and that some hidden, more ancient fear was better left in the past. And dead. Dead. A suicide, she reminded herself. He set you free when he killed himself.

"We should call your brother," she said.

"Why?"

"Because he has many connections in law enforcement. Maybe someone he knows could analyze this letter. Fingerprint it. Test it. Tell us something about it."

"I think that whoever's sending it has probably thought of those things. And anyway, he hasn't broken any law. At least, not yet. I think we should wait until I figure the whole note out. Shouldn't take too long."

"Well," Diana said quietly, "we do know one thing."

"What's that?" the daughter asked.

The mother stared at the daughter, as if Susan were incapable of seeing something directly in front of her.

"Well, he put the first note in the mailbox. And you found this one where?"

"At the front door."

"Well, that tells us he's coming closer, doesn't it?"

NEW WASHINGTON

The western sky had a metallic sheen to it, like highly polished steel, a wide, cold, unyielding expanse of clarity. He turned away from the glare, shielding his eyes momentarily.

"You'll get used to it," Robert Martin said casually. "Sometimes, out here, this time of year, it seems like someone's shining a light in your face. Spend a lot of time squinting at the horizon."

Jeffrey Clayton didn't reply directly. Instead, as they drove down a broad street, he turned and let his eyes course over the parade of modern office buildings, one after the other, set back from the highway. They were all different, yet the same: wide green expanses of landscaped lawns dotted with groves of trees; vibrant blue, man-made ponds and reflecting pools sweeping up to solid gray architectural shapes that spoke more of money spent than creativity of design, a marriage of function and art where there is little doubt which takes precedence. His eyes kept traveling, and he realized that everything was new. Everything was sculpted, spaced, and orderly. Everything was clean. He recognized the logos of major corporation after corporation. Communications, entertainment, industry. The Fortune 500 on display. He thought: If there is money being made in this nation, it has a presence here.

"What's the name of this street?" he asked.

"Freedom Boulevard," Agent Martin replied.

Jeffrey smiled briefly, sure there was irony hidden in the name. The traffic was light, and they traveled at a steady, unhurried pace. He continued to absorb his surroundings, finding something hollow in the newness of it all.

"Wasn't this desert once?" he wondered aloud.

"Yes," Martin answered. "Mostly scrub grass, arroyo, and tumbleweed. Lots of dirt and sand and wind a decade ago. Dam a river, divert water, maybe circumvent a few environmental laws—and it blooms. The technology is expensive, but, as you can guess, that wasn't the greatest factor."

Jeffrey thought this an interesting idea: replace one sort of nature with another. Create an idealized, corporate vision of what the world *should* look like, and impose it on the messy, not quite up-to-snuff world that is actually provided. A land within a land. Not unreal, but surely not authentic, either. He wasn't sure whether this made him uncomfortable or unsettled.

"Turn off the water, and I guess in another ten years this place'd be a ghost town," Martin said. "But no one's turning off the water."

"Who was here? I mean, before . . ."

"Here, in New Washington? Nothing was here. At least not much. A couple of hundred square miles of mostly nothing. Rattlesnakes and gila monsters and buzzards. Once upon a time, part was federally owned lands, part was an old Indian reservation that was annexed, and part was seized by eminent domain. Some well-to-do ranchers were a bit miffed. Same thing was true for the entire state. People who lived in the areas designated for development were paid off and moved out before the bulldozers arrived. It was just like every time in history when this nation expanded; some people got rich, some people got displaced, some people just got shoved into the same poverty, someplace else. No different from, say, the 1870s. The only thing that wasn't maybe the same was that this was expanding *inward*, not outward into uncharted territory, but into territory that no one cared all that much about. Now they care, because they've seen what we can do. And what we're gonna do. This is a big place. There's still lots of empty space, especially to the north of us, near the Bitterroot Range. Room for more expansion."

"Is there a need for expansion?" Jeffrey asked.

The detective shrugged. "Any territory is looking to grow. Especially a place dedicated to safety. There's always a need for expansion. And always more people who want a piece of the real American vision."

Clayton quieted again, and let Martin drive.

They had not discussed the purpose for his presence in the Fifty-first State—not once throughout the long flight west, across the midsection of the nation, over the great spine of the continental divide, and finally slip-sliding down into what had once been the isolated northern portion of the state of Nevada.

As they drove, Jeffrey had a sudden, unwelcome memory.

The orderly procession of buildings dissipated before his eyes, replaced with a hard, concrete city world, a place that had once known the exaggerations of wealth and success, but like so much else in the past decade, had fallen into a shabby, threadbare disrepair. Galveston, Texas, less than a half-dozen years earlier. He remembered: a warehouse. The door had been jammed open, and it rattled in a steady, penetrating cold wind that came in off the muddy brown Gulf waters. The ground-floor windows were all jagged with broken glass; it had rained earlier in the morning, and the reflections of dim light from the street threw grotesque snakes of shadows onto the walls.

Why didn't you wait? he abruptly asked himself. This was a familiar question, one that accompanied this particular memory every time it arrived unbidden into his waking consciousness, and frequently when it intruded in his dreams.

There was no need to hurry. If you'd waited, he reminded himself, backup would have arrived, sooner or later. A SWAT team with night vision eyewear and heavy weaponry, body armor and military discipline. Enough officers to form a perimeter around the warehouse. Tear gas and bullhorns. A helicopter with a spotlight hovering overhead. There was no need for you and those two detectives to go inside before reinforcements arrived.

But they wanted to, he replied to his own question. They were impatient. The hunt had been long and frustrating and they could sense it was ending, and he was the only one who knew how dangerous the quarry would be, in its own lair, cornered.

There is a children's story. Rudyard Kipling's tale of the mongoose who follows a cobra into its hole. It is cautionary in its vision: fight your battles on your own ground, not the enemy's. If you can. The problem is, he thought, you can't.

He'd known that, but said nothing that night, even though help was already heading their way. He wondered why, but was aware of the real reason. In all his studies of killers and their killings, he'd never seen one in that luminescent moment of power when they had someone under their control and were centered on the task of creating a death. That was what he'd wanted to see, and wanted to feel firsthand: to be there at that royal instant when all the killer's reason and madness coalesced into an act of singular savagery and depravity.

He'd seen too many pictures. He'd taped hundreds of eyewitness recollections. He'd visited dozens of crime scenes. But all these portions of information had come one step removed. He'd never been there as the moment was actually happening, to see for himself all the madness and magic wrapped together. And this—he couldn't bring himself to call it curiosity, because he knew it was something significantly deeper and stronger and more powerful ricocheting around within him—made him keep his mouth shut when the two city detectives had drawn their weapons and gingerly slid through the warehouse entrance, only a few feet ahead of him. Cautiously, at first, but then picking up speed and leaving care behind when they heard the first high-pitched scream of terror coming from deep within the darkened, gloomy space.

It was all a mistake. An indulgence. An error in judgment.

We should have waited, he thought, regardless what was happening to someone. And we should never have made the noise we did, entering that man's domain, going deep into the hole that he called his home, where he was intimate with every angle, every shadow, and every loose board on the floor.

Never again, he insisted.

He breathed in hard. The results of that night were a strobe-light memory pulsating within his chest: one detective dead, another blinded, a seventeen-year-old prostitute still alive, but only barely, and undoubtedly ruined for life. He, himself, wounded severely, but not crippled—at least in no discernable, easily apparent manner.

And the killer, arrested, spitting and laughing, not really angered by the end of his murderous spree. It was more like he'd been *inconvenienced*, especially with the unique satisfaction of what had happened within the warehouse. He was a small man, an albino with white hair, red eyes, and a ferretlike pinched face. He was young, almost the same age as Clayton, with a young man's wiry muscles and a huge red and green tattoo of an eagle sweeping across his pasty white chest. And all the killing that night had given him great pleasure.

Jeffrey wiped the vision of the killer from his imagination, refusing to conjure the singsong pitch of the killer's voice as he was led away amidst all the pulsating lights from the assembled police vehicles.

"I will remember you," he'd called out as Jeffrey had been wheeled into an ambulance.

He's gone, Clayton thought now. On Death Row in Texas. Don't ever go back there, he told himself. Never into a warehouse like that. Never again.

He stole a quick glance at Agent Martin. Does he know that's why I chose anonymity? he wondered. Why I no longer do precisely what it is he's asked me to do?

"There it is," Martin said abruptly. "Home sweet home. Or at least, my workplace."

What Jeffrey saw was a large building, unmistakably governmental in nature. A little more functional, a little less designed than all the other offices they'd cruised past. A little less opulent in appearance, which was not to say shabbier, but simply more stolid, like someone's older brother walking through a playground of younger children. It was sturdy, unforgiving gray concrete, with a cube's sharp edges and a uniformity that made him suspect that the people who worked there were probably as rigid and dull as the building itself.

Martin swung the car into a parking lot at the side of the building. He slowed and quickly said: "Hey, Clayton, see that man up ahead?"

Jeffrey spotted a single man, dressed in a modest blue suit, carrying a leather briefcase and walking amidst the rows of late-model cars.

"Watch him for a moment, and you'll learn something," the agent added.

Jeffrey watched as the man paused by a small station wagon. He saw the man remove his suit coat and take it and his briefcase and toss them into the rear seat. He took a moment to roll up the sleeves of his white, button-down shirt and loosen his tie before climbing behind the wheel. The car backed out of the space and exited. Martin swung his own vehicle into the vacated spot.

"What did you see?" the detective asked.

"I saw a man on his way to an appointment. Or maybe heading home with a touch of the flu. That's it."

Martin smiled. "You got to learn to open your eyes, Professor. I would have thought you'd be more observant. How'd he get into his car?"

"He walked up and got in. No big deal."

"Did you see him unlock the door?"

Jeffrey shook his head. "No. He probably has one of those electronic remote control locks. Just about everybody does. . . ."

"You didn't see him point an infrared light at the vehicle, did you?"

"No."

"Hard to miss that, right? You know why?"

"No."

"Because the car wasn't locked. That's the whole point, Professor. The car wasn't locked, because it didn't need to be. Because whatever he left inside it was safe. Because no one was going to come and steal it out of this lot. No teenage mugger with a handgun and a habit was going to pop out from behind another car and demand his wallet. And you know what? No security cameras. No security guards patrolling the area. No Dobermans or electronic motion detectors or heat sensors. This place is safe because it *is* safe. Safe because no one would ever think to take something that didn't belong to them. Safe because of where we are."

The detective shut off the engine.

"And safe is how I mean to keep it."

There was a large sign inside the vestibule of the building:

WELCOME TO NEW WASHINGTON

LOCAL REGULATIONS ENFORCED AT ALL TIMES

PASSPORT VIOLATIONS PUNISHABLE BY IMPRISONMENT

NO SMOKING

HAVE A NICE DAY

Jeffrey glanced over at Agent Martin. "Local regulations?"

"It's quite a list. I'll get you a copy. It's pretty much what we're all about."

"What about passport violations? What do they mean by that?"

Martin smiled. "You're in violation of the passport rules right now. That's part of the package here. Access to the proposed state is controlled, just as it would be to any other country, or to a private estate. You need permission to be here. To get permission, you have to go to Passport Control. But it's okay. You're my guest. And once you have permission, you can travel freely throughout the state."

Jeffrey spotted a sign that pointed toward IMMIGRATION, and peered down a corridor to a large room, filled with desks, a clerical worker at each one, working diligently at a computer screen. He hesitated, watching the people work, then had to hurry to keep up with Martin, who was quick-marching down an adjacent hallway, following a sign that indicated SECURITY SERVICES. A third sign pointed people toward DAY CARE. Their feet made slapping sounds against the polished gleam of the terrazzo floor and echoed off the walls.

After a moment they entered another large room, not as large as Immigration, but substantial nonetheless. There was a clean, white glow to the room, the overhead fluorescent lights blending with the ubiquitous green of computer screens. There were no windows, and the hum of air-conditioning mingled with voices muffled by glass partitions and soundproofing. He thought it looked as he would have envisioned a corporate office, not a police station, even an ultramodern one. There was none of the dirtiness of crime littering the atmosphere. There was no lurking rage or anger, no hidden madness, no fury, no restraints. There were no broken chairs or scarred desktops created by crazed detainees struggling against cuffs. No loud noises, no obscenities. Just a steady drone of efficiency and the syncopation of steady work.

Martin paused at a desk, greeted by a young woman dressed in a trim white shirt and dark slacks. A small vase with a single yellow flower in it was perched on the corner of the desk.

"So, Detective, back finally. We missed you around here."

Agent Martin laughed and replied: "I bet. Would you ring through, let the boss know I'm here?"

"With the famous professor, I see."

The secretary looked up at Jeffrey. "I have some paperwork for you, Professor. First, a temporary passport and identification. And then some documents you should read and sign at your convenience."

She handed him a folder.

"Welcome to New Washington," she said. "We're all certain that you're going to be able to help out . . ."

As she said this, she turned toward Agent Martin and added, with a coy smile, ". . . with whatever problem the detective doesn't seem to be able to figure out on his own and won't tell anyone about."

Jeffrey glanced down at the document folder and started, "Well, Agent Martin is more optimistic than I am, but that's because I know more about—"

He was interrupted by the hulking detective: "We're expected inside. Come on."

He grasped Clayton by the arm and steered him away from the secretary's desk toward the door to an office. As he did he pulled Clayton close to him and hissed a whisper: "No one, got it! No one knows! Keep your mouth shut!"

There were two men sitting behind a polished rosewood desk inside the office. Two red leather armchairs had been arranged in front of the desk. In contrast to the sleek, utilitarian look of the main room they'd passed through, this office had a more antique and decidedly richer feel. The walls were lined with oak bookshelves crammed with legal texts, and there was an Oriental carpet on the floor. A thick green leather couch rested against one wall, between a standing American flag and a flag of the proposed Fifty-first State. One wall was filled with framed photographs, but Clayton didn't have the time to inspect these closely, though he did recognize a picture of the president of the United States, which he thought was obligatory for a government office.

A tall, reedlike man with a bald pate sat directly behind the desk. To his side was a smaller man, thicker built, older, with a square jaw and a face twisted like a retired boxer's. The bald man waved Jeffrey and Agent Martin into the two armchairs. To the professor's right another door opened, and a third man entered. He appeared younger than Jeffrey, and wore an expensive blue pin-striped suit. He sat on the couch and simply said: "Get on with it."

The bald man leaned forward with a smooth, predatory motion, not unlike an osprey balanced on a naked tree branch, eyeing the movements of rodents in the grass.

"Professor, I am Agent Martin's superior in State Security. The man to my right is also a security administrator. The gentleman on the couch is a representative from the territorial governor's office."

Heads nodded, but no hand came forward in greeting.

The stocky man to the side of the desk spoke bluntly. "I want it repeated for the record that I object to the professor being summoned here. I object to involving him in this case whatsoever."

"We've been over that," the bald man said. "Objection noted. Your opinions will be reflected in after-case notes and disposition documents."

The man snorted in agreement.

"I'd be happy to leave," Jeffrey said. "Immediately, if you so desire. I don't want to be here anyway."

The bald man ignored this statement. "Agent Martin will have filled you in on the preliminaries, I suppose. . . ."

"Do you have names?" Jeffrey asked. "Who am I talking with?"

"Names aren't necessary," the young man said, shifting about, making the leather creak beneath his seat. "All records of this meeting are strictly controlled. In fact, your presence here is under strict secrecy guidelines."

"Maybe I think names are necessary," Jeffrey said stubbornly. He glanced quickly at Agent Martin, but the hulking detective had slunk back deep into the armchair, concealing his expression.

The bald man smiled. "All right, Professor. If you insist, then: I'm Tinkers, he's Evers, and over there, the man on the couch, is Chance."

"Very funny," Jeffrey said. "And I'm Babe Ruth. Or Ty Cobb."

"Would you prefer Smith, Jones, and—say, ah, Gardner?"

Jeffrey didn't reply.

"Perhaps," the bald man continued, "we could call ourselves Manson, Starkweather, and Bundy? That almost sounds like a law firm, doesn't it? And more in keeping with your line of work, no?"

Jeffrey shrugged. "All right, Mr. Manson. Whatever you say."

The bald man nodded and grinned. "Fine. Manson, it is, then. Now let me perhaps make this conversation easier, Professor. Or at least smoother. Here are the financial parameters of your visit, which I'm sure you will find of interest."

"Go on."

"Yes. Now should your investigation provide information that is later developed by others into evidence leading to an arrest, we will pay you a quarter of a million dollars. Should you actually identify and locate our subject, and assist in the apprehension of this individual, we will pay you one million dollars. Both sums, or any sum in between that we feel is warranted by the extent of your contribution to the solution of our problem, will be tax-free and in cash. You, in return, must promise that no information you acquire, no impression you form, no memory of your visit here in the slightest, is ever recorded by any physical or electronic means, and that no trace of your visit here, or its purpose, is ever uttered, or publicized in any fashion whatsoever. No interviews to newspapers. No book contract. No academic papers even with the limited circulation of law enforcement agencies. What I'm saying is this: the events that have brought you here, and which ensue from this time on, never officially happen. And for this absolute secrecy, you will be well rewarded."

Jeffrey sucked in breath slowly between his teeth. "You must really have a problem," he said slowly.

"Professor Clayton, do we have an arrangement?"

"What help do I get? How about access . . ."

"Agent Martin is your partner. He will provide access to any and all records, documents, locations, witnesses—whatever you need. He will handle all expenses, arrange for lodging and transport. There is only one target here, and that takes precedence over any concern, especially financial."

"When you say *we* will pay you, precisely who is the *we* involved?"

"That would be cash from the governor's discretionary fund."

"There must be a catch. What's the catch, Mr. Manson?"

"There is no hidden catch, Professor," the bald-headed man said. "We are under considerable pressure to bring this investigation to a speedy and satisfactory conclusion. You are not unintelligent. Two security officers and a politician should tell you that there is much at stake. Hence our generosity. But, also our impatience. Time, Professor. Time is of the essence."

"We need answers, and we need them swiftly," the younger man from the governor's office interjected.

Jeffrey shook his head. "You're Starkweather, right? Do you have a girl-friend, because if you do, you should start calling her Caril Ann. Well, I told the detective, Mr. Starkweather, and I'll repeat it for you: these cases don't lend themselves to easy explanations or quick solutions."

"Ah, but your inquiries were singularly successful in Texas. How did that come about? Especially with such dramatic results."

Jeffrey wondered if there was a note of sarcasm in the man's question. He ignored it.

"We knew the areas commonly frequented by the prostitutes our killer was preying upon. So, without much fanfare, we quietly began arresting all the streetwalkers—nothing exciting that might have gotten the attention of the press, just typical Saturday night vice sweeps. But instead of booking them, we enlisted their aid. We provided a significant percentage of them with small, electronic tracing devices. They were miniature, with a limited range, activated by a single button. We had the women sew them into their clothes. The theory was, eventually one of the women would get snatched by our man, and that she'd be able to trigger the tracer. We monitored the tracers around the clock."

"And this succeeded?" the stocky man asked eagerly.

"Sort of, Mr. Bundy. There were a number of false alarms, as we expected. And then three women were killed while wearing the devices before one managed to trigger it successfully. She was younger than the others, and our target must have been less threatened by her because for once he took his time in restraining her, giving her the opportunity to signal us. And because he never saw her punch the alarm, which would have caused him to flee, we got there in time to save her life, but only just barely. A mixed result, I'd say."

The stocky man, Bundy, interrupted. "But proactive. I like that. You took steps. Creative. That's what we should do. Something like that. A trap. I like that. A trap."

The young man also spoke rapidly. "I agree. But any steps like that need to be cleared through the three of us, Agent Martin. Understand?"

"Yes."

"I don't want there to be any doubt on this. There are political ramifications to each and every aspect of this case. We must always err on the side that allows us the most control and secrecy, but still eliminates our problem."

Jeffrey smiled again. "Mr. Starkweather. Mr. Bundy. Please keep in mind that the likelihood of even identifying the man who is creating your *political* problem is minimal. Creating the circumstances that would allow us to set a trap for him are even more remote. Unless you want me to wire every young woman within the boundaries of your state, after putting out some sort of general alert."

"No, no, no . . ." Bundy said quickly.

Manson leaned forward and spoke in a low, conspiratorial tone: "No, Professor, obviously we do not want the sort of widespread panic that this suggestion entails." He made a sweeping, dismissive gesture with his hand before continuing. "But, Professor, Agent Martin has led us to understand that you might have a special connection to our elusive subject that will facilitate this discovery. This is true, no?"

"Perhaps," Jeffrey responded, much too swiftly for the uncertainty of the word he used.

The bald man nodded, and leaned back slowly. "Perhaps," he said with a raised eyebrow. He rubbed his hands together with a washing motion. "Perhaps," he repeated. "Well, one way or the other, Professor, the money is on the table. Do we have an agreement?"

"Do I have a choice, Mr. Manson?"

The desk chair beneath the bald man squeaked as he swiveled about momentarily.

"That is an interesting question, Professor Clayton. Intriguing. A question of philosophical import. Psychological import. Do you have a choice? Let us examine it: financially, of course, obviously not. Our offer is most generous. While it will not make you fabulously wealthy, it is still far more than you could reasonably expect to make by teaching overfilled classes to psychotically bored undergraduates. But emotionally? Given what you know—and what you suspect—and what is possible, ah, I don't know. Could you choose to leave that behind, without answers? Wouldn't you be condemning yourself to a prison of curiosity for the rest of your life? And then, of course, as well, there is the technical side of all this. After bringing you out here, do you think we would be eager to see you simply depart, without helping, especially when we've been persuaded by Agent Martin that you are the only person in the country truly capable of solving our problem? Would we just shrug our shoulders and let you walk out of here?"

This last question hung in the air.

"It's a free country," Jeffrey blurted.

"Is it, now?" Manson replied.

He leaned forward again, in the same predatory style that Jeffrey had noticed earlier. He thought that if the bald-headed man were to abruptly adopt dark robes and a hood, he would have qualified in style and appearance for a major role in the Spanish Inquisition.

"Is anyone truly free, Professor? Are any of us, here in this room right now, really free, knowing, as we do, about this source of evil at work in our community? Does our knowledge not make us prisoners of his evil?"

Jeffrey didn't reply.

"You raise interesting questions, Professor. Of course, I would have expected nothing less from a man of your academic reputation. But, alas, this is not the time for us to discuss these most sublime issues. Perhaps at some other, more convivial juncture we could share our thoughts. But for now, that is less critical. So, I ask you again: Do we have an agreement?"

Jeffrey took a deep breath and nodded.

"Please, Professor," Manson said sharply. "Speak loudly. For the record."

"Yes."

"I thought as much," the bald-headed man said. He gestured toward the door, signaling that the meeting was concluded.

COFFEE EMERALD
THANT

Diana Clayton no longer liked to leave the house.

Once a week she would make an obligatory trip out to the local pharmacy to pick up her supply of painkillers, vitamins, and the occasional experimental drug, all of which seemed to have little effect upon the depressing, steady procession of her disease. While waiting for the pills, she made false, cheery small talk with the young, immigrant Cuban pharmacist, whose accent was still so thick she could barely make out what he was saying, but whom she enjoyed for his eternally optimistic manner and constant suggestions that one bizarre concoction or another would help save her life. Then she would cautiously walk across the four lanes of Route 1, gingerly dodging the traffic, and down a single block of a side street to a small, well-shaded, cinder-block library that was set back away from the garish strip malls that littered the Keys highway.

The assistant librarian, an older man perhaps ten years her senior, liked to flirt with her. He would be expecting her arrival, perched on a high seat behind one of the iron-barred windows, and buzz her through the double-locked security doors without hesitation. Although he was married, the librarian was lonely, pleading that his wife had time only for their two pit bulls and compulsively following the fortunes of the stars of television soap operas. He was an almost comic Lothario, doggedly following Diana through the meager stacks of shelves, whispering invitations to cocktails, to dinner, to a movie—anything that would give him an opportunity, convinced, as he was, to express to her that she was his only true love. She found his attentions both flattering and annoying, in almost equal parts, and so she rebuffed him, but did not totally discourage him, although she told herself that she had every intention of dying before actually having to tell the librarian once and for all to leave her alone.

She read only the classics. At least two each week. Dickens, Hawthorne, Melville, Stendhal, Proust, Tolstoy, and Dostoevsky. She devoured Greek tragedies and Shakespeare. The most modern work she read was an occasional foray into Faulkner and Hemingway, the latter out of a sense of Keys loyalty and because she liked particularly what he wrote about death. It always seemed, in his books, to have romantic, heroic qualities, selfless sacrifice even at its most sordid, and this gave her some encouragement, even if she knew it only to be fiction.

After obtaining her books, she would take her leave of the librarian, an extraction that usually required some diligence on her part as she fended off his latest entreaties. She'd then walk one more block, down yet another sunswept side street, to an old, weather-beaten Baptist church. There was a single, tall palm in the front yard of the white clapboard church, too high to provide much shade, but it had a splintered wooden bench at its roots. Diana knew that the choir would be practicing, their voices sliding like a wind from within the darkened church, out to the bench, where it was her custom to sit and rest and listen.

There was a sign next to the bench:

NEW CALVARY BAPTIST CHURCH
SERVICES: SUNDAY, 10 A.M. AND NOON
BIBLE CLASS: 9 A.M.
THIS WEEK'S SERMON: HOW TO MAKE JESUS
INTO YOUR SPECIAL BEST FRIEND
REV. DANIEL JEFFERSON, PREACHER

Several times over the past months, the preacher had come out and tried to persuade Diana that it was more comfortable and considerably cooler inside the church, and that no one would mind if she listened to the choir practice in the greater safety within. She had turned him down. What she liked was listening to the voices as they rose into the heat and sun above her. She enjoyed straining to make out the words. She did not want someone telling her about God, which she knew the preacher, who seemed a kindly sort, would inevitably do. And more important, she did not want to offend him by refusing to listen to his message, no matter how sincerely he presented it. What she wanted was to hear the music, because she'd discovered that while concentrating on the joyous noise of the choir, she forgot to feel the pain in her body.

This, she thought, was a small miracle in and of itself.

Promptly at three P.M., choir practice concluded. Diana would rise from the bench and slowly walk home. The regularity of her sortie, the uniformity of the route she traveled, the antlike pace that she adopted, all made her, she knew, into an obvious and modestly attractive target. That no mugger seeking her meager funds, or a junkie in need of the painkillers, had as yet discovered her and murdered her was something of a surprise, and, she thought with a modest astonishment, probably the second miracle attached to her weekly journey.

She sometimes allowed herself the luxury of thinking that being slaughtered by some beady-eyed drifter or strung-out teenager would not be so terrible, and that what was truly terrifying was staying alive, as her disease tortured her with a patient enthusiasm she thought devilishly cruel. She wondered if experiencing a few moments of terror wouldn't in an odd way be preferable to the drawn-out horrors of her disease. Recognizing an almost exhilarating freedom in her attitude, she stayed alive, and persisted in taking her medication and internally fighting and battling with the illness each waking moment. She thought this combativeness stemmed from a sense of duty and stubbornness and a desire to not leave her two children, though they were grown and adults, alone in a world that no one seemed to trust any longer.

She wished that either one had produced a grandchild.

A grandchild, she believed, would be pure pleasure.

But she understood this was not in the cards, meanwhile allowing herself to fantasize what some future grandchild would be like. She invented names, and pictured faces, and constructed future memories to replace the real ones she wished for. She envisioned vacations and holidays, Christmas mornings and school plays. She could sense holding a grandchild in her arms and dabbing away the tears caused by a cut or scrape, or feeling the steady, intoxicating breathing of the child as she read to him or her. She thought this an indulgence on her own part, but not an evil one.

And the fictional grandchild she didn't have helped to leaven her worries about the children she did.

Diana thought that their odd estrangement and the solitude each had adopted was often as painful as her disease. But what pill could they take to shorten the distance they put between each other?

On this particular afternoon, as she walked the last few yards to her own driveway, thoughts of her children troubling her, the sound of "Onward Christian Soliders" still ringing in her ears, copies of *For Whom the Bell Tolls* and *Great Expectations* under her arm, she saw a huge, angry thunderhead forming off to the west. Great gray-black clouds had gathered into a soaring ball of fierce energy, hanging ominously in the sky as a distant threat. She wondered if the thunderhead would push toward the Keys, bringing bursts of lightning and dangerous sheets of blinding rain, and she hoped her daughter would arrive safely home before the storm.

Susan Clayton left her office that evening in a phalanx with other employees of the magazine, under the watchful eyes and automatic weapons of the building security force. She was escorted to her car without incident. Generally, the drive from downtown Miami to the Upper Keys took her slightly more than an hour, even traveling in the high-speed unrestricted lanes. The problem, of course, was that almost everyone wanted to drive in those lanes, which required a certain cold-bloodedness at a single car length and one hundred miles per hour. Rush hour, she thought, more closely resembled a stock car race than some benign evening commute; all that was missing was the grandstand filled with rednecks hoping for a crash. On the freeways out of downtown, they would not often have been disappointed.

She enjoyed the drive, for the adrenaline-filled rush it prompted, but more because it had a cleansing effect on her imagination; there was simply no time to concentrate on anything other than the road and the car in front and the car behind. It cleared her head of daydreams, of office worries and fears about her mother's illness. On those occasions when she was unable to focus solely on the drive, she'd developed the mental discipline to swing the car out of the high-speed lane and into slower-moving traffic, where the risks were not as high and she could let her mind wander.

This was one of those days, which frustrated her.

She glanced with envy at the flow to her left, blurred vehicles glistening in the spillover light from the downtown business sections. But almost as quickly as she felt the jealousy of the unconfined speed to her left, she realized her own head was filled with the remaining words of the anonymous writer's message: Previous *always* coffee emerald thant.

She was persuaded that the style of the puzzle would be the same as before, and more or less the same as her reply had been; a simple word game where each word had a logical connection to some other word, which would be the answer to the puzzle and give her the writer's reply.

The trick was figuring out each. Wondering whether they were independent or linked—whether there was some hidden quotation or added twist that would obscure further what the man was trying to say. She doubted this. Her correspondent *wanted* her to figure out what he was writing. He just wanted it to be clever, reasonably difficult, and cryptic enough so she would write another reply of her own.

Manipulative, she thought.

A man who wants to be in control.

What else? A man with an agenda?

Absolutely.

And what was that?

She was not certain, but was sure it was one of two possibilities: sexual or emotional.

A car in front of her braked sharply and she slammed down her foot, feeling the instancy of panic rising in her gorge as the brakes pulsated, and without forming the word *crash*, prickly heat overcame her. She could hear tires all around her squealing in pain, and expected the noise of metal crushing metal. But this did not happen; there was a momentary silence, and then the traffic started moving forward again, picking up speed. A police helicopter thundered overhead; she could see the waist gunner leaning out over the barrel of his weapon, watching the flow of vehicles. She imagined a bored expression on his face, behind the dark, tinted Plexiglas of his helmet and face shield.

What do I know? she asked herself.

Still very little, she answered.

But that's not the game, she insisted. The game is for me to find out eventually. At the end, it wouldn't be a puzzle if he didn't want to be uncovered. He just wants to control the pace.

This is dangerous, she recognized.

There was a bar, the Last Stop Inn, about halfway between Miami and Islamorada, located on the periphery of an upscale shopping plaza that serviced some of the fancier walled suburbs. The bar was the sort of place she liked to frequent, not every day, but enough days so she had a nodding familiarity with several of the bartenders and occasionally recognized some of the other regular customers. With them, of course, she shared nothing, not even conversation. She just liked the false familiarity of faces without names, voices without personalities, camaraderie without history. She pulled across the highway, heading to the exit that would take her to the bar.

The parking lot was about three-quarters filled. An odd chiaroscuro of lights streaked the glistening black macadam; the first glow of evening mingled with the erratic sweep of headlights from the adjacent highway. The nearby mall sported covered wooden walkways and carefully planned plantings. These were mostly palms and ferns, intended to create a false jungle and make shopping resemble a trip to some designer's vision of a polite rain forest filled with expensive boutiques rather than unruly wild animals. The security force at the mall dressed up in the khaki colors of big-game hunters

and wore pith helmets, though their weaponry was more urban in orien-
tation. The Last Stop Inn had adopted some of the pretentiousness of its
neighbor, but without quite the same financial commitment. Their own plantings had created shadows and darkened corners around the periphery of the
parking area. Susan walked swiftly past a stubby, thick palm that stood sentry-
like at the entrance to the bar.

The main room of the place was shadowy and poorly lit. There were
some small tables with a pair of waitresses moving diligently amidst the
groups of businessmen sitting around martinis with their ties loosened. A
single bartender, not one she recognized, was hard at work behind the long,
dark mahogany bar. He was young, with shaggy hair and sideburns like
some 1960s rock star, a little out of place in his appearance, clearly someone
who wished he had another job, or perhaps did have another job but needed
to fix drinks to earn a living. There were about two dozen people occupying the stools in front of the bar, enough to make the area crowded but
not oppressive. The place didn't quite qualify as a singles bar—although
probably a third of the clientele were women—it was more a spot where
drinking was paramount, but assignation possible. It had less energy than the
bars devoted to making connections; the sound of voices was modest, the
piped-in music low-key, not urgent. It was a place that seemed willing to
accommodate anything that could be done with a drink in hand.

Susan took a seat near the end, three chairs away from any other patron.
The bartender sidled over to her, wiped the surface of the polished wood
with a hand towel, and, with a nod, acknowledged her request for scotch on
the rocks. He returned almost immediately with the drink, set it in front of
her, took her money, then moved back down the length of the bar.

She pulled out her notebook and a pen, arranged them next to her drink,
and hunched over, beginning to work.

Previous, she said to herself. What did he mean? Something that went
before.

She nodded to herself: Something in the first message *I have found you.*

She wrote down that phrase at the top of the page, then beneath it wrote:
Coffee Emerald Thant.

Again, she told herself, these are simple word plays. Does he want to be
known as clever? How deep are they? Or is he beginning to get eager, and
therefore made them easy enough so I won't waste much time before coming up with an answer?

Does he know my deadline schedule at the magazine? she wondered. If
so, he'd know I have until tomorrow to figure this out and invent an appropriate reply that I can run in the regular game column.

Susan took a long pull from the scotch, swallowing the liquor, then licking at the edge of the glass with her tongue. The scotch dropped within her like a siren's promise. She told herself to drink slowly; when she'd last seen her brother, she watched as he swallowed a glass of vodka as if it were water, gulping it down without pleasure, only eager for the loosening within that the alcohol would give him. He runs, she thought. He runs and plays sports with recklessness, and then drinks any pulled muscles away. She sipped again at her own drink and thought: Yes, *Previous* means something from the first message. And I already know *Always*. She looked at the words, balanced them together and abruptly said out loud: "I have always . . ."

"I do, too," said a voice behind her.

She swiveled in her seat, startled by the words.

The man hovering behind her was holding a drink in one hand, smiling loosely, with an aggressive eagerness that instantly put her off. He was tall, thickset, probably fifteen years her senior, balding, and she saw the wedding band on his finger. He was a subtype she recognized instantly: the low-ranking, passed-over-for-promotion, executive on the make. Looking for a little one-time-only good deal. No names sex before heading home to a microwave dinner, a wife who couldn't care less what time he returned home, and a pair of sullen teenagers. Probably even the dog wouldn't bother to wag its tail when he came through the door. She shuddered briefly. She saw him take a sip from his drink, and he added: "I have always wanted the same."

"What do you mean?" she asked.

"Whatever it is you've always whatever it is, that's what I've always, too," he said rapidly. "Buy you a drink?"

"I've got one."

"Buy you another?"

"No thanks."

"What'cha working so hard on?"

"My business."

"Maybe I could make it my business, too, huh?"

"I don't think so."

She let the man hang behind her. She pivoted back on her stool as he stepped closer.

"Not very friendly," the man said.

"That a question?" Susan replied.

"No," he said. "An observation. Don't you wanta talk?"

"No," she answered. She thought she was trying to be polite, but decisive. "I want to be left alone, finish my drink, and get out of here."

"Come on, don't be so cold. Let me buy you a drink. Let's talk a bit. See what happens. You never know. I bet we've got a lot in common."

"No thanks," she said. "And I don't think we've got a damn thing in common. Now, excuse me, I was in the midst of something."

The man smiled, took another pull from his drink, and nodded. He leaned toward her, not drunkenly, because he wasn't drunk, and not overtly menacingly, because to this moment he'd only seemed optimistic, perhaps slightly hopeful, but with a sudden intensity that made her pull back.

"Bitch," he hissed. "Fuck you, bitch."

She gasped.

The man leaned closer, and she could smell the heaviness of his after-shave and the liquor on his breath.

"You know what I'd like to do?" he asked in a whisper, but it was the sort of question that doesn't require an answer. "I'd like to cut your fucking heart right out and stomp on it while you watch."

Before she had a chance to respond, the man turned abruptly and disappeared down the bar, moving steadily, his broad back quickly enveloped in the shifting sea of other business suits, anonymous once again.

It took her a couple of moments to compose herself.

The burst of obscenities had struck her like so many slaps across the cheeks. She breathed in quickly and told herself: Everyone is dangerous. No one is safe.

She felt twisted inside, her stomach knotting, feeling clenched like a fist. Don't forget, she reminded herself. Don't let your guard down, not even for an instant.

She pushed her drink to her forehead, although she wasn't warm, then took a long pull at it. The bitter liquor sloshed in the glass; she took another long pull, and looked up to see the bartender working with his back to her. He was pouring ground coffee into an espresso machine. She doubted he'd seen the man approach her. She swiveled about in her chair, but no one appeared to be paying any attention to anything other than the space a few inches in front of them. The shadows and noise seemed contradictory, unsettling. Leaning back, she cautiously glanced down the bar at the tangle of people, trying to see if the man was still there, but she could not pick him out. She tried to fix his face in her head, but all she remembered was the ring and the sudden fury in his whisper. Turning back toward the message on the pad in front of her, she stared at the words, then looked over again at the bartender, who had placed a carafe beneath the machine's opening, standing back to watch the steady drip of black liquid.

Coffee, she thought abruptly. Coffee is made from beans.

I have always bean/been.

She wrote this down, and then lifted her head.

She felt as if she was being watched, and spun around again, looking for the man. But again she could not pick him out of the crowd.

For a moment she tried to shake the sensation, but could not. She carefully picked up her notepad and pencil and placed them in her handbag next to the small .25-caliber automatic pistol that lurked in the bottom of the satchel. She made a joke, when she touched the reassuring cool blue metal of the gun: At least I'm not alone.

Susan examined her situation: a crowded room, dozens of unreliable witnesses, probably no one who would even remember that she'd been there. She mentally retraced the steps to the parking lot, measuring the distance to her car, recalling every shadow and darkened spot where the man who said he wanted to cut out her heart might be waiting. She thought of asking the bartender to walk her out, but doubted he would. He was alone behind the bar, and he'd risk his job if he left his post.

She took another sip of her drink. You're being crazy, she thought. Stick to the light, avoid the shadows, and you'll be fine.

She pushed away what little remained of her scotch and picked up her satchel, placing the long leather strap over her right shoulder, so she could surreptitiously drop her right hand into the midst of the bag, grip the pistol, and slide her finger up against the trigger guard.

The crowd at the bar burst into laughter, some joke spoken loudly. She pushed away from her seat then and moved swiftly through the knot of people, head slightly down, walking steadily. At the end of the bar, off to her left, was a set of double doors with a sign for the ladies' room. Above the doors, in red, she saw EXIT. This made quick sense to her; pause in the bathroom, give the man some more time to get lost out front in the parking lot, expecting her to emerge from the main entrance, then take whatever back exit existed out to her car, changing her route, approaching from a different direction.

If he was waiting for her, she would gain the advantage. Maybe even end-run him completely.

She made the decision instantly, heading through the doors, finding herself in a narrow back corridor. There was only a single, bare lightbulb, which threw sheets of light across dirt-stained yellowed walls. The corridor had several cases of liquor stored in it. On one wall a second, smaller, hand-printed sign with a thick, crudely drawn black arrow pointed her toward the bathrooms. She assumed the exit would be located just beyond them. It was quieter in the corridor, the bar noise slicing away as the soundproofed doors swung shut behind her. She quick-marched down the corridor and took a turn to her left. The narrow space continued for another twenty feet, ending in two doors, across the hallway from each other—one marked MEN, the other LADIES. The exit was between them. To her dismay, she saw two other things: a red sign on the exit door that said EMERGENCY ONLY/ALARM WILL SOUND, and a thick metal chain and padlock looped over the door handle and fastened to the adjacent wall.

"So much for an emergency," she whispered to herself.

She hesitated a second, took a single step back toward the corridor leading to the bar, and swiveled her head about, making certain she was alone, then decided to head into the ladies' room.

It was a small space, just enough room for a pair of stalls, with two sinks on the opposite wall. Incongruously, there was only one mirror mounted between the twin sinks. The bathroom wasn't particularly clean, nor well-appointed. The fluorescent light would have made anyone appear sickly, regardless how much makeup they had caked on their face. In a corner there was a red metal combination condom and Tampax dispenser. The smell of too much disinfectant filled her nostrils.

She sighed deeply, headed into one of the stalls and, with a sense of resignation, sat down on the toilet. She'd just finished and was reaching for the toilet flush handle when she heard the bathroom door open.

She hesitated, listening for the clicking sound of high heels against the stained linoleum floor. But instead she heard a scraping, shuffling sound, followed by the thud of the door being shoved closed.

Then she heard the man's voice. "Bitch," he said. "Come out of there."

She pushed herself back in the stall. There was a small bolt lock on the stall door, but she doubted it would survive even a modest kick. Without replying, she reached down into her handbag and removed the automatic. She slipped off the safety catch, brought the weapon up into a firing position, and waited.

"Come on out," the man repeated. "Don't make me come get you."

She was about to reply with a threat, something along the lines of "Get out or I'll shoot," then thought better of it. With a great surge of control over her accelerated heart, she calmly told herself: He doesn't know you're armed. If he was smart, he'd know, but he's not. He's not really crazy drunk, just mostly angry drunk and being stupid, and he probably doesn't deserve to die, although maybe if she thought about it, she might reach a different conclusion.

"Leave me alone," she said, with just a small shakiness in her voice.

"Come on out, bitch. I've got a surprise for you."

She heard the noise of his zipper moving up and down.

"A big surprise," he said, laughing.

Her opinion changed. She tightened her finger against the trigger. I will kill him, she thought.

"I'm not moving. You don't get out of here, I'm gonna scream," she said. She kept the weapon pointed at the stall door, aimed straight ahead. She wondered if a round would be able to penetrate the metal and still carry enough force to wound the man. It was possible but unlikely. She steeled herself: When he kicks in the door, don't let the noise and shock affect your aim. Keep your arms steady, your aim low. Fire three times; save some shots in case you miss. Don't miss.

"Come on," the man said. "Let's have some fun."

"Leave me alone," she repeated.

"Bitch," the man said again, back in his whispering mode.

The stall door buckled as he kicked it sharply.

"You think you're safe?" he asked. He knocked on the door like a salesman visiting a home. "This ain't gonna hold me."

She didn't reply, and he knocked again.

He laughed. "I'm gonna huff and I'm gonna puff and I'm gonna blow your house down, you little pig."

The door boomed as he kicked it a second time. She sighted down the barrel, holding her breath. She was surprised the door had held.

"What do you think, bitch? Third time the charm?"

She thumbed back the hammer of the pistol and straightened her shoulders, ready to fire. But the third kick didn't immediately arrive. Instead she heard the ladies' room door open suddenly, with a slam of its own.

There was a second's delay before she heard the man say: "So, who the fuck are you?"

There was no response.

Instead she heard a long grunt, followed by a gurgling noise and short, quick, panicked breaths. There was a thudding sound and a hissing noise, followed by a crash and a kicking sound, more like a tap-dancing clamor, rapid, ending quickly after a few seconds. There was a moment of silence, and then she heard a long, drawn-out bubbling noise, like the sound of someone releasing air from a balloon. She could see nothing, and was unwilling to step out of the shooter's stance to bend down and try to see under the door.

She could hear a few short breaths of exertion. The sink started to run water, stopping with a squeak. Then there were a few footsteps and she heard the unhurried sound of the door opening and closing.

She continued to wait, holding the pistol in front of her, trying to imagine what had happened.

When the weight of the pistol threatened to drag her arms down, Susan breathed out, and was aware of the line of sweat on her forehead and the sticky sensation of fear beneath her arms. She told herself: You cannot stay here forever.

She was unaware whether it had been seconds or minutes, the long or the short, since the third person had entered and exited the bathroom. All she knew was that silence had filled the space, and that, save for her own quick gasps seizing air, she could no longer hear anything. Adrenaline started to make a throbbing racket in her head as she lowered her weapon and reached out for the bolt lock on the stall door.

She released the lock slowly and carefully pulled back the door.

She saw the man's feet first. They were sticking up, as if he were sitting down on the floor. He wore expensive brown leather shoes, and she wondered why she hadn't noticed that earlier.

Susan stepped from the bathroom stall, turning toward the man.

She bit her lip hard and fast to stifle the scream that tried to hurtle out from within her.

He was slumped down in a sitting position, jammed in the narrow space beneath the twin sinks. His eyes were open and staring at her in a sort of doubting astonishment. His mouth was agape.

His throat was sliced open, a wide, red-black crease in the skin, like some especially ironic, secondary smile.

Some blood had collected on his white shirt, smearing his chest, then pooled beneath him. His pants zipper was open and his genitals were exposed.

Susan reeled back away from the body.

Sensations of shock, fear, and panic raced through her like so many electric currents. She had trouble processing not merely what had happened, but what she was to do. For a second she stared down at the automatic still in her hand, as if having forgotten that she'd used it, that somehow it had been her shot that killed the man staring blankly in death's surprise. She jammed the weapon into her satchel as a wave of nausea washed through her body. She gulped air and fought off the impulse to vomit.

Susan was unaware that she had stepped backward, almost as if punched, until she felt the wall behind her. She told herself to look at the body, and then, to her astonishment, realized she already was, and that she'd been unable to take her eyes off of it. Trying to gather her wits, she reminded herself to try to acquire details, and was suddenly struck with the thought that her brother would know exactly what to do. He would know precisely what had happened and why and how and what the relevant statistics were that put this particular killing into some larger social context. But these thoughts only made her dizzier, and she pushed her back hard against the wall, as if she could make it give way and not have to step past the body in order to leave.

She continued to stare. The man's billfold was open by his side, and she thought it looked as if it had been ransacked. A robbery? she wondered.

Without thinking, she reached out, as if to touch it, then drew back, as if she'd reached for a poisonous snake. She told herself to touch nothing.

She whispered to herself: "You weren't here." She took another deep breath and added: "You were never here."

She tried to organize her thoughts, but they were racing around, on the verge of panic. Insisting on control, she felt some semblance of order returning to her heart after a few seconds. You are not a child, she reminded herself. You have seen death before. Although, she knew that this death was closer than any she'd ever witnessed.

"The toilet!" she said out loud.

She had not flushed the toilet. DNA. Fingerprints. Stepping back into the stall, she grabbed some paper and wiped the door lock. Then she pushed down the handle. As the toilet gurgled, she stepped out again and glanced down at the body. A coldness came over her.

"You deserved it," she said. She wasn't totally sure she believed this, but it seemed as fitting an epitaph as any. She gestured at the man's crotch. "What were you going to do with that?"

Susan forced herself to stare one more time at the wound in the man's neck.

What had happened? A straight razor, she guessed, or a hunting knife, slashed across the jugular. A moment of panic as he realized he was dead, then he must have dropped to the floor like a stone.

But why? And who?

These questions made her pulse begin to race once again.

Moving gingerly, as if unwilling to awaken a sleeping animal, she opened the bathroom door and stepped out into the corridor. She saw a single, partial shoe print, etched in maroon blood, on the floor. She stepped over this as the door closed behind her, checking to make certain she wasn't leaving the same telltale mark behind. Her shoes were clean.

Susan walked down the corridor and took the right turn back to the soundproofed, double doors leading to the bar, picking up her pace. She told herself not to hurry. Briefly, she considered going to the bartender and telling him to call the police. Then, as swiftly as this thought entered her mind, she erased it. Something had happened that she was an integral part of, but just how, and what her role had been, she was unsure.

She layered ice over her emotions, and stepped back into the barroom.

Noise enveloped her. The crowd had grown in the few minutes she'd been in the back room. She glanced at some of the few women in the bar, and thought it would not be long before one of them needed to make the same trip. Her eyes scoured the men.

Which one of you is a killer? she wondered.

And why?

She did not want even to attempt an answer. She wanted to flee.

Moving steadily, quietly, almost as if tiptoeing, trying to avoid attention, she turned for the main exit. A small group of businessmen was heading out, and she followed them, acting as if she were part of their group, stepping away from them as she passed into the night outside.

Susan gulped at the black air like it was water on a hot day. She lifted her head and surveyed the edges of the bar's building, her eyes creeping up the few light stanchions that shed weak yellow light into the parking lot. She was searching for video cameras. The better establishments always monitored the inside and the outside, but she could find no cameras, and murmured a small thank-you to the cheapness of the owners of the Last Stop Inn, wherever they were. She wondered whether a camera had perhaps picked up her meeting with the man at the bar, but then doubted it. Regardless, if there was a video, the police would find her eventually and she could tell them what little she knew. Or lie and tell them nothing.

Without noticing, she'd picked up her pace, moving rapidly amidst the cars until she reached her own. Unlocking the door, she tossed herself behind the wheel, jamming the key into the ignition. She wanted to thrust the car into gear and get away as quickly as possible, but again, as she had earlier, she grabbed hold of her emotions and demanded they obey common sense and safety. Slowly and deliberately, she started the car and put it into reverse. She peered into the mirrors and backed the car out of the space. Then, still clamping down on her thoughts and feelings as if they might betray her at any moment, she fled in a constrained, leisurely fashion. She was not aware that a professional criminal would have admired the steadiness of her hand on the wheel and the coolness of her departure, although that thought did occur to her many hours later.

Susan drove for about fifteen minutes before deciding she'd distanced herself enough from the man with the slashed throat. A sucking sort of weakness was penetrating her core, and she felt as if her hands needed to come off the wheel and shake.

She lurched the car into another parking lot, pulling into an empty, well-lighted space directly across from the solid square building of a large, national electronics chain. The store had a massive red neon sign out front, which sent a smear of color against the dark sky.

She wanted to assess what had happened at the bar, but it remained elusive. I was trapped in the ladies' room, she told herself, and the man came in and he was going to rape me, maybe, or maybe he was just going to expose himself, but one way or the other, he had me cornered, and then another man came in and without saying anything, he never said a word, he simply killed the man and stole his money and left me behind. Did he know I was there? Of course. But why wouldn't he say something? Especially after saving me?

This was a difficult construction for her, and she rolled it over in her mind. *The killing man saved me.*

She found herself staring at the huge red sign at the front of the electronics store. The sign was saying something to her, but it seemed distant, not unlike hearing someone far away playing a single chord on a musical instrument over and over. She continued to peer at the sign, allowing it to distract her from her thoughts of what had happened that night in the bar, and finally she spoke the name out loud, but in a soft voice: "The Wiz."

Then she asked herself: What is it?

She felt a quick dryness in her throat.

Emerald.

The Wizard of Oz lived in the Emerald City.

She sang to herself: ". . . the wiz, the wiz, the wiz, the wiz, what a wonderful wizard he is, he is . . ."

She pulled her notepad from her satchel, shoving the pistol out of the way to reach it. *Previous Number/always Coffee Emerald Thant.*

Susan felt a cascade of abrupt sensations: fear, curiosity, a bizarre satisfaction. The last word, she thought, I should have seen that earlier. Much earlier, because it is the easiest. In the mid-1960s, the same era that produced her message to her correspondent, the secretary general of the United Nations came from Burma. He wasn't as well known as some of the men who'd preceded him, or some who'd followed, but he still was known to her. Last name: Thant. First name, as was the custom in that nation: the letter U.

She said out loud: "Previous Number Coffee Emerald Thant."

Susan wrote on her pad:

I have always bean wiz u.

Her hands quivered abruptly, and she dropped her pencil to the floor of the car as she grabbed at the steering wheel to steady herself. She breathed in sharply, and in that second she could not tell herself with any certainty whether this was leftover fear from what had happened earlier that night, or new fear boiling up from the words she'd just written on the page in front of her, or some even darker combination of the two.

A TASK FORCE OF TWO

Agent Martin had acquired a small office, separated from the main security headquarters of the state, a floor above the State Office Building's day care center. There, the two men were to set up their investigation. He'd had computers and file cabinets moved in, a secure telephone line, and a handprint-controlled entry system that was designed to prevent anyone from entering, other than the two of them. On one wall he'd placed a large topographical map of the Fifty-first State; next to that, a blackboard. Each man had a simple, orange-colored steel desk; there was a small wooden conference table, a refrigerator, coffee maker, and in an adjoining room, two foldout beds, a bathroom, and a shower. It was a utilitarian space, a place of minimums. This lack of clutter pleased Jeffrey Clayton. And when he sat at his computer screen in the morning, he realized he could just make out the haphazard sounds of children at play penetrating the soundproofing beneath his feet, rising up to where he sat. He found this reassuring.

He thought his problem twofold.

The first issue, of course, was whether the man who'd left three bodies in twenty-five years spread-eagled in desolate areas was his father. Clayton felt a dizzy sort of emotional drunkenness when he formulated this question in his head. The pedantic academician within him demanded: What do you know of these crimes? He answered within himself: Only that three bodies were left in such a highly distinctive style that in a world of probabilities, little doubt existed they were left by the same man. He knew as well that his partner in the investigation was obsessed with the first murder, which had done something unsaid to him twenty-five years ago.

Jeffrey unleashed a long sigh, exhaling like a spent balloon.

He felt swamped by questions. He knew little of that first murder, little of Agent Martin's relationship to it, little of what his father may have had to do with it. He was afraid of seeking any answers in any area, almost crippled by what he might uncover. Jeffrey discovered that he was internally debating with himself, holding full conversations between warring segments of his imagination, trying to negotiate between the most livid nightmares within him.

He fastened onto the meeting he'd had with the three officials, Manson, Starkweather, and Bundy. *At least I will be well paid for opening up my past.*

The irony of his situation was almost humorous, and almost impossible as well.

Find a killer. Find your father. Find a killer. Clear your father.

He abruptly felt sick to his stomach.

Quite a legacy he left to me, he told himself. Out loud he said: "And now, for the reading of the last will and testament. I leave to my long-lost son my entire . . ."

He stopped in mid-sentence. *What?* What did he bequeath me?

He paused, staring at the documents that were collecting on his desk. Three crimes. Three folders. He was just beginning to understand how profound his dilemma was. The secondary issue he was facing was just as problematic: Regardless of *who* was committing the crimes, how did he go about finding him? The scientist within him cried out for a protocol. A list of tasks. A set of priorities.

That I can do, he insisted. There has to be some scheme to uncovering the killer. The trick is to determine what will work.

Then he realized: two schemes. Because finding his father—his late father, the father that part of him believed had been severed from his life a quarter century ago and who had died anonymously and separately—was a different investigation than finding some unknown and as yet undefined killer.

Another irony, he thought. It will be much easier for Agent Martin and State Security if it *is* my father committing these crimes. He made a mental note that the officials would press in that direction at every opportunity. It was, after all, the ostensible reason for bringing him in. And the alternative—that this was simply some new, anonymous, terrifying man—was the worse of the two nightmares for them, because someone unidentified would be far, far harder to catch and stop.

Of course, he knew to catch either, he had to create a series of intimacies—a knowledge of the crimes, which would lead to an understanding of the criminal. If he could understand the killer, he could couple that knowledge with the evidence acquired, and determine in which direction they would lead.

He both welcomed and dreaded this process. He thought himself not unlike some crazed yet dedicated scientist who carefully injects himself with a virulent, tropical disease in order to truly study its effects and fully comprehend the nature of the illness.

Infect yourself with these murders and then understand them.

With all the enthusiasm of an undergraduate getting ready for a final exam in a course where his classroom attendance has been spotty at best, Jeffrey began to read through the entire case files of the three killings, saving Agent Martin's interview with his father for the end.

When he turned to these final pages, he felt an emptiness within. He could hear his father's voice—glib, sarcastic, unafraid, always with a touch of anger—sounding effortlessly across the decades. He paused for a moment to assess his own memory: What do I remember about that voice? I remember that it was always curling with the smoke of near rage. Did he yell? No. An outward anger would have been far better. His silences were far worse.

The man's words jumped out at him. "Why is it you think I can help you, Detective? What makes you think I'm a player in this game?"

"Is not murder a means of finding truth? Truth about oneself, truth about society? Truth about life?"

"Are you not a philosopher as well, Detective? I thought all policemen were philosophers of evil. They have to be. It is an integral part of their territory."

And finally: "I'm surprised, Detective. Surprised that you wouldn't know a thing or two about history. My field, history. Modern European, to be precise. The legacies of bright, white men. Great men. Men of vision. And what has the history of these men taught us, Detective? It has taught us that the urge to destroy is as creative as the desire to build. And any competent historian will tell you that in the end probably more has been built out of ashes and rubble than out of peace and plenty."

Agent Martin's responses—and his own questions—had been noncommittal, brief. He'd merely urged answers, not entered into the debate. It was a good technique, Clayton thought. Textbook stuff, just as Martin had told him before. A technique that should have worked. One that would have worked probably ninety-nine times out of a hundred.

But not this time.

The more his father was asked, the more he grew oblique, obtuse. The more he was queried, the more distant and elusive he became. He did not rise to any of the bait trolled through the interview by the detective. Nor did he say anything incriminating.

Unless, Jeffrey thought, you viewed everything he said as incriminating.

He rocked in his seat, abruptly nervous. He could feel droplets of sweat sliding down beneath his arms. He suddenly reached out and seized a ballpoint pen off of his desktop. He dropped it to the floor and, lifting his shoe, ground it hard underfoot. Anger surged within him. *It's there,* he thought. *What he was saying was simple: Yes, I am who you think I am—but you cannot catch me.*

Jeffrey dropped the interview onto the desktop, unable to read any further. I know you, he thought.

But just as quickly, he denied this to himself: Do I?

There was a swooshing sound as the door to the office opened up behind him. He swiveled around and saw Agent Martin walking briskly through the entrance, slamming the door behind him. The electronic lock gave out a solid thunk.

"Making any progress, Prof?" he asked. "Earning your paycheck yet? Fast on your way to your first million?"

Clayton shrugged, trying to hide the surge of emotions he'd just experienced. "Where have you been?"

The detective dropped into a chair, and his tone changed. "Checking on the disappearance of our second teenage girl. The one I told you about back in Massachusetts. Seventeen years old, pretty as a cheerleader—blonde, blue eyes, skin so new and fresh it must have felt like she was hardly a day removed from the cradle, and gone, as of a Thursday two weeks past. The agents handling the case haven't come up with anything that even barely resembles evidence of a crime. No convenient witnesses. No signs of struggle. No helpful tire tracks, no unaccounted for fingerprints or bloodstained jacket. No book bag abandoned by the side of the road. No ransom note from some kidnapper. One minute she was on her way home, and now she's not. The family is still hoping for a teary-eyed phone call from a wayward child, but I think you and I both know that's not going to happen. They had Boy Scouts and volunteer personnel searching the adjacent woods for a couple of days, but they didn't turn up anything. You know what's pathetic? After the foot search got called off, the family hired a private chopper service with an infrared detector to do a grid search of the area she disappeared in. The camera's supposed to pick up any source of heat. Military technology at work. Anyway, it should pick up the presence of wild animals, decomposing bodies, anything. So far, they've found some mule deer and coyotes and a couple of stray dogs as they fly around at more than five grand a day. Good work, if you can get it. Pathetic."

Jeffrey took a few notes. "Maybe I should interview the family. The girl disappeared how?"

"Walking home after school. The school's in a less constructed area of the state. One of those newly developed expansion areas I was talking about. Pretty rural countryside. In two years it'll be a typical suburb, with a Little League field and a community center and a couple of pizza parlors. But that's all in the process of coming about. Lots of designer's drawings in various stages of completion. Right now it's still pretty raw. Not much traffic on the nearby roads, especially after the local construction crews were sent to their barracks. She'd stayed late to work on some decorations for a school dance, then declined a ride from her friends. Said she needed to get some fresh air and some exercise. She'd missed volleyball practice to work on the decorations. Fresh air. It killed her."

Martin spat out the last words, swiveling his chair in frustration. "Of course, no one knows that for certain so far. The fact that that damn helicopter search didn't turn up her corpse has got everyone encouraged that she's alive and just someplace else. Family's sitting around their kitchen trying to figure out whether she had some secret teenage life, hoping that she took off with a boyfriend, maybe headed to Vegas or L.A., and that the worst that'll happen is that she'll get some purple tattoo of a dragon, or maybe a rose, scorched into the skin of her thigh. They've ransacked the girl's room, trying to find a hidden diary that would have some hackneyed teenage expression of undying love for someone they didn't know about. They want her to be a runaway. They're praying she's a runaway. They insist she's a runaway. No luck so far."

"She ever run away before?"

"No."

"But it's still possible, isn't it?"

The detective shrugged. "Yes. And maybe someday pigs will fly. But I don't think so. And neither do you."

"True enough. But how do we know she was abducted by our . . ." He hesitated. ". . . subject? There are construction crews in that area? Has anyone questioned them?"

"We're not idiots. Yes. And background checks as well. And one of the little added safety features we have here is that all outside workers have to be bonded. And they're constantly monitored by security while they're here. Come to work in this state, and you wear one of those handy electronic bracelets, so we know where you are at all times. Of course, we pay construction workers about twice the going rate in the other fifty, which makes the trade-off worthwhile. Still, even with all sorts of precautions, that was the first place we looked. So far, negative, negative, negative."

Agent Martin paused, then continued in his hip-hop, sardonic fashion. "So, what have we got? A teenage girl who disappears one day without a trace and without an explanation. Presto! Ladies and gentlemen, taa-daaa! The amazing disappearing act! Let's not kid ourselves, Professor. She's dead. She died hard and in more than enough terror for anyone. And right now she's someplace distant, spread out like a crucifixion with her damn finger sliced off, and a lock of her hair missing from her scalp and her crotch. And right now, because I've got no other real good idea, I have acquired the singular belief that your father—excuse me, your late father, the guy you probably continue to think is dead—is the person we're looking for."

"Evidence?" Jeffrey asked. He knew he'd asked this question before, but it still jumped from his lips, carrying much of the same doubting sarcasm his father must have had when the subject of a missing teenage girl had been raised. "I still haven't heard anything positive that connects my old man to this, or any of the other cases."

"Come on, Professor. All I know is that she fits the overall type of young woman, and now she's gone without any other viable explanation. Just like those old alien abduction stories that used to fill the tabloids. Zap! Bright lights, big noise, science fiction, and gone. Trouble is, this ain't no alien. At least, not the sort of alien those scribblers had in mind."

Jeffrey nodded.

The detective continued: "You've got to understand where you are, Professor. When all those corporate honchos first got the idea for a statewide crime sanctuary more than a decade ago, it was to be simply and precisely that: safe. Here there has to be an obvious explanation for anything out of the ordinary, because that is the foundation upon which the entire area rests. Hell, we even legislate ordinary. Ordinary is the law of the land. It's in every breath you take here. It's what makes this place so goddamned attractive. So, in a way, it would be more reasonable for me to go to those parents of that teenage girl and say, 'Yes, ma'am, and yes, sir, your little darling girl *was* abducted by aliens. She was just out walking and all of a sudden got sucked right up into some big fucking flying saucer,' because that would ultimately make a helluva lot more sense, since we exist in order to be the opposite of the rest of the nation. Those parents could understand that. . . ."

He paused, caught his breath, then added: "I'll bet that back home in your little college town, when that girl disappeared from your class, why, nasty as it was, I'll bet you didn't lose any sleep over it, did you, Professor? Because it just wasn't all that unusual. Happens every day, or maybe not *every* day, but enough days, right? It was just some of that old-fashioned bad luck. A poor deal of the deck. A little visitation by the commonplace, homegrown version of savagery and tragedy. Everyday stuff. No big deal one way or the other. Life, such as it is, goes on. Wouldn't even make a headline, right?"

"You're correct."

"But here, Professor, we *promise* you safety. We promise that it's safe to walk home alone after dark. That you can leave your doors unlocked and your windows open. So when the state cannot live up to its promise, well, that would make front-page news, no? You don't think some reporter at the *New Washington Post* would find that worth scribbling about?"

"I see your point."

"Do you? Well, even if you don't, you will, soon enough. Read the bylaws. Read the rules for living here. You'll get the picture. People don't disappear. Not here. Not without some explanation that comes from the rest of the world."

"Well," Jeffrey said, "this child did, and it tells us something important, doesn't it?"

"What's that, Prof?"

Jeffrey lowered his voice so that it seemed to come from some croaking, deep location within him.

"Someone's not playing by the rules."

Agent Martin scowled.

Jeffrey took a deep breath. "Of course, if it turns out this girl actually did take off with some boyfriend in a leather jacket and driving a chopper, well, then all bets are off. On the other case, the young lady whose body you *did* manage to find, how much time between disappearance and discovery?"

"A month."

"And the other two cases?"

"A week."

"And twenty-five years ago?"

"Three days."

Jeffrey nodded. "Assume, Detective, it is the same man committing these acts. An assumption we're basing only on the most meager of facts. But still, assume it so, for an instant. Then he's learned something, hasn't he?"

Agent Martin nodded. "It would seem so." He coughed hard once, before adding a single, frightening word: "Patience."

Jeffrey rubbed a hand across his forehead. His skin felt cold, clammy to the touch.

"I wonder how he's learned that?" he asked.

Martin didn't reply.

The professor pushed himself away from his seat and, without speaking, walked into the small bathroom connected to the back of the office. He closed the door behind him, locked it, and bent over the sink. He thought he would throw up, but all that emerged was noxious, bitter bile. He splashed cold water on his face and said to himself while searching his eyes in the small mirror: I am in trouble.

It took a few moments for Jeffrey to regain his composure. He stared hard at his image, as if checking to make certain there was no residue of anxiety in his eyes, and reentered the office, finding Martin swiveling about in his desk chair, grinning at his discomfort.

"So, I wouldn't call the paycheck waiting for you at the end of all this precisely easy money, Prof. No, not at all easy . . ."

Jeffrey sat down in his own seat and thought hard for an instant.

"I don't suppose we'll get lucky, but one thing did occur to me. This latest girl was leaving a school, and the first victim, back a quarter century ago, was at a private school, and then the girl who was abducted from my class was a student as well. So, Detective Martin, maybe instead of sitting there grinning and finding the situation *you* got me into so damn amusing, you might start acting like an investigator."

Martin stopped rocking in his seat.

Jeffrey pointed at the computer. "Your computer, there, tell me, what magic can it do?"

"This is a State Security computer. It can access any data bank in the state."

"Then let's take a look at the faculty and staff of the school where she was staying late. I suppose you can get pictures and biographies up on the screen? Can you separate them by age? After all, we're looking for someone in his sixties. Maybe late fifties. White male."

Martin turned to the screen and started to punch in codes. "I can cross-reference with Passport Control and Immigration," he said.

As the detective worked, Jeffrey asked: "Precisely what information does Immigration obtain?"

"Picture, fingerprints, DNA chart—although they only started doing that in the last year or so—IRS forms for the past five years, personal references, verifiable family history, auto, home, medical records. If you want to live here, you must allow the state extensive access to your personal life. That's the drawback that prevents some rich folks from moving here. Some people would rather live in, say, San Francisco, with a personal bodyguard and behind walls topped with razor wire, and keep their lives—and how they made their money—obscured."

Agent Martin looked up from the computer. "What this says is there are twenty-two names that more or less fit the profile. White, male, over fifty-five, and connected with that school."

"Maybe this will be easy. Put their pictures up on the screen, slowly."

"You think?"

"No, I don't. But imagine how stupid we'd look if we failed to perform the obvious. The answer to your question, which you haven't yet asked, is no, I don't think I could recognize my father after twenty-five years. But I might. I'm not sure. A chance in a million? Worth trying, I guess."

The detective grunted, and punched in additional keys. One by one pictures and accompanying personal information flicked onto the computer screen.

For an instant Jeffrey was fascinated.

This was the ultimate voyeurism, he thought.

The minutiae of lives flashed in electronic color on the computer screen. An assistant principal had had a messy divorce more than a decade earlier, and his ex-wife filed an abuse claim that was determined to be unfounded; the varsity football coach had failed to declare some income derived from a stock transfer and been flagged by the IRS; a social studies professor had a drinking problem, at least his three DUI convictions a dozen years earlier would lend one to suspect that, and had completed a twelve-step program. But the biographies went further, complete with peripheral information—the English teacher whose sister had been hospitalized for schizophrenia, the janitorial service head whose brother died of AIDS. Detail after detail flickered on the screen in front of him.

Each biography was accompanied by a full-face and right and left profile picture, and a complete medical history. Heart, kidney, liver problems, outlined in quick medicalese. But it was the photographs of each subject that he was interested in. He scanned them carefully, as if measuring the length of the nose, the jut of the chin, trying to find the architecture of each face, and comparing it to the child's vision that he kept contained deep within some emotional closet within him.

Jeffrey found himself breathing slowly, shallow gasps of air. He calmed himself and exhaled through slightly pursed lips. He was surprised to realize that he was relieved.

"No. Not there. Not to my knowledge."

He rubbed a hand over his eyes.

"In fact, no one who even looked close. Or what I might have supposed looked close."

The detective nodded. "It would have been too lucky."

"I'm not sure I could recognize him, anyway."

"Sure you would, Prof."

"You think so? I don't. Twenty-five years is a long time. People change. People can be changed."

Martin didn't reply for an instant. He was staring up at the last picture on the screen. This was a white-haired school administrator whose parents had been arrested as teenagers at an antiwar demonstration.

"No, you'll remember," he said. "You may not want to, but you will. So will I. He doesn't know it, does he? But there are two people now within the state who've seen his face and know him for what he is. We just have to find a way to put that picture up on this screen and then we're in business."

The detective swiveled away from the computer. "So, what's next, Professor?" He leaned back in the seat. "Want to look at the pictures of every white male in the territory that's over fifty-five? Wouldn't be more than a couple of million. We could do that."

Jeffrey shook his head.

"Didn't think so," Martin replied. "So, what is it, then?"

Jeffrey hesitated, then spoke in a low, iron voice. "Let me ask the stupid question here, Detective. If you're so damn convinced that the man performing these acts is my father, what have you done to isolate him? I mean, what steps have you taken to find him here? He must be registered with your immigration service, right? You were so damn clever at finding me, what about him?"

The detective grimaced slightly, making a face. "I would not have come searching for you, Professor, if I hadn't exhausted those avenues. I'm not an idiot."

"Then if you're not an idiot," Jeffrey said with a sense of satisfaction, "you have a file somewhere that you haven't turned over to me, which details everything you've done to find him so far. And how you've failed."

The detective nodded.

"I want that," Jeffrey said. "Now."

Agent Martin hesitated. "I know it's him," he said quietly. "I've known it since I saw the first body."

He reached down and slowly unlocked the bottom drawer of his desk. He removed a sealed yellow manila envelope and tossed it over to Clayton.

"The history of my frustration," the detective said with a small laugh. "Read it at your leisure. You'll find that your old man had one area of expertise which seems to have defeated me. At least, so far."

"What was that?"

"Disappearing," the detective said. "You'll see. Anyway, let's get back to the present. What do you want to do first, Professor? I'm at your disposal."

Jeffrey thought for an instant as he fiddled with the tape that sealed the envelope. "I want to see where you found the most recent body. The one we've got listed as number three. Then we're going to work out a plan of investigation. And like I said, maybe we could talk to the family of this latest disappearance."

"And find out what?"

"They all have something in common, Detective. Something links them together. Age? Appearance? Location? Or something more subtle, like, maybe they're all left-handed blondes. Whatever, that something is what makes them prey. The challenge is to find out what it is. Once we know that, then maybe we'll understand the rules the killer is playing by. And then, maybe we can play his game."

The detective nodded. "Okay," he said. "Sounds like the start of a plan. Give you a chance to see a bit of the state, too. Let's go."

Jeffrey gathered the case file of the murder victim. He saw that her name—*Janet Cross*—was written in black felt-tip pen on the outside of the folder that contained the crime scene analysis, autopsy report, and raw police investigative notes. He told himself: I don't want to know your name. I don't want to know who you were. I don't want to know that you had any hopes or dreams or beliefs, that you were someone's beloved daughter, or perhaps someone's hope for the future. I don't want you to have a face. I just want you to be number three, nothing else. He put the case file and the sealed envelope into a leather satchel.

The professor stood and walked over to the chalkboard. He drew a line down the middle of the green slate, with a piece of dull yellow chalk. He thought there was something vaguely amusing in what he was doing; in a world that relied so heavily on the instantaneous electronics of computers, an old-fashioned chalkboard was probably still the best tool for trying theories, standing back, staring at them, then erasing the ideas that were not fruitful. He'd requested the chalkboard; he'd used one in the Galveston investigation, and in Springfield as well. He liked the chalkboard; it was an antique, like murder itself.

He fingered the piece of chalk for an instant, aware that the detective was watching him; then, on the right-hand side of the board, he wrote at the top of the board: SUSPECT A: *If the Killer Is Known to Us.* Then on the opposite side, he wrote: SUSPECT B: *If the Killer Is Not Known to Us.*

He underlined the word *Not.*

Agent Martin nodded as he read the words.

"All right," he said, approaching the board. "That makes sense. There's gonna come a point where we're gonna be able to erase one side or the other. First job, let's find something which will allow us to do that." He tapped the left-hand side, raising a small puff of chalk dust from *Not*. "My money says we're erasing this part first."

THE FOUND GIRL

The two men drove north through the Fifty-first State, heading toward the rocky foothills where some months earlier the body of the young woman they were designating number three had been discovered. Jeffrey Clayton listened idly to the rhythmic thump of the auto's wheels as they struck against electronic sensing devices embedded in the freeway macadam. They traveled fast, although in a distant control room their speed and progress could be monitored on a computer-driven map of the entire state roadway system. But they were left alone. Agent Martin had called in a traffic code to headquarters as they set out; no State Security helicopter would sweep overhead and demand they slow down to the rigidly enforced speed limit.

Periodically they swept past exit ramps leading to populated areas. These all had aggressively upbeat names like Victory, Success, or Happy Valley—or else the made-up sort of name designed to evoke clean, outdoor life, according to some executive in an office: Wind River or Deer Run. The entrance to each of these areas was announced in a different, color-coded sign. Clayton finally asked why.

"Simple," Agent Martin responded. "Different color means a different sort of housing. There are four levels inside the state: yellow, for town homes and condos; brown, for two- or three-bedroom single family homes; green, for four- or five-bedroom houses; and blue, for estates. It's all based on a housing concept Disney came up with for the first of their private town, outside Orlando—only taken a bit further."

Clayton tapped at a red sticker that adorned the side window. "Red?" he asked.

"That means all access."

They were passing a green sign for a place called Fox Glen. Clayton gestured and said: "Show me."

With a grunt, the detective steered the car down the exit ramp with a jerky motion. "Good choice," he said cryptically.

Almost instantly they were in the midst of a suburban development, a place of wide lawns and stands of pine trees. Sunlight filtered through the branches, occasionally reflecting sharply off the metal hood of a well-polished, late-model car lingering in a driveway. Small rainbows formed as the sun struck the spray from sprinkler systems automatically watering the yards. The houses themselves appeared spacious, each situated on an acre or two, set back from the modest roadway. More than one had screened-in pools.

Clayton could see that there appeared to be several basic designs for each house; he recognized Colonial, Western, and Mediterranean. The houses were all painted white, gray, or beige, or were stained with a clear coat that accentuated the wooden clapboard siding. Within the framework of each design, though, there were small differences—an atrium, a screened-in porch, or half-moon windows—so that the neighborhood appeared to be the same, but not completely; similar, but not wholly. Or, he thought, unique but not very, which he recognized was a contradiction in terms but seemed appropriate. The architecture of the development was subtle; it seemed to state that every home was distinct but that the totality was uniform. He wondered if the same could be said of the occupants of the homes.

It was midday, and it was mild, warming slightly as the sun rose overhead. The neighborhood was quiet; with the occasional exception of a woman patiently watching small children at play on side yard swing sets and wooden jungle gyms, the streets were empty. Clayton looked around for signs of decay or clutter, but everything was too new. After a few blocks, he spotted a pair of women in brightly colored jogging outfits, running slowly behind glinting tubular-steel strollers, each containing a baby. They were both young, perhaps his own age, although he abruptly felt older. The women waved as they rolled past.

He noticed something else: no security fences.

"Not bad, huh?" the detective asked.

"No," Clayton conceded. "Seems nice. Are there rules restricting the types of housing?"

"Of course. Rules about color. Rules about design. Rules about what you can and can't have. All sorts of rules, except they're not called rules. They're called covenants, and everybody signs the appropriate agreement before moving in."

"Nobody objects?"

The detective shook his head. "Nobody objects."

"Suppose you had a fancy art collection, one that required pressure sensors and alarms, could you have that installed?"

"Yes. Maybe. But any system would have to be registered, inspected, and approved by State Security. Any state-authorized architect could do the paperwork. It's part of the package."

Martin slowed the car down, pulling to a stop in front of a large, modern design. The house, however, was clearly empty; a FOR SALE sign hung by the driveway. The lawn was slightly thicker than the others on the block, and the plantings hadn't been trimmed. It gave the professor the impression of a gangly teenage boy, mostly presentable, but with unkempt hair and in need of a shave, as if he'd stayed up too late the night before and had too many illegal beers.

"That's where Janet Cross lived," the detective said quietly, gesturing to the files on Clayton's lap. "She was an only child. Family finally moved out, two, maybe three weeks ago."

"Where'd they go?"

"Minneapolis, I heard. Back to where they started. They had relatives there."

"The neighbors? What did they think?"

Agent Martin put the car in gear and rolled down the street. "Who knows?" he replied after a moment.

Clayton started to ask another question, but stopped himself. He glanced over at the detective, who was staring straight ahead. The professor thought he'd just heard a remarkable response. The neighbors should have been questioned thoroughly. Did they see anything? Hear anything? Had they noticed anyone out of the ordinary hanging around in the days before the young woman's abduction? And afterward? Hadn't they protested to the authorities? Hadn't they formed neighborhood anticrime associations and held meetings and discussed crime watch patrols? Hadn't they insisted on added security and talked of mounting video cameras to monitor the streets? In a second he thought of half a dozen or more separate responses that would be typical of the middle-class response to violent crime. They might be useless responses, but they would be responses nonetheless.

He breathed out slowly and instead asked: "She disappeared how?"

"Walking home after baby-sitting at a house no more than three blocks away. Just close enough so there wasn't any need to call for a ride. Just early enough, too. The couple she was sitting for had made an early dinner reservation and then caught the eight o'clock showing of some flick. They came home, forked over a couple of bucks, and she was out the door and never seen again after eleven P.M."

"Drive over to the house where she'd been working," he told Martin, who grunted in assent.

Clayton leaned back in his seat, letting his imagination work. He stared down the quiet suburban street and found it easy to envision a thick coating of night covering the area. Was there a moon that night? Find out, he told himself. The stands of trees would make for shadows, cutting off any light from the sky. And there were few street lamps—and they were certainly not the high-intensity, sodium vapor style that illuminated much of the rest of the nation's dark spots. There would be no need, and the homeowners would likely complain about the brightness filtering through their windows.

Clayton understood. If you buy into the myth of safety, then you would never want to have something bright every night reminding you that you could be wrong.

He continued to envision the moment. So, she was walking alone, long after night fell, hurrying a little, because even here the night would be unsettling and even if she thought she had nothing to fear, still, she was alone. A quick pace, listening to her sneakers slap against the sidewalk, holding her homework books close to her chest, just like some portrait painted by Norman Rockwell. And then what? A car moving slowly behind her, lights extinguished? A voice coming from one of the shadows? Did he stalk her like some nocturnal predator?

He could answer that question. Yes.

Clayton made a notation to himself: The assault would have been swift. Noiseless and sudden. Total surprise, because a scream would have ruined the collection. So, what would he need to accomplish that?

Was it the night that was perfect for hunting, and did number three just happen to be in the wrong place by an accident of fate? Or was she the prey that he'd already selected and studied—this night merely affording him an opportunity, one that he'd been waiting patiently for?

Clayton nodded to himself. An interesting distinction. One type of hunter moves stealthily through the forest, searching. The other hunkers down behind a blind, waiting for the victim he knows is en route. Find the answer.

There is always a connection in violent death. An agenda. A set of rules and responses that all add up, like some hellish mathematical equation, into a murder.

What was it, this time? Jeffrey Clayton's mind churned with questions, not all of which he was eager to answer.

They had reached the end of the block and turned into a second street of homes, ending in a cul-de-sac a half mile from the start. As the detective drove around the small, landscaped circle, he pointed down an incline toward a house set back a little farther than most of the others. By accident of construction, the next house on the cul-de-sac was angled away, its drive-way hitting the road through a thick, tangled green hedge. A third house, across the divide, was also situated so its view was back down the roadway, not toward the circle. It was up a small rise as well, behind a pair of large pine trees.

"Stop the car," Clayton said abruptly.

Martin looked at him oddly, then complied.

Clayton let himself out and walked a few paces away, staring back at each house, measuring.

The detective rolled down his window. "What?" he said.

"Right here," Clayton replied. He could feel a clammy, cold sensation crawl over his skin.

"Here?"

"This is where he waited."

"How do you know?" Martin asked.

Clayton gestured quickly toward the three houses. "Can't be seen. Not from any of the houses. It's like a blind spot. No street lamp. Dark car, after night. Just park and wait."

The detective got out of the car and looked around. He paced off briefly, turned, stared back at where Clayton was standing, then paced back. He frowned, looked back at the angles created by the houses, measuring the intersection mentally. After a moment he nodded and whistled.

"Probably right, Professor. Not bad. Not bad at all. These houses are all hidden. As soon as she's another thirty yards down the street, why, she'd be up on the sidewalk and visible from both sides. And closer to the houses, too, to hear her scream. If she did scream. If she could scream." The detective paused, once again letting his eyes sweep the area. "No. You're probably right, Professor. Don't know why I couldn't see it myself. My hat's off to you."

"Was there a search, after the disappearance? Of this area?"

"Of course. But you must understand, it wasn't until I saw her body that we understood what we were up against. And by that time . . ." His voice trailed off.

Clayton nodded and got back into the car. He peered around another time, questions battering him. The baby-sitter's clients, they would be driving in.

How did he manage to avoid being seen by their headlights? Simple. He arrived afterward. How did he know she would be walking home and not getting a ride? Because he'd seen her before. How did he know the neighbors wouldn't be coming or going as well? Because he knew their schedules, too.

Clayton quietly took a deep breath and told himself that it was not a terrible thing for him to be able to drive down a quiet residential suburban street and immediately find the best place for a killer to wait. He told himself that it was necessary to be able to look at the neighborhood through the killer's eyes, because otherwise they would have no chance of finding the man, and so this ability was something to be praised and not feared. Of course, he knew this was a lie. Nevertheless, he grasped hold of it, clutching it inwardly, because the alternative was something he did not want to contemplate.

They drove a few minutes, exiting the upscale housing development, and Clayton saw a small park. He noticed a black cinder running trail around the perimeter, some tennis courts, a basketball hoop, and a toddler play area that was busily being used by several children. A small gathering of women sat on a set of benches a few feet away, talking, paying the sort of moderate attention to their children that speaks of safety. As they drove past the park, he saw that the houses on the opposite side were smaller, more closely aligned, and nearer to the sidewalk. The street signs were suddenly brown.

"Now we're in Echo Woods," Martin said. "A brown development. Middle-class, but the other end of that spectrum. Right on the edge of town."

They emerged from the suburb onto a wide boulevard with low-slung malls on either side. They were of southwestern design, with red-tiled roofs and light beige stucco walls, even on the large grocery store that occupied almost a block in the center of the mall. Clayton started reading the names of stores and realized that they, too, were clustered: upper scale clothing boutiques and gadget stores at one end of the mall, discount and hardware stores at the opposite end. Restaurants, pizza parlors, and fast-food outlets were spread throughout the mall.

"So much for shopping," the detective said. "Welcome to the town of Evergreen. Suburb of New Washington."

There was almost an old-fashioned New England feel to the center of the small town. It was dominated by a wide, green, grassy common. At one end Clayton saw the white spire of an Episcopal church outlined against the clear blue of the western sky. To its right there was another spire, topped with a cross: a Methodist church. Across the edge of the common, a Jewish synagogue faced the churches, with a golden Star of David unapologetically perched on its roof. They were all modern, free-form designs. Nearby, he saw a trio of buildings, each with white clapboard walls. One was marked TOWN OFFICES. The next was STATE SECURITY SUBSTATION 6. And the third read: COMPUTER CENTER.

There was also a small sign, pointing down a side road, for EVERGREEN REGIONAL SCHOOL AND HEALTH CENTER.

Agent Martin nodded and pulled the car to a halt by the edge of the common. Clayton saw there was even a statue at one end, a World War II–era soldier in heroic pose rising above a pair of old, black-painted cannons. He wondered whether the town had imported some fictional hero to celebrate.

"See, Professor. Everything you need. Organized and handy. Get the picture?"

"I think so."

"Minimum three places of worship in each community. They vary, of course. Could be Mormon. Could be Catholic. Could even be Moslem, for Christ's sake. But always three. One church, that's exclusivity. Two, that's competition. Three, that's diversity. And just enough of that to be strong, but not divisive, if you see what I mean. An ethnic mix that strengthens rather than divides. Same with the way the communities are planned. Each economic group is represented—but they all rub shoulders together in town or at the shopping mall. We can drive out past the estates, if you're interested. Add to that a single kindergarten through high school building and a combination health club and mini-hospital, and what else do you need?"

"Computer Center?"

"Every house is connected through fiber optics. If you want, you can do your shopping, vote in a town election, file your taxes, gossip, exchange recipes, or sell stocks—whatever—from your home. Electronic mail, scheduling music lessons, whatever. Everything's on some town billboard somewhere. Hell, teachers can send out assignments on the computers and kids can send in their homework the same way. Everything's connected nowadays. Library, grocery store, high school basketball team schedule, and ballet class recitals. You name it."

"And State Security can monitor any transmission or transaction?"

Martin hesitated before replying. "Of course. But we don't advertise that. People are aware, but after a year or two they forget. Or they don't care. Probably, Mr. and Mrs. Jones don't really give a damn that State Security can read all the invitations to their dinner party and monitor their arrangements with the caterer. They probably don't even care that we can tell when they wrote out their check to pay for liquor or floral arrangements. And we know if that check clears, too."

"I don't know," Clayton replied. He was staggered. His own world seemed to drift away like the last dream before waking. He suddenly had trouble remembering what the university looked like, or what his own apartment smelled like. All he recalled was a sense of fear. Cold, fear, and dirt. But even that seemed distant. The detective turned the car, and a momentary burst of sunlight and glare crowded Clayton's eyes. He put up a hand to shade them, squinting ahead. It took him a moment before his eyes adjusted and he could see clearly again.

"Did you want to drive past some of the estates? They're on the outskirts of town. But they're more isolated. Usually set way back on ten, maybe more acres. More privacy. That's pretty much the only advantage to the highest economic rung. You can live in greater isolation. But hell, we've found that some of the richest folks prefer the green areas, which are more upper-middle-class in nature. They like being perched on a golf course, or located near the town recreation center. Curious, that, I guess. Anyway, you want to try to see an estate area? They're harder to see from the street, but you can still get the general idea."

"Do they use the same base designs, like the other developments?"

"No. They're all custom jobs. But because the number of architects and contractors are limited by the state licensing procedures, there are some similarities."

An idea struck Jeffrey, but he kept it to himself. Instead he gestured to the access ramp leading back to the freeway. "I want to see where the body was found," he said.

With an assenting grunt, Martin steered his car toward the ramp.

"What about you, Detective? Are you a brown? Yellow? Green or blue? Where does a cop fit into this scheme of things?"

"Yellow," he said slowly. "A town home right outside downtown New Washington so I don't have a long commute. No wife anymore. We separated a dozen years ago. Fairly amicably, or at least as easily as these things can be, I guess. It was before I came to work here. She lives in Seattle now. One kid in college. One kid out working. Both grown up. Don't need their old man much anymore. I don't see either too much. So, I live alone."

Clayton nodded, because that seemed the polite thing to do.

"It's unusual, of course, here."

"What do you mean?"

"The state frowns on single adult men. The state is about family. Single men, for the most part, just screw things up. We have to accommodate some—people in my situation, for example, and no matter how many pre-immigration surveys we perform, there are still some divorces, although we're one-tenth the national norm—but for the most part, no. To get in, and

stay in, you need a family. Can't get in if you're a loner. Not too many singles bars in the state. Actually, like zero."

Jeffrey nodded again, but this time because something had occurred to
him. He started to open his mouth, then clamped down hard. Biding his own
counsel. He thought: There's much I don't know yet. But I'm beginning to
learn things.

He leaned back in his seat as the detective accelerated. The foothills
seemed visibly closer, rising above the flat plain, green and brown and
slightly darker than the rest of the world. At first he thought them only a
short distance away, then recognized that they still had several hours of
driving to do. In the West, he reminded himself, distances are deceptive.
Things are generally farther away than one thinks. He thought the same was
true of most homicide investigations.

In early afternoon they reached the area where the body of number three
was found. It had been more than an hour since they'd passed the last populated area, and the highway road signs were warning them they were less
than a hundred miles from the newly drawn border to southern Oregon. It
was rough country, heavily forested, oppressively quiet. They passed few
other vehicles. Clayton thought they were in the midst of one of the hard
places of the world; a place of silence and loneliness. There was little development in the region, just an emptiness that would be hard to fill artificially.
The mountains they approached seemed forbidding, granite gray, white-
capped and harsh. An unforgiving territory.

"Not much here," Clayton said.

"Still wild," Martin agreed. "Won't be forever, but still is." He hesitated,
then added, "There are some psychological studies, and some half-assed scientific polls, that show that people are comfortable and in favor of wild
areas, as long as they're limited in scope. We designate state forests and
camping areas, then pretty much leave them alone. Makes the nature freaks
happy. The construction slowly creeps up toward them. That'll happen here,
too. Five years. Maybe ten." He gestured with his right arm. "Logging road,
up ahead. No more logging, of course. The greenies won that battle. But the
state keeps the roads viable for campers. Great fishing and hunting up here.
And convenient. Three hours' drive time from New Washington. Less than
that from New Boston and New Denver. They're in the process of creating a
whole new industry. Talking about putting rustic lodges and fly-fishing and
hunting specialty shops up here. There's a helluva lot of money to be made
off organized nature."

"That's how she was found, right? A pair of fishermen?"

The detective nodded. "A couple of insurance executives who'd scheduled a day off to look for wild rainbow trout. Found more than they expected."

He turned off the highway, the car suddenly bumping and pitching like a small boat caught in a choppy inlet. Dust curled up behind them, and the sound of gravel rock striking the undercarriage was like so many pistol shots. The yawing back and forth made both of the two men grow quiet. They drove this way for perhaps fifteen minutes. Clayton was about to ask how much farther when the detective pulled the car to a halt in a small turnout.

"People like it," Martin said. "Seems like a pain in the ass to me, but people like it. I'd have paved the damn road, but I'm told the psychologists say that people prefer the sense of adventure bouncing along gives them. Allows them to think that the thirty grand they dropped on their all-wheel-drive sports utility vehicle was worth it."

Clayton stepped from the car and immediately saw a narrow trail leading through the scrub brush and trees. There was a brown wooden plaque and a map encased in plastic at the edge of the turnout at the trailhead.

"We're getting there," the detective said.

"She was left here?"

"No. Farther in. A mile or so. Maybe a little less."

The path through the trees had been cleared and was not hard to traverse. It was just wide enough for the two men to walk abreast. Beneath their feet the forest floor was brown pine needles. An occasional scrambling noise could be heard, when they spooked a squirrel or chipmunk. A pair of blackbirds objected to their passage with discordant noise, clattering away through the trees.

The detective stopped. It was cool in the shadows, but he was sweating hard, a big man's sweat. "Listen," he said.

Clayton stopped, and could just make out the sound of rushing water.

"River's about fifty yards away. We figured these two guys were pretty pleased. It's not a tough hike, but they were in waders and carrying rods and backpacks and all that sort of stuff. And it was pretty hot, too, that day. Over seventy degrees. Try to imagine it from their eyes. So they were hurrying along, probably not taking care to notice anything on the way."

The detective gestured forward, and Clayton went ahead.

"Janet Cross," Martin muttered, a step behind the professor. "That was her name."

The river noise increased with each step, filling Clayton's ears. He stepped through a final stand of trees and was suddenly perched on an embankment, perhaps six feet above where the water bubbled and rushed through a series of rocky, boulder-strewn riffles. The water seemed sinuous, alive. It was fast water, muscular, pouring through a small gorge like an angry thought. The sun bounced off the surface, making it seem a dozen different colors of blue-green streaked with frothy white foam.

Martin stood beside him.

"Blue-ribbon, the fishermen call it. Trout hold just about everywhere. Tricky to fish, they tell me, because it's all speed and swirling about. And if you slip off one of those rocks, well, that would be some major trouble way out here. But it's still a great place."

"The body?"

"The body. Yes. Janet. Nice girl. They're always nice girls, aren't they, Professor? An A student. Heading to the university. A gymnast, too, I understand. Wanted to study early childhood development." The detective slowly lifted his arm and pointed at a large, flat boulder perched on the edge of the river. "Right there."

The rock was at least ten feet wide, like a tabletop tilted slightly back toward where they were standing. He thought the body must almost have appeared framed or mounted, like a trophy.

"The two fishermen—hell, at first they thought she was just sunbathing naked. Just a first impression, you know, because there she was, spread out, what'd we say—like a crucifix. Anyway, they called to her, and nothing, so one of them wades out and jumps up, and there you have it."

Martin shook his head. "Her eyes must have been open. Birds had pecked them out. But no other animal damage to the body. And decomposition was minimal; she'd been there maybe twenty-four to forty-eight hours before those guys came along. Don't think they'll be fishing this stretch of the river much anymore."

Jeffrey looked down and saw that the rock where the body had been found was a short ways from the shore, resting on a gravel bed in less than a foot of water. It overlooked a modest pool; a pair of larger boulders at the head of the pool split the river's energy, thrusting the fiercest water to the far embankment, creating a small slick of slower water behind the flat rock.

He did not know a great deal about fishing, but suspected that the rock was a prime location. From its back edge one could easily cast across the pool. The man who left the body in that spot, he thought, must have observed that as well.

"When you processed the area—" he started, but the detective cut him off.

"All rock. Rock and then water. No footprints. And there'd been some rain the previous evening as well. And no lucky bit of clothing snatched off by some thorn, either. We went over the entire area, right back to the parking place, with the proverbial fine-tooth comb. No tire prints, either. All we had was one body, right here, just as if she'd been dropped from Heaven."

Martin was staring out over the stream, directly at the spot. "I was in the first team to get here, so I know the scene wasn't contaminated to any degree."

He shook his head. His voice was flat, affectless.

"You ever see something which reminds you of a nightmare? Not a dream you once had, or a fantasy. Not even one of those odd little déjà vu situations that everybody gets. No, I was standing right here, and there she was, and it was just like I was right in a nightmare I'd once had, and one that I thought was long gone. I saw her arms spread out, and her legs pinned together, and no blood or obvious signs of a struggle. I knew right then, just as soon as I'd taken my first breath, that we weren't gonna find shit to help us. And I knew when I got closer I was going to see that missing finger . . . and I knew, Professor, I knew right then what I needed to know, which was who did it."

The detective's voice trailed off, swallowed by the sound of the water racing past them.

Jeffrey did not entirely trust his own voice, and certainly had the sense not to make any smartass reply. He could see Martin staring down at the flat rock, and knew the detective could see the girl's body resting there just as clearly as the day it was found.

"He wanted the body found," Clayton said.

"That's what I thought, too," Martin replied slowly. "But why here?"

"Good question. He probably had a reason."

"Isolated, but not exactly hidden. Out here, he could have found a spot where she'd never have been discovered. Or, at least, by the time she was, she'd have been nothing more than skeletal remains. Hell, he could have dumped her in the river. From the forensic point of view, that would have made even more sense—if the point is to avoid any telltale link we might find between him and the victim. Instead he carried her here, which, no matter how small she was and how strong he is, is still a haul, and arranged her body like it was some sort of blue plate special."

"He will be considerably stronger than he appears to the public," Jeffrey said. "What did she weigh—maybe one hundred fifteen?"

"She was slight. Thin and slight. One fifteen is probably on the high side."

Jeffrey was letting his thoughts spill out as words. "He carried her down that path for a mile, and then placed her here because he wanted her found in just that way. This isn't somebody being dumped and abandoned. This is a message."

Martin nodded. "I thought much the same. But that wasn't the sort of opinion it was wise to express. Politically, you know." He crossed his arms and stared at the flat rock and the endless flow of water that curled around its edges.

Jeffrey agreed with what the detective had said. He recalled a quote from a famous politician in Massachusetts, that all politics are local, and wondered if the same was true of murder. He began to process the site internally then, adding, subtracting, thinking hard about what it said about a man who would carry a body a mile through the empty woods, just to leave it on a pedestal where it would be found within a day or two.

He didn't say it out loud, but he thought: A careful man. A man who plans, and then carries out his plans with precision and confidence. A man who understands exactly what the effect of what he does will be. A man who understands the science of detection, and the nature of forensics, because he knows he leaves nothing of himself behind with his victim. What he leaves is a statement, not a trail.

Then, he added, again to himself: A dangerous man.

"The two guys who found her, the fishermen . . . what did they think?"

"We told them it was a suicide. Shook them up pretty bad."

A beeper on the detective's belt went off then, its electronic noise seeming alien amidst the trees and the splashing sounds of the river. Martin looked at it oddly for an instant, as if his reverie of memory was difficult to shake loose. Then he switched it off, and, in almost the same motion, retrieved a portable telephone from his suit coat pocket. He quickly punched in a number and rapidly identified himself, then listened closely, nodding.

"All right," he said. "We're on our way. Probably ninety minutes." He snapped the phone shut. "Time to go," he said. "They found our runaway."

Jeffrey noticed that the burn scars on the detective's throat were flushed with red. "Where?" he asked.

"You'll see."

"And?"

Martin shrugged bitterly. "I said they found her. I didn't say she came walking through the front door to her house into the waiting arms of her angry yet overjoyed parents."

He turned and started quickly back up the path toward the road and the spot where they'd left the car. Clayton hurried after him, the sound of cascading water fading behind him.

The professor saw the glow of lights from at least a mile away. The spotlights seemed to carve away the crust of darkness. He rolled down his window and could hear the stolid dissonance of electric generators filling the night. They had driven hard and fast, across a desertlike expanse, heading west toward the California border. The detective said little during the drive, other than to point out that they were again traveling into an undeveloped area of the state. But the topography had changed; no longer rocky hills and trees, but flat scrubland. It was the sort of country that western writers waxed eloquent about, Clayton thought, but which to his untrained, East Coast eye seemed to be territory where God must have been momentarily distracted as he went about his business of forming the earth.

Several hundred yards away from the generators and spotlights, there was a solitary roadblock. A State Security policeman in trooper's gear, standing next to a set of orange highway cones and several glowing flares, flagged them over, then waved them forward when he saw the red sticker in the car window.

Agent Martin stopped anyway. He rolled down his window and briskly asked: "What are you telling people?"

The trooper nodded, making a small salute, and replied: "Broken water main washing away the road. We're detouring people all the way over to Route Sixty. Luckily, there's only been a dozen or so vehicles."

"Who found her?"

"A pair of surveyors. They're still here."

"Are they state residents or bonded outsiders?"

"Outsiders."

Martin nodded, then pulled the car ahead. "Keep your mouth shut," he said to Clayton. "I mean, you can ask questions if you need to, do your job. But don't draw any additional attention to yourself. I don't want anybody asking who you are. And if they do, I'll just say you're a specialist. That's the sort of generic description that generally satisfies everyone, but doesn't really mean a helluva lot if you actually think about it."

Jeffrey didn't reply. The car shot forward, and then the detective pulled in behind a pair of glistening white panel trucks, each bearing the State Security logo on its sides, but no other designation. Jeffrey glanced at the trucks and saw them for what they were: crime scene analysis units. But in a state where there wasn't supposed to be any crime, they wouldn't want to advertise their presence. He smiled to himself. A small hypocrisy, to be sure, but one he appreciated. He suspected there were others inside the Fifty-first State that he was unaware of. He stepped from the detective's vehicle. The night had an edge of cold to it, and he turned up the collar of his jacket.

Another trooper signaled them, and pointed. "Quarter mile in," the man said, gesturing toward the source of the lights.

Martin walked ahead rapidly, and Clayton jogged to keep up with him.

The banks of klieg lights cut a swath through the darkness. Jeffrey immediately saw there were different teams at work within the area framed by light. He spotted three separate search teams carefully processing the sandy dirt and rock, looking for any fibers, footprints, tire tracks, or other telltale indication of who had been that way before. He observed them for a few moments, like a coach watching tryouts for a team. They were moving too fast, he thought. Not enough patience. And probably not enough experience, either. If there was something to miss, they would miss it. He turned and saw another team working around the body, obscuring it, at first, from his view. This group of men was perched up on a small dusty plateau. Among them he saw a man in shirtsleeves, despite the coolness of the night, bent over, his white latex gloves catching an occasional piece of light from the throbbing kliegs, which made his hands glow with an otherworldly brightness. Jeffrey assumed he was the medical examiner.

He followed Detective Martin, meanwhile surveying the area. He had one quick, bitter thought: It's what I should have expected. Maybe what I did expect.

He shook his head as he walked forward. They won't find a thing, he told himself.

The security agents parted to let the two men through, and Clayton caught his first glimpse of the body at almost the same moment the detective uttered a brief, harsh obscenity.

The teenager was naked. She'd been placed on the surface of a wide, flat, gravelly area. Her face was to the ground, obscured, her arms stretched out ahead of her, her knees drawn up beneath her torso. Her position reminded Jeffrey of the way Moslems prostrated themselves as they prayed in the direction of Mecca. He noticed that she, too, was pointed to the east.

He looked closer and saw that something had been carved into the skin of her exposed back. Postmortem, he realized; there was no bleeding around the edges of the slice marks. In fact, there was little blood anywhere—only a small dark stain collected under the girl's chest, a residue of death, and, he knew, merely the last fluid insult. She'd been killed someplace else, then brought here.

He looked at her hands and saw that the index finger had been removed from her left hand. Not her right, as with the other victims, but the left. This made him raise an eyebrow involuntarily. He could not tell immediately what other damage had been done to the body. He couldn't see her face; it was pressed down into the dirt, beneath her outstretched arms.

Supplication, he thought.

Martin was pointing at the torso and loudly demanding from a white-gloved technician: "What's the cause? How was she killed?"

The technician bent down and indicated a small red area just at the base of the girl's skull, where her long, brownish blonde hair was matted with blood.

"Entry wound," the man said. "We'll see where it came out on the other side. Looks to be large. Large enough, at least. Nine millimeter, probably. Maybe .357. We'll know more when we turn her. Maybe the bullet's still in there."

Jeffrey stared again at the carved shape in her back, then recognized it for what it was. He stepped back. The lights made him feel hot, flushed. He wanted to move into the dark, where it was cooler and he felt he could breathe. He walked a short way from the body, then turned and looked back toward all the men gathered around. He bent down and touched the sandy dirt, rubbing some between his fingers. When he looked up, he saw Martin approaching him.

"Not our guy, goddamn it," the detective said. "Christ, what a mess. Gonna be a boyfriend or maybe the neighbor whose kids she watched or some pervert at her school who teaches gym class or works for janitorial services and somehow slipped through the immigration checks, goddamn it, or something else, goddamn it, but not our guy. Shit! This isn't supposed to happen! Not here. Somebody's screwed up big-time."

Jeffrey leaned back up against a large rock. "Why don't you think it's our guy?" he asked.

Martin stared hard at him for a moment before replying. "Hell, Professor, you can see as well as I. Body position different. Cause of death, gunshot, that's different. Something carved in her back, that's different. And her goddamn finger. From the wrong hand. The other three were from the right hand. This is left."

"But killed someplace else then brought here. What were the surveyors doing when they found her?"

Martin knitted his brows for an instant, then replied: "Preliminary site work for a new town. This was their first day up here. They'd been at it since this morning, were just getting ready to wrap it up for the day and decided to do one more set of numbers when they found her. Guy spotted her right through the viewfinder. So what?"

"So, somewhere there's a schedule, right? Or something that told people that they'd be here sooner or later?"

"That's right. It was in the papers. Always is, when a new town starts to get planned. It goes out over the electronic billboards, too."

"You know what that is, carved on her back?" Clayton asked.

"Not a clue. Some sort of geometric shape."

"A pentagram."

"Okay, a pentagram. So what?"

"Shape commonly associated with devils and devil worship."

"No shit. You're right. You suppose we've got some crazy coven running around out here? Naked and baying at the moon and fucking each other and talking about cutting the throats of chickens and cats? Some sort of Southern California craziness? That's all I need now."

"No. Though that's an interpretation the killer might have—maybe even probably—thought you'd make. Something you'd have to check out that would take time and energy. Lots of time and lots of energy."

"What are you getting at, Professor?"

Jeffrey hesitated, staring up into the sky. He blinked at the expanse of blue-black space, dotted with stars. He thought: I should learn astronomy. It would be nice to know where Orion is, and Cassiopeia, and all the others. That way I could look up into the nighttime and feel as if I understood it all, that there was order and organization to the heavens.

He lowered his eyes and looked at the detective. "It's our guy," Jeffrey said. "He's just being clever."

"Tell me why."

"The others have been angels, eyes open to God, arms wide to greet him. This one has the mark of Satan on her back and she's praying to the earth. And her finger is gone from the left. The left is the devil's hand. The right, Heaven's. At least in some traditions. All he's done is turn some things around. They are the same, except different. Heaven and Hell. Isn't that the dichotomy that we're forever struggling with? Isn't that precisely what you're trying to avoid right here?"

Martin snorted in disgust. "Sounds like a lot of religious gobbledygook," he said. "Socioreligious crap. Tell me: Why the handgun, not a knife, like before?"

"Because," Jeffrey said coldly, "it's not the killing that's turning him on. I don't think he cares what device he uses to dispatch the young women. It's the entirety of the act. It's stealing the child and possessing her, physically, emotionally, psychologically, then leaving her where she'll be found. Where is the thrill in painting a picture and then never showing it to anyone? Where is the satisfaction in writing a book and never allowing it to be read?"

Another question occurred to him. How do you make your own mark in history, when so many others have made the same marks over so many centuries?

"How do you know?" Martin demanded slowly. "How can you be sure?"

I know because I know, Jeffrey said to himself.

But he did not answer the question out loud.

It was well after midnight when Martin dropped Clayton off in front of the State Office Building. There was the usual late-night "get some sleep we'll get at it in the morning" back and forth, and then the detective pulled away from the curb, leaving the professor standing alone outside the hulking concrete form. The other corporate buildings were all shut down for the night, darkened save for an occasional light illuminating the company's sign and logo. The parking lots were empty; there was a modest glow in the distance from the downtown of New Washington, but even this minimal source of humanity was compromised by the quiet that enveloped the professor. He shrugged hard, partially against the chill in the air that had dogged him all night, but mostly because of the sense of isolation that swept over him.

He turned away from the darkness and quick-marched through the State Office doors. In the center of the vestibule there was a security and directory station, with a single uniformed officer behind a large desk. His face was lit up by the glow from a small television screen. He waved at Clayton.

"Late night, huh?" he asked, not really expecting an answer. "Wanna sign in for me?"

"Who's winning?" Jeffrey asked. The sheet he was handed was blank. No other after-hours visitors. His would be the only name on the page.

"Score's tied," the man replied. He didn't identify the teams playing as he collected the sign-in clipboard and turned back to the game.

Jeffrey thought for a moment about conversation, then measured the exhaustion within him and decided that no matter how lonely he might feel, sleep was preferable to the security guard's opinions of life, sport, and duty, regardless of what they might be. He trudged over to the elevator, rode it up to the floor where his office was located, and walked down the hallway slowly, the sound of his sneakers filling the empty corridor.

He placed his hand on the electronic security lock and the door unlocked with a thunk. Pushing his way into the office, he headed toward the adjacent bedroom, trying to clear his mind of what he'd seen that day, what he'd heard, and what he believed to be true. He told himself that there was much he had to reduce to writing, that it was important to keep a record of his observations and a diary of his thoughts, so that when it came time to make a case in a court of law, he would have the benefit of a clear record of everything he'd absorbed. As a corollary to this duty that he'd defined for the upcoming day, Clayton realized he'd acquired some information that was appropriate to his blackboard. He recalled the two columns he'd created, and glanced back at the blackboard just as he was heading into the bedroom.

What he saw made him stop short.

He leaned hard against the wall, breathing sharply.

He looked around quickly, to see if anything was missing, then his eyes returned to the board. He thought: This must be an accident. A cleaning crew, perhaps. There's probably some easy explanation.

But he was unable to think of any except the obvious.

Jeffrey let out a long slow whistle and told himself: Nothing is safe.

He remained like that, staring at the chalkboard for several minutes, his eyes lingering on an empty space. The category *If the Killer Is Not Known to Us* had been erased.

Moving slowly, like a man in a darkened room taking care not to stumble, he approached the blackboard. He fingered a piece of chalk in his hand, turned around abruptly, as if he thought someone might be watching, and then, fighting off the turbulence that careened about within him, carefully replaced the words that had been removed, thinking all the time: Let's just have it be the two of us who know you've been here.

DIANA CLAYTON'S
WORRIES

Diana Clayton looked at her daughter and thought that there was much to be afraid of, but that it was somehow important not to display the resonances of her fear, no matter how deeply they sounded. She sat stolidly in a corner of the worn, white cotton sofa in her small, decidedly cramped living room, drinking slowly and deliberately from a cold bottle of imported beer. When she lowered the bottle from her lips, she rested it on her thigh, moving her fingers slowly up and down the neck in a motion that in the younger woman would have been genuinely sexy, but for her merely displayed the residue of her nervousness.

"There's no real way to tell if there's a connection," she said brusquely. "It could have been anyone."

Susan was standing. She had slumped into an armchair, then moved across the room to a stiff-backed wooden rocker; then, uncomfortable there, she'd risen again and paced back and forth about the room in a style not unlike the pained frustration of a large fish pulling against a taut line.

"That's right," she said, suddenly sarcastic and breaking into language she knew would unsettle her mother, if not exactly offend her. "It could have been anyone. Just any old fellow who just happened to follow me and this poor asshole into the ladies' room, and just happened to have a handy hunting knife on his person, which, immediately assessing the situation, he decided to use on that dumb fuck, which he did, expertly and enthusiastically. And then, realizing that I had now been rescued from a fate worse than death, quietly exited, because he knew this would be an awkward moment for a lengthy introduction and he's not all that big on the normal social graces anyway."

She glared across the room. "Give me a break, Mother. It had to be him." She exhaled slowly. "Whoever the hell *he* is."

The daughter held up the piece of notepaper with the man's cryptic message. *"I have always been with you,"* she said sullenly. "Good thing he was there tonight."

Diana thought her daughter's words rattled in the small space of the room. "You were armed," she said. "What was going to happen?"

"That poor drunken bastard was going to kick in the damn door, and I was going to shoot him right between the eyes or between the legs, whichever seemed more appropriate given the circumstances."

Susan muttered a quiet obscenity or two, then walked to the window and peered out into the night. She could see little, and so cupped her hands around her temples to cut away the living room light and pressed her face against the glass. She could see the darkness glisten with warmth, steaming from the rainstorm that had struck and passed earlier that evening, leaving behind nothing except a few ripped palm fronds knocked to the roadway, streaks of moisture puddled up in potholes and street depressions, and a residual heat that seemed to be buttressed by the passing storm, as if renewed or encouraged. She let her eyes assess the darkness, uncertain in that moment whether she would prefer to see the emptiness, which would underscore their isolation, or actually spot the shape of a man moving furtively through the shadows, lurking just beyond the periphery of their yard, which she thought likely.

She saw no one, which convinced her of nothing. After a moment she reached out and lowered the shade with a clatter.

"What really bothered me," she said slowly, as she turned to face her mother, "the more I thought about it, was not what happened, but *how* it happened."

Diana nodded, to encourage her daughter to keep talking, thinking that this was precisely what was bothering her as well.

"Go on," the older woman said.

"You see, there wasn't any hesitation," Susan continued. "Not an appreciable one, at least. One second there's this abusive drunk with God knows what on his mind, but certainly at a minimum rape, banging away at the door. Then I hear the other door open and the bastard has just enough time to say 'Who the fuck are you?' and then whoosh! That knife or razor or whatever had to be in his hand, ready to operate. He came walking through that bathroom door *already* knowing what he was going to do, and he didn't take a second to assess anything. Not a second to worry, to wonder, to think twice, to posture, or maybe just threaten the guy. He must have stepped forward, and bang!"

Susan took a single step into the room and swept her arm through the air in a quick slashing motion.

" 'Bang' is wrong," she said quietly. "There was no 'bang!' It was faster than that."

Diana bit down hard on her lip before speaking. "Think," she said. "Was there anything there that might have suggested this crime was something other than what you're saying? Was there anything—"

"No!" Susan interrupted. Then she paused, reflectively picturing the scene in the ladies' room of the bar. She remembered the crimson color of the blood pooling beneath the dead man and how starkly it showed against the light-colored linoleum bathroom floor.

"He was robbed," she added slowly. "At least his wallet was open and it had been thrown down beside him. That's something. And his pants were unzipped."

"Anything else?"

"Not that I can remember. I got out of there pretty quick."

Diana thought hard about the empty wallet. "I think we should call Jeffrey," she said. "He could tell us for certain."

"Why? This is my problem. All we'll do is scare him. Unnecessarily."

Diana started to respond. Then she thought better of it. She looked at her daughter and tried to see behind the angry glare and stiff shoulders, and she felt a huge gloomy depression within herself because she understood that she'd once upon a time been so possessed with saving them physically that she hadn't been able to see what else needed saving. Collateral damage, she said to herself. The storm blows down a tree, which falls against a high-power wire, which drops into a puddle, charging the water with a fatal jolt of electricity, which kills the unsuspecting man out walking his dog as the sky clears and the stars come out above. That's what happened to my children, she thought bitterly. I saved them from the storm. But that was all.

Doubt hardened her voice. "Jeffrey is an expert in homicide. All sorts of homicides. And, if we're really being threatened—which we also don't know for certain, but which is a real possibility—he has a right to know about it, because he may have some expertise that would help us in that situation as well."

Susan snorted. "He has his own life and his own problems. We should be certain we need help before asking for it."

She said this as if making some sort of definitive point, as if her words proved something. But her mother was unsure what this was.

Diana wanted to argue, but felt a sudden, abrupt shaft of pain crease her insides, and she snatched a breath savagely out of the still room air to stifle it. The pain was like a shock to her system, buzzing about within her, setting all her nerve ends on edge. She waited for the surge to settle, then ebb, which it did after a moment or two. She reminded herself that the cancer within her didn't care much about emotions, and it certainly didn't give a whit about what other problems she might have. It was the precise opposite of the homicide that her daughter had experienced that night. It was slow and nastily patient. It might cause as much pain as the man's knife, but it would take its own time to cause that pain. There would be nothing swift about it, although it would be just as singularly fatal as a knife wound or a gunshot.

She felt a little dizzy, but fought that off with a series of deep breaths, like a diver preparing to submerge beneath the surface of the water.

"All right," she said carefully. "What does that open wallet you saw tell you?"

Susan shrugged, and before she could answer, her mother continued.

"This is what your brother would tell you: that we live in a violent world where there is little time and little inclination for anyone to actually *solve* a crime. The police exist to try to maintain order, which they do with some ruthlessness. And when a crime occurs that has an easy answer, they will provide it, because that helps to keep the routine of life flowing bumpily along. But most of the time, unless the victim is important, it will be ignored and merely chalked up as yet another example of these lawless times. And some half-drunk oversexed junior executive doesn't sound to me like a case where there's going to be some political importance. And, assuming for a moment that some detective is interested in the case, what is he going to see? An open wallet and unzipped pants. A robbery homicide, just like that. Bingo. And what he's going to figure is that there were some working girls in that not exactly high-class bar, and that one of them, or their pimp, did the job. And by the time this overworked detective figures out that this which seems so damn obvious isn't at all what happened, he'll have a very cold case and little desire to do anything about it other than file it away at the bottom of his pile of a hundred other cases. Especially when he finds out there wasn't any helpful security camera in the bar conveniently recording all the comings and goings. So, all that is what your brother would tell you the killer achieved, merely by helping himself to the man's cash and leaving the wallet lying there. Simple as that."

Susan listened, then hesitated before replying: "I could still go to the cops myself."

Diana shook her head vigorously. "And how is it that you think they'll help us when you instantly create for them a wonderful suspect in the homicide? That is: yourself. Because they sure as hell aren't going to believe for an instant that someone *else* is watching over you, anonymously. Surreptitiously. Someone who doesn't have a face or a name or an identity other than a pair of cryptic notes left for you outside our house, and just happens to be skilled enough to dispatch anyone who comes along and threatens you. Just like some sort of uniquely evil guardian angel."

Diana stopped short then.

Again her head spun and pain surged through her body.

There was a vial of pills on the coffee table in front of her, and she slowly and deliberately reached out and shook two into the palm of her hand. She gulped them down, chased by the last bitter, warm swig of beer in the bottom of the bottle.

But it wasn't the disease making its presence felt that truly pained her. It was the final words that she'd spoken. *A uniquely evil guardian angel.* Because she could think of only one person with the qualifications to fit that specific description.

But he's dead, goddamnit! she shouted to herself. He died years ago! We're free of him!

She said none of this out loud. Instead she let this sudden fear fix itself within her, at a location uncomfortably close to the steady stabs of pain that wracked her body.

They ate dinner that night in relative silence, without further discussion of the notes or the killing, and certainly no additional conversation about what they might do, then repaired to their own rooms in the small house. Susan stood at the foot of her bed knowing that she was both exhausted and energized at the same time. Sleep, she considered, was imperative, yet would be elusive. With a shrug, she turned away from the bed and tossed herself into her desk chair. She fingered the keyboard in front of her computer and told herself that she had to concoct another message for the man she believed had saved her.

She dropped her head into her hands, shaking it back and forth.

Saved by the man who threatens me.

She smiled wryly, thinking that she would probably appreciate this irony a helluva lot more were it happening to someone else. Then she lifted her head and clicked on the computer.

She toyed with words and phrases, but couldn't find anything she liked, mainly because she didn't know what it was she wanted to say.

In frustration, she pushed herself away from the desk and went to her closet. Arranged on the back wall were all her weapons, the assault rifle, several pistols, and boxes of cartridges. On an adjacent shelf there were some fly reels and lines, a filleting knife in a sheath, and three clear, Myran fly boxes cluttered with brightly colored deceivers and cockroach tarpon flies, some snapping shrimp imitations, crazy Charlies, and dull brown crab flies that she used when she fished for permit. She lifted one box and shook it.

She thought it was an odd thing: the most successful flies were rarely the most lifelike imitations. Often the lure that caught the best fish was merely a suggestion of shape and color, an enticement, not a reality, hiding a deadly saltwater-hardened steel hook.

Susan put the box back on the shelf and reached out for the long filleting knife. She removed this from the black, fake leather sheath and held it in front of her. She ran her finger down the dull edge. The blade was narrow, curved slightly, like an executioner's self-satisfied grin at the moment of death, and razor sharp. She flipped the knife over and gently placed her finger on the cutting edge, taking care not to move it one way or the other, because that would slice open her finger. She held her hand in this precarious fashion for several seconds. Then, abruptly, she swept the knife upward, brandishing it a few inches from her face.

Something like this, she told herself. She made a slashing motion in the air in front of her, similar to the one she'd made earlier in the living room with her mother. She listened carefully, though, as this real blade sliced the still air.

It makes no sound, she thought. Not even a whisper to warn you that death is hurrying in your direction.

She shuddered, and replaced the knife in its sheath and back on the shelf. Then she returned to her computer. Quickly she typed:

Why are you following me?
What is it you want?
And then, she added, almost plaintively: *I want to be left alone.*

Susan looked at the words she'd written, and with a deep breath started to translate them into a puzzle she could put in her column in the magazine. *Mata Hari,* she whispered to her alter ego, *find something truly cryptic and difficult that will take him some time to decipher, because I would like to have a few days free to figure out what I'm going to do next.*

Diana rested on the edge of her bed considering the cancer that was steadily eradicating her insides. She thought it was interesting, in a perverse sort of way: this alien disease that had fastened itself to her pancreas in what she believed was some sort of arbitrary and capricious decision. After all, she'd gone through most of her life worrying about so many things, but it had never occurred to her to imagine that this organ deep within her would emerge as her betrayer. She shrugged, wondering, as she had on several occasions before, what her pancreas actually looked like. Was it red? Green? Purple? Were the tiny flecks of cancer black? What did it do for her, other than now, when it was slowly killing her? Why did she need it in the first place? Why did she need any of them, liver, colon, stomach, intestines, kidneys—and why hadn't they been infected? She tried to envision her own tissues and organs as if they were some machine, like an engine running roughly because of poor quality fuel. She wished, for an instant, that she could plunge her hand deep into her body and rip out the offending organ, then toss it to the floor and defy it to kill her. She was filled with anger, an outrageous, reverberating fury that some hidden, insignificant pipsqueak of an organ could rob her of life. I must take charge, she thought. I must take control.

She recalled the moment she'd seized her own future, and thought: I must do the same with my death.

She stood up and walked across her small bedroom.

The rain in the Keys is fierce, she thought, a sudden bursting forth, like earlier that evening, when it seems as if the heavens are enraged and they let loose a total black deluge that blinds and shakes the whole world. It was different the night she fled from her husband; that was a cold, harsh rain, spitting and hissing around her, unsettling, giving support to all the fears erupting within her. It had none of the decisiveness of the Keys storms that she'd come to be so familiar with; on the night she fled her home and her past and every connection she'd ever had with anyone or anything in her first thirty years, that had been a rain of doubts.

In a corner of her bedroom closet she kept a small lockbox, which she searched for behind some canvases, old tubes of paint, and brushes. She took a second to berate herself; there is no reason to stop painting, she said. Even if you are dying.

She was unaware that her own actions were unknowingly mimicking her daughter's. But where Susan had searched out a knife from her closet, Diana seized hold of a small box of well-hidden memories.

The lockbox was made out of cheap, black metal. There had once been a small padlock that secured it, but Diana had misplaced the key, and she'd been forced to cut the padlock off with a metal rasp. Now it was secured only by a simple clasp. She thought that was probably true of most memories; no matter how deep one thinks they are locked away, in reality they're secured only by the flimsiest of containers.

Standing by the side of her bed, she opened the box slowly, spreading its contents on the bedspread in front of her. It had been years since she placed anything inside, years since she'd removed anything. At the top were some papers, a copy of her will—splitting everything she owned, which she knew was not much, equally between the two children—an insurance policy for some small sum of money, and a copy of the deed to the house. Beneath these papers there were several loose photographs, a short, typed list of names and addresses, a single letter from an attorney, and a glossy page torn from a magazine.

Diana picked up the sheet of paper first and sat down heavily. At the bottom margin of the page was a number: 52. Adjacent to that, in a preciously small script, were the words: *The St. Thomas More Academy Bulletin. Spring 1983.*

There were three columns of type on the page. The first two were under the listings *Marriages* and *Births*. The third was headed *Obituaries*. There was only a single entry in this column and it was to this that her eyes were drawn:

It is with regret that the Academy has learned of the recent passing away of former history teacher Jeffrey Mitchell. Professor Mitchell, a violinist of note, is remembered by many students and faculty for his energy, his diligence and wit, displayed during his few years at the Academy. He will be missed by all who love the study of history and classical music.

Diana wanted to spit. Her mouth tasted of bile.

"He will really be missed by all the people he didn't get a chance to kill. . . ." she whispered furiously to herself.

She held the page from the magazine and remembered the sensations she felt on the day she'd seen the entry. Astonishment. Relief. And then, curiously, she'd expected to feel a surge of freedom, an exhilarating burst of escape because the entry told her that her worst fear—that of being found— had been removed. But this release from anxiety had not occurred. Instead, what had taken place within her was a constancy of doubt. The words told her one thing, but she would not allow herself to fully believe it.

She set the sheet of paper down and picked up the letter.

At the top was the letterhead of an attorney with a small firm in Trenton, New Jersey. The letter had been addressed to a *Ms. Jane Jones* at a post office box in North Miami. She had driven north two hours in the hot sun, out of the Keys, for the sole purpose of renting the box at the largest and busiest mail facility in the city, simply for the receipt of this letter.

Dear Ms. Jones:

I understand that is not your real name, and ordinarily I would be reluctant to communicate with a fictitious individual, but under the circumstances, I will try to cooperate.

I was contacted by Mr. Mitchell, your estranged husband, some two weeks prior to his death. Curiously, he told me that he had had a premonition of dying, and that was why he wanted to be sure his meager affairs were in order. I prepared a will for him. He left a substantial collection of books to a local library, and the proceeds from the sale of his remaining possessions was donated to a local church group and chamber music society. He had a few investments, and modest savings.

He informed me that the day might arrive when you would seek information about his death, and I was instructed to release what I knew about his passing, and to make one other, additional statement.

This is what I learned of his death: It was abrupt. He was killed in a collision with another vehicle late at night. Both were traveling at high speeds, and they struck head on. It was necessary to use dental records to identify the victims. The police in the small Maryland town where this event took place were persuaded on the basis of interviews with survivors that your estranged husband actually directed his vehicle into the path of the onrushing tractor-trailer. His death was listed as vehicular suicide.

Mr. Mitchell's body was subsequently cremated and ashes interred at Woodlawn Cemetery. He made no prior provision for a headstone, only for the minimal funeral. As best as I can tell, no one attended. He said he had no other living relatives, and no real friends.

In our few conversations, he never mentioned any children, and did not indicate anything that should be left to them.

The statement he had me prepare to issue to you, should you ever contact this office was, according to his instructions, his gift to you. That statement is: "For better or for worse, through richer or through poorer, in sickness and in health, until death do us part."

I am sorry I can provide no further information.

The lawyer had signed the letter with a flourish: *H. Kenneth Smith*. She'd wanted to call him, because it seemed to her that the letter suggested more than it answered, but she resisted this temptation. Instead, upon reading the letter, she immediately closed her post office box account, leaving no forwarding address.

Now, she set the letter down on the bed next to the St. Thomas More Academy Bulletin obituary and stared at the two.

She remembered. In a way, the children still seemed like babies when they arrived in South Florida. She had hoped so; she'd wanted to find a way to eradicate any memory of their first life in the house up in New Jersey. She had made a conscious effort to render everything different—the clothes they wore, the food they ate. Any fabric or taste or smell that might remind them of where they'd fled from, she'd removed. Even their accents. She'd worked to develop some of the southernisms of the Upper Keys. Bubba speech, the locals called it. Y'alls and sho'nuffs and the like. Anything that might make it seem to them, as they grew older, that their lives had started right there.

She reached into the lockbox and removed a typed list of names and a small packet of photographs. Her hands quivered as she held these on her lap. She hadn't looked at them in many years. One by one she held them up.

The first few were of her parents, and of her own sister and brother, when they were all young themselves. They were taken on a New England beach, and the swimsuits and the beach chairs and umbrellas and coolers were dated and therefore slightly ludicrous. There was one picture of her father carrying a long surf rod, dressed in waders, with a swordfish-billed hat pushed back from his forehead, displaying a large grin and pointing at the immense striped bass that he toted by the gills. He's dead, now, she thought. He must be. Too many years have gone by. I wish I knew for sure, but he must be. He would be proud to know his granddaughter was as expert a fisherman as he was. He would have loved it if she'd taken him out, just once, on that skiff of hers.

She set this photograph aside and picked up another, of her mother, standing with her brother and sister. They all had their arms linked together, and it was obvious that she'd managed to snap the shutter just at the punch line of a joke, because all their heads were thrown back in unmistakable, unrestrained laughter. That was what she liked about her mother, that she always seemed able to laugh at anything, no matter how hard it had been. A woman who defied bad news, Diana thought. I must have gotten my stubbornness from her. She must be dead, too, now. Or else far too old and filled with forgetfulness. She looked down at the picture a second time and felt a sublime loneliness within her, and for an instant she wished she could remember the joke that had been told at that moment. Nothing else, she thought, but just to know the joke again would be nice.

She sighed deeply. She looked at her brother and sister and whispered "I'm sorry" to the two of them. For a moment she wondered if it had been harder on all of them, when she disappeared. Birthdays, anniversaries, Christmases. Probably weddings, births, deaths, all the ordinary commerce of life in a family, sliced away from her with a single deadly psychological sword stroke. She hadn't given them a word of explanation, not even a syllable of connection. It was the one thing that she'd known utterly and completely the night that she fled Jeffrey Mitchell and the house she'd shared with him.

If she was to have a life for herself and her children, it had to be somewhere safe. And the only way she could guarantee safety was to never surface, because then he would find her. She knew this with total certainty.

I died that night. And was reborn as well.

She set the photographs down and glanced at the typed list. It contained the names and the last addresses she knew for all her relatives. It was for her own children someday, she hoped. There would come a day, she believed, when reconnection was possible.

She had thought it might have happened when she received the lawyer's letter. Evidence of his death. It had remained in the lockbox for decades. And it was all she'd been waiting for. She suddenly asked herself: Why hadn't she emerged, when it arrived?

She shook her head.

Because a large part of her didn't believe it. Enough of a part of her that she wouldn't risk her life and her children's lives, no matter how persuasive the lawyer's letter was.

There was a small manila envelope in the bottom of the lockbox, the last remaining item. This she removed gingerly, as if it was fragile. She opened it slowly, for the first time in many years.

It, too, was a photograph.

In the picture, she was much younger and sitting in an armchair. She frowned when she saw her face. Mousy. Hiding behind glasses. Timid and indecisive. Weak. A five-year-old Susan was clinging to her lap, all bottled energy. Seven-year-old Jeffrey was standing next to her, but leaning toward her, his face all serious and concerned, as if he somehow knew that he'd already aged far beyond his years. His hand was tightly gripped in her own.

Standing behind the three of them, behind the back of the chair, apart a slight ways, was the elder Jeffrey. The camera had been on automatic, set up across from them, and by standing back just a few inches, his features had been blurred.

He never wanted his picture taken. For a moment, she stared at his face. Bastard, she thought.

Jeffrey would know, she realized. He would know how to take the picture and have it scanned by an optical computer, which could enhance the features, making them clear and distinct. And then they could electronically age him, so they'd know what he now looked like.

She stopped in mid-thought. "But you're dead," she said out loud. The face in the picture made no reply.

She'd done everything she could, Diana thought. She had tried her best to keep tabs on him, diligently read the St. Thomas More Academy bulletins, and surreptitiously subscribed to the *Princeton Packet*, the weekly paper that covered Hopewell. She'd considered hiring a private detective, but, as always, she understood one critical fact: all information can flow two ways. Every effort she made to find out about him, no matter how subtle, could travel back to her. So, over the years, she had simply scoured what few avenues she felt relatively safe within. These were mainly public sources, like newspapers and bulletins. She culled the alumni magazines of every school he'd attended, or anywhere he'd taught. She read obituaries and newspapers and paid careful attention to real estate transactions. But mostly it had been fruitless, especially in the many years since the lawyer's letter. Still, she'd continued. She'd been very proud of this. Most people would have concluded they were safe, but she did nothing of the sort.

She looked up and addressed her husband as if he were standing there in the room with her. Either a ghost, or flesh and blood, it made no difference to her.

"You thought you could fool me. All along, you thought I would do precisely what you wanted, what you expected, and what you desired. But I didn't, did I?"

She smiled.

That must pain you no end, she thought.

If you are alive, it must be an unrelenting sore.

And if you are indeed dead, then I hope it drives you to fury in whatever Hell you've found.

Diana Clayton took another deep breath.

She stood and gathered the items from her bed, replacing them in the lockbox. She thought of what had happened to her daughter, and the messages she'd received.

It's all a game, she thought bitterly. It was always a game.

She decided, in that moment, that no matter how angry it might make her daughter, she would call her son. If it is him sending the notes, she thought, if after all these years he's finally found us, then Jeffrey has the right to know, because his danger is just as profound as our own. And he has the right to be a player in this game as well.

She walked over to a small bedside table and removed the telephone from its cradle. She hesitated a moment, then dialed her son's number in Massachusetts.

The telephone rang infuriatingly. She counted ten rings, then let it ring on for an additional ten. Then she hung up.

She sat down hard on the bed.

Diana knew she would not sleep that night. She reached out for her pain pills and swallowed a pair without water, gulping hard, knowing they would do nothing for the real pain within her, a sudden, awful, black-tinged dread.

A PLACE OF
CONTRADICTIONS

Jeffrey Clayton shifted about uncomfortably on the polished hardwood of the church pew while the congregation surrounding him dipped their heads in silent prayer. It was many years since he'd been in a church during a service, and he was uncomfortable with the enthusiasm that surrounded him. He sat in the last row of the Unitarian church in the town where the young woman he could only mentally refer to as number four had made her home.

The town, named Liberty, was still in the midst of construction. Idle bulldozers were lined up on a swatch of light brown dirt that would soon become the town common. There were stacks of metal girder frames and mounds of cinder blocks at other locations.

The day before, there had been continual construction noise: the beeping and bellowing of earth-moving equipment, the high-pitched whine of machinery, the rumbling of truck diesel engines. This day, however, was Sunday, and the beasts of progress were silent. And from where he sat, inside the church, there was none of the sense of saws, nails, and raw materials. It was new and sparkling on the bright morning, shafts of colored light streaming through a large stained-glass window depicting Christ on the cross, though the artisan who'd created the window had envisioned a Savior less afflicted by the pain of his early death than absorbed by the joy of the Heaven awaiting him. The bright light that illuminated the Christ figure's crown of thorns threw multicolored hues and rainbow projections on the unyielding white walls of the church.

Jeffrey scanned the congregation. The church was filled, and, with the exception of himself, exclusively with families. The majority were white, but there were a few black, Hispanic, and Oriental faces intermixed. He guessed the median age of the adults was slightly older than he was, and the median for the children as perhaps junior high school age. There were some babies in arms, and some older teenagers who seemed to have more interest in each other than in the service. All were scrubbed, pressed, and combed. He ran his eyes over the faces of the children, trying to find the one who resented wearing the Sunday finery, but with a few tentative possibilities— one boy whose tie was askew, another whose shirt had come untucked, a third who squirmed in his seat despite his father's arm draped over his shoulders—he couldn't find an obvious candidate for rebellion. No Huck Finns here, he thought.

Jeffrey ran his hand over the polished reddish-brown mahogany pew and noticed, as well, that the black jacket of the hymnal was hardly worn. He looked back up at the stained-glass figure and thought: There must be a set of priorities and a schedule somewhere, because it took some craftsman a good deal of time to create that vision and then render it so meticulously. So he received his commission, complete with dimensions and specifications, months before the first bulldozer moved, before the town hall was built, or the supermarket, or the shopping mall.

The choir rose. They wore deep burgundy robes, trimmed in gold. Their voices soared through the church, but he paid little attention. He was waiting for the sermon to begin, and he moved his gaze over to the minister, who was shuffling through some notes, sitting off to the side of a podium. He rose just as the final notes of the hymn started to fade from the rafters.

The minister kept eyeglasses on a chain around his neck, occasionally raising them to a perch on the bridge of his nose. Oddly, he gestured only with his right hand, leaving his left glued rigidly at his side. He was a short man, with thinning, longish hair that sprung wildly from his head as if caught in a breeze, although the air in the church was still. His voice was larger, however, than he was, booming forth over the congregation's heads. "What is God's message when he delivers to us an accident that robs us of someone we love?"

Tell me, please, Jeffrey thought cynically. But he listened carefully. This was the reason he was at the church.

This particular service was not specifically devoted to victim number four. A small, private family service had been held midweek in a Catholic church a few yards away, across the still dusty area that would be watered, sodded, and turn green when the growing season grew stronger. He had insisted to Agent Martin that everyone attending the service for the murdered girl be videotaped, and that every vehicle, even those that merely drove past the service ostensibly on some other errand, be identified. He wanted to know the names and backgrounds of anyone connected with the interment of the young woman. Anyone who showed even the most meager interest in her death.

Those lists were being prepared, and he planned to cross-reference them against teachers, workers, lawn maintenance men—anyone—who might have come into contact with her. Then he would cross-reference the list an additional time against every name that had been compiled in the course of investigating the murder of victim number three. This, he knew, was fairly standard procedure when it came to examining any serial crimes. It was a time-consuming and frustrating process, but occasionally—at least in the literature of multiple killers—the police would get fortunate and a single name would show up on each list.

He held out little hope for this.

You know, don't you? he suddenly demanded of his mental image of the killer. You know all the standard techniques? You know all the traditional avenues of inquiry?

The minister's voice crashed through his reverie.

"Are not accidents God's way of choosing from amongst us? Where he decides to impose his will upon our lives?"

Jeffrey had clenched his fist tightly. I need to know the link, he thought. What is it that's driving you to these young women? What is it that you are saying?

The answer to this question eluded him.

Jeffrey lifted his head and started to pay closer attention to the service. He hadn't come to the church seeking divine inspiration. His curiosity was of a different nature. He noticed the billboard outside the church the day before, promoting the Sunday sermon by title: "When God's Accidents Happen to Us." He'd considered it an odd choice of words: *accident.*

What did it have to do with the depravity he'd seen the final results of a few days earlier?

That's what he was eager to learn.

What accident?

He had kept this question to himself, not sharing it with Agent Martin, who was now impatiently waiting for him outside the church.

Jeffrey continued to listen. The minister boomed on, and the professor waited to hear a single word: *murder.*

"So we ask ourselves: What is God's plan when he takes someone so young and filled with promise from our side? For there is a plan, we can rest assured . . .”

Jeffrey rubbed his nose. Helluva plan, he thought.

“. . . And sometimes we learn that by taking the very best of us to his bosom, what he is really asking of us who stay behind is to redouble our faith and renew our commitment and rededicate our lives to the doing of good and the spreading of love and devotion . . .”

The minister paused, letting his words flow over the faces lifted toward him.

“. . . And if we follow that path that he has made so clear, despite our grief and our sorrow, we will bring ourselves and all who remain here on earth that much closer to him. That is what he is demanding of us, and it is a challenge that we will rise to!”

The left hand that the minister had kept at his side now pointed eagerly toward the heavens, as if signaling whoever it was that was up above and monitoring his words that he’d reached his conclusion. The minister hesitated a second time, giving his words added resonance, then finished:

“Let us pray.”

Jeffrey bowed his head, but not in prayer.

Because of what I have not heard, I just learned something important, he told himself. Something that made his stomach clench with a small knot of intense anxiety, an anxiety that had nothing to do with the murders he was examining, but everything to do with the place where he was examining them.

Agent Martin was sitting at his desk, playing with jacks. The small child’s rubber ball made a muffled thumping sound, and occasionally the hulking detective would miss, curse, and start over again, rattling the game pieces on the flat surface of the steel desktop.

“One . . . two . . . three . . .” he mumbled to himself.

Jeffrey looked over from where he was writing on the blackboard. “It’s ‘onesies, twosies, threesies,’ etcetera,” he said. “You need to get the terminology straight.”

Martin smiled. “You play your game,” he replied, “and I’ll play mine.” He swept all the pieces off the desk into his right hand in a single, sharp gesture and turned his attention to what Clayton was writing.

The two primary categories remained at the top of the board. Jeffrey had filled in additional information, however, loosely under the heading *Similarities*, which detailed the body positioning of each victim, the locations, and the absent index fingers. Victim number four, of course, had made some of these details problematic. Jeffrey had discovered a certain skepticism on

Martin's part, and a reluctance to see—as he did—that the differences in the careful positioning of the corpse and the removal of the left index finger, as opposed to the other victims' right fingers, only suggested the same man. The detective had an obstinate streak, which made him shake his head and say: "The same is the same. Different is different. You want different to be the same. It doesn't work that way."

The side of the board that read *If the Killer Is Not Known to Us* had considerably fewer entries. Clayton hadn't told the detective that it had been erased and he'd replaced it; not that the security of the office had been compromised.

Clayton hadn't taken any steps to hide the information about the killings—the crime scene reports, autopsy results, witness statements, and the like—that filled the office filing cabinets. Most of these were also contained in computer files as well, and Jeffrey assumed that anyone with the capacity to make his way past the electronic locks on the work space also had the ability to read anything generated on their computer.

Instead, he'd stopped in a local stationery store and purchased a small, leather-bound notebook. In an era of computer think pads and high-speed communications, the notebook was almost an antique. But it had the singular virtue of being modest enough to fit into his jacket pocket, and thus would remain on his person at all times. Therefore, it was private, and not beholden to an electric current or a computer code to be secure. It was rapidly filling with Jeffrey's concerns and observations, all of which seemed to underscore a doubt he was as yet unable to formulate, but which was gathering momentum within him.

On one of the first pages, he'd written: *Who erased the blackboard?* and then, beneath that, had written four possibilities:

1. A maintenance worker, making some mistake.
2. Some political figure, e.g. Manson, Starkweather, or Bundy.
3. My father, the killer.
4. The killer who is not my father, but wants me to believe that he is.

He had already effectively ruled out the first by finding the building maintenance schedules and speaking briefly with the people on duty. They had revealed two interesting things: that they were told by Agent Martin that any clean-up in the office had to be performed under his direct supervision, and that State Security could override virtually any computer-driven locking system, anywhere in the state.

He had also ruled out the politicians, at least in theory. Although the message in the erasure was precisely what he knew they wanted, it was too premature in his investigation to exert that sort of pressure on him. The pressure, he knew, would arrive soon enough. It always did, politics caring little for anything, save timing. And he doubted that such pressure would have the subtlety of the message contained in the simple act of erasing something he'd written on the blackboard.

Which left, of course, two possibilities. The same two possibilities that had plagued him from the beginning.

He was, as always, churning with questions, many of which he'd scribbled into his notebook late at night. If the small act of erasing a few words from a blackboard was performed by the killer—regardless of who he was—what did it mean?

He had answered this question in his book with a single word, written in black, block pencil and underscored three times: *Lots.*

"So, what's next, Professor? More interviews? Want to go talk with the medical examiner and get a really firsthand idea how our latest died? What have you got in mind?"

Martin was grinning, but it was the grin that Clayton had come to associate with anger.

He nodded. "There's an idea. You go over to the medical examiner and tell him we need his final report by this afternoon. Use all your powers of persuasion. The man seems reluctant."

"He's unaccustomed to his task. The state medical examiner's office here is usually more concerned with making certain that schoolchildren are properly inoculated and that Immigration isn't allowing any infectious diseases to arrive here willy-nilly from one of the other fifty, or abroad. Autopsies of murder victims aren't on the dance card. Not usually."

"So, go light a fire."

"And what is it, Professor, that you'll be doing while I'm off being irritating as only I know how?"

"I'm going to sit around and outline every forensic aspect of each crime, so that we can focus on the similarities."

"Sounds fascinating," the detective said as he rose from his chair. "Sounds really critical, too."

"You never know," Jeffrey responded. "Success in these sorts of investigations usually comes from some element of drudge work."

Martin shook his head. "No," he said, "I don't think so. That's true for a lot of murder investigations, sure. That's what they teach you in the academies. But not here, Professor. Here, something else will be required."

The detective started for the door, then paused. "That's why you're here. To figure out what that something else is. Try to remember that. And work on it, Professor."

Jeffrey nodded, but Martin had exited before seeing his response. He waited a few minutes, then quickly rose, seized his notebook and his jacket, and left, having absolutely no intention of doing what he'd told Martin he was going to do, but with a clear agenda in his head of what he needed to find out.

The offices of the *New Washington Post* were located near the center of the city, although Jeffrey was not certain that *city* was the correct word to describe the downtown area. It was certainly not like any urban area he'd ever visited; it was a place of almost rigid order in the guise of routine organization. The grid of streets was uniform, the plantings by the roadway well-tended. Sidewalks were wide and well-spaced, almost like a promenade. There was little of the mishmash of design and desire that characterizes most cities. And none of the sometimes frenetic disorder of modern and old butting up against each other.

New Washington was a place that had been thought out, sketched, measured, and modeled before a single shovelful of dirt was dug from the earth. Not that everything was the same. On the surface, at least, it was not. Different designs and different shapes marked each block. It was, however, the overall newness of everything that overwhelmed him. But though different architects had designed different buildings, it was clear that at some point every design had been channeled past the same eyes belonging to the same committee, and thus the city had imposed on it not so much a uniformity as an agreement of vision. That's what he found oppressive.

But he recognized, as well, that his sensation of distaste was likely to be highly transitory. As he walked down Main Street, he noted that the sidewalk had been swept clean of any overnight debris, and realized that it wouldn't take long to become accustomed to the new world that had been created in New Washington, if only because it was neat, uncluttered, and quiet.

And safe, Jeffrey reminded himself. Always safe.

There was a receptionist inside the newspaper office who smiled at him as he entered through a double set of swinging glass doors. On one wall, prominent issues of the newspaper had been blown up to gigantic size, the headlines crying out for attention. This, he thought, was not an untypical entryway for a newspaper; but what surprised him was the selection of blowups. At other newspapers one was likely to see famous editions from the past, which would reflect a mingling of successes, disasters, and enterprises, all of great import to the nation—Pearl Harbor or V-E Day, Kennedy's assassination, the stock market collapse, Nixon's resignation, the day man walked on the moon—but here the mock-ups were completely upbeat and

considerably more local: GROUND BROKEN FOR NEW WASHINGTON, STATE-
HOOD PUSH SEEN LIKELY, NEW TERRITORY OPENED IN NORTH, AGREEMENTS
REACHED WITH OREGON AND CALIFORNIA.

Only good news, Jeffrey thought.

He turned away from the wall and smiled at the receptionist. "Does the
paper have a morgue?"

The woman's eyes opened wider. "A what?"

"A library. Where past editions are kept."

She was young, well-brushed, better dressed than one would have expected for her age and her position.

"Oh, of course," she answered quickly. "I just never heard anyone use
that other term. Where dead people are kept."

"In the old days, that's what newspaper libraries were always called," he
replied.

She smiled. "Learn something new every day. Fourth floor. Stay to the
right. Have a nice day."

He found the library without any difficulty, located farther down a corridor from the newsroom. He paused for a moment, staring in at the men and
women working at desks, behind computer screens. There was a bank of
television monitors tuned to the cable all-news stations, suspended above a
central editing desk. The room was quiet, save for the ubiquitous plastic
clacking of computer keys being struck and an occasional voice breaking out
into laughter. Telephones buzzed quietly. It all seemed slick and efficient to
him, and lacking any of the romance that newspaper work once carried. It
did not look like a place for intensity and crusades, of outrage and indigna-
tion. No one that even remotely resembled Hildy Johnson or Mr. Burns.
There was no urgency. It looked how he cynically imagined a large insurance company office would appear, company drones processing information
for homogenized dissemination.

The librarian was a middle-aged man, a few years older than Jeffrey and
slightly overweight, with a wheezy quality to his voice, as if he were laboring constantly underneath the cloud of a head cold or asthma. "Library's
closed to the public right now," he said, "unless you have an appointment.
General hours listed on the plaque to the right." He gestured with a hand as
if to dismiss the visitor.

Jeffrey produced his temporary identification passport. "This is official
business," he said, mustering as much officiousness as he could. He suspected the librarian was the type who would be protective of his turf for a
few moments, then back down and ultimately prove helpful.

"Official?" The man stared at the passport. "What sort of official?"

"Security."

The librarian looked up curiously. "I know you," he said.

"No, I don't think so," Jeffrey responded.

"Yes. I'm sure of it," the man persisted. "I'm sure. Have you been in here before?"

Jeffrey shrugged. "No. Never. But I need help finding some files."

The man stared at the passport, stared again at his visitor, then nodded. He pointed the professor over to an empty chair in front of a computer screen, then pulled up a chair next to him. Jeffrey noticed that the man seemed to be sweating, though it was cool in the library. The librarian also kept his voice down, though there was no one else around, which Jeffrey thought was the normal state for librarians.

"All right," the man said. "What do you need?"

"Accidents," Jeffrey replied. "Accidents involving teenagers or young women. In say the past five years."

"Accidents? Like car wrecks?"

"Like anything. Car wrecks would be fine. Shark attacks, being struck by meteors. Anything. Just accidents involving young women. Especially where the young woman disappeared for some time before being found."

"Disappeared? Like poof?"

"That's right."

The librarian rolled his eyes. "Unusual request." He grunted. "Key words. Always need key words. That's how everything is filed in the data bank. We identify common words or phrases, then electronically file them. Like *City Council* or *Super Bowl*. I'll try *accident* and *teenager*. Give me some more key words."

Clayton thought, then said: "Try *runaway*. Try *missing* and *search*. What are some other words that newspapers use to describe an accident?"

The librarian nodded his head: "*Mishap* is one. Also most accidents always get an automatic adjective, like *tragic*. I'll punch that in as well. Five years, you say? Actually, we've only been in business for a decade. Might as well go all the way back."

The librarian fiddled with the keys. Within a few seconds the computer had processed the request, and for each key word an answer blipped up, listing the number of entries where the words existed. By punching *Directory* on the keyboard for each, the computer would give him each story's headline and the date and location it appeared in the paper. The librarian showed him how to pull each story up on the screen and how to split the screen to compare stories.

"All right, have at it." The librarian stood up. "I'll be around and about, if you have any questions or need any help. Accidents, huh?" He looked hard at Jeffrey once again. "I know I've seen your face," he said before shuffling off.

Jeffrey ignored him and turned to the computer screen.

He worked his way through the entries methodically, not satisfied with what he was coming up with until he thought of the obvious and typed in a pair of key words: *death* and *fatal*.

These words gave him a more operable list of seventy-seven separate articles. He examined them, and realized they represented twenty-nine different incidents spread over the ten-year period. These he began to read through, one at a time.

It did not take him much longer to realize what he was looking at. In the period of a single decade, twenty-nine women—the oldest a twenty-three-year-old recent college graduate visiting her family, the youngest a twelve-year-old who had gone off to a tennis lesson—had experienced fatal accidents inside the Fifty-first State. None of these "accidents" were of the garden variety acts of some capricious God, who might place a teenager on a bicycle in the path of a speeding car one afternoon. Instead, Jeffrey read about young women who mysteriously disappeared on camping trips, abruptly decided to run away from home in the midst of the most normal of activities, or never showed up at their destination after scheduling some sort of routine lesson or appointment. There were some bizarre headlines claiming that wild dogs, or wolves reintroduced into forest areas by conservation-minded ecologists, had set upon one or two of the young women. There were a series of outdoor mishaps, falls from cliffs, drownings in streams, and unfortunate exposures to hypothermia that had done in several others. There were several described as despondent, and suggestions that they'd run away from their families in order to take their own lives, as if this were somehow something absolutely normal for a teenage girl to do, as opposed, say, to systematically destroying herself with bulimia or anorexia.

The *Post* had handled each case in boringly similar fashion. Story one: GIRL DISAPPEARS UNEXPECTEDLY. (Page three, below the fold.) Story two: AUTHORITIES LAUNCH SEARCH. (Page five, single column, left, no photo.) Story three: REMAINS OF GIRL DISCOVERED IN RURAL, UNDEVELOPED AREA. FAMILY MOURNS ACCIDENT VICTIM.

There were a few departures from this unimaginative approach, cases that simply ended with the unfortunate variation of the GIRL DISCOVERED story, replaced by the AUTHORITIES CALL OFF FRUITLESS SEARCH story. No story had ever landed on the newspaper's front page, up with the stories about new corporations relocating to the Fifty-first State. No story had ever probed beyond official statements issued by State Security spokesmen and -women. And at no time had any enterprising reporter ever mentioned any similarities between one incident and any previous incidents. Nor had any reporter ever compiled a list such as the one he was preparing.

This surprised him. If he could see the number of cases, surely some reporter could as well. The information was sitting in their own computer library.

Unless, of course, they'd seen it but wouldn't run it.

Jeffrey rocked back in his desk chair, staring at the computer screen. For a moment he wished that the newsroom he'd passed actually was filled with insurance company workers, because at least they would know the actuarial tables listing the percentages of likelihood of death for teenage girls by these alleged misadventures.

Not a chance, he said to himself. How about alien abductions, too, he scoffed, remembering that was the same image Agent Martin had once used with him.

He repeated this to himself, under his breath: "Not very goddamn likely."

Jeffrey tried to guess what number of the deaths were actually as described. A couple, he figured. There were bound to be some teenagers who actually *did* run away, and probably some who *did* take their own lives, and maybe there *had* been a camping accident. Maybe even two. He calculated quickly. Ten percent would mean three deaths. Twenty percent would be six. That still left some twenty deaths over ten years. At least two a year.

He continued to rock in his chair.

The methodical killers in history would have found that a reasonable output of homicidal energy. Not spectacular, but adequate. Their counterparts, the psychotic killers enmeshed in their own sprees of death, would probably consider the numbers modest, as they looked up from their own perches in Hell. They preferred volume and instant gratification. The greed of death. Of course, they were easier to catch because of their excesses.

But the steady, quiet, dedicated killers occupying the ring of torment next to them would nod their heads in appreciation of a man so in control of his passions that he limited himself. Like the wolf that culled the sick or injured from the herd of caribou, never taking so many that the source of his sustenance was actually threatened.

Jeffrey shuddered.

He began to print out the stories of cases he believed were part of this pattern, and meanwhile could see why they'd wanted him here. The authorities were running out of plausible excuses.

Wild dogs and wolves. Snakebites and suicides. Eventually someone was going to refuse to believe. And that would be a problem, indeed. He smiled to himself, as if at least a part of him found it amusing.

They don't have two victims, he thought.

They've got twenty.

Then his smile faded as he asked himself the obvious question. *Why didn't they say so at the start?*

A printer to his side began spitting out the sheets of stories, the paper racheting through the platen as he waited. He looked up and saw the newspaper librarian walking toward him, carrying a copy of the *Post*.

"I knew I'd seen you before," the man wheezed in a self-satisfied tone. "Why, you were on the front of the 'Around the State' page just the other week. You're a celebrity."

"What?"

The man thrust a newspaper at him, and he looked down and saw his picture, two columns wide, three columns deep, on the bottom of the break page of the paper, the front of the second section. The headline above the picture, and over the story that accompanied it, read: STATE SECURITY HIRES CONSULTANT TO INCREASE SAFETY. Clayton glanced at the date on the paper and saw that it was from the day he arrived in the Fifty-first State.

He read:

> ... In their continuing efforts to maintain and improve personal safety inside the state, State Security has called on well-known Professor Jeffrey Clayton of the University of Massachusetts to perform a wide-ranging examination of current plans and systems.
>
> Clayton, whom a spokesman said is hoping soon to qualify to move to the state, is an expert at various criminal procedures and styles. The Security spokesman said, "This is all part of our continual efforts to outthink criminals before any should try to arrive here. If they know there's no chance to succeed at their games here, they're far more likely to stay where they are, or head someplace else. ..."

There was more, including a quote from him that he'd never made. Something about how happy he was to be visiting, and how he hoped to return one day.

He put the paper down with a start.

"Told you so," the librarian said. He glanced over at the sheets of paper spitting from the computer printer. "This got something to do with what you're here for?"

Jeffrey nodded. "This story," he said, "how widely was it disseminated?"

"All our papers. And it went out electronically, too. Any house that wants to read the day's news on their home computers can do that instead of getting newsprint on their fingers."

Jeffrey nodded. He stared at his picture on the newspaper page. So much for secrecy, he thought. There was never any intention of keeping my presence here quiet and anonymous. The only thing they want to keep quiet is the real reason I'm here.

He swallowed hard, felt a calm, frigid, deep chasm within him creak open. But at least now he knew why he was there. He did not precisely form the word *bait* in his head, but had the unpleasant sensation the worm must feel as it dangles from a hook and is heartlessly lowered into the cold, black waters occupied by its predators.

As he stepped out onto the sidewalk, the double doors to the newspaper closed behind Jeffrey with a vacuum-swooshing sound. For a moment he was blinded by the noontime sunlight as it reflected off the glass facade of an office building, and he pivoted away from the source of the light in his eyes, inadvertently raising his hand to shield his vision, as if he were afraid of injury. He took a few quick steps down the sidewalk, picking up his pace, moving rapidly. Earlier, he'd ridden a bus downtown from the State Security offices. It was a modest distance, no more than two miles. He walked faster as thoughts flooded him, and after a while was jogging.

He dodged through the lunch-hour pedestrian traffic, ignoring the stares and the occasional cursed complaint of an office worker or two who jumped out of his path. His jacket billowed out behind him, his tie flapping in the wind he created. He pulled his head back, took a great gulp of air, and sprinted hard, as if at the start of a race, trying to put distance between him and the other competitors. His shoes creaked and complained against the sidewalk, but he ignored them and the thought of the blisters he'd have later. He started to move his arms in a pumping motion, adding speed, crossed a street against a red light and heard a furious honking behind him.

By now he was no longer paying attention to his surroundings. Running hard, he turned away from the center of the city, heading down the boulevard toward the State Office Building. He could feel sweat trickling beneath his arms and dampening the small of his back. He listened to his breath as it raspily tore at the clear western air. He was alone now, in the midst of the corporate headquarters world. When he saw the State Office Building loom up, he slowed abruptly, gasping by the side of the street.

He thought: Leave. Leave now. First plane out. Screw the money.

He smiled and shook his head. Won't do that.

He put his hands on his hips and spun around, trying to catch his breath. Too stubborn, he thought. Too curious.

He walked a few yards, allowing himself to cool down. He stopped at the entrance to the building and stared up at it. Secrets, he told himself. There are more secrets here than you imagined.

For an instant he wondered if he himself were like the building. A solid, unprepossessing exterior masking lies and half-truths. He continued to stare at the building, and told himself the obvious: No one is to be trusted.

In an odd way, this observation gave him some encouragement, and he waited until his pulse returned to normal before entering the building. The security agent looked up from his bank of cameras.

"Hey," he said, "Martin is looking for you, Professor."

"I'm here now," Jeffrey responded.

"He didn't look none too happy," the guard continued. "Of course, he never looks all that happy, does he?"

Jeffrey nodded as he walked past. He ran his jacket arm over his forehead, mopping off the sweat that had gathered there.

He expected to see the detective stomping about their office when he walked through the door, but the room was empty. He looked around and saw a message alert on his computer screen. He punched up his mail file and read:

Clayton, where the hell are you? You're supposed to keep me informed as to your whereabouts twenty-four hours. All the fucking time, Professor. No exceptions. Not even to go to the damn john. I'm out looking for you. You get back first, you'll find prelim autopsy report of latest possible vic is under computer file *newdead 4*. Read it. I'll be back shortly.

He was about to turn to this file when he noticed that the message counter at the top of the screen indicated there was a second electronic message in his mail file. What other complaints do you have, Detective? he wondered as he scrolled to this second note.

But any residual irritation fled immediately when he read the message. It was unsigned and without salutation, just a series of words blinking in green in the center of a black screen. He read it through twice before pushing back a few inches from the computer, as if the machine were dangerous, and somehow capable of reaching out for him.

He read: WHEN YOU WERE A BABY, YOUR FAVORITE GAME WAS PEEKABOO.

AND THEN, WHEN YOU GREW A LITTLE OLDER, IT WAS PLAYING HIDE-AND-SEEK. CAN YOU STILL PLAY THOSE GAMES, JEFFREY?

Jeffrey put a sudden cap on the flood of emotions that penetrated all the years of solitude and loneliness he'd built around himself. He felt a quickening within him, part fear, part fascination, part terror, part excitement. All these feelings rumbled around within him, and he struggled to keep them in check. The one thing he allowed himself to think clearly was a single response, meant only for him, certainly not for his employers, and one that he suspected his quarry—although suddenly he did not know if that was the right word to describe the man he was searching for—already knew the answer to.

Yes, he said inwardly. I can still play those games.

GRETA GARBO
TIMES TWO

When they thought they were alone in the world, they both developed an odd sense of security, thinking they could rely upon each other for support, companionship, and protection. Now that they were less certain of their isolation, it disrupted the routine of their relationship; mother and daughter were suddenly nervous, almost distrustful of each other, certainly afraid of what awaited them outside the walls of their small house. In a world that seemed so often devoted to violence, they had managed to build strong barriers, both emotional and physical.

Now, both Diana and Susan Clayton independently felt those barriers being eroded by the undefined presence of the man sending the notes, like a concrete abutment jutting into the water, beaten by the constant waves, slowly dissolving, flaking away, crumbling and disappearing beneath the gray-green ocean. Neither fully understood the nature of their fear; that some man was stalking them was true, but they found the nature of his approach confusing.

Diana refused to share her wildest fear with her daughter; she needed more proof, she told herself, which was a sort of half-truth in and of itself. Mostly, she refused to listen to the insistence that had driven her to the lockbox in her closet and forced her to search out the meager evidence she had of her onetime husband's death. She told herself that the contents of the box were hard facts, but this created a turmoil of argument within her, the sensation one has when pummeled by the conflict between what one wants to believe and is afraid to believe.

In the days since the incident in the bar, the mother had fallen into an external silence, while a cacophony of harsh sounds, doubts, and disease racheted about within her.

Her inability to contact her son only made this discord worse. She had left a series of messages with his department at the university, had spoken to a dizzying array of secretaries, none of whom seemed to know precisely where he was, but all certain that he would get the message and return her call promptly. One even went so far as to say she'd tape the message to his office door, as if this would somehow guarantee success.

Diana was reluctant to push harder, because she thought that would add a sense of urgency, close to panic, to her request, and she did not yet want to give in to that particular sensation. She was willing to acknowledge that she was nervous. Upset, even. Worried, to be sure. But panic seemed a harsh state, and one she hoped was still far distant.

Nothing has happened yet that we cannot handle, she told herself.

But despite the phony positiveness of this insistence, she found herself relying heavily—far more heavily than before—on her medications to calm herself, to help her sleep, to rid herself of worry. And she took to mixing her narcotics liberally with alcohol despite all the physician's warnings to the contrary. A pill for pain. A pill for increasing the red blood cell count as they futilely and microscopically lost their fight against their white cell counterparts deep within her. She had no hope that chemotherapy would help. There were also vitamins for strength. Antibiotics to prevent infections. She would line the pills up and think historically: Pickett's charge. A valiant and romantic effort against a strongly entrenched and implacable army. Doomed before they started.

Diana would wash the batch down with orange juice and vodka. At least, she told herself ruefully, the orange juice is local and probably good for me.

At more or less the same time, Susan Clayton noticed that she was suddenly taking precautions that she'd previously disdained. In the days after the bar incident, she no longer got on an elevator unless several other people accompanied her. She didn't stay late at her desk. If she went anywhere, she requested an escort. She had the sense to vary her daily routine as much as possible, trying to find safety in variety and spontaneity.

This was difficult for her. She thought of herself as a stubborn person, not a spontaneous one, although her few friends in the world probably would have told her she had her own self-assessment backward.

When she drove to and from her office, Susan now made a habit of flashing between the high speed and the slow lanes; for a few minutes she would be speeding at a hundred miles per hour, only to abruptly slow almost to a crawl, swerving between the two extremes in a style she thought would undoubtedly frustrate even the most dedicated stalker because it certainly frustrated her.

She wore a handgun constantly, even around the house after arriving home from her office, concealed beneath the leg of her jeans in a holster strapped to her ankle. This, however, did not fool her mother, who knew about the weapon but thought it wiser to say nothing, and who, on another level, wholeheartedly approved.

Both women found themselves frequently glancing out the windows, hoping to catch sight of the man they knew was out there somewhere. But they saw nothing.

Meanwhile, the troubled feelings Susan contained were redoubled by her inability to come up with an appropriate puzzle in which to send her latest message. Word games, literary crostics, crosswords—all had proved inadequate. For the first time, perhaps, Mata Hari had drawn a blank.

This made her increasingly angry.

After several tense evenings, sitting around the house filled with an unruly writer's block, facing an approaching publishing deadline, she tossed her pad and pencil to the floor of her bedroom, slapped off her computer screen, kicked some reference books into a pile in the corner, and decided to head out in her skiff.

It was late in the afternoon, and the muscular Florida sunlight had started to lose its tight grip on the day. Her mother had taken up a large, white pad of drawing paper and was busy sketching with some chalks, sitting in a corner of the room.

"Mother, damn it, I need some air. I'm going to take the skiff out and catch us a couple of snapper for dinner. I won't be long."

Diana looked up. "It will be getting dark soon," she said, as if this were a reason for not moving.

"I'm just going to run a half mile out. Little hole out there I know. Almost straight out, straight back. Won't take me long, and I need something to do other than sitting around trying to figure out how to write this bastard back and say something that will get him out of our lives."

Diana didn't think there was anything her daughter could write that would achieve that end. But she was encouraged that Susan was being decisive, which she found reassuring. She made a little wave with her hand.

"Some fresh grouper would be nice," she said. "But don't be long. Be back before dark."

Susan grinned. "It's just like ordering at the grocery store. I'll be back in an hour."

Although it was late in the year, there was a midsummer heat filling the end of the day. In Florida there can be a daunting relentlessness to the heat. Usually this is primarily true of the summer months, but occasionally other times of the year ride some southern push of air. The heat has a presence that saps strength and muddies thoughts. It was this sort of night approaching; calm, liquid, still. Susan was a veteran fisherman, an expert in the waters that she'd grown up on. Anyone can look into the sky and see thunderheads and water spouts and know the danger they can suddenly bring, with their punishing winds and tornado speed. But sometimes the dangers of the water and the night are more subtle, hidden beneath a breathless sky.

As she cast off she hesitated a second, then shrugged off the sensation of jeopardy, thinking it had nothing to do with what she was doing, which was a common enough excursion, and everything to do with the residual fear the man and his notes had delivered to her. She idled her skiff down the narrow waterway channel toward the open bay, then thrust her throttle down, abruptly filling her ears with noise and her face with a blast of wind.

Susan bent to the speed, reveling in the buffeting and tugging it brought to her, thinking she was out there in this world she knew so well precisely to get rid of her feelings of anxiety.

She immediately decided to run past the close-in spot she'd told her mother about, and turned the skiff sharply, feeling the long, narrow hull dig into the light blue chop as she headed toward a more productive, distant location. She felt the restraints of land drop away behind her, and was almost disappointed when she reached the site she'd selected.

For a moment after cutting the engine, she sat bobbing on the tiny wavelets. Then, with a sigh, she turned to the business of catching the dinner. She dropped a small anchor, baited a hook, and tossed the line out. Within a few seconds she felt an unmistakable tug.

Within a half hour she'd half filled a small cooler with snapper and grouper, more than enough for the dinner she'd promised her mother. The fishing did for her what she'd hoped. It freed her mind of fears, and encouraged her. Reluctantly, she reeled in her line. She stored her equipment and stood, looking around her, and realized that perhaps she'd stayed out a little too long. As she stood and watched, it seemed the last gray streaks of day faded around her, slipping from her grasp. Before she could even turn the skiff toward home, she was enveloped by night.

This concerned her. She knew the way back, but knew also that it would be much more difficult now. When the last light faded, she'd been caught in a clear, quiet, viscous, slippery world where the usual boundaries between solid land, the ocean, and the air had all turned into a shifting mass of black. She was abruptly nervous, knowing she'd crossed some line of caution that had suddenly taken the world she loved and made it unsettling and perhaps even dangerous.

Her first instinct was to point the skiff toward shore and run hard for a few minutes, trying to find some familiar landmark out of the varied shades of night in front of her. She had to force herself to throttle the engine back, but she did.

Ahead she could see the hilly shapes of a pair of humpbacked hammocks, and she knew there was a narrow channel between them that would lead her into some open water. Once clear, she'd be able to see some distant lights, perhaps a house or headlights on the overland highway. Something that would orient her to civilization.

She idled forward, trying to find the cut between the two hammocks. She could just make out some of the tangle of mangrove trees as she swept close, and she feared she'd run aground before finding the deeper water. She tried to calm herself, insisting that spending an uncomfortable night on the boat battling mosquitoes was the worst that could happen. She steered carefully, sliding forward, the engine making a burbling sound behind her, her confidence growing as she moved into the space between the hammocks. She was just congratulating herself for finding the channel when the boat's hull ground onto the muddy sand of an invisible flat. "Damn it!" she shouted, knowing she'd strayed too much to one side or the other. She thrust the engine into reverse, but the prop was already churning against the bottom, and she was smart enough to cut the engine completely, before it tore itself loose.

She angrily cursed the night, letting her invective flow wildly from her lips, a solid succession of "goddamns" and "Jesus fucking Christs," the sound of her voice reassuring her. After a moment of damning God, the tides, the water, the treacherous flats, and the darkness that had made it all impossible, she stopped and listened for a few moments to the sound of wavelets slapping against the hull. Then, still speaking out loud to her boat, she raised the engine with the electric tilt, the sound a whining noise. She'd hoped this would set her adrift, but it did not.

Still cursing and complaining, Susan grasped her push pole and tried to push herself free. The boat moved slightly, she thought, but not enough. She remained grounded. Replacing the push pole in its holder, she moved to the side of the skiff. She stared at the water surrounding the boat and told herself it was probably only six inches deep. The boat drew eight. She would only get her ankles wet. But she needed to get out, put both hands on the prow and invest a shove with all her strength. She needed to rock the boat free of the grip of sand. And if that didn't work, well, she told herself, then she was stuck until daylight and the tidal change, when fresh seawater would flood across the flat and float her free. For an instant, as she perched on the gunnel, ready to step from the security of the skiff, she considered waiting and allowing nature to do the hard work for her. But she told herself not to be so prissy, and with a decisive move vaulted out of the skiff, into the water.

Warm as a bath, it swirled around her calves. The bottom was a mushy ooze beneath her shoes. She instantly sunk down a few inches. She started swearing again, keeping up a steady stream of words. She put her shoulder to the bow and with a deep breath, started to push. She groaned with exertion.

The skiff did not move.

"Oh, come on," she pleaded.

Again she dropped her shoulder to the prow, this time pushing up and trying to rock the skiff. Beads of sweat broke out on her forehead. She grunted hard, felt the muscles of her back tighten like a drawstring cinching up a pair of pants, and the skiff scraped backward a few inches.

"Better," she said.

She pushed again, taking a deep breath and shoving hard. The flats boat scratched back another half foot toward deeper water.

"Progress, goddamn it," she grunted. One more effort and it would be floating.

She didn't know how much strength she had left, but was determined to use it on this attempt. Her feet had dug down deep into the sucking sandy bottom. Her shoulder was creased from where she'd thrust it against the boat. Again she pushed, letting out a small shout as the skiff ground backward and then came free. Susan stumbled as she shoved, losing her balance and gasping as she tumbled forward and the skiff slid away from her. Salt-water splashed up into her face and she flopped into the water, onto her knees. The skiff scooted back like a puppy afraid of being disciplined, bobbing on the surface no more than a dozen feet away. "Damn it, damn it," she said, cursing the wet, but actually delighted that she was loose. She rose up, shook as much of the sea from her face and hands as she could, and, jerking her feet free from the muck of the flat, stepped after the skiff.

But where she expected to feel the loose bottom beneath her feet, there was nothing.

Susan pitched forward again, losing her balance, crashing into the black water. She knew instantly that she'd stepped into the channel, and twisting her face up out of the expanse of black, she gasped for air. Her toes searched for some purchase on the bottom but found nothing. The dark water seemed to suck her in. She breathed out hard, fighting an instant wave of panic.

The skiff rocked on the gentle surface hardly more than ten feet distant.

She did not allow herself to imagine what her situation truly was, that she was treading water in the dark, while a gentle current pushed the safety of her boat steadily away from her. She kept her head, took a deep breath of the silky night air, and made several quick, powerful overhand strokes through the water, kicking hard with her feet, sending small explosions of white phosphorus up behind her. The skiff floated tantalizingly in front of her, and she swam hard to its side, reached up, and grabbed the gunnel with both arms.

For an instant she hung there, dangling by the side of the skiff, pressing her cheek up against the smooth fiberglass of the boat like a mother would press the cheek of a lost child. Her feet hung down into the water, almost as if they were no longer a part of her. It was only then that she realized how terribly tired she was. She held herself there for a moment, resting. Then she gathered what remained of her strength and lifted herself up, thrusting one leg over the gunnel, trying to grip the skiff with her belly. For a second she hung precariously, then she tightened her grip, kicked hard with the leg still drooping into the water, and tumbled into the boat.

Susan lay there, staring up into the sky, gasping for breath.

She could feel the adrenaline pumping through her temples, could feel her heart thumping away within her chest. She was overcome with an exhaustion far greater than what her actual expenditure of energy demanded, an exhaustion that had much more to do with fear than exertion.

The stars above her blinked benignly. She looked at them and said out loud: "Never, never, never, never get out of the boat at night. Never lose contact. Never lose grip. Never, never, never let this happen again."

She pushed herself to a sitting position, back up against the gunnel. She gathered her breath and, after another moment, wobbled to her feet. "All right," she said out loud. "Try again. Find the channel, goddamn it, not the sand. All ahead slow."

She wanted to laugh, but realized she still hadn't maneuvered through the channel. "Not out of the woods quite yet," she said.

As she plopped herself down behind the steering console and reached for the ignition, a great sheet of gray-black water crashed beside her, spraying her face and hands and making her shout out in surprise. There was a huge thudding thump as a fin whacked the side of the skiff, a burst of white foamy energy erupting inches from her hand.

The explosion knocked her from her seat to the deck of the skiff.

"Jesus Christ!" she shouted.

The water swirled by the boat, then quieted.

Her heart jumped.

"What the hell are you?" she demanded, struggling to her knees.

The question was answered only by silence and the return of the night.

She stared out over the currents but could see no sign of the fish that had surfaced next to her skiff. Again she calmed herself. Jesus, she thought, what was in the water with me? Bull shark? Could have been. Maybe a big tiger or a hammerhead? Jesus Christ, he must have been right there, right on the edge of the flat, looking for his evening meal, and I was right in the water, right beside him, splashing away. Jesus. She had a sudden vision that the fish had been beneath her the entire time, staring up, waiting, confused as to what she was, but closing on her just the same. She exhaled rapidly, blowing out a burst of air.

Susan shuddered, trying to puff out the fear that remained within her. She understood there was nothing else she could do, and, with a slightly shaky hand, she slowly lowered the engine, hit the ignition, and thrust the transmission into forward. Moving at barely more than an idle, she pointed the skiff in the direction she thought would carry her to shore.

We'll just get home tonight, she told herself, then no more fishing for a while. As she motored forward at little more than the speed a baby would have crawling across an unfamiliar floor, she thought to herself that her mother would not be with her for much longer and that she had to start preparing for that reality quickly. She was at a loss, however, to imagine what those preparations were.

Diana Clayton had been engrossed in her sketch, and when the light faded around her, making the last few lines and shadings of her drawing difficult to see, she looked up as she reached for the light switch and realized her daughter was late in returning.

Her first instinct was to head to the window, but too often in the past few days she'd caught herself staring out as if she no longer trusted the world she was familiar with. This time she would not act like some decrepit, dying old woman, which was what she thought she might be, and have confidence in her daughter to return home safely. So, instead of peering out, she moved quickly through the small house, turning on the lights, turning on far more lights than they would ordinarily have used. Eventually, there was not a single bulb that wasn't burning inside every room. She even flicked on the closet lights.

When she returned to where she'd been sketching, she looked across at the charcoal drawing and abruptly asked, out loud:

"What did you want from me?"

She'd drawn the face on the pad with a tight-lipped smile and a sense behind the eyes that he knew something no one else did, a sort of self-congratulatory amusement that she recognized only as evil.

"Why did you pick me out?"   •

In the picture he was a young man, and she thought of herself as an old woman, aged by disease. She wondered if his own disease had aged him as precipitously as well, but somehow she doubted it. His disease would more likely act as some sort of Ponce de León elixir, she thought angrily. Perhaps the years have given him a little more flesh in the jowls, and the hairline has receded a bit. Maybe there are some thicker lines on his forehead, and around the edges of his mouth and eyes. But that would be all. He will still be strong, and always confident.

In the sketch, she had not drawn his hands. The memory of them made her shudder. He'd had long, delicate fingers, which concealed great physical strength. He played the violin quite well, able to draw from the instrument the most evocative of sounds.

He always played alone. In the basement, in a room he had there, where neither she nor the children were allowed. The sound of the instrument would creep like smoke through the house, less a noise than it was a smell, or a sensation of cold.

She closed her eyes, gritting her teeth, thinking that the hands she could not draw had touched her body. Deeply, intimately. His attentions had been oddly infrequent, but when they arose, they were insistent. Sex had not been a junction of two people, it had been him simply using her, whenever he felt like it.

Diana felt her throat tighten.

She shook her head hard, disagreeing with herself.

"You're dead," she said out loud, facing the sketch. "You died in a car wreck and I hope it hurt."

She picked up the sketch pad, looked deeply at the caricature in front of her, then closed the book. She thought the lines of his mouth were duplicated in her daughter; his forehead also belonged to her son. The chin the three of them shared. The eyes—and what they'd seen—she hoped, were his alone. I was young and I was lonely, she remembered, and I was quiet and bookish and I had no friends. I never had any friends. I was never popular and I was never pretty, so there were never any boys hanging around, calling me up for dates. I wore glasses, and I pulled my hair back tightly, and I never wore any makeup and I wasn't funny or amusing or athletic or anything that would attract anyone else. I was uncoordinated and, except for my studies, couldn't talk about anything or anyone. And before he came along, I thought that was all there was to life, and more than once I thought that maybe I would end it all before it had all begun. Depressed and suicidal. Why was that? she suddenly asked herself. Because my own mother was a mousy, quiet, weak-spirited woman, with an addiction to diet pills, and my father was a dedicated academic, a little cold, a little remote, who loved her but cheated on her, and every time he did, grew more ashamed and more detached from us all. I lived in a household filled with secrets and not eager to seek truths, and after growing up, I was anxious to get away, and then when I did, I found there wasn't much out there for me.

She looked down at the sketch pad, which had slipped to the floor. *Except you.*

She abruptly reached down for the pad and flipped open to the picture, and in the same breath shouted: "I saved them! Damn it, I saved them and I saved myself from you!"

Diana Clayton half rose and threw the pad across the room, where it slapped against the wall and fluttered to the floor. She fell back in the chair, leaned her head back and closed her eyes. *I'm dying,* she thought. *I'm dying, and now when I deserve peace, I have none.* She opened her eyes and saw the sketch staring back at her. *Because of you.*

She stood, walked slowly across the room, and picked up the pad. She dusted it off, closed it, then gathered the charcoals and the rag that she'd used to shade the paper, took them all to the closet in her bedroom and thrust them into the corner, where she hoped they would be hidden away.

She stepped back and slammed the closet door. I will not think about it, she demanded of herself. It was finished then, that night. It does no good to remember these things.

Not believing any of the lies she'd just told herself, Diana went back out to the living room of her sanctuary, to wait for her daughter to return home with the promised dinner. She waited in silence, surrounded by the blazing light, until she heard the familiar noise of her daughter's footsteps coming up the walkway in the dark outside.

The fresh fish fillets, sautéed in a little butter, white wine, and lemon, were delicious and revived their spirits. Mother and daughter each had a glass of wine with the dinner as well, and they shared an off-color joke or two, which put some laughter into the house where there hadn't been any for some time. Diana didn't talk about the sketch she'd drawn. Susan didn't mention why she was late returning with the dinner. For an hour they both managed to make things seem almost as they'd once been, an acceptable illusion.

After the dishes were washed and put away, Diana repaired to her own room, and Susan went to hers, where she flicked on the computer and again set about the frustrating task of building a puzzle for the man she thought was watching her. This observation made her smile, but not with any humor: the idea that the man could very easily be outside her door, or beneath her window, or lurking in the dark shade beside any of the palms that stood sentry in the yard—but that even though he could be close enough to reach out and touch, her means of communication was clever word games.

She had an idea, and she formed a box on her computer screen. Within the box she wrote:

Are you the man who saved me?
What is it that you want?
I want to be left alone.

She stared at the message for a moment and thought that what she had were two questions and a statement. She separated the two elements of the message, so that she had:

Are you the man who saved me?
What is it that you want?

and

I want to be left alone.

The first pair, she decided, could be jumbled and concealed. She started to rearrange the letters and came up with:

Theme where a navy do amuse?
Why is tit a tat, now a tut?

She liked those. Susan considered the last sentence of the message, then had an idea, smiled once, impressed with her cleverness, and whispered to herself, "You haven't lost your touch quite yet, Mata Hari." She wrote:

On the bull's ancient island you make a mistake that makes you gag,
and reminds you of the most famous thing she ever said.

She was pleased. She shipped the page electronically to her computer at work, barely an hour before the magazine deadline would shut down all additions, and probably minutes before some harried editor would contact her in a near panic. Then she turned off her own machine and went to bed with a sense of satisfaction. She slept instantly and, for the first time in days, dreamlessly.

, Susan woke up a few seconds before her alarm clock sounded. She switched the device off before it buzzed, rose and quickly stepped into the shower. After toweling off, she dressed rapidly, eager to get to her office, see the layout proofs for that week's contest column and then what it would bring. She tiptoed down the hallway to her mother's room, opening the door quietly and peering around the corner. Diana still slept, which her daughter assumed was a good thing, thinking that the rest would help restore her. Part of what was so debilitating about her disease was the way the pain robbed her of genuine rest, so that exhaustion constantly added its burden to the array of other agonies within her.

Susan saw on the bed stand the vials of pills that were a constant in what remained of her mother's life. Moving quietly, she went to the small table and gathered them up. She carried these with her into the kitchen.

She looked at the labels carefully, then removed the correct morning dosage from each container and lined them up like a platoon on review on an empty white china plate. There were a half-dozen pills to start the day. One red. One tan. Two white. Two different two-tone capsules. Some were small, others large. They stood at attention, waiting for a command.

Susan went to the refrigerator, took out some freshly squeezed orange juice, poured a glass, and hoped her mother would not drink half then refill it with vodka. She put the glass next to the pills. Then she took out a knife, found a cantaloupe and a honeydew, sliced them up carefully, and arranged the half-moon pieces fancily on another plate. Finally, she found a sheet of paper and wrote the following mundane note:

> Glad you got some sleep. I left for work early. Here is some break-
> fast and today's medicines. See you tonight. We can finish off the
> fish for dinner.
>
> XXX
> Susan

She looked around the kitchen, to see if anything was out of place, decided all was right, and stepped out of the house through the back door. She locked the door behind her and peered up into the sky. It was already warm, already blue. A few bulbous high white clouds meandered past. A perfect day, she thought.

Perhaps an hour after her daughter's departure, Diana Clayton wakened with a start.

Sleep still clouded her eyes, and she choked out a small shout of fear, lashing the air with both fists at the same time, persuaded in that eerie vapor between the senses that someone had been standing over her bed. She punched at the emptiness around her.

She coughed hard, and realized she was sitting up in bed. She peered around the room wildly, half expecting to see someone hiding in a corner.

She listened carefully, as if she could pick out the sound of the intruder's breathing and separate it from her own short bursts. She wanted to lean over and examine beneath the bed, but couldn't bring herself to do that. Her eyes fixed on her closet door, thinking perhaps the intruder was hiding in there, but then she realized that the door concealed enough terrors already, held in the lockbox, drawn on a sketch pad, and she let herself fall back onto her pillows, still gasping.

It was the dream, she said to herself. In her last dream of the night, she'd been with her daughter and looked down and saw that both of them were suddenly sliced across the throat, like the man in the bar. That sight had catapulted her from sleep to wakefulness. She put her hand up to her neck and felt a damp, slithery gathering of sweat dripping down between her breasts.

She waited until her breathing returned to a normal pace and her heart slowed its rat-a-tat drumbeat in her chest before swinging her feet out of the bed. She wished there was a pill she could take for fear, and turning, saw that the supply of vials was missing from her bed stand. For a moment this confused her, and she rose, tossed an old, white cotton bathrobe around her shoulders, and padded across the wooden floor to the kitchen. She spotted the lineup of containers almost before she had a moment to worry.

She also saw the melon slices, popped one into her mouth, and saw the juice and the note. She read what her daughter had left for her and smiled. She thought: I have been selfish, keeping her close to me. She is a special child. Both of them are special children, in their own ways. They have always been. And now that they're grown, they are still special to me.

On the plate in front of her a dozen pills were nicely arranged. She started to reach for them. It was her habit to scoop them all into her hand, toss them like a handful of peanuts into her mouth, and wash them all down with a gulp of juice.

She was not sure what made her stop. Perhaps the rattling sound, which took her a moment to assess. Something broken, she thought. What could be broken?

She looked out the window, into the bright blue sky. She saw one of the palms swaying in a brisk, morning breeze. She heard the rattling sound again, only this time it seemed closer. She took a step or two through the kitchen and saw that the rear door seemed loose. The rattling sound came from it, as the wind sucked it open and then banged it shut.

This was out of place, and she knitted her brows.

Susan always locks the doors when she leaves early, she thought.

She walked across the kitchen and stopped short.

The dead-bolt lock was thrown, but the door was not closed. She looked closer and saw that someone had taken a screwdriver or a small clawhammer and ripped the wood around the lock. Like much of the wood in the Florida Keys, the constant exposure to heat, humdity, rain, and wind had ravaged the door frame, making it softer, infirm, almost rotten. A burglar's delight.

Diana stepped back fast, as if the evidence of a break-in were infectious. *Am I alone?*

She kept her wits about her. Susan's room, she told herself. She padded that way in a half run, expecting someone to come bursting out at her. She leapt across the room and threw open the closet door, seizing one of her daughter's handguns from the closet shelf. She spun about, in the shooter's stance her daughter had shown her, thumbing back the hammer of the small revolver and sliding the safety release off in the same motion.

She was alone.

Diana listened carefully but could hear nothing. At least nothing that made her think the intruder was still around. Still, moving with an exaggerated caution, she went from room to room, checking each closet, corner, beneath the beds, anywhere a man might hide. Nothing had been disturbed. Nothing was out of place. There was no sign that anyone else had been inside the house, a realization that made her begin to relax.

She returned to the kitchen and went back to the door, inspecting the frame more closely. She would have to call a handyman that day, she thought. Get someone over and fix it immediately. She shook her head, and for a moment held the cool metal of the gun up to her brow. What had frightened her so severely a moment earlier was quickly passing into a modest irritation as she mentally went through her brief list of workmen who might be available at short notice. She examined the ripped wood again. "Damn it to hell," she muttered out loud. A vagrant probably. Or maybe teenagers who'd dropped out of school. She'd heard about a couple of enterprising local seventeen-year-olds who'd made a tidy profit stealing televisions, stereos, and computers during daytime hours, while families were at school or work. The scratch marks on the door frame told her that whoever had savaged the lock was an amateur. Someone who jammed a piece of metal into the wood and put their muscle to it. Someone in a hurry, not being careful. Someone who must have thought the house was empty and that a little bit of noise wouldn't disturb anyone.

They must have arrived sometime after Susan left, she realized. They were probably halfway into the house when they heard her awaken. That must have frightened them off.

She smiled to herself and lifted the pistol.

If they'd only known. She didn't think of herself as much of a warrior, and certainly no match for a pair of teenage boys. She looked at the weapon. Maybe it would have evened things out, she thought. But that was only if she could have reached it in time. She tried to imagine sprinting through the house ahead of a pair of teenagers. Not a race she would expect to win.

Diana shook her head.

She sighed and told herself not to think how close she'd just come to dying hard. Nothing had happened. Nothing more than an inconvenience, and one that was certainly common, not just in the Keys and in the cities, but everywhere. A moment of great and significant routine nothing. A nonevent, hardly worth talking about or paying any attention to, that could have resulted in death. They heard the noise she made getting up, and this scared them off, which was a good thing, because had they made it a step or two farther into the house, they probably would have just decided to kill her, in addition to robbing her.

She envisioned the pair of teenagers. Long, greasy hair. Earrings and tattoos. Nicotine stains on their fingers. Punks, she thought. She wondered if that word was still in common use.

Diana turned from the door and went back to the kitchen table. She placed the handgun down on the counter and slid another sweet piece of melon into her mouth. The sugary juices reinvigorated her. She picked up the glass of orange juice and reached once again for the pills her daughter had left out for her.

And then she stopped.

Her hand wavered in the air a few inches from the tablets.

"What's wrong?" she asked herself abruptly.

A coldness spread through her.

She counted the pills. Twelve.

That's too many, she thought. I know that. Usually it's no more than six.

She picked up the vials, read each one, counted again and said out loud: "Six. Should be six."

There were twelve on the plate.

"Susan, did you make a mistake?"

This didn't seem possible. Susan was a cautious type. Organized. Sensible. And she'd put out medications many times before.

Diana moved to a corner of the kitchen, where there was a small computer plugged into the telephone line. She punched in the code for the local pharmacy, and within a few seconds the computer screen blinked with the image of the pharmacist.

"Hey, good morning, Mrs. C! How you feeling this nice day?" The man's accent burst through his greeting.

Diana nodded a greeting. "Just fine, Carlos. I just have a small question about my medication. . . ."

"I got your records right here. Whassa matter?"

She looked at the pills. "Is this right? Two megavitamins, two pain-killers, four Clopamine, four Renzac—"

"No, no, no, Mrs. C!" Carlos interrupted. "The vitamins, that's okay, maybe even double the painkillers, okay, too, but not all time. Probably jes' make you fall asleep right away. But the Clopamine and Renzac are very powerful. Very strong medicines! Thass much too much. One each! No more, Mrs. C! This very important!"

A clammy sensation penetrated her stomach. "So four of each would be . . ."

"Don't even think this! Four each make you very sick."

"How sick?" she interrupted.

The pharmacist paused. "This probably kill you, Mrs. C. Four each at the same time. Very dangerous."

She didn't reply.

"Especially wid those painkillers, Mrs. C. They jes' gonna knock you out, and you not even gonna know you got such a big trouble with the Clopamine and Renzac. Issa good thing you called, Mrs. C. You ever have any questions with all these medicines, I know, is hard to keep them all time straight. You just call me, Mrs. C. And if you cannot get me onna phone, jes' don't take nothin'. Maybe painkiller, but thass all. These cancer drugs, Mrs. C, they are *muy fuerte*. Very strong."

Diana's hand was shaking slightly.

"Thank you so much, Carlos," she managed to stammer. "You've been most helpful." She punched the keyboard and disconnected the line. Care-fully, she returned the extra pills to their proper containers, fighting off a vision of the once-familiar face of the man who'd broken into the house, seen their daughter's note, and instantly saw the opportunity it presented. This must have seemed like a great joke to him. He must have left grin-ning, maybe even laughing out loud when he reached the street outside, after deliberately placing a lethal dosage of the medications that were supposed to be keeping her alive on the breakfast table waiting for her.

PEEKABOO

Jeffrey Clayton, frozen in his seat, at first unsure what to do, was still staring at the message on the computer screen when Agent Martin burst through the door, red-faced and furious. "Peekaboo," Clayton said to himself as the detective slammed the door and immediately burst into invective:

"Clayton, you son of a bitch, I told you the rules! I'm with you all the fucking time! No little day trips without me along! Goddamn it, where have you been? I've been looking all over for you."

The professor didn't immediately reply to the question, nor to the anger. He swiveled in his seat and glared at the detective. He understood the reasons behind Martin's fury—after all, what good is a lure if you're not actually watching it more or less constantly, so that when the target of one's hunt rises from whatever depths of concealment and exposes himself, you're ready to seize the opportunity. His own anger at being used in this way started to choke in his throat—but he had the ability to stifle it. He knew instinctively that it would be better for him if he didn't let on that he'd figured out the real reason he was there in the Fifty-first State. And, after all, the evidence of the soundness of Martin's plan was all too obvious on the monitor screen at his desk. For a brief second he thought of hiding the message he'd received, but without actually making a decision, he found himself gesturing slowly at the words in front of him.

"He's here," Jeffrey said quietly.

"What? Who's here?"

Jeffrey pointed. Then he rose, walked over to the blackboard, and as the detective slipped into his seat to read the computer screen, erased the half side of the board with the title: *If the Killer Is Not Known to Us.*

"Won't need that," he said, more to himself than Martin. He realized that he was erasing what had already once been erased, for him, which he'd refused to acknowledge. When he turned back, he saw that the burn scars on the detective's neck and hands were red and darkening fast.

"I'll be damned," Martin muttered.

"Can you trace it?" Jeffrey asked suddenly. "The message came over a phone line. We ought to be able to backtrack to the source number."

"Yes," Martin responded eagerly. "Yes, goddamn it, I think I can. I mean, I ought to be able to." He hunched over the keyboard and started to punch letters. "Electronic avenues are tricky, but they pretty much always travel both ways. You think he knows that?"

Jeffrey thought that was possible, but he wasn't sure. "I don't know," he said. "Probably some fourteen-year-old whiz kid at the local high school not only knows how, but could do it in about ten seconds. But how technically adept is he? No way of telling. Just see what you can come up with."

Martin continued with the keyboard, and momentarily hesitated. "There," he said abruptly. "I'll be damned. I think we've got him. Bastard."

He laughed suddenly, but without humor.

"Easier than I thought," the detective said. He lifted his fingers from the keyboard and twiddled them in the air. "Magic," he declared.

Jeffrey bent over his shoulder and saw that the computer had generated a single telephone number under *Source of message.* The agent moved the computer cursor up to the phone number and typed in another request. The computer then demanded a security code, which Martin entered.

"That will take us past the security lock," he said.

As he spoke, the computer coughed up an answer, and Clayton saw a name and address appear beneath the phone number.

"Got you, you bastard," Martin said again, triumphantly. "I knew it! There's your fucking daddy," he said angrily.

Clayton read the entry:

Owner: Gilbert D. Wray; Secondary Owner/Wife: Joan D. Archer; Occupant Children: Philip, 15, Henry, 12. Address: 13 Cottonwood Terrace, Lakeside.

He stared at the address. It seemed oddly familiar to him.

There was some additional information, which listed the man's occupation

as a business consultant and his wife's merely as a housewife. It gave their
date of arrival in the Fifty-first State as six months earlier, and their former
address was a hotel in New Washington. Before that, the family had lived
in New Orleans. Jeffrey pointed this out to the detective. Martin, already
reaching for a telephone, quickly replied:

"That's normal. People sell their homes and move in, stay in a hotel
while they're waiting to clear Immigration and close on their new house.
Come on, damn it!"

The person on the other end of the line must have answered at that
moment, because the detective said: "This is Martin. No questions. I want a
Special Action team to meet me in Lakeside. Right now. Priority One."

Adjacent to the computer, a printer started to hum, and four sheets of
paper slid through the exit portal. The detective reached for them, stared at
them momentarily, then handed them to Clayton. The first picture was a
passport photograph of a man in his early sixties, thick-necked, with a brush-
cut, military-style haircut and thick, black-rimmed eyeglasses. This was followed by a photograph of a woman close in age to the man, with a pinched
face and a slightly skewed nose, like a fighter's. The two children were also
pictured. The older of the two had a sullen, barely concealed anger about
him. Beneath each picture were height, weight, identifying marks and a
modestly detailed medical history, Social Security numbers, and driver's
license. Bank account numbers and credit information was also listed as well
as the children's academic records. Jeffrey realized there was more than enough
information for any competent policeman to investigate the person—or find
them, if they were wanted.

"Say hi to your dad," Martin said briskly. "Say hi and then say 'bye."
While Jeffrey stared blankly at the photographs without even the vaguest
sense of recognition, the detective rose from his seat and walked across the
office to a locked file cabinet in the corner. He fumbled with the combination for a moment before opening a drawer, reaching in, and removing a
glossy black Ingram submachine pistol. "American made," he said. "Although some of the other agents are partial to foreign models. Can't see why.
Not me. Like my weapons born and bred right here in the good old U.S. of
A." The detective grinned as he snapped a clip loaded with stubby, evil-
looking, Teflon-tipped .45-caliber rounds into place with a resounding click
and confidently slung the weapon over his shoulder.

The State Security substation in Lakeside was a traditional design, New
England in character, a redbrick, white-shuttered, old-style police station on the
outside, a modern, computer-driven observatory on the inside, a world of gray

steel lockers and beige, plastic computers, all housed beneath recessed ceiling lights with heavy, industrial-strength brown carpeting on the floors that muffled any noise. The windows to the outside were mere decorative accessories, since the real method employed at the security station of looking out at the world beyond the walls was electronic. Computers, video monitors, and sensoring devices. Martin had parked their car in a concealed rear area, then briskly walked inside, a set of doors buzzing open to allow his entry into a small vestibule where the Special Action team was assembled, waiting for him.

There were six members of the team—four men, two women. They were dressed in civilian clothing. The women wore stylish, bright jogging outfits. One of the men was in a conservative navy blue suit and rep tie, another in a tattered gray sweat suit that he had dampened, so it would appear he'd been working out. The two other men were dressed as telephone line repairmen, jeans, work shirts, hard hats, and brown leather utility belts. All were occupied with their weapons when Jeffrey first saw them, working the bolts on their Uzis, checking the clips for full loads. He saw, as well, that the weapons could all be concealed; the businessman placed his in an attaché case; the two women placed theirs in similar baby strollers, the workmen in their tool kits.

Martin handed the team copies of the pictures. He moved to a computer screen and within seconds had punched in the address and been rewarded with a three-dimensional topographical site plan of the property at 13 Cottonwood Terrace. Another series of entries produced architect's renderings for the house. A third entry produced a satellite picture of the property. The security agents gathered around these, and within a few moments had ascertained where each member of the team would position him- or herself.

"We'll use a standard high-caution approach," Martin said.

"Any particular model?" a security agent dressed as a workman asked.

"Model three," Martin replied briskly.

The team all nodded. Martin turned to Clayton and said: "That's a regular assault model. Multiple subjects, single location, multiple exits. Moderate likelihood of arms. Risk to arresting agents, mid-range. We practice these things all the damn time."

The team leader, the blue suit, coughed as he stared at the computer picture of the house and adjusted his tie as if he were going to some executive presentation. He asked a single question: "Arrest or eliminate?"

Martin glanced sideways at Clayton. "Arrest. Of course," he replied.

"Sure," one of the workmen said, as he slid the action on his pistol back and forth, making an irritating clicking sound as he spoke. "And what level of force are we authorized to use in making this arrest?"

Martin answered that briskly: "Maximum."

"Ah." The workman nodded. "I would have thought so. And what is our subject accused of?"

"Crimes of the highest level. Red One."

This response caused some eyebrows to shoot up.

"Red-level crimes?" one of the women asked. "I don't know that I've ever been involved in apprehending a red-level criminal. Certainly not Red One. What about his family? Are they red levels, too? How do we handle them?"

Martin paused before answering: "There is no hard evidence of their involvement in any criminal activity, but we should assume they have knowledge and have provided assistance. After all, they're the bastard's family." He glanced at Clayton, who didn't respond. "That would make them accessories to red levels. They should be taken into custody as well. Got lots of questions for them. So, let's just secure everyone at the site, okay?"

The team leader nodded and started handing out body armor. One of the women pointed out that it was a school day, and probably the boys were in school, and maybe they could be picked up there. A computer check, however, of the day's attendance at the Lakeside High School showed neither in attendance. Agent Martin also ran a computer weapons check, and discovered none registered to Subject Wray or to Wife Archer. He made a quick series of other computer requests, vehicle types, then office schedule. The computer showed that the subject worked out of a home office, which Martin pointed out, telling the team that probably meant he was at home. He quickly checked to see if Subject Wray had made any travel plans, but couldn't find any with airlines or high-speed rail connections. Nor did he find any immigration records of recent automobile travel in and out of the state. When the computer came back with all negative responses, Martin shrugged and said, "The hell with it. He sounds like a real homebody. Let's just go get this guy and figure out the rest later."

As Martin rose from his seat, he reached out and handed Jeffrey a loaded nine-millimeter pistol. But as he shoved it toward the younger man, he asked, in a sardonic tone: "So, Professor, you sure you want in on this little party? You've already earned your cash, or at least some of it. You want to sit this one out?"

Jeffrey shook his head and hefted the weapon, as if measuring its weight. He was thankful that Martin had given him the semiautomatic. The machine pistols the agents were carrying tore hell out of everything, and he wanted to leave both people and scene intact at 13 Cottonwood Terrace.

"I want to see him."

Martin smiled. "Sure you do. It's been a long time."

Jeffrey adopted an academic tone. "There's a lot we can learn here,

Detective." He gestured at the Ingram hanging by a strap over Martin's shoulder. "Let's try to keep that in mind."

The detective shrugged. "Sure. Whatever. But advancing scientific knowledge ain't my first priority." He smiled again. "But I understand your concern. This isn't exactly the sort of family reunion I would have chosen, but hey, you can't pick your own blood, can you?"

Martin pivoted, gestured to the team, and quick-marched out of the quiet of the police station. The sun was just beginning to set in the west, and when Jeffrey turned toward it, he had to shade his eyes against a final, blinding glare. It would be dark within a few minutes, he thought, half an hour at most. First a fading gray, followed by night. They should move swiftly to take advantage of the last of the light.

The team separated into different vehicles. Wordlessly, Jeffrey slid into the seat next to Martin, who by now was incongruously humming an old tune that Clayton recognized. "Singin' in the Rain." It's not raining, Clayton thought, and he wasn't sure there was all that much to be happy about. The detective accelerated, the tires squealing as they exited the security sub-station, and it occurred to Clayton that the arrest was probably a secondary priority to the detective. He wondered for a moment about the conversation he'd heard, about levels of offenses. "So what the hell do you mean *red*-level crime?" he asked.

Martin hummed for a few more bars before replying. "Just like the different housing areas get colors, so does all antisocial activity in the state. The color defines the state's response. Red, obviously, is the highest. Or worst, I guess. Pretty rare around here. That's why the team was surprised."

"What's a red crime?"

"Usually economic. Like embezzling funds from your company. Or social, like teenage drug use at the community center. But of sufficient seriousness that a subject might respond violently to arrest. Hence, of course, the team approach. But in the history of the state, we've only had a dozen or so homicides, and those have all been spouse against spouse killings. We still have a problem with hit-and-run accidents, which are, in the old system of justice, considered something like manslaughter. Those would be red crimes as well, but lower level. A two or a three."

Jeffrey nodded, noting the lies, but saying nothing.

"The thing about it is," the detective continued, "Immigration is supposed to forestall that sort of propensity to violence and alcohol abuse in preoccupancy psychological testing of applicants. There have also been some instances of teenagers getting into fights. Like over girls or high school basketball games, where rivalries are intense. Those can create lower red-level crimes."

"But my father—"

"We should have a different color for him. Maybe scarlet. That has a nice literary quality to it, don't you think?"

"And arrest? What did the team leader mean by *eliminate*? There seemed to be some question. . . ."

Martin didn't reply at first. He took up humming once again, getting about halfway through a verse before interrupting himself. "Clayton, don't be naive. The point is: your old man doesn't get away. If someone has to use deadly force, then so be it. You've been through this on other cases before. You know the rules. In this situation, they're no damn different here than they would be in Dallas or New York or Portland or anyplace bad guys like to ruin lives. You understand that, right? So, say the word, and I'll drop you by the side of the road and you can wait in this nice green area beneath a nice shady tree, twiddling your thumbs while I go apprehend your fucking father. You want out, just say the word. Otherwise, what happens, happens."

Jeffrey shut his mouth and asked no more questions. Instead he watched the shadows thrown by tall pine trees spread across the manicured lawns of the quiet, prim, and perfect suburban world.

Detective Martin stopped the car a half block from the house. He adjusted a radio earpiece, ran a quick check with the members of the Special Action team, and ordered everyone to move into position. The two workmen were to situate themselves at a telephone switching box on the north side of the property, the businessman and the sweat suit on the south end. The two women with strollers had the back covered as they paced slowly along, seemingly engaged in idle gossip. Martin and Clayton were to drive up to the front door, and as they knocked, the team would close in. The procedure was simple, swift, standard. Enacted correctly, not even the neighbors would realize there was an arrest being made until subsequent backup units arrived. Four additional State Security vehicles with uniformed officers were lined up a block away, awaiting orders.

"All set?" Martin asked, but he pulled forward without waiting for a reply.

Jeffrey felt himself breathing sharply.

He understood that in some remote location he was being pummeled by emotions. He understood, too, that a sense of excitement was overcoming all the questions he had, and obscuring his feelings. He felt an odd coldness, almost like a child the moment he realizes there is no Santa Claus, just myth and adults. He searched within himself, trying to find some reasonably concrete emotion to latch on to, but could not.

He felt almost bloodless. Hard and iced over.

The detective swung the car up a circular drive toward a modern, two-story, four-bedroom house that, like the town they'd come from, mimicked a New England colonial design. The world was an indistinct gray, light fading about them rapidly, the unmarked police cruiser's headlights merely blending with the half-light of dusk more than illuminating the house.

The house was dark inside. He could see no movement within.

Martin braked the car abruptly. "Here we go," he said, quickly stepping out.

He swung his machine pistol behind his back, concealing it from anyone who might be staring out a window, and quickly approached the front door. "At the door now!" he whispered into his mouthpiece. "Everyone close in."

Gesturing for Clayton to step to the side, he knocked sharply.

Out of the corner of his eye, Jeffrey saw the other team members rushing the house. Martin knocked again, loudly. This time he shouted: "State Security! Open up!"

There was still no sound from within.

"Shit!" Martin said. He peered in through the window next to the door. "Everyone in!"

The detective stepped back and delivered a kick to the front door that resounded like a cannon shot. The door swayed and buckled, but didn't yield. "Goddamn it!" He turned to Clayton. "Get the damn door buster out of the car! Do it now!"

As Jeffrey went to the car for the sledgehammer that would take out the door, he heard the team members shouting in the distance, and at the same time he could hear their words crackling over the radio earpiece the detective wore, almost like the stereo effect of a speaker system. Martin snatched the receiving piece from his ear. He gestured wildly to him. "Come on, goddamn it!" Clayton seized the iron battering ram from the backseat and carried it to the detective.

"Give me the fucking thing!" Martin shouted, grabbing it from Clayton. He stepped a foot or two back from the door, swung the door buster back angrily, then crashed it into the wood. This time splinters flew. Martin grunted with exertion, then swung the hammer a second time, the door bursting open with a shattering crash. The door buster was dropped, thudding to the floor, and Martin swung his machine pistol to the front and in the same motion leapt through the door, shouting, "I'm in, I'm in!"

Jeffrey followed right behind.

Martin slammed up against a wall, pirouetting as he covered the darkened vestibule with his weapon, simultaneously pulling the chambering mechanism on the pistol. It made a loud, metallic click.

Which echoed.

The echoing sound was the first impression Jeffrey had. It made him stumble mentally for a moment, and then he understood what it meant. He slumped next to the detective and whispered: "You can relax. Tell the others to come on in through the front door."

Martin continued to swing the weapon in a right to left arc in front of him. "What?"

"Tell the others to join us. Tell them to stand down their weapons. There's no one here but us."

Jeffrey straightened up and started to search the half darkness for a wall light switch. It took him a second before he found one, connected to the track lighting in the ceiling. He flicked it on and the two of them were suddenly encased in light and could see what Clayton had already perceived: the house was empty. Not merely of people, but of furniture, carpets, drapes, and life.

Martin took a few tentative steps forward, the sound of his feet against a wooden floor echoing in the empty space, just as the noise of his weapon had moments earlier.

"I don't get it," he said.

Jeffrey didn't reply. But he thought: Well, Detective, you thought it would be just that simple? A little computer magic, and bingo! Not a chance.

The two men walked into an empty living room. Behind them, they could hear the noise of the Special Action team, which had assembled in the front entranceway. The team leader in the suit came into the room.

"Nothing, huh?"

"Not so far," Martin replied. "But I want this entire place searched for any signs of activity."

"Red One," the man in the suit said. "Sure."

Martin glared at him, but the team leader ignored him.

"I'm going to clear out the backup. Tell them to resume regular patrols."

"Thanks," Martin said. "Damn."

Jeffrey walked slowly through the empty room. There's something here, he thought. There's something here to learn. This emptiness means as much as anything else. You just have to figure out how to interpret it. As he considered this, he heard voices from the vestibule. He turned around and saw that Martin was standing in the center of the living room, his machine pistol drooping at his side, his face red with anger. The detective seemed about to say something to him, when the action team leader stuck his head back into the room.

"Hey, you want to talk to one of the neighbors? They just came waltzing up the driveway to see what the hell all the excitement was about."

Jeffrey said quickly, "Yes, I do," and walked past Martin, who snorted and followed him to the entranceway.

A middle-aged man wearing khaki slacks, a purple cashmere sweater, and holding the leash to a yapping small terrier bouncing around at his feet, was talking with two of the team members. One of the women in jogging suits looked up as she unstrapped her bulletproof vest and said: "Hey, Martin, you probably want to hear this."

The detective stepped forward. "What do you know about the owner of this place?" he asked.

The man turned and shushed the dog unsuccessfully. "Nobody owns it," he said. "Been on the market for almost two years."

"Two years? That's a long time."

The man nodded. "Usual turnover in this neighborhood is six months. Eight, max. It's a real nice development. Got a write-up in the *Post* once, just after it was completed. Real good master plan, real good access to downtown, real good schools."

Jeffrey stepped up. "But this house is different? Why?"

The neighbor shrugged. "I think people believe it's got bad luck. You know how people can be superstitious. Number thirteen and all. I told them they should just change the number."

"Bad luck? How, exactly?"

The man nodded. "I don't know if you'd exactly call it bad luck. And it's not like it's haunted or anything. Just a bad association, that's all. And I don't see why the rest of us should suffer because of one little incident."

"What little incident?" Jeffrey asked.

"And anyway, what are you folks doing here?" the man asked abruptly.

"What little incident?" Jeffrey demanded again.

"The little girl that disappeared. It was in the paper."

"Tell me."

The man sighed, jerked on the leash when the dog started to sniff at the leg of one of the Special Action team, and shrugged.

"The family that used to live here, well, they moved out after the tragedy. People find that out, it turns them off. There are too many other real nice houses around the block or over in Evergreen. You don't want to buy the one that has a bad history already."

"What sort of bad history?" Jeffrey asked. His patience was being stretched.

"Nice family. Robinson was their name."

"I'm sure. And?"

"Little girl wandered off out back late one afternoon, right before dinnertime. We're on the edge of a real big conservation area. Lots of woods and wildlife. Fourteen years old, you'd figure she would have had the sense to stick close to home. Especially right before dinnertime. I could never figure that out. Anyway, she wanders off, her folks start calling for her, the neighbors all get out with flashlights, and even Security shows up with a helicopter, but not a sign of her. They never found her again. No sign of anything, but mostly people figured it was wolves, maybe, or wild dogs carried her off. Some people thought it was some Sasquatch-type animal. Not me, of course. Don't believe in that sort of foolishness. I figured she just ran off to get back at her parents after some fight. You know how teenagers are. And she takes off, gets lost, and that's all there is to it. There are some caves in the foothills, everyone figured that was where her body was taken or ended up or whatever, but hell, you'd need an army to search the area completely. At least, that's what the authorities said. Lot of people moved away after that. I think maybe I'm the only person in the neighborhood left who remembers. Didn't bother me all that much. My kids are grown."

Jeffrey stepped back, leaning up against one of the empty white walls of the house. Now he remembered where he'd seen the address before; it had been in one of the news stories he'd collected from the *Post*. He had a vague, elusive memory in his mind's eye of a picture of a smiling girl with braces on her teeth. That had been in the paper as well.

The man shrugged. "You'd think that the Realtors would keep that history part quiet when they show the house. It's a nice place. Ought to have people in it. Another family. I guess eventually it will."

The man jerked his dog's leash again, although this time the terrier was sitting quietly on the floor.

"And leaving it empty, hell, it brings all the property values down for everybody else."

Martin demanded suddenly: "Have you seen anyone here lately?"

The neighbor shook his head. "Who did you think was here?"

"What about workmen, Realtors, landscapers, anyone?" Clayton asked.

"Well, I don't know. I wouldn't have noticed those types."

Detective Martin thrust the computer-printed pictures of Gilbert Wray and his wife and family at the man.

"These familiar? Ever seen these people?"

The man stared, then shook his head. "Nope," he said.

"How about the names. Recognize the names?"

The man paused, then shook his head. "Never heard of them. Hey, what's all this about, anyway?"

"None of your goddamn business," Martin snapped as he grabbed the photographs from the man's hand. The terrier yapped and leapt aggressively at the big detective, who simply stared down at the dog.

Jeffrey thought Martin was about to ask another question, or perhaps kick the animal, when one of the team members called out from within the house: "Agent Martin! I think we've got something."

The detective gestured to one of the women officers standing to the side. "Take a statement from this fellow." He added, with a touch of bitterness: "And thank you for your help."

"No problem," the neighbor said haughtily. "But I'd still like to know what's going on. I have some rights, too, Officer."

"Sure you do," Martin said brusquely.

Then Martin, with Clayton stepping swiftly behind him, followed the sound of the officer's voice. It came from the kitchen area.

It was one of the men dressed as a telephone worker. "I found this," he said.

He pointed at a polished gray stone countertop across from the kitchen sink. There was a small, inexpensive laptop computer sitting on the counter, plugged into an electric outlet on the wall and to an adjacent telephone jack. Next to the machine was a simple timing device, the sort available in any electronics store. The computer screen glowed with a series of geometric shapes that kept shifting position, forming and reforming in a haphazard electronic dance, changing color—from yellow to blue to green and red—every few seconds.

"That's where he sent the message to me," Jeffrey said quietly.

Agent Martin nodded.

Jeffrey approached the computer carefully.

"That timing device," the workman said, "think it's attached to a bomb? Maybe we should get Special Handling in here."

Clayton shook his head. "No. The timer is there so he could leave this thing behind, and it would automatically send the message after he was far away. But we should still have a crime scene unit process the computer for fingerprints, and this whole area, too. Won't find any, but we should do that."

"But why would he leave it here where we could find it? I mean, he could have sent the message to you from any public spot."

Jeffrey glanced at the timer. "Another part of the same message, I suppose," he replied, but of course, he wasn't supposing anything. The choice of this particular location was highly intentional, and he had a pretty solid idea what that message was. His father had been here before—perhaps not inside the house, but certainly outside; with the wild animals that would be blamed for the child's disappearance, he thought sardonically. He must have found this terrifically amusing. Jeffrey realized that many of the killers he'd come into contact with over the years would have been genuinely entertained by the idea that authorities in the Fifty-first State were probably far more interested in concealing the killer's activities than the killer himself. He exhaled slowly. Every one of the killers he'd known and studied over all his adult years would have found that wonderfully ironic. The cold ones, the crazy ones, the calculating ones, and the impulsive ones. Without fail, they would have laughed themselves blue in the face, bent over, clutching at their sides, tears rolling down their cheeks at the utter hilarity of it.

He stared down at the small computer screen and watched the shifting and changing shapes. Some killers are like that, he thought with frustration. Just when you think they have one shape and one color, they alter themselves just enough to throw you off. In sudden frustration, he reached out rapidly and punched the Enter key on the computer, to get rid of the designs swirling irritatingly in front of him. The twisting geometric shapes instantly disappeared, replaced by a black screen with a single unsigned message blinking in yellow:

> *Peekaboo.*
> *Did you think I was stupid?*

AN INTERESTING CHARACTER
FROM HISTORY

Once again Agent Martin led Clayton through the antiseptic maze of office cubicles in the security headquarters for the Fifty-first State. Their presence caused some stir; people at desks, on the telephones, or peering at computer screens paused whatever they were doing and watched the progress of the two men through the room, so that their passing caused a ripple of quiet. Jeffrey thought that perhaps word had already spread of the abortive raid at the empty house. Or perhaps people had finally figured out why he was there in the new state, and this made him, if not a celebrity, at least an object of some intrigue. He could sense eyes following them as they passed.

The secretary guarding the entrance to the director's suite said nothing, but waved them ahead.

As before, the director was sitting behind his desk, rocking slightly in his chair as they entered. He had his elbows on the polished, shiny wood surface, his fingertips together, giving him a predatory appearance as he leaned forward. To Jeffrey's right, sitting on the sofa, were the other two men from the first meeting: the older, bald-headed man whom he'd called Bundy, whose tie was loosened and whose suit had a slightly rumpled look, as if he'd slept on the couch; and the younger, sharply dressed man from the governor's office, whom he'd nicknamed Starkweather. The younger man looked away as he came into the room.

"Good morning, Professor," the director said.

"Good morning, Mr. Manson," Jeffrey replied.

"You've had coffee? Something to eat?"

"I'm fine," Jeffrey said.

"Good. Then we can get on with business." He gestured toward the two chairs drawn up in front of the wide mahogany desk, motioning, as he had before, to sit. Jeffrey arranged some papers and notes on his lap, then looked at the director.

"I'm glad you could come here this morning and give us a little update on your progress," Manson began, only to be interrupted by Starkweather, who muttered, "Or lack of progress." This caused the director to glare in his direction. As before, Agent Martin was sitting stolidly, waiting to be asked a question before he would open his mouth, an experienced bureaucrat's sense of preservation surrounding him.

"Oh, I don't think that's a totally fair assumption, Mr. Starkweather," the director said. "I think the good professor knows far more than he did when he first arrived here. . . ."

Jeffrey nodded.

"The issue before us, as always, is how best to put the professor's knowledge to use. How does it serve us? What advantages does it give us? Am I correct, Professor?"

"Yes," he replied.

"And I'm correct in thinking that we have at least made one critical decision, am I not, Professor?"

Jeffrey hesitated, cleared his throat, and nodded again. "Yes," he said slowly. "It would appear that our subject is indeed related to me." He could not bring himself to say the word *father*, but Mr. Bundy did for him:

"So the sick bastard that's screwing everything up is your father!"

Jeffrey half turned in his seat. "It would appear so. It would be possible, still, I think, to suspect an extremely clever deception. That is to say, someone who had been intimate with my father and acquired knowledge and details only my father had in his possession. But the odds of this sort of deception taking place are extremely small."

"And, after all, what would be the point?" Manson asked. He had a soothing, unruffled voice, like synthetic lubricant, in sharp contrast to the bluster and frantic tones of the other two men. Jeffrey thought that Manson was probably a formidable man because of his restraint. "I mean, why create this deception? What exactly would be the purpose? No, I think we can safely assume that the professor has at least achieved the first task we set out for him: he has accurately identified the source of our *troubles*."

Manson paused, then added, "My congratulations, Professor."

Jeffrey nodded, but thought it might have been more correct to state that the source of their troubles had accurately identified him, a scenario that they might reasonably have expected after placing his name and picture in the newspaper so prominently. He did not say this.

"I thought he was here to find the son of a bitch so we could take care of him," Starkweather said. "I would think any real congratulations could hold off until that point."

The rumpled man, Bundy, quickly agreed. "Understanding and progress aren't the same thing," he said. "I'd like to know if we're closer to identifying the man so that he can be apprehended and we can get on with the rest of life. Need I remind you that the longer we are delayed, the greater the threat to all our futures."

"That would be *political* futures?" Jeffrey asked with an edge of sarcasm. "Or perhaps *financial* futures. Of course, they're likely to be one and the same."

Bundy shifted on the couch, leaning forward with irritation, mouth open to speak when Manson held up his hand.

"Gentlemen, we've been through this and around this and over this a half-dozen times." He turned halfway toward Clayton, at the same time picking up an old-fashioned letter opener from his desk. The opener had a carved wooden handle and reflected sunlight from the blade. Manson worked its sharp edge against his palm, as if testing the blade's cutting surface. "This has never been considered to be an easy arrest, even with the good professor's able assistance. And it will remain difficult to achieve, despite what we've learned. Even here, where we have so many advantages of law. But in a rapid amount of time, we've made great strides. True, Professor?"

"I think that is accurate."

He thought the word *accurate* was being bandied about the room with a bit too much frequency, but he didn't say this out loud.

Manson smiled, shrugging in the direction of the other two men. "This investigation, Professor . . . can you recall a similar investigation from the annals of history? From the literature of this sort of killer? Or perhaps from all those FBI files you're so familiar with?"

Jeffrey coughed, thinking hard. He hadn't anticipated this question, and he felt suddenly like one of his own undergraduates abruptly called on to quickly answer an oral examination.

"I can see elements of other cases—famous cases. After all, Jack the Ripper allegedly contacted the police and the press. David Berkowitz sent his Son of Sam messages. Ted Bundy—no offense, Mr. Bundy—had a chameleonlike ability to blend in with his surroundings, and it was only when his compulsions grew unmanageable that he was arrested. I'm sure I could think of others. . . ."

"But these would only be elements of similarity, no?" Manson asked. "Can you think of a time that a killer has allowed his very identity to be known—to his own offspring, at that?"

"I can't think of an instance where a killer's offspring were utilized in the hunt for him, no. But in history there have been some . . . well, *relationships* between killer and police pursuers, or with the press that gave them notoriety. . . ."

"That's not precisely what we have here, is it?"

"No. Of course not."

"And what does that tell you, Professor?"

"It suggests many things. A sense of grandiosity. A sense of egotism. But foremost, it tells me that our subject has created many layers—a blanket of misinformation—that will conceal the connection between who he once was and who he is now. And when I say who he *is*, I only mean his current identity. That is to say, his job, his home, his life. The essential core of his personality hasn't changed. Or if it has, it's changed for the worse. But his exterior will be different. Different socially—and what I mean is, he'll no longer be the history teacher that I knew at age nine. And different physically as well. I would imagine there are some changes in his actual appearance. And he must believe that it is totally, completely, absolutely safe, to have done what he's done so far."

He paused, then added: "Arrogance is a word that leaps to mind."

"Well, then, what the hell are we supposed to do!" Bundy nearly shouted. "This sick bastard keeps killing, and we can't do anything about it! If this gets out, forget it! People will be leaving the state in droves. It will be like the gold rush in reverse."

No one spoke.

This is all about money, Jeffrey thought. Safety is money. Security is money. What is the price of being able to leave one's home without setting an alarm, or even locking the doors?

The room stayed quiet for another moment, until Jeffrey said: "I'm not certain people will continue to believe that their teenage children are being carried off by wolves."

Starkweather snorted. "They'll believe what we tell them," he insisted.

"Or wild dogs. Or hiking accidents. Aren't you running low on plausible explanations? Or even semiplausible?"

Starkweather didn't exactly reply. Instead, he said: "I always hated those damn dog stories."

"How many killings have there been?" Jeffrey demanded in a low voice. "I found possible evidence of more than twenty. How many are there?"

"When did you do that!" Martin burst out. Clayton simply shrugged.

The room returned to silence.

Manson swiveled around in his chair, making a small, squeaking sound, and stared out the window, leaving the questions hanging in the air. Jeffrey heard Martin mutter an obscenity under his breath, and he suspected it was directed at him.

"We don't know exactly how many," Manson finally replied, still staring out the window. "There could be as few as three or four. As many as twenty or thirty. Does the number truly matter? The crimes are not linked by their appearance in death; they are linked by the type of victim, the consistency in the mode of abduction. Surely you can see, Professor, how unique a situation we find ourselves in. Repetitive criminals are either identified by the source of their interest or by the results of their depravity. It's that secondary element that led us to you, and to our conclusions about the three spread-eagled bodies posed so similarly and provocatively. But then there are these other disappearances, so similar in nature. But the bodies arrive— when they do—in . . . how shall I say it? In different *styles*. Like this latest, that you believe is the work of the same man—though others . . ." Without moving his chair, he looked back over his shoulder briefly at Agent Martin. ". . . disagree. This young woman disappeared in similar fashion, then was found in a prayerful position. Utterly *dis*similar. Questions abound."

Manson spun back toward Jeffrey. "There is rhyme and reason to it all, Professor. But you must find the tune for us. There are deaths and disappearances, and we all believe fervently that they're caused by a single man. But what is the pattern? If we knew that, we could take steps. Find answers for us, Professor."

Again there was silence in the room, broken after a moment or two by Bundy, who sighed with discouragement before speaking.

"So, I suppose this latest identity, what's his name, Gilbert Wray and his wife, Joan Archer, and the family are all fictional? And useless to us? No progress there, right?"

Agent Martin replied to that question. He spoke in a flat policeman's voice. "After the unsuccessful raid at the Cottonwood house, we checked further with Immigration and discovered that many of the necessary records and required documents for the Wray family were either missing or nonexistent. Preliminary investigation suggests that these personae were entered into computer files from an unknown terminal within the state merely in anticipation of our heading to that particular location. There is the possibility that our subject created these persons and installed them in the computer systems as some sort of diversion. He may have done this in days, or even hours, before our arrival at the Cottonwood house. It would appear from this and other information we have developed . . ." Here, the detective paused and shot a quick glance at Jeffrey. ". . . that he has significant access to State Security computer systems and is extremely knowledgeable about our current passwords."

Jeffrey recalled his surprised reaction when he realized that the blackboard in his own office had been erased. "I think it would be safe to say that our subject has the knowledge to bypass almost any security system currently in place in the state," he said, without supporting the statement with a specific example. He pointed at a stack of papers on Manson's desk. "I wouldn't assume those were safe from his eyes, Mr. Manson. Perhaps he has rifled the drawers of your desk."

Manson nodded gravely.

"Damn," Starkweather said. "I knew it. I knew it all along."

"Knew what?" Jeffrey demanded of the young politician.

Starkweather shrugged angrily, slumping forward. "That the bastard is one of us."

This comment silenced the room for several seconds.

Jeffrey had an immediate question or two, but did not voice them. He did, however, make a mental note of what Starkweather had said.

Manson rocked in his chair and made a whistling noise between his teeth. "Where, Professor, do you suppose our subject came up with the name? Gilbert D. Wray. Does it mean anything to you?"

"Say it again," Jeffrey said abruptly.

Manson didn't reply. He merely leaned forward again.

"What?" Bundy asked, as if speaking for Manson.

"The name, damn it. Say it again, quickly."

The rumpled man shuffled about on the sofa. "Gilbert D. Wray. Wray. Like *ray of sun* I guess. Wasn't there an old-time actress—back almost a century ago, Kay Wray, I think? No, Fay Wray. That's right. She was in the original *King Kong*. Blonde and famous for her scream, I remember. Is there another pronunciation?"

Jeffrey leaned back in his chair. He shook his head. "I apologize," he said, quietly directing his words toward Manson. "You would think I'd have recognized the name when I first saw it. But I didn't speak it out loud. How stupid of me."

"Recognize?" Manson asked. "How so?"

Jeffrey smiled, but felt a withering, sick sensation within. "Gilbert D. Wray. Say it again with a little Frenchified touch. How about Gilles de Rais?"

"Who's that?" Bundy asked.

"An interesting character from history," Jeffrey responded.

"Yes?" Manson said.

"And Joan D. Archer. Children Henry and Charles. And they came here from New Orleans. How obvious. I should have seen it right away. What a damn idiot I am."

"Seen what?"

"Gilles de Rais was an important figure in thirteenth-century France. He became a famous military leader in their fight against the British invaders. He was—as history tells us—the chief military assistant and one of the most fervent supporters of Joan of Arc. Saint Joan. Or, as she was also known, the Maid of Orleans. And the warring parties? Like two squabbling children, Henry of England and the Dauphin, Charles of France."

Again the room was momentarily silent.

"But what has that to do—" Starkweather began.

Jeffrey interrupted him. "Gilles de Rais, in addition to being exceptionally brilliant militarily, and a rich nobleman to boot, was also one of the most horrific and prolific murderers of children that we have ever encountered. It was believed that he slaughtered more than four hundred children in sadistic, sexual rituals inside the walls of his estate, before being discovered and ultimately beheaded. An intriguing man. A prince of evil, who fought with devotion and immense bravery at the right hand of a saint."

"Jesus Christ," Bundy whistled. "I'll be damned."

"Gilles de Rais certainly was," Jeffrey said softly, "although he probably presented a fascinating question for the relevant authorities in the great hereafter. What precisely does one do with such a man? Perhaps every century or so he's given a day off from eternal torment. Would that be reward enough for a man who more than once saved a saint's life?"

Nobody answered this question.

"Well, what do you make of our subject using the name?" Starkweather demanded angrily.

Jeffrey paused. He had discovered that he enjoyed seeing the politician's discomfort. "I would say that our subject, which is to say, my father, is . . . well, he's interested in the moral and philosophical issues surrounding absolute good and absolute evil."

Starkweather stared at Jeffrey with a considerable anger built from frustration, but said nothing. Jeffrey, however, filled the momentary pause by saying:

"As am I."

For a few seconds Jeffrey thought that his statement would signal the end of the session. Manson had lowered his chin to his chest and appeared to be thinking heavily, although he also continued to stroke his palm with the blade of the letter opener. Abruptly, the director of security slapped the weapon down on his desk, making a cracking sound like that of a small-caliber pistol going off.

"I think I'd like to speak with the professor privately for a moment or two," he said.

Bundy started to protest, then quickly stopped.

"Have it your way," Starkweather said. "You'll update us again within a few days, a week at the most, all right, Professor?" This last statement contained both an order and a question.

"Whenever you like," Jeffrey said.

Starkweather rose, gesturing to Bundy, who struggled up out of the thickness of the sofa and followed the man from the governor's office through the side door.

Agent Martin had also risen. "You want me to stay or go?" he asked.

Manson pointed to the door. "This won't take more than a few minutes," he said.

Martin nodded. "I'll wait right outside."

"That would be fine."

The director waited until the agent had exited before continuing in a low, even voice: "I am troubled, Professor, by some of what you say, but more in what you imply."

Jeffrey shrugged. "How so, Mr. Manson?"

The director rose from his seat behind the desk and went to the window. "I don't have enough of a view," he said. "It's not exactly right, and it has always bothered me."

"I beg your pardon?"

"The view," he said, gesturing with his right arm out the window. "I can see toward the mountains off to the west. It's very scenic, but I think I'd prefer more of a view of construction. Of something being built. Come here, Professor."

Jeffrey rose, stepped around the desk, and stood next to Manson. The director seemed smaller up close.

"It's very pretty, isn't it? Panoramic vista. Postcard perfect, no?"

"I would agree."

"It is the past. It is ancient. Prehistoric. Within my vision there are trees that date back centuries, land masses that were formed eons ago. In some of those forests there are places where no man has ever walked. From where I sit, I can look out and see nature much as it was when people first struggled across the continent."

"Yes. I can see that."

The director tapped the windowpane. "What you see is the past. It is also the future."

He turned away, pointing Jeffrey back to his seat, and then he sat down as well.

"Do you think, Professor, that America has somehow lost its way? That the ideals that our proverbial forefathers carved out of this nation have been eroded? Dissipated? Forgotten?"

Jeffrey nodded. "That is an increasingly popular view."

"Where you live, in the disintegrating America, there's violence. There's no respect. There's no sense of family. There's no sense of the greatness we have had, and the greatness we can achieve, is there?"

"It's taught. It's a part of history."

"Ah, but teaching it and experiencing it are far different, are they not?"

"Of course."

"Professor, what do you think the point of the Fifty-first State is?"

Jeffrey didn't answer.

"Once, America was filled with adventure. Bursting with confidence and hope. America was a place for dreamers and people of vision. No longer."

"Many would agree with that."

"So, the question for some, who hope that our third and fourth centuries can be as great as our first two, is how do we replace that sense of national pride."

"Manifest destiny."

"Precisely. I haven't heard that phrase since I was in school, but it is precisely what we need. What we must re-create. Anyway, you cannot import it, as we did once, taking the best of the world and throwing them into this massive stew of a nation. You cannot create a sense of greatness by giving people more freedoms, because that's been tried and all it has done is led inevitably to more disintegration. Once we were able to install hope and glory and a sense of national purpose and unity by fighting a world war, but that is no longer feasible because the weapons of today are too large and impersonal. World War Two was fought by individuals, willing to sacrifice themselves for ideals. That is no longer possible when modern weaponry allows war to be antiseptic, robotic, fought by computers and technicians in distant locations directing devices through the skies. So, what is left?"

"I don't know."

"What's left is a single belief, and it's what we are all devoted to here in the Fifty-first State. And that belief is that people will rediscover their values and their sense of sacrifice and betterment, that they will become pioneers again, if only they're given a land as pristine and filled with promise as this nation was once."

Manson leaned forward in his seat, spreading his hands wide. "They must have no fear, Professor. Fear defeats everything. Two hundred years ago, the people who stood where we stand now, and looked up at those same mountains, and saw those same vistas, they knew challenge. They knew hardship. And they overcame the fear of the unknown."

"True enough," Jeffrey said.

"The challenge today is to overcome the fear of what is known."

Manson paused, now leaning back in his seat.

"So, this is the idea behind our state: we create a world within a world. A nation within a nation. We create opportunity and safety. We take what was once a given in this nation, and, once again, we provide it. And do you know what will happen then?"

Jeffrey shook his head.

"It will grow. Outward. Steadily, inexorably."

"What are you saying?"

"I'm saying that what we have here will slowly, but surely, take over the remainder of the country. It may take generations—just as it did once before. But eventually our way of life will crush all the horror and depravity that you know outside the state. Already we're beginning to see the communities just beyond our borders start to adopt some of our laws and some of our tenets."

"And these laws and tenets?"

Manson shrugged. "You've seen many of them already. We curb some First Amendment rights. Freedom of religion exists. Freedom of speech— well, less so. And the press? It belongs to us. We limit Fourth Amendment rights. We control the rights of search and seizure. We restrict Sixth Amendment rights; you can no longer expect to commit crimes and buy your freedom through some slick attorney. And you know what, Professor?"

"Yes?"

"People give them up without a whimper. People are willing to trade their right to be free of an unwarranted search for a world where they don't have to lock the front door of their house when they go to bed. And those of us here are gambling that there are many more like us, beyond the borders. And that slowly what we have will take over the nation."

"Like an infection?"

"More like an awakening. A nation roused from a long sleep. We're just up a little earlier than the rest."

"You make it sound attractive."

"It is, Professor. Let me ask you: When have you ever, personally, employed any of those Constitutional safeguards? When have you ever said: 'Now's the time for me to exercise my First Amendment rights'?"

"I can't recall an instance. But I'm not sure I don't want them, should I ever need them. I don't know about giving up fundamental freedoms. . . ."

"But if those same freedoms are enslaving you, wouldn't you be better off without them?"

"That's a difficult question."

"But people already are allowing themselves to be imprisoned. They live in gated communities. They hire security services. They walk around armed. Society is little more than a series of walls and jails. To keep evil out, you must lock yourself in. Is that freedom, Professor? But that's not the way it is here. In fact, did you know, Professor, that we are the only state in the nation with successful handgun control laws? And no alleged hunter here owns an assault rifle. Did you know that we are hated by the NRA and its old Washington lobbyists?"

"No."

"You see, you think when I say we've taken away Constitutional rights, that I am automatically some right-wing conservative. On the contrary. I am safely without political designation, because I can pursue what is necessary from either end of the political spectrum. Here in the Fifty-first State the Second Amendment to the Constitution means what it says—not what some lobbyist with deep pockets insists despite all evidence to the contrary. And I could go on, Professor. For example, there are no laws in the Fifty-first State restricting, for example, a woman's reproductive rights. But there is much debate about this. Consequently, the state controls all access to abortion. We set guidelines. Reasonable guidelines. That way, not only do we keep the debate limited to the issue, but we also protect the physician who performs the service."

"You, too, are a philosopher, Mr. Manson."

"No. A pragmatist, Professor. And I believe the future walks with me."

"You may be right."

Manson smiled. "Now, do you see what a threat your father, the killer, is?"

"I'm being educated," Jeffrey replied.

"What he is achieving is simple: he is utilizing the very foundations of the state to perform his evils. He makes a mockery of everything we stand for. He makes us seem like impotent hypocrites. He strikes not only at these children, but at the core of our ideals. He is using us against ourselves. It is like rising one morning to discover a cancerous lump in the very lungs of our state."

"Do you think that a single man can threaten so much?"

"Ah, Professor, not only do I think this, I know it. History tells us as much. Just as it has told your father, the onetime historian. A single man, acting alone, with a unique and warped vision and the dedication to act upon it, can cause great empires to crumble. There have been numerous solitary assassins throughout history, Professor, who have successfully altered the course of the tides. Our own history is replete with Booths and Oswalds and Sirhan Sirhans whose shots have killed ideals as well as men. We must prevent your father from being such a killer. If we do not stop him, he will assassinate our vision. Singlehandedly. So far, we have been fortunate. We have been able to obscure the truth of his activities. . . ."

"I thought the truth set men free."

Manson smiled and shook his head. "That is a quaint and antiquated concept. Truth only brings more misery."

"That is why it's controlled here?"

"Of course. But not in some Orwellian ideal, feeding disinformation to the masses. What we are is . . . well, *selective*. And, of course, people still talk. A rumor can be far worse than any truth. So far we seem to have contained your father's activities. That will not last, not even here, where the state manages to control its secrets better than anywhere else in the nation. But as I said, I'm a pragmatist. No secret is ever truly safe until it is dead and buried. Made a part of history."

"Safety is fragile."

Manson sighed deeply. "I have enjoyed this session, Professor. I have other business that demands my time—though none that is quite so urgent. Find your father, Professor. Much rides on your success."

Jeffrey nodded. "I'll do what I can," he said.

"No, Professor. You must be successful. At any cost."

"I'll try," Jeffrey said.

"No. You'll succeed. I know this, Professor."

"How can you be sure?"

"Because we're speaking of many things, layer after layer of truths and intrigues, Professor, but of one thing I am absolutely certain."

"And that is?"

"That fathers and sons always struggle for the same prize, Professor. That is your fight. It always has been. Mine, perhaps, is different. But yours . . . well, it goes to the core of your being, does it not?"

Jeffrey found himself breathing hard.

"And its time has arrived now, has it not? Did you think you could go through your entire life without doing battle with your father?"

Jeffrey felt his voice grow raspy. "I thought that was a confrontation that would be purely psychological. A fight against a memory. I thought he was dead."

"But it does not turn out that way, does it, Professor?"

"No." Jeffrey felt as if his tongue was suddenly failing him.

"And so the fight takes on some different dimensions, does it not?"

"It would seem so, Mr. Manson."

"Fathers and sons," Manson continued. His own voice was soft, with a small lilt to it, as if he found everything he'd said to have some deep amusement. "They're always a part of the same puzzle, like two similar pieces being jammed into a slightly misshapen space. The same weave of fabric, pulling against each other. The son struggles to outdistance his father. The father seeks to limit his son."

"I may need some help," Jeffrey blurted.

"Assistance? And who could help you in this most elemental of struggles?"

"There are two other parts of the same machinery, Mr. Manson. My sister and my mother."

The director smiled. "True enough," he said. "Though I suspect they will have battles of their own to fight. But, Professor, do what you must. If you need to enlist reinforcements, please do so. In this fight, you have complete and total freedom."

This last statement, of course, Jeffrey knew instantly for a lie.

Agent Martin did not ask what Jeffrey had spoken about with his supervisor. The two men trudged silently side by side back through the building, toward their office, as if contemplating the task before them. As they approached the office, a secretary carrying a manila envelope appeared from an elevator. She stepped out carefully, threading her way past a dozen four-year-olds linked together by a fluorescent orange rope, a day care class heading out to the playground. The young secretary smiled, waved good-bye to the children, then moved rapidly toward the two men.

"This is for you, Agent," she said briskly. "Expedited and rush-rush, hurry-up, and all that. A couple of interesting details. I don't know if it'll help you in whatever the case is, but it sure got the quick and dirty treatment in the lab."

She handed Martin the envelope.

"You're welcome," she said, when he didn't thank her. With a quick, measuring look at Jeffrey, she turned and headed back to the bank of elevators.

"That is?" the professor asked as he watched the young woman disappear with a pneumatic swoosh.

"Preliminary laboratory report on the portable computer we seized at Thirteen Cottonwood." The detective ripped open the envelope. "Goddamn it," he muttered.

"Yes?"

"No workable prints. No hair fibers. If he'd picked up the damn thing with sweaty palms, we might have been able to get a DNA match from residue. No such luck. The damn thing was clean."

"He's not stupid."

"Yeah. I know. He already told us that, remember?"

Jeffrey did remember. "What else?"

Martin continued to scan the report. "Well," he said after a moment, "here's something. Maybe your old man isn't the perfect killer after all."

"What's that?"

"He left the serial number of the machine intact. The lab guys were able to do a little tracing."

"And?"

"Well, the lot number of the machine corresponds to computers the manufacturer shipped to various outlets in the Southeast. That's something. Apparently, your old man didn't think much of their warranty program, because he never mailed in the warranty registration."

"He knew he wasn't going to keep the machine that long."

Agent Martin shook his head. "Probably paid cash for the damn thing, too."

"I would suspect that is correct."

Martin rolled up the report and slapped it against his leg. "I wish we could come up with just one thing, that's all, one thing that I didn't think your fucking old man had already considered."

The two men were at the door to their office, about to enter. Martin unwrapped the report again and stared at it as he unlocked the door. He looked up at Jeffrey.

"Why do you suppose the bastard went all the way to South Florida to buy the computer? I mean, there are a lot closer places, and we'd have just the same trouble tracing it. You think maybe he went there on a vacation? Or business? That gives us something, huh?"

"Where?" Jeffrey asked abruptly.

"South Florida. That's where the computers with those serial numbers were sent. At least, according to the computer company's manifests. There's maybe a hundred stores in that region that it could have been sent to. Mostly down below Miami. Homestead. The Upper Keys. Why? That mean something to you?"

It did. There was only one reason for his father to purchase the computer in that location and then deliberately fail to remove something as obvious as a serial number etched on the rear of the machine in plain view. He wanted to leave behind the means for his son to find out what he'd done. It meant that after all those years, he'd found them. The father whom they'd fled, who they thought had died, had brought his son to his own door, and also discovered where his onetime wife and daughter still hid.

Jeffrey, filled with a sudden, profound despair, wondered whether they had any secrets left.

He pushed past Martin, ignoring the detective's sudden questions, heading to the telephone to call his mother and warn her. He didn't know, of course, that she was sitting in the kitchen of the small house where she'd once prayed that her daughter and her son would be able to restart their own childhoods, and where they'd all thought they were safe for all those years. Nor could he have known that she was watching a local repairman diligently cut wood and replace the broken door frame and dead-bolt lock, and that his mother was inwardly desperate to warn him of precisely the same thing he was about to tell her.

WHAT WAS STOLEN

In her office cubicle, Susan Clayton wondered how long it would take for her latest puzzle to be deciphered. She had thought that sending the encoded message would give her some rest and some time to determine what she and her mother would do next. But she'd been wrong about this; anticipating a reply only made her more nervous. It forced her into a false mathematics; she had electronically shipped the latest addendum to her regular puzzle the night before; the magazine would be on newsstands by the end of the week, more or less the same time it would be available to online computer subscribers. The questions she'd sent in puzzle form weren't that difficult—a day, perhaps two, to decode and assess them. Then he would concoct a reply.

But how that response would arrive was a puzzle beyond her.

She found herself wedged into a corner of her work space, alert to the sound of anyone approaching. She told the building security and the office receptionists that anyone asking for her was to be photographed through the video monitors and that any identification produced by someone asking for her—whether false or not—was to be seized. When they asked what was the matter, she replied that she was having problems with an old boyfriend. This was a convenient lie that seemed to cover almost any potential ill.

She tried telling herself that fear was like a prison, and that the more she was afraid of the man, the greater his advantages.

The problem was: *What did he want?*

Not generally. But specifically.

If she knew the answer, Susan thought she could act. Or at least take some positive steps. But in the absence of a firm idea of the rules of the game, she was at a loss as to how best to play, and certainly unable to guess how to win. And, she realized, with a dryness on her lips that she should have associated with fear, she did not yet know what the stakes of this particular game were.

She thought of her namesake. Mata Hari knew what was at risk when she played at being the spy.

Lose that game and there was only one possible result: death.

She had played, and she had lost. Susan took a long, deep breath, and in that moment wished that she'd come up with some other pseudonym. Penelope, she thought. She kept the suitors at bay with her ruse of weaving and unraveling, until the day Odysseus returned home. That would have been a safer alter ego for her to choose.

It was closing in on noontime, and she turned and glanced out her window. She could see the downtown Miami streets filling with office workers. It reminded her of a documentary she'd once seen about an African river during the dry season; the water level had dropped just enough to bring all the animals that relied upon it into dangerously close proximity to the crocodiles that lurked in the muddy stream. The documentary had shown the balance between need and death, a world of risk. She'd been fascinated by the connection between the killers and the killed.

Now, as she stared from her window, it struck her that the world was closer to this natural terror than ever before; the office workers exited their buildings in groups, heading toward any number of downtown restaurants, exposing themselves to whatever risk the street in daytime might hold. Most of the time, they were safe. They'd walk out into the sunlight, enjoy the breeze, ignore the homeless beggars sitting with their backs to the cool, concrete building walls, like so many crows on a wire. Don't think that one might be in the midst of some mad homicidal rage, twisting inside, she thought. Don't think that some predatory street gang might be moving down an adjacent side street. At noontime the world belongs to the sun, the authorities, the people who belong. Going out for lunch? Sure. Nothing to it.

Of course, every so often someone went out to lunch and died. Just like the animals that were forced by circumstances to drink a few feet away from the crocodile's jaws.

Natural selection, she thought. Nature making us stronger, culling the weak and the stupid from the herd. Like animals.

There was a group forming in the center of her office. She could hear voices raised in discussion. Chinese or a salad bar? For which would you be willing to risk your life? For a moment she thought of joining them, then decided against it.

She reached down and checked the automatic pistol in her pocketbook. A round was chambered, the hammer cocked back. The safety, however, was on, but all it would take was a simple flick of the thumb and the slightest pressure on the trigger, and the weapon would fire. The day before, she'd taken a screwdriver and small jeweler's pliers and adjusted the pull tension on all her weapons. Barely more than a touch would fire any of the guns, including the automatic rifle hanging by the peg in the rear of her closet. She thought: There is no time left, in this world, to wonder whether one is doing the right thing. There's time only to point and shoot.

The luncheon group and their loud voices crowded into an elevator. Susan waited another moment, then, slinging her pocketbook over her shoulder, positioned so she could slide her right hand into the bag and grip the pistol's butt, she rose and exited alone. She realized she was making herself vulnerable to any number of threats, but also that in a world of constant and random danger, she'd developed an odd immunity, because there was really only one threat abroad in that world that meant anything to her.

Heat like a drunkard's insistent breath hit her as she stepped outside her office building. For a moment she paused, watching waves of filmy air rise from the concrete sidewalk. Then she stepped forward, slipping into the flow of office workers, her hand still wrapped around the pistol's handle. She saw that there were police officers on every street corner, hidden behind dull black crash helmets and mirrored sunglasses, idly fingering the triggers of their slung automatic weapons. Protecting the productive, she thought. Guarding the staffers as they went about the routine of life. As she walked past one pair, she could hear their portable radio crackling with the tinny, disembodied voice of a police dispatcher, updating the officers about the action in different parts of the city.

She paused, staring up at one of the buildings, seeing the sun reflect from its glass facade like an explosion. We live in a war zone, she thought. Or an occupied territory. There was a whoop-whoop-whoop sound of a police siren in the distance fading fast.

Six blocks from the building there was a small sandwich shop. She headed in that direction, although unsure whether she was really hungry or simply needed to be alone amidst the flowing crowds of people. She thought probably the latter. Still, Susan Clayton was the sort of person who needed some artificial purpose in her actions, even if this alleged task covered up some deeper desire. She would tell herself that she was hungry and needed to get something to eat, when all she really wanted was to get out of the small, enclosed space of her work cubicle, whatever the risk. She was aware of this flaw within her, but had little interest in trying to change.

As she walked she noticed the mumbling of the beggars, lined up against the walls of the offices, hiding in the meager shade, trying to avoid the noontime sun. There was a constancy to their pleadings. Spare change? A quarter? Help me out?

Like virtually everyone else, she ignored them.

Once, there had been some shelters, some programs, some community efforts to assist the street people, but those ideals had dissipated over the years. The police, as well, had ceased sweeping the streets; too much effort, not enough return. No place to put them once they were arrested. And dangerous, too, in its own way: too much disease, infectious and contagious. Diseases of dirt. Diseases of blood. Diseases of despair. Consequently, almost every city had a shadow city within it; a place where the homeless made their homes. In New York, this would be abandoned subway tracks. The same was true for Boston. Los Angeles and Miami had the advantages of weather; in Miami, the world beneath the thruways had been taken over, filled with makeshift cardboard and rusty steel shelters and scrofulous living areas. In Los Angeles, the aqueducts were now like squatter's camps. Some of these shadow cities were decades old now, and almost qualified as neighborhoods that could be shown on some map, just as surely as gated and walled suburban areas.

As she walked briskly down the sidewalk, a barefoot man incongruously wearing a thick brown winter coat, seemingly oblivious to the oppressive Miami heat, lurched a step toward her with his demand for spare change. Susan sprang away, turning to confront him.

He had his hand out, palm up. It shook.

"Please," he said. "Can you spare something?"

She stared at him. She could see suppurating wounds beneath a layer of grime on his feet. "Another step and I'll blow your ass away," she replied.

"I don't mean no harm," he said. "I need something to . . ." He hesitated briefly. ". . . eat."

"More likely drink. Or shoot up. Fuck you," she said. She did not turn her back on the man, who seemed to hover on the edge of the building's shadow, as if stepping into the harsh sunlight that filled most of the sidewalk would be like stepping from a precipice.

"I need help," the man said.

"We all do," Susan answered. She gestured with her left hand toward the wall. "Sit back down," she said, keeping her right hand gripped on her weapon. She was aware that the flow of other office workers was diverting itself around her, that she was like a rock thrust up from the middle of a stream.

The homeless man raised his hand to a nose dark with dirt and blotched red with skin cancers. His hand continued to shake with an alcoholic palsy, his forehead glistening with a rancid sweat that also matted streaks of gray hair to his scalp.

"I meant no offense," he said. "Are we not all God's children under his great roof? If you help me now, will not God come and help you at your moment of need?"

He gestured to the sky. Susan did not remove her eyes from him. "He may," she said. "Of course, he may not."

The man ignored her sarcasm, plowing ahead, a rhythmic lilt to his voice, as if the thoughts tumbling through his madness were sweet.

"Is not Jesus waiting just beyond those clouds for all of us? Will we not all have a cool drink from his cup and know true joy and have all our earthly pains vanished in that second?"

Susan remained quiet.

"Are not all his greatest miracles to come? Will he not return to this earth someday in order to carry each and every one of his children in his great hands right to the very gates of paradise?"

The man smiled at Susan, showing rotted teeth. He'd folded his arms in front of him, as though cradling a child, rocking gently back and forth.

"This will come to pass. For me. For you. For all of his children on earth. I know this to be true."

Susan saw the man's eyes had swept upward, as if his conversation was directed to the rare blue sky above. His voice had lost any of the raspiness of disease and despair, replaced with a sort of joyous exuberance of belief. Well, if you have to be deluded, she thought, then this man's delusion was certainly benign. Carefully, she dug her left hand into her purse, hunting until she found a couple of loose coins in the bottom. She brought these out and flipped them toward the man. The coins clinked and rattled on the sidewalk, and he immediately ripped his eyes from the sky and dropped down, looking for them.

"Thank you, thank you," the man said. "God bless you."

Susan stepped away, heading rapidly down the street, leaving the man mumbling in his singsong voice behind her. She'd gone perhaps a dozen feet when she heard him say:

"Susan, you will know peace, too."

Hearing her name made her spin about. "What?" she shouted. "How did you know—"

But the man was now thrust back against the building, lowered to a crouch, rocking back and forth in some odd, crazed reverie that meant something only to himself.

She took a step back toward him. "How did you know my name?" she demanded.

But the man just stared blankly ahead, as if blind, muttering to himself. Susan strained to hear his words, and what she could just make out was: "Soon we will all travel on his highway to the very gates of Heaven."

She hesitated a moment, then turned away from the man.

Susan or *soon.*

It could have been either word, she thought.

She started to walk away, filled with doubts, half turned back a final time and saw that he'd disappeared. Again she reversed direction, and took a few quick steps back to where he'd been hunkered over, her eyes scanning the street, trying to spot him. She could see nothing save the flow of office workers. It was as if he'd been a hallucination.

For a moment she stood rooted in place, filling with an undefined dread. Then she shook herself free of the sensation, like a dog shaking raindrops from its coat, and continued on her path to the lunch she didn't want.

When the counterman asked for her order, she first considered yogurt and fruit, then changed her mind and asked for ham and Swiss on a hard roll with plenty of mayonnaise. The counterman seemed to hesitate, and she said, "Hey, we only go around once." This made him smile, and he quickly made her sandwich, putting it and a bottle of springwater in a paper bag.

Susan walked another six blocks with the sandwich, to a small park tucked on one side of a shopping mall, right up against the bay. There were two mounted police officers at the park entrance, watching the people enter. One had slung his automatic rifle across the saddle and was leaning forward, a modern caricature of some old-time western dime novel. She expected him to say "Howdy, ma'am," but instead the policeman simply eyed her from behind dark glasses, giving her the same scrutiny he gave everyone else. She assumed to get into the park and sit and eat a sandwich a few feet away from where Biscayne Bay lapped at wooden pilings, one had to be clearly a franchised member of society. No derelicts or homeless allowed in at midday. The night would probably be different. Then, it would likely be suicidal for someone like herself to enter the small park, no more than a hundred yards of shoreline. The shade trees and benches that were so inviting in the heat of the day would take on a whole different aura after the sun set; they would be places of concealment. That's what was so difficult about life, she thought: the odd duality to everything. What was safe at noon would be hazardous eight hours later. It was like the tides in the Upper Keys, which she was so familiar with. One minute they would flood an area with water, making it safe to pass. The next, they would turn, ebbing the safety away. People, she thought, were probably much the same.

She found a bench where she could sit alone, eating her sandwich and staring at the expanse of water, defiant in the face of too many calories and too much artery-clogging fat. There was just enough breeze to kick up a light chop on the bay, as if the sheen of green-blue water were alive. She watched a pair of tankers leaving the Port of Miami. They were fat-bottomed and un-gainly ships, beating their way through the crowded channels like a pair of dull bullies in a schoolyard.

She swigged at the springwater, which was warming rapidly in the day's heat. She thought, for a moment, that she could sit there and ignore every-thing; who she was, what was happening to her. Her reverie was burst, how-ever, by a rapidly approaching siren and the insistent thrash-throbbing noise of a helicopter. She twisted around and saw a police chopper scooting low by the edge of the bay, its siren wailing. As she watched, she saw a pair of teenagers running parallel to the water, heading from the downtown toward the park. In the same glance, she saw the pair of mounted officers moving to intercept the pair.

The arrest was swift. The chopper hovered, and the men on horseback corraled the pair, much as they would in some western rodeo. If the two younger men were armed, they didn't show it. Instead, they both pulled up, raising their hands and facing the policemen. She could see both teenagers were grinning, as if they had little to fear, and that the pursuit and arrest were as familiar to them as the sun rising each morning. From where she was sit-ting, she saw that the shirt and pants of one of them were stained with red-brown streaks of blood. Somewhere, she thought, the owner of that blood lies dying. Or, at the least, hurt beyond pain.

She turned away, crumpling the remains of her lunch and tossing it into an adjacent wastebasket, then brushing the crumbs from her clothes. Her eyes swept the park. There were perhaps a dozen other people there, some eating, others just strolling. Almost everyone was patiently, quietly, watch-ing the action just outside the park's gates, as though it were a show pro-vided for their amusement. She rose from her bench and glanced back at the arrest. Several police cruisers with flashing lights had joined the situation. There was one dog unit as well, and a German shepherd strained at his leash, barking, snarling, fangs bared. As she watched, the helicopter rose abruptly and, with a graceful, almost balletic dip and swerve, peeled away into the sunlight. The thumping sound of its rotors faded from her hearing, as did the barking of the dog, replaced by the lonely slapping noise her own shoes made against the hot pavement.

Susan headed back toward her office, but took the long way around, keeping near the bay as long as possible before striking inward. She was on a small side street, a piece of real estate that seemed to have been ignored by the contractors and developers who had covered most of the downtown with a variety of skyscrapers and hotel complexes, filling the area with concrete shapes and walls, so that the few streets that remained were surrounded by cement. There was the acidic smell of cleaning fluid in the light breeze, mixing with the salt air that stirred across the bay; she assumed that some wall covered with graffiti was getting the high-pressure hose and solvent treatment from a county prison work crew. This was a Sisyphean task; once clean, the wall would simply become a new target for the same vandals, who enjoyed dodging the nighttime patrols. They were remarkably efficient.

She continued down the street, but paused mid-block, in front of a significantly smaller, older building, almost, she thought, a house, tucked between the rear of a hotel complex and an office building. It was something from a time warp, a genteel, old Miami shape, reminiscent of a time when the city had been merely a swampy town with a growing population and too many mosquitoes, and not a hip-hop, electrified, neon metropolis. The building sat behind a small, well-groomed grassy swatch. A walkway demarcated by rows of flowers led to the front. There was a wide veranda running the length of the building, and an imposing set of double doors that she guessed were hand-carved from some ancient stand of Dade County pine—the preferred construction material a century earlier, a wood that, when dried, was as hard as granite and seemingly impervious to even the most determined termite. The wide jalousie windows had horizontal wooden hurricane shutters shading them from the sunlight. The building itself was only two stories high, topped with a burnished red tile roof that seemed to be baking in the midday light.

Susan stared at it, thinking that in the midst of the concrete and steel that made up the downtown, it was an antique. It was incongruous, out of place, and oddly beautiful because it spoke of an independence of age in a world dedicated to the immediate and the instant. She realized she rarely saw things that were old anymore, as if there were some unspoken prejudice against things built to last a century or longer.

She took a step forward, curious about who would occupy such a building, and saw a small brass plaque on one of the pillars supporting the veranda. Moving closer, she read: THE LAST PLACE. RECEPTIONIST INSIDE.

Susan hesitated, then opened the double door slowly. Inside, it was shaded and cool. A lazy pair of wooden paddle fans hung from a high ceiling, spinning indefatigably. There was deep, brown, wooden trim framing the white walls, and a polished wooden floor the color of maple leaves in November. To her right there was a wide, sweeping stairway that rose to a landing, and to her left a single mahogany desk with an antique banker's lamp on one corner and a solitary computer screen on the other. A middle-aged woman with frizzy, gray-streaked hair that jumped from her scalp like odd and abrupt thoughts looked up at her as she entered.

"Hello, dear," she said.

Her voice seemed to echo. Susan thought it was not unlike someone speaking in a research library. She glanced around again before replying, wondering where the security was. She could see no spy cameras mounted in the corners, no electronic surveillance, motion detectors, alarm system, or automatic weapons. Instead, there was a somber quiet, but not a complete one, for she caught the distant strains of a symphony playing somewhere within the building.

"Hello," she replied.

The woman gestured her over. Susan padded across a blue and red Oriental carpet.

"Is it you who needs our services, or are you thinking of someone else?"

"I'm sorry . . ."

"Is it you who is dying, or someone close to you?"

Susan stopped in midthought. "No, not me," she blurted. The woman smiled.

"Oh," she said. "I'm glad. You look so young, and when you came through the door, I took one look at you and thought it would be far too unfair for someone as young as you to need to be here because I suspect you've got lots of living yet. That's not to say we don't get our share of young people. We do. And, try as we might, it's hard not to feel they've been cheated, no matter how easy we make it for them. I think it's easier for all involved when the person passing is elderly. What does the Good Book say? The fullness of years. Three score and ten?"

"This is a hospice?" Susan asked.

The woman nodded. "What did you think it was, dear?"

Susan shrugged. "I didn't know. It seemed so different, outside. It seemed old. Something out of the past, not the future."

"Dying is about the past," the woman replied. "About seeing where you've been. Appreciating all the moments that have gone by." She sighed. "It's getting much harder, you know."

"What?"

"Dying peacefully. Dying with satisfaction. Dying with dignity and love and affection and respect. Nowadays people seem to die for all the wrong reasons." The woman shook her head, sighed again. "Death seems all hurried and tough now," she added. "Not gentle. Unless you're here. We make it . . . well, gentle."

Susan found herself agreeing. "You make sense."

The woman smiled again. "Would you like to look around? We have only a couple of clients now. There are some empty beds. And there should be one more, by this evening." The woman cocked her head toward the distant strains of music. "The Pastorale Symphony," she said. "But the Brandenburg concertos work every bit as well. And there was one woman, last week, who listened to Crosby, Stills and Nash over and over. Do you remember them? They were before your time. Old rockers from the Sixties and Seventies mainly. 'Suite Judy Blue Eyes' and 'Southern Cross' mostly. It made her smile."

"I wouldn't want to disturb anyone," Susan said.

"Would you like to stay and see some films? We're showing some Marx Brothers comedies this evening."

Susan shook her head.

The woman seemed to be in no hurry. "As you wish," she said. "And are you sure there's no one—"

"My mother is dying," Susan blurted.

The woman behind the desk nodded slowly. There was a small silence.

"She has cancer," Susan said.

Again silence.

"Inoperable. Chemotherapy didn't really work. She was in a brief remission, but now it's back and it's killing her again."

The woman remained quiet.

Susan could feel tears welling up in her eyes. She thought that her insides were suddenly being twisted and then ripped by a great, cruel claw.

"I don't want her to die," she gasped. "She's always been there and there's no one else. Except my brother, but he's away. There's just me. . . ."

"And?"

"I'll be alone. We've always been together, and now we won't. . . ."

Susan was standing awkwardly in front of the desk. The woman motioned toward a chair, and, with a small hesitation, Susan slumped into it, taking a single breath and then giving in to the tears completely. She sobbed unremittedly for several minutes, while the woman with the electric hair waited, a box of tissues in her hand.

"Take your time," the woman said.

"I'm sorry," Susan blurted.

"Nothing to be sorry about," the woman replied.

"I don't do this," Susan said. "I don't cry. Never before. I'm sorry."

"You're tough? And you think that's important?"

"No, it's just, I don't know. . . ."

"No one shows emotion anymore. Do you drive home sometimes at night and think that we are all becoming inured to pain and distress? That society only acknowledges achievement? Success. Being tough."

Susan nodded. The woman once again smiled. Susan saw that she had an odd, wry tilt to the corners of her lips, as if she saw sadness within every humor and the tear behind every laugh.

"Toughness is overrated. Being cold isn't the same thing as being strong," the woman said.

"When do people come . . . ?" Susan gestured toward the stairs.

"Near the end. Sometimes as long as three to four months before passing. But usually two to four weeks. Just enough time for them to put their internal selves at rest. We recommend that the external selves be handled beforehand."

"External?"

"Wills and lawyers. Estates and legacies. Once here, people are more interested in what they will leave behind of their spirit. Not so much goods and stocks and cash. That sounds far more religious than I mean it to be. But that's the way things seem to work. Your mother . . . how much time?"

"Six months. No, that's too short. A year, perhaps. Maybe a little longer. She doesn't like it when I speak with the doctors. She says it's upsetting for her. And even when I do, it's hard to get a straightforward answer out of them."

"Perhaps that's because they're unsure themselves?"

"I suppose so."

"It seems sometimes we expect death to be precise because he is so final. But he's not." She smiled. "He can be erratic and capricious. And he can be cruel. But he doesn't control our living, only our dying, and that's why we are here."

"She won't talk about what's happening to her," Susan said. "Other than to mention the pain. I think she wants to be alone. To shut me out, because she thinks that will protect me."

"Oh, dear, I don't know that that is wise. Death is best faced with the comfort of family and friends. I would urge you to take a more active interest and to tell your mother that her passing is a moment that you need to share. And you still have time, from the sound of it."

"What should I do?"

"Place your relationship with your mother in order. And help her to take care of the business of dying. Then, when it comes close, bring her here and the two of you can sort out the emotion of dying. Say what needs to be said. Remember what needs to be remembered."

Susan nodded. The woman opened a dark drawer and pulled out a business card and a slick, glossy, magazine-style brochure.

"This should answer some of your questions," she said. "Is there anywhere your mother wants to go, someplace she might want to see, something specific and important that she might want to do? I would urge you to do it now, before she weakens and sickens further. A trip, an experience, an accomplishment, can sometimes make passing easier."

"I'll keep that in mind," Susan said. She took a deep breath. "A trip. An experience. An accomplishment. While she still has the strength."

"Sounds a little like some Far Eastern mantra, doesn't it?" The woman laughed briefly.

"But it makes sense. Something to . . ."

"Focus on, other than pain and loss and fear of the unknown."

"A trip. An experience. An accomplishment." Susan stroked her chin with her forefinger. "I'll tell her."

"Good. And then I'll look forward to speaking with you again. When it gets closer. You'll know the time," the woman added. "Sensitive people, like you seem to be, they always know the time."

"Thank you," Susan said, rising. "I'm glad I came in." She hesitated again. "I noticed there's not even a lock on the door. . . ."

The woman shook her head.

"We're not scared of death here," she said briskly.

As Susan stepped from beneath the shaded overhang on the front veranda, the sun creased across the lip of the roof of an adjacent skyscraper, blinding her for a moment. She put her hand to her forehead, like a sailor searching the horizon, and saw the derelict she'd spoken with earlier in the day teetering nervously on the sidewalk in front of the hospice, seemingly waiting for her. When he saw her, the man held his arms wide, as if mounted on a cross, and broke into a wide smile.

"Hello! Hello! There you are! Greetings!" he shouted, like some bizarrely happy Christ figure, enjoying his crucifixion.

She paused, without replying. She could feel the heft of the pistol in her satchel.

"Someday we'll all climb the stairway to Heaven," he yelled up to her.

"Led Zeppelin. The untitled album. Nineteen seventy-one," Susan muttered to herself. She descended the hospice stairs slowly, walking toward the man on the sidewalk. In a louder voice she replied: "Don't you think you should try to have delusions that are, at the very least, original? You don't want to be quite that derivative."

The derelict's head was tossed back. His brown overcoat almost reached the ground. She saw that his threadbare pants were held up by a filthy, tattered, rainbow-hued piece of cloth.

"Jesus will save us all. . . ."

"If he has the time. And the inclination. Which I sometimes doubt . . ."

"He will reach out to each and every one of us . . ."

"If he doesn't mind getting his hands dirty."

". . . and he will deliver his word right to our waiting ears."

"That's assuming we're willing to listen. I wouldn't count on that, either."

Abruptly, the man's arms dropped to his sides. His head tilted forward, and Susan could see a glint in his eyes, which she took to be the ordinary, benign sort of madness.

"His word is the truth. He told me so."

"I'm happy for you," Susan said, starting to push past the man, heading up the street.

"But he's here!" the derelict cried out.

"Sure," Susan said, tossing the word back over her shoulder. "Sure he is. Jesus has decided the perfect place to start the Second Coming is Miami. Works for me," she said sarcastically.

"But he *is* here, and he gave me a message that he insisted was just for you!"

Susan had gone a few feet past the man, but now stopped and turned back. "For me?"

"Yes, yes yes! That's what I was trying to tell you!" The man was grinning, showing blackened, decayed teeth. "Jesus told me to tell you that you will never be alone, and that he will always be there to save you! He said that for years you have wandered in the terrible darkness of not knowing him, but that is now to change, hallelujah!"

Susan felt a sudden, icy darkness within her.

Are you the man who saved me?

Theme where a navy do amuse?

What is it that you want?

Why is tit a tat, now a tut?

Two questions, encoded, answered by a derelict who seemed to be following her. She shook her head.

"Jesus told you this? When?"

"Just a few minutes ago. He appeared in a great flash of white light. I was blinded, Lord, blinded by the magnificence of his presence, and terrified, too, and I averted my gaze, but he reached out his hand to me and I knew peace, right in that second, a great and complete peace, and he gave me a task that he said was crucial, that would ease his Second Coming to this earth. Help to pave the way, he told me. Clear the path, he said. He brought me to this place here, and then he told me to become his voice. And then he gave me some money, too. Twenty bucks!"

"What did he tell you?"

"He told me to seek out his special child and to answer her two questions for her."

Susan could hear a quaver in her voice. She wanted to shout, but her words came out in something closer to a whisper, breathless, rapidly evaporating, dried up by the day's heat.

"Did he say anything else? Anything at all?"

"Yes, he did!" The derelict wrapped his arms around himself in joy and ecstasy. "He has made me into his very messenger, here on this earth! Oh, the joy of it!" The derelict shuffled his feet, almost as if breaking into a little jig.

Susan struggled to keep herself calm. "And what was this message? That you were to deliver to me?"

"Ah, Susan," the man said, unmistakably this time using her name. "Sometimes his messages are mysterious and strange!"

"Still, what did he say?"

The derelict calmed himself and tilted his head forward, as if in deep and dedicated thought. "I didn't understand it, but he made me repeat it over and over until I got it right."

"What?" It was difficult to keep panic from her tone.

"He said to tell you: 'I want what was stolen from me.' "

The derelict paused, his lips moving to himself. "Yes," he said, smiling again. "I got it right. I'm sure. I wouldn't want to get it wrong. It might mean he wouldn't select me a second time."

"Anything else?" she asked. Her voice trembled.

"What else do we need?" the derelict replied with a great braying laugh of satisfaction and joy. He turned away from her and headed down the street—a half stumble, half skip, like a child's walk—toward the satin blue waters of the bay. His voice was raised in a hymn of his own making, praising the Second Coming of a man he thought came from Heaven but whom Susan suspected really emanated from some far rougher place. She wanted to sit, to take things carefully, to assess what she'd heard, but instead found herself walking away swiftly. As she picked up her pace, she abruptly looked back, trying to spot the man who was stalking her, but all she could see was a suddenly empty street. In the distance there was traffic, police, and people. She snatched a deep breath of superheated air and ran hard for the false comfort and safety of the anonymous crowd.

THE MAN WHO
HID THE LIE

When she heard her son's voice on the telephone, Diana Clayton felt parallel surges of delight and fear. The first was ordinary mother's affection for her too distant child. The second was a more complicated emotion, which contained elements of anxiety that she'd thought had long been hidden and were now bursting like seeds throughout her. At the root of this fear was the understanding that nothing they'd come to understand as their lives was quite right, and that much was about to change.

"Mother?" Jeffrey said.

"Jeffrey," she replied, "thank goodness. I've been trying and trying to reach you."

"You have?"

"Yes. I left message after message at your office, and at your home on the machine. Didn't you get them?"

"No. Not a one."

Jeffrey made a mental note of this fact, thought it a curious thing, then realized it only spoke of the efficiency of the security forces of the Fifty-first State. He rapidly plugged the telephone into the computer pickup, and seconds later his mother's face appeared on the screen in front of him. He thought she appeared gaunt, troubled. He realized she must have seen his reaction, because she said:

"I've lost weight. It's inevitable. I'm okay."

He shook his head. "Sorry. You look fine."

Both let this small lie rest.

"Are you in much pain? What do the doctors say?"

"Oh, screw the doctors. They don't know anything," Diana responded. "And what's a little hurt? It's no worse than when I broke my leg the summer you were fourteen. When I fell off the damn roof. Do you remember?"

He did. The roof had sprung a leak, and she climbed up with a bucket of pitch to try and patch it, slipped, and fell. It was a single-story thud, which could have been far worse than the fracture and bruises she'd received. He'd driven her to the hospital emergency room despite the fact that he was two years shy of obtaining his driver's license.

"Of course I remember. Remember the doctor, after wrapping that plaster cast, how he looked when he asked how you were getting home, and I had the car keys?"

Both mother and son laughed at the shared memory.

"I think he figured we wouldn't make it a single block before I crashed the car and we were both right back there in the emergency room."

Diana Clayton smiled, nodding. "You were always a good driver," she said.

Jeffrey shook his head. "Safe and steady. Mr. Dull. Not as good as Susan. She can really handle machines."

"But too fast."

"That's her style."

Diana nodded again. "You're right. She has to be patient so much of the time. Patient and thoughtful and careful and exact. It must be terribly boring for her sometimes. That's why she lets speed into her life. It's something different."

Jeffrey did not reply. He simply fixed his eyes on the image of his mother's face on the screen in front of him. He thought that he'd been wrong not to pay more attention to her. There was a momentary silence between the two, and then he said:

"I think I have a problem. We have a problem."

Diana knitted her brows. She took a deep breath and said what she'd hoped she'd never have to say: "He did not die. And he's found us."

Jeffrey nodded. "Has he—" he started to ask.

His mother interrupted him. "He's been here. Inside the house while I was asleep. He's been following Susan and sending her word games and puzzles. She's responded in kind. I don't know exactly what he wants, but he's been toying with us. . . ."

She hesitated, then added: "I'm afraid. Your sister is tougher than me. But maybe she's a little afraid, too. She doesn't know yet. I mean, at first I was hoping that it wasn't him. I just couldn't believe it, after all these years. But now, I'm sure it is. . . ."

She stopped and she stared at the image of her son in front of her.

"How did you know?" she asked abruptly. Her voice had a ragged, high-pitched quality. "I thought it was just me. I thought . . . I mean, how did . . . what, has he contacted you, too?"

Jeffrey nodded slowly. "Yes."

"But how?"

"He committed some crimes, and I was contracted to help solve them. I didn't believe it was him, either. I was no different from you. It was as if I'd somehow been allowed to believe a lie all those years."

"What sort of crimes?"

"The sort of crimes that you would never speak about."

Diana closed her eyes for a moment, as if trying to shut away the vision that accompanied what they were talking about.

"And now, I'm supposed to find him for the police here," her son continued. "But instead of finding him, it appears he's found me."

"He's found you. Oh, my God. Are you safe? Are you at home?"

"No, I'm not at home. I'm out West."

"Where?"

"The Fifty-first State. I'm in New Washington. That's where he's been committing his crimes."

"But I thought . . ."

"Yes, I know. It's not supposed to happen here. That's why they hired me. At least, that's what I thought when I was brought here. Now, I'm not sure."

"Jeffrey, what are you saying?" Diana Clayton asked.

Her son hesitated before replying.

"I think," he said slowly, measuring his words carefully, because they came not from any evidence of the head, but from evidence stemming from the heart, "that he brought me here. That everything he's done was designed to deliver me right here to his doorstep. That he knew he could create deaths which would prompt the authorities here to seek me out and bring me here. I feel like I'm a part of a game that I've only just started to understand the rules to."

Diana held her breath for a second, then released it slowly, letting it whistle between her lips.

"He plays at death," she said abruptly.

Behind her, she heard the sound of a key in the front door lock, and a second later footsteps and the call, "Mother!"

"Your sister's home," she said. "Early."

Susan walked into the kitchen and instantly saw the image of her brother on the video screen. As always, a mingling of emotions creased her heart.

"Hello, Jeffrey," she said.

"Hello, Susan," he replied. "Are you all right?"

"I don't think so," she answered.

"What is it?" Diana asked.

"He's here. Again. He contacted me. The man who's been sending the notes . . ."

"He's not a man," Diana interrupted sharply. Her daughter looked at her wildly, surprised. "I know who it is."

"Then . . ."

"He's not a man," the mother repeated. "He's never been a man. He's your father."

Silence seized them all. Susan sat down hard at the kitchen table, nodding, taking in shallow breaths of air, like a fireman crawling through a smoke-filled apartment.

"You knew, and you didn't say anything?" she asked, a ridge of fury crawling slowly along the precipice of her words. "You thought it might be him, and you thought I shouldn't know?"

Tears began to slide from the corners of Diana's eyes. "I wasn't sure. I didn't know for certain. I didn't want to be like the little boy who cried wolf. I was so convinced he was dead. I thought we were safe."

"But he isn't and we aren't," Susan replied bitterly. "I suppose we never have been."

"The question is," Jeffrey interrupted, "what does he want? Why find us now? What is it that he thinks we can give him? Why not just get ahead with his life—"

"I know what he wants," Susan said abruptly. "He told me. Not him, exactly, but he told me. And not in so many words, either, but . . ."

"What?"

"He wants what was stolen from him."

"He wants what?"

"What was stolen. That was his latest message to us."

Again they were quiet, considering the phrase. It was Jeffrey who responded first. "But what the hell, I mean, what exactly was stolen?"

Diana looked pale, and tried to hide the quaver that tripped her words as she spoke. "That's simple," she said. "What was stolen? You and your sister. Who was the thief? I was. What did I rob him of? A life. At least, a life that he'd invented. And so he was forced to invent another, I suppose."

"But what do you think that means?" Susan asked.

"I would guess, in a word, revenge," Diana replied softly.

"Don't be crazy. Revenge against Jeffrey and me? What did we do—"

"No, that doesn't make sense," her brother interrupted. "But it does where Mother is concerned. She's probably in great danger. Actually, I think we all are, probably in different ways and for different reasons."

"I want what was stolen from me," Susan said quietly. "Jeffrey, you're right. His relationship, if that's the right word, with each of us is distinct. Separate. I mean, to him, Mother is one issue, you're another, and I'm the third. A different agenda for each of us."

She paused, looked up, and saw her brother nodding in agreement. "There's one way of looking at this," she went on. "Imagine we're all parts of a jigsaw puzzle—a psychological jigsaw puzzle—and when we get fit together, it will create one coherent picture. The problem for us, obviously, is figuring out what that picture is, beforehand. And figuring out how it will all fit together . . ."

She took a deep breath.

". . . before he fits it together for us."

Jeffrey rubbed a hand across his forehead, smiling. "Susan, remind me never to play cards with you. Or chess. Or even checkers. I think you're absolutely right."

Diana had dabbed the tears away from her eyes. She spoke quietly once again, repeating herself. "He plays at death. That's the game. And now, we're the pieces."

The truth of this statement was clear to all three.

Jeffrey's voice was raised, and he thought he sounded like he must in classes, posing a question to students. "I don't imagine that it makes any sense to try to hide again," he said slowly. "Perhaps we could defeat the game by splitting up, heading in three separate directions. . . ."

"Not very damn likely," Susan said briskly.

"Susan's right," Diana added, turning to the screen. "No," she said, "I don't suppose it would, even if we could. We must do something else this time. And probably what I should have done twenty-five years ago."

"What's that?" Susan asked.

"Outplay him," her mother replied.

Susan had an iron grin on her face, not a look of amusement, or pleasure, but of cruel determination. "Makes sense to me. All right. If we're not going to hide, then where are we going to confront him? Here? Back in New Jersey?"

Again the three of them paused.

"Jeffrey, you're the expert on that sort of question," his sister said.

Jeffrey hesitated. "Confronting one's father is not the same thing as confronting a killer. Even if they are one and the same. We ought to decide which we intend to do. Confront our father, or confront a killer."

The two women did not reply. He waited a second, then added with a snap of certainty: "Grendel's lair."

Diana looked confused. "I don't quite understand. . . ." But Susan's face twitched into a wry half smile. She clapped her hands together in modest, only partly mocking, applause.

"What he means, Mother, is that if you want to destroy the monster, you must wait for him to come to you and then you must seize hold of him, and you cannot him let go, no matter what happens, even as he pulls you into his own world, because that's where your fight will both start and finish."

They were all silent for a few seconds, until Susan half raised her hand, like a schoolchild not completely sure of her response but not wishing to miss the opportunity to be called on.

"I've only got one other question," she said, some of the confidence in her voice wavering. "So the three of us track him, and find him before he finds us. Beat him to the punch, I guess. Then we confront him. Killer or father. What precisely is our purpose? I mean, what do we do at that meeting?"

None of them, yet, had the answer to this question.

Susan and Diana agreed to get the next flight west, which departed from Miami the following morning. In the interim, Jeffrey had his mother ship him an electronic copy of the letter she'd received from the attorney and copies of the announcement of her husband's death from the St. Thomas More Academy Bulletin. He told them only that he would have them met at the New Washington airport, and that he would arrange for their housing. These were tasks he immediately distributed to Agent Martin.

"All right," the detective said, "after I get finished being your secretary, what is it you're going to do?"

"I'm going to be gone for a day. Maybe two. You make certain that my mother and sister are safe, secure, and under no circumstances is there to be any attention drawn to their arrival. They will fly in under phony names, and you're to whisk these phony personae right through your fancy-Dan immigration checkpoints without so much as a twitch on any computer screen anywhere or a burp from any government drone. That would include the issuing of their temporary passports. No computer entries. None whatsoever. This whole damn system is compromised, and I don't want our subject to note the arrival of a mother and daughter. He'd recognize their ages, origination, you name it, and he'd be ahead of us before we'd even had a chance to figure out our plan of attack."

The detective grunted in assent. Unhappy, but clearly in agreement. Jeffrey thought that Robert Martin was probably keeping quiet because he'd figured that three baits were probably even more likely to raise their quarry. And the suggestion of a plan of action probably appealed to him as well.

"My sister will be armed. Well-armed. No problems there, either."

"A gal after my own heart."

"I don't think so."

"And you, Professor, you're going where?"

"On a sentimental journey."

"Moonlight and soft music? Guitars strumming in the background? And where might that take you?"

"I need to go home," Jeffrey said. "Not for long, but I need to go there."

"You're not going back to that dump you call a university," Martin said brusquely. "That's not part of our arrangement. You're here for the duration, Professor."

Jeffrey responded quietly, but sourly. "That's not my home. That's where I work. I'm going back to my home."

"Well, regardless," Martin said, shrugging as if disinterested, "you should take a friend along." The detective reached into a desk drawer and removed a nine-millimeter semiautomatic pistol, which he tossed to Jeffrey with a small laugh.

He managed a fitful sleep on the red-eye east, waking only from dreams that seemed insistent on turning into nightmares as the plane began to descend into Newark International Airport. It was just after dawn, and the bleakness of the northeastern winter was lurking in the near weeks ahead. A gray, dark haze of smog and pollution hung over the city, fighting the shafts of early morning sunlight that tried to penetrate through to the earth. From his window, Jeffrey thought the world a place of concrete and macadam, tightly compacted, fenced in by steel and brick, surrounded by rusty chain link and barbed wire.

As the plane slowly circled to the north of the city, he could see the scars of riot, huge expanses of charred blocks left to rubble and neglect. From the air he could make out the lines where beleaguered police and national guardsmen had formed ranks and stopped the tides of arson and looting as easily as he could see the areas that had been allowed to consume themselves. As the jet engines throttled back and the landing gear thumped down, he found himself oddly longing for the open spaces and clean designs of the Fifty-first State. He shook this thought from his head, rubbing his eyes to clear them of the half sleep of the flight, and hunched his shoulders forward in anticipation of the cold.

There was heavy, stop-and-go traffic when he exited the airport in the car he'd rented. The traffic continued all the way to the turnpike, and then in fits and starts for another twenty miles, so that by the time he reached Trenton, the state capital, he hit the morning rush hour.

He took the Perry Street exit, the ramp cutting past the cinder-block and glass square of the Trenton *Times*. There were large black soot streaks dancing down the side of the stolid, old building, increasing in size and shape near the loading dock, where battered, dark blue and yellow delivery trucks were lined up, waiting for the morning press run. A half-dozen drivers were outside, gathered around a fire in an old steel drum, waiting for the signal to begin loading.

He turned and drove a few blocks closer to the capitol building, close enough so he could see the golden domed roof glistening in the light. He was waved through a police barricade midway—a barbed-wire and sandbagged line that separated an area of urban blight and burned-out, boarded-up shells of buildings from reconstructed row houses created by urban renewal. The police presence was scattered, but insistent—enough to make certain that no surges of frustration swept down the streets where money had been spent, heading angrily toward the capitol. He found a place to park and proceeded on foot.

The attorney's office was barely a block away from the legislative buildings, in an old-fashioned, converted brownstone house that maintained an antique, insistent elegance to its exterior. There was a sally-port entrance, which required him to be buzzed in at both the external and internal doors by a sullen and bored-looking security guard.

"Got an appointment?" he asked, checking a clipboard.

"I'm here to see Mr. Smith," Jeffrey replied.

"Got an appointment?" the guard repeated.

"Yes," Jeffrey lied. "Jeffrey Clayton. Nine A.M."

The guard looked hard. "Not here," he said. He instantly produced a large-caliber handgun, which he trained on the professor. Jeffrey ignored the weapon.

"Must be a mistake," he said.

"Don't make mistakes," the man said. "You should leave now."

"How about calling Mr. Smith's secretary? You'll do that, won't you?"

"Why should I? You're not on the list."

Jeffrey smiled, reaching slowly into his jacket and removing his temporary security pass from the Fifty-first State. He guessed the man would not take note of the limited dates stamped on the front, but would instead see the badge and golden eagle symbol.

"The reason you should do as I ask," he said slowly, handing over the pass, "is because if you don't, I'm going to come back here with a warrant, a search team, and a SWAT squad, and we're going to bulldoze your boss's office, and then when he finally figures out who screwed up so fucking bad and brought all this trouble down square on his head, he's going to know it was the dumb shit at the front door. How's that for a good enough reason?"

The security guard picked up the phone and said, "Got a police type out here wants to see Mr. Smith without no appointment. You wanna come out and talk to the man?"

He hung up the phone and said, "Secretary'll be right out." He continued to train his weapon directly on Jeffrey's chest. "You armed, S.S. man?" When Jeffrey shook his head, having left his own weapon in the glove compartment of the car, the security guard motioned him toward a metal detector. "We'll see about that," he said. He looked disappointed when Jeffrey did not set the device's alarm off. "You got one of those new high-tech plastic handguns, maybe?" he asked, but before Jeffrey could reply, a woman emerged from an inner office. She was young, prim, officious, with a man's tightly styled white shirt buttoned to her throat, which Jeffrey, in a fit of disrespectful internal humor, thought probably meant she was sleeping with the attorney, who was cheating on his dowdy country-club-addicted wife. The conservative, nonsexy clothes were probably designed to hide her real occupations. He smiled at the fantasy, but didn't think he was wrong.

"Mister?"

"Clayton. Jeffrey Clayton."

The security guard handed her the Fifty-first-State identification card.

"And your business here, so far away from the brave new world out West?" The woman's sarcasm was crystalline.

"Mr. Smith represented a man some years ago who is now the subject of a significant investigation in our territory."

"All communications and business between Mr. Smith and his clients is strictly confidential."

Jeffrey smiled. "Of course it is."

"So, I don't think he can help you." She handed him back the identification.

"As you wish," Jeffrey said. "But on the other hand, I would have thought an attorney might want to make that decision for himself. Of course, if you suspect he'd prefer to simply see his name on an indictment, or as a headline in the local paper, without any advance warning, well, that's up to you."

In an odd way, Jeffrey was enjoying himself. Bluffing was not his usual style, and not something he got to do very often.

The secretary stared hard at him, as if trying to find the deception in some curve of his smile or wrinkle in his chin. "Follow me," she said. "I'll see if he can spare two minutes." She turned on her heel, adding, "That would be one hundred and twenty seconds. No more."

She led him into an anteroom. It was filled with expensive, uncomfortable Victorian furniture. The carpet on the floor was Oriental, large and handmade. An antique grandfather clock stood in the corner, keeping poor time and ticking loudly. The secretary motioned toward a stiff-backed sofa, and retreated behind a desk, rapidly distancing herself from Jeffrey. She picked up a telephone and spoke quickly into the mouthpiece, concealing her words from him, then hung up and said nothing. After a moment a large wooden door swung open and the lawyer emerged. He was cadaverously thin, with a shock of gray hair gathered in a ponytail that plunged down the back of his tailored blue shirt. He wore leather braces, holding up hand-sewn gray pinstripes. His Italian shoes were polished to a reflective sheen. His hand was large, bony and strong, and he gripped the professor's hard.

"And what trouble is it that you would make for me, Mr. Clayton?" the lawyer said between tightly pursed lips.

"That would depend, of course," Jeffrey answered.

"On what?"

"On what you've done."

The lawyer smiled. "Then clearly I have nothing to be worried about. Ask a question, Mr. Clayton."

Jeffrey handed the man the letter he'd sent to Diana. "Ring a bell?"

The attorney read the letter slowly. "Barely. This is very old. I remember the case vaguely . . . a terrible auto accident, just as I said. Bodies burned beyond recognition. Tragic loss of life . . ."

"He did not die."

The attorney hesitated, then said: "That's not what it says here."

"He did not die. Especially in an auto accident. Especially in a suicidal auto accident."

The attorney shrugged. "I wish I could remember. This is most curious. You think this man somehow didn't die, even though I attended his funeral? Or at least I must have, because that's what I wrote. Do you think I'm in the habit of attending phony funerals?"

"This man, as you put it, was my father."

The attorney shot a thin gray eyebrow upward. "Really? But still, dying young, I suspect, despite what most children may believe, is not a crime."

"That's true. But what he *has* been doing, is."

"Which would be?"

"Homicide."

Again the attorney paused. "A dead man involved in murder. How intriguing."

The attorney shook his head. "I do not think I have any additional information for you, Mr. Clayton. Any conversations or correspondence I had with your late father were privileged. That privilege might not survive his death. That would be arguable. But if, as you suddenly claim, he is alive, then, of course, the privilege would still be fully intact, even after all these years. But anyway, this is all ancient history. Extremely ancient history. I doubt I even have the file anymore. My practice today is considerably larger and considerably different than it was back when I wrote that letter to your mother. So, I believe you to be mistaken, and in either regard, I cannot help you. Good day, Mr. Clayton, and good luck. Joyce, show the gentleman out."

This, the prim secretary seemed most eager to do.

The grounds at the St. Thomas More Academy were surrounded by a twelve-foot-high, wrought-iron fence that would have merely been decorative if not for the warning signs stating that the fence was electrified. Jeffrey presumed that the fence extended a half-dozen feet beneath the earth as well. A guard met him at the gate and escorted him into the academy. They walked down a tree-lined path, between stolid redbrick buildings. In the spring, Jeffrey thought, green ivy would be thick on the sides of the dormitories and classrooms; but now, with winter nearing, the brown vines were stems and stalks that crawled up the brick like so many ghostlike tentacles. From the steps of the administration building he could see a wide expanse of dull green playing fields, streaked with the brown sod of use. The escort wore a blue blazer and a red school tie, and Jeffrey noted the outline of an automatic weapon beneath the jacket. He was sullen, quiet, and when a church bell pealed, signaling the end of a class period, he pushed Jeffrey through a set of wide, glass doors. Behind them, classrooms started to disgorge students and the deserted walkways abruptly jammed with a clogged flow of students.

The headmaster's assistant was an elderly woman, with a helmet of teased blue hair and horn-rimmed glasses perched on the end of her nose. She had a friendly but efficient manner that made Jeffrey think that in a world wracked by changes, the old schools were the slowest to change. He wasn't certain whether this was a good or a bad thing.

"Professor Jeffrey Mitchell, my goodness, I don't believe anyone has mentioned that name to me in years. Decades. And you're saying he was your father? My goodness, I don't even recall knowing he was ever married."

"He was. I'm trying to find anyone who might have known him. And anyone who might remember his death. I'm afraid I never knew him. Not really. Divorce at an early age."

"Ah," the woman said, "too frequent the case. And now you're . . ."

"Just trying to fill in a few gaps in my own life," Jeffrey said. "I'm sorry to come upon you unannounced. . . ."

The woman looked at him in more or less the same manner that she might when confronting a student who'd failed some test because he had the flu. Understanding, but not totally sympathetic.

"My own memory is limited," she said. "I recall a young man of promise. A handsome young man of considerable promise. And great intellect. History, I think, was his field?"

"Yes. I believe so."

"Alas, there are too few of us around anymore who might recall anything. And your father was here only a few years, if I remember correctly. I knew him only for a few weeks, before he resigned, and then not really. His departure coincided with my arrival. And I was here, in administration, and he was faculty. And now, twenty-five years is a long time, even at a school such as this. . . ."

"But . . ." Jeffrey caught a hesitation in her voice.

"I suppose you should see old Mr. Maynard. He's mostly retired now, but he still teaches a section of American history. My memory tells me he was department chair when your father was here. He was the department chair for more than thirty years. He might have some knowledge of your father."

The history teacher was sitting at a desk, peering out a second story window, across one of the playing fields, when Jeffrey knocked and entered the small classroom. Maynard was an old man with closely cropped gray hair, a salt and pepper beard, and a boxer's nose, broken and rebroken, flattened and misshapen. He had a gnomelike look, and swiveled in his seat almost like a child playing on a grown-up's chair as Jeffrey walked in. When he saw that his visitor was not a student, he made a small, blushing smile, a coy look that contradicted his bulldog appearance.

"You know, sometimes I can look out over the fields and remember specific games. I can see the players, just as they were. I can hear the sound of the ball and voices and whistles and cheers. Getting old is awful. Memories take over realities. They are a poor replacement. So . . ." He looked hard at Jeffrey. ". . . you seem familiar, but not exactly. I usually can remember all my former students, but I cannot place you."

"I wasn't a student."

"No? Then how is it that I can help you?" he asked.

"My name is Jeffrey Clayton. I'm seeking some information. . . ."

"Ah," the teacher said, nodding. "That's good. There are so few left. . . ."

"I beg your pardon?"

"Seekers of information. Nowadays, people simply accept what they're told. Especially young people. As if knowledge for knowledge's sake is an antiquated and useless endeavor. They only want to know what will help them on some standardized test. Get them into a prestigious college. Get them a good job where they don't have to work hard. Get them some money and some success and a big house in a safe place and a big car and luxury. No one wants to learn because learning is intoxicating. But you are perhaps different, young man?"

Jeffrey smiled, shrugging. "I've never really correlated knowledge with success."

"But still, you come seeking information. Exceptional. What sort of information?"

"About a man you once knew."

"And this would be?"

"Jeffrey Mitchell. Onetime teacher in your department."

Maynard rocked in his seat, eyes fixed upon his visitor. "This is most curious," he said. "But not completely unexpected. Even after so many years."

"Do you remember him?"

"I do indeed." He continued to stare at Jeffrey. After a moment he said: "You are, I suspect, related to Mr. Mitchell?"

"Yes. He was my father."

"Ah, I should have guessed. I can see a distinct resemblance in the face. And the physical nature as well. He was tall and thin, such as yourself. Trim and athletic. A man of conditioning, both of the mind and the body. Do you play the violin as well? No? Ah, too bad. He was quite gifted. And so, son of this man I once knew but not particularly well, what is the information you come seeking?"

"He died. . . ."

"So I was told. So I read."

"Actually, he didn't die."

"Ah, interesting. And does he live today?"

"Yes."

"And you?"

"I have not seen him since childhood. Nine years old. Twenty-five years."

"And like some orphan, or better, some child tearfully put up for adoption, you have gone in search of the man who abandoned you?"

"Abandon might not be the right word. But in a way, yes."

The history teacher rolled his eyes upward, spun in his chair, took another long look out the window over the playing fields, and then swung back to Jeffrey.

"Young man, this is not a journey I would recommend you take."

Jeffrey stood in front of the desk, hesitating. "And why not?" he asked.

"You expect to gain something from this information? Fill some hole in your life?"

Jeffrey did not think that was precisely what he was searching for, but thought that at least in part there was some truth there. He hesitated, thinking it might be wise for him to actually determine what it was he wanted to learn. But instead of blurting this out, he said:

"Do you remember him?"

"Of course. He made a singular impression upon me."

"Which was?"

"He was a dangerous man."

This reply made Jeffrey pause. "How so?"

"He was the most unusual of historians."

"Why do you say that?"

"Because most of us are merely intrigued by the vagaries of history. Why this happened. Why that happened. It's a game, you see, like tracing a map through paper that is not quite thin enough."

"But he was different?"

"Yes. At least that was my impression. . . ."

"And?"

The older man hesitated, then shrugged. "He loved history because— and this is only an impression, mind you—he intended to use it. For himself."

"I don't understand."

"History is often a compilation of the mistakes of man. I had the feeling that your father thirsted to learn because he intended not to make the same mistakes."

"I see—" Jeffrey started.

"Ah, but you don't. Your father taught European history, but that was not his true field."

"Which was?"

The small man smiled again. "Merely an opinion. A feeling. Not really evidence." He stopped, then sighed. "I am growing old. Just one class now. Seniors. They don't really care for my style. Brusque. Belligerent. Provocative. Question theories. Question conventions. That's the problem with being a historian, you know. You don't much like the modern world. It's all these old times that you long for."

"You were saying. His real field?"

"What do you know of your father, Mr. Clayton?"

"What I know, I do not like."

"Judiciously put. This will seem a harsh thing to say, Mr. Clayton, but I was overjoyed when your father told me he was leaving. And not because he wasn't a good teacher, because he was. Probably one of the best I've ever seen. And popular as well. But we'd already lost one student. An unfortunate young woman snatched from the campus and most brutally treated. I did not want there to be a second."

"You think he had something to do with it?"

"What do you know, Mr. Clayton?"

"I know the police interrogated him."

The old man shook his head. "Police!" he snorted. "They didn't know what to look for. A historian knows, you see. He knows that all events are a combination of many factors. Of the mind, of the heart, of politics and economics, of accident and coincidence. Of the capricious forces of the world. Do you know that, Mr. Clayton?"

"In my field of expertise, that would certainly be true."

"And what is your field, if I may be so bold?" the old man asked, rubbing the end of his broken nose.

"I am a professor of criminal behavior at the University of Massachusetts."

"Ah, how intriguing. Your field, then, is . . ."

"My field is violent death."

The old teacher smiled. "And so was your father's."

Jeffrey leaned forward, asking a question in his body language. The historian rocked in his seat.

"I did wonder why," the older man continued, "sometimes over the years, no one ever came seeking answers about Jeffrey Mitchell. And, as years passed, sometimes I allowed myself to think that that famous car accident was actually real and that the world had managed to dodge a small but deadly bullet. That's a cliché. I shouldn't allow myself to speak in clichés, even now when I'm old and they don't have as much use for me here, or anywhere, they once did. A historian should always doubt. Doubt the easy answer. Doubt the idea that dumb, blind luck has brought good fortune to the world, because it rarely does. Doubt everything. Because it is only through that doubt and some skepticism to season it that one can hope to find truths of history. . . ."

"My father . . ."

"Did you want to know about death? Were you curious about killing? About torture? About all the times the darker side of human nature erupted? He was the man to see. He was an encyclopedia of evil: the auto-da-fé, the Inquisition, Vlad the Impaler, the Christians in the catacombs, Tamerlane the Conqueror, burning heretics during the Hundred Years' War. This is what he knew about. What portion of the woman's kidney did Jack the Ripper deliver to the authorities with his famous challenge? Your father knew. Billy the Kid's preferred weapon? A forty-four-caliber Colt revolver—not dissimilar to the Charter Arms Bulldog forty-four that David Berkowitz, the Son of Sam, utilized. The exact formula for Zyklon B? Your father could tell you that as well, and also the temperature of the ovens at Auschwitz. How many men died in the first moments after they blew the whistles at the Somme and went over the top? He knew. Ethnic cleansing and Serbian death camps? Tutsis and Hutus in Rwanda? He had all the details of those depravities at his fingertips. He knew how many blows from the knouter's whip it would take to kill a man sentenced to be punished in the czarist gulags of prerevolutionary Russia, and he knew how long it took for the guillotine's blade to fall, and he would have told you, with a little smile of his own, that Monsieur Guillotin, the device's inventor, absolutely and disingenuously assured the French authorities when first they considered employing his construction that the hellish machine's hapless victims would feel no more than 'a little tickle on the back of the neck.' He could tell you any of those things, and far more."

The old man coughed. "If you want to know your father, then you must know death."

Jeffrey made a small waving gesture with his hand, as if to clear some of the smell of memory from before him. "He frightened you?"

"Of course. He boasted to me once that history, if nothing else, showed how easy it was to kill."

"Did you tell this to the police?"

The history teacher shook his head. "Tell them what? That their suspect was seemingly intimate with the historical details of the lives and deaths of every greater and lesser killer in the modern world? And this proves what?"

"It was probably information they could have used."

"The girl was killed. A number of people here, your father amongst them, were questioned. But he was not alone. A couple of other teachers, a janitor, a food service employee, and the women's junior varsity lacrosse coach were also questioned. Just as the others, he was released without any charges, because there existed no evidence against him. Just suspicions. Shortly thereafter, he abruptly resigned. A few weeks later, the astonishing news of his death. Alleged death, as you say. But news nonetheless. A minor shock. A momentary surprise. A small curiosity, perhaps, because of the unusual timing. But few questions were raised and fewer answers produced. Instead, life went on. It always does, in schools such as these. Regardless of what happens in the world, the school goes on, just as before, just as it will."

Jeffrey thought there were similarities between the school and the state he was working for. Both believed that in their own fashion they could shut out the rest of the world. Both had the same problems maintaining that illusion.

"Do you recall, by any chance, what he said? When he resigned."

Old Mr. Maynard nodded, then leaned forward. "I had two meetings. They have remained with me, even over the decades. A historian must be like that, you know, Mr. Clayton. You must have a journalist's eye for details."

"And?"

"We met twice. The first time was shortly after the police inquiry. I ran into your father by accident in the local convenience store. We were both making some purchases. It's still there, right up the road outside the school. You know, cigarettes, newspapers, milk and soda, food that is in a state somewhere far beyond inedible . . ."

"Yes."

"He made some jokes. First about the state lottery, then about the police. He seemed to think it nothing. Did you know, Mr. Clayton, that your father possessed an easygoing, devil-may-care attitude? He used this offhand manner to conceal much about himself. Certainly, he managed to hide his sense of precision and exactitude. More like a scientist, I suppose. He would be amusing, diffident, yet underneath, calculating and cold. Are you like that, Mr. Clayton?"

Jeffrey did not reply.

"He was a most frightening man. There was a looseness, a lasciviousness, about him. Sharklike. I recall feeling quite chilled by the conversation we had that night. It was like speaking with a hungry fox at the door to the henhouse and being told there was nothing to worry about. Then, a week later, he suddenly appeared at my office. Most abrupt. With hardly a how do you do he announced he would be leaving the following week. No real explanation, other than to say he had inherited some funds. I asked about the police, but he simply laughed and said he didn't think they were much to be concerned about. I asked what he intended to do, and he said—and this I remember distinctly—he said there were people he needed to find. Those were his words. I remember them most clearly. *People he needed to find.* He had an eye like a hunter. I began to ask him for more details, but he turned on his heel and exited my office. When I went to check again with him, he had already left. Cleaned out his lockers and bookcases. I called his home, but the telephone had already been disconnected. Perhaps the next day, I drove around to his home, but it was empty and a FOR SALE sign adorned the front. He was, in a word, gone. I had barely time to assess this disappearance when we received word of his death."

"When was this?"

"Well, I recall we were most fortunate, because it was only a week before the Christmas break, and we only had to take over a few sections of his classes. We were interviewing replacements when we were informed of the auto accident. New Year's Eve. Drinking and high speed. Not, alas, all that uncommon. There was an unpleasant, freezing rain that night all over the eastern seaboard that prompted many accidents, your father's being one. At least, that is what we were led to believe."

"Do you happen to recall how you were told of the accident?"

"Ah, an excellent question. An attorney, perhaps? My memory is not as precise on that point as I might wish it to be."

Jeffrey nodded. This made some sense to him. He knew which attorney had made that call.

"And his funeral?"

"Odd, that. No one I knew was given even the slightest information of time, location, what have you, and therefore no one attended. You might go to the Trenton *Times* microfilm library and check."

"I will do that. Can you recall anything else that might assist me?"

The old historian smiled wryly. "But, my poor Mr. Clayton, I doubt I have told you anything that will assist you. Much that might disturb you. Some that might give you nightmares. Certainly a great deal that will trouble you today, and tomorrow, and probably far longer still. But help? No, I do not think knowledge like this helps anyone. Especially not a child. No, you'd have been far wiser and far more fortunate if you had never asked these questions. It is rare, but sometimes even that awful blank of not knowing is preferable to the truth."

"You may be correct," Jeffrey replied coldly, "but I did not have that option."

Jeffrey smelled the thick odor of smoke, but couldn't tell where it was coming from. The midday sky was a muddy gray-brown canopy of haze and smog, and whatever was burning merely added to the dreariness of the world.

He stopped a few blocks shy of the house where he'd spent his first nine years, on the main street of the small town renowned for a single crime so many years earlier. As an undergraduate, he'd once spent some time in a university library, searching through the dozens of books about the kidnapping, seeking pictures of his hometown in that earlier era. Decades ago it had been an insistently quiet place, a rural area dedicated to farms and privacy, a microcosm of the benign, traditional world of small-town America, which was probably what had attracted the world-famous aviator to Hopewell in the first place. It was a place that afforded him an illusory state of sanctuary, while at the same time did not remove him from the political mainstream that he'd immersed himself in. The aviator was an unusual man, who seemed both disturbed and attracted to the limelight of attention that his transatlantic feat had delivered to him. Of course, the subsequent notoriety of the kidnapping had changed all that. Changed it abruptly, by the invading press that covered the case, and the wild circus trial of the accused man, held right up the road in Flemington; changed it more subtly in the years that followed by giving Hopewell an odd reputation based on a single act of evil. It was like an insoluble dye in the water, something the town could never rid itself of, no matter how idyllic a place it was. And, over the years, the character of the town had changed as well. The farmers sold their lands to developers, who subdivided and put up luxury housing to accommodate the business people of Philadelphia and New York who thought they could escape the city life by moving away—but not far. The town suffered from its proximity to both cities. There are few things in the world, Jeffrey thought, more potentially devastating to the land than being convenient.

His own home had been older, a remodeled relic dating back to the time of the kidnapping, although it was located on a side street near the center of the town, and the aviator's estate was actually several miles into the countryside. He remembered his home to be large, spacious, filled with dark corners and surprising shafts of light. He had occupied a front bedroom on the second floor, which had a mildly Victorian half-circular shape. He tried to recall the room, and what he remembered was his bed, and a bookcase, and the fossil of some ancient prehistoric crustacean that he'd found along a nearby riverbed, and which, in their hurry to leave, he hadn't packed and for years had regretted leaving behind. The rock had a coolness to its touch that fascinated him. He'd liked to run his fingers over the shape of the fossil, almost expecting it to come alive beneath his hand.

He started the car up now, telling himself he wasn't there to do anything except acquire information. This trip to the house they'd fled was nothing more than a stab in the dark.

He drove down his street, fighting memories all the way.

When he pulled to a stop, and before he looked up, he reminded himself: *You didn't do anything wrong*—which he thought was an odd message. Then he turned to the house.

Twenty-five years is an awkward filter. So is the distinction between being nine and thirty-four. The house seemed smaller to him, and despite the weak sunlight battling against the gray sky, it appeared lighter. Clearer than he expected. It had been painted. Where he remembered a slate-gray shade on the clapboard siding, with black shutters on the windows, now it was white, trimmed in dark green. He remembered a large oak tree that once stood in the yard, throwing shade over the front of the house, but it was gone.

He stepped from the car and saw a man, hunched over, tending to some shrubbery by the front steps, a rake in his hands. Not far away from him was a FOR SALE sign. The man turned his head at the sound of Jeffrey's door closing, and he reached for something, which the professor assumed was a weapon, but nothing was presented. He approached the man slowly.

The man looked to be in his mid-forties, thickset, with extra weight around his midsection. He wore jeans that were creased and pressed, and an old-fashioned pilot's jacket with a fur collar.

"Can I help you?" he asked as the professor approached.

"Probably not," Jeffrey replied. "I just lived here briefly, when I was a child, and happened to be passing through, and thought I'd take a look at the old place."

The man nodded, reassured that he wasn't being threatened. "Want to buy it? Give you a good deal."

Jeffrey shook his head.

"You lived here? When?"

"Maybe twenty-five years ago. How about yourself?"

"Nah, not that long. We bought it three years ago from a couple that had been in it only two, maybe three years. They got it from some other folks that were just passing through. Place has had a lot of owners."

"Really. Why do you suppose?"

The man shrugged. "I don't know. Bad luck, I guess."

Jeffrey looked quizzically at him.

The man shrugged again. "Truth is, no one I ever knew had any luck here. Me, I just got transferred. To fucking Omaha. Jesus. Got to uproot the kids and the wife and the fucking dog and cat and move to God know's what out there."

"Sorry."

"Guy before me, he got cancer. Before that, family had a kid that got hit by a car, right down the street. Heard that someone seemed to remember a murder that had taken place in the house, but hey, no one knew anything, and I even looked it up in the old papers, but couldn't find nothing. House was just bad luck. At least I didn't get my ass fired. Now that would've been some real bad luck."

Jeffrey looked closely at the man. "A murder?"

"Or something. Who knows? Like I said, nobody ever knew nothing. You wanta look around?"

"Maybe for a minute."

"Place has probably been redone maybe three, four times since you were here."

"That's probably true."

The man led Jeffrey up through the front doors, into a small hallway, and then on a quick parade through the downstairs, into the kitchen, a family room that had been added on, the living room and a small room that Jeffrey remembered as his father's study, now filled with a stereo and a wall-sized television set. He found his mind working quickly, mathematically, figuring an equation that had rested deep within him. It all seemed cleaner than he remembered. Lighter.

"My wife," the man said, "she's the one with the taste for modern art and pastels on the walls. Which was your room?"

"Upstairs, to the right. Circular wall."

"Yeah. My home office. I put in a buncha built-in bookshelves and my computer. You want to see?"

Jeffrey had a sudden memory, of hiding in his room, head on his pillow. He shook his head.

"No," he said. "That's all right. It's not that important."

"Suit yourself," the homeowner said. "Hell, I keep giving tours to real estate agents and their clients, getting pretty good at the selling spiel." The man smiled and started to walk Jeffrey back to the entrance. "Hell, must be sorta weird for you, after all these years, it looking so different and all."

"A little strange. It seems smaller than I remember."

"That stands to reason. You were smaller then."

Jeffrey nodded.

"Why, my guess is, the only room that's the same is the basement room. Nobody's ever figured that one out."

"I'm sorry?"

"That funny little room just past the boiler in the basement. Hell, I'll bet half the folks that owned this place never knew about it. We only learned 'cause we had a termite guy in, and he noticed it when he was banging on the walls. Can't hardly see the door. In fact, there wasn't any damn door when he found it. Place had been sealed up with Sheetrock and plaster. But when the bug guy gave it a whack, it sounded all hollow, and he and I, we got curious and opened it up."

Jeffrey stopped. "Like a hidden room?" he asked.

The man spread his hands wide. "I dunno. Maybe once. Like a concealed hiding-type place? Been a long time. You wanta see?"

Jeffrey nodded.

"Okay. Not too clean down there. That okay?"

"Just show me, please."

There was a small door behind the stairs, which Jeffrey remembered led to the basement. He didn't remember spending much time down there. Dusty, dark, forbidding to a nine-year-old. He paused at the top of the stairs as the homeowner banged his way down. Something else, he recalled. Another reason? A dead-bolt lock on the door. A wayward memory struck him: faint strains of violin music, concealed. Hidden, like the room.

"Is this the only way down?" he asked.

"No, there's an outside entrance, too, by the side. A door and a shaft, the old-fashioned way people'd get down to a coal bin. Of course, that's long gone."

The man flipped a light switch and Jeffrey saw piled boxes and an old rocking horse. "Can't use this for much more than storing shit," the man said.

"Where's the door?"

"Over there. Behind the oil burner, of all places."

Jeffrey had to squirm past the burner, which flicked on with a thumping sound as he squeezed past. The door the man referred to was a sheet of pressed wood covering a small square hole in the wall that rose up from the floor to Jeffrey's eye level.

"I put that piece of crap wood there," the man said. "Like I said, used to be Sheetrock, same as the wall. Couldn't hardly tell it was there. Been sealed up for years. Might have once been a coal storage room that got refinished. Lotsa old houses have those. They got closed up, same as the coal mines."

Jeffrey pushed the board aside and bent down. The homeowner leaned forward and handed him a flashlight that had been left on a nearby circuit breaker box. There were cobwebs covering the entrance, and the professor swept them aside, then bent over slightly and entered the room.

It was approximately six by nine feet, with an eight-foot ceiling that was covered with a double-thick piece of soundproofing. There was a single, empty light socket in the center of the ceiling. No windows. It smelled musty and tomblike. The air was like the inside of a crypt. The walls were painted with a bulky coating of vibrant glossy white, which reflected the beam as it passed. The floor was gray cement.

It was empty.

"See what I mean?" the homeowner said. "Like what the hell good is this place? Not even for storage. Too damn hard to get in and out of. Maybe a wine cellar once? Could have been. Sure gets cold enough. But I don't know. Somebody used it for something once upon some time. You got any recollection? Hell, it reminds me of a cell at Alcatraz, except even there I bet you got a window to look out of."

Jeffrey slowly moved the flashlight around the walls. Three were empty. One had a pair of small, three-inch diameter metal rings fixed at either edge.

He trained the light on the rings.

"Do you have any idea what these rings might be for?" he asked the homeowner. "Do you know who installed them?"

"Yeah, I saw those when me and the termite guy first came in here. Not a clue, friend. You got any suggestions?"

He did, but he did not speak any of them out loud. Indeed, he knew precisely what they were used for. If someone were hung from the rings, they would hang suspended over the white wall like a snow angel. He walked closer and ran his finger over the smooth white paint next to the rings. He wondered whether he would find that there were cuts and grooves in the wallboard filled with spackle, then painted over. The sorts of marks that fingernails might make in panic and desperation. He didn't think the paint would successfully survive a quality examination by a forensic scientist; there would undoubtedly be microscopic particles of a victim left behind. But twenty-five years earlier, Agent Martin hadn't come up with enough evidence for even the most sympathetic of judges to issue a search warrant. Decades later, the termite man discovered the room while looking for an infestation, not realizing he'd found one of a totally different dimension. Jeffrey didn't know whether the New Jersey State Police would have been nearly as clever. He doubted it. He doubted they'd had any idea what they were looking for.

Jeffrey bent down and ran his finger over the cold cement floor. The light didn't reveal any staining. No telltale blotch of faded maroon. How did he get around that? There should have been blood and all the other matters of death all over the place. Jeffrey answered his own question: plastic sheeting. Available in any hardware store. Easily disposed of in any landfill. He sniffed hard, searching for the telltale odor of cleaning solvents, but none had lasted over the decades.

He slowly turned around, taking in the tiny room. Not much here, he thought. Then he realized that was to be expected.

As he knelt there he remembered his father's voice, telling him after some quiet, tension-filled evening at the dinner table to remove his plate and utensils to the sink, rinse them, and place them in the dishwasher. *Always clean up after yourself.* The sort of admonition that all parents direct toward their children.

For his father, though, it was a message that meant far more.

The professor stood up. From what he'd seen, he could not guess whether the tiny room had seen one horror or a hundred. He suspected the first, but would not rule out the second.

He had a sudden idea, and knew the name of a man—besides his father—who might be able to answer that question for him.

As he was about to leave the killing room, Jeffrey felt an abrupt chill, as if he were on the verge of being feverish, a twinge in his stomach, almost a suggestion of nausea to come. He realized he had learned much in a very small space, and he hated himself in that moment with a great and undefinable loathing, for being able to understand every bit of it.

The library at the Trenton *Times* bore little resemblance to the modern, computerized office at the *New Washington Post*. It was located in a cramped, desultory side room, not too far from a cavernous, low-ceilinged space filled with old, steel desks and unsteady typing chairs, which housed the news staff at the paper. A distant wall was devoted to windows, but they were covered with a thick coating of gray grime and dirt, and gave the room the sensation of being perpetually at dusk. The library was occupied by rows of metal filing cabinets, a pair of no-longer-modern computers, and a microfilm machine. A young clerk, his cheeks pockmarked from a difficult bout with teenage acne, wordlessly cued up the antique microfilm for Jeffrey.

He read through the paper's coverage of the murder of the young woman at St. Thomas More Academy, and it was exactly what he'd expected: lurid details about the discovery of the body in the woods, but not quite the level of detail the police forensic teams had acquired. There were obligatory quotes from policemen, including one from a young Detective Martin, about interrogating a number of suspects and following up a number of promising leads, which was police shorthand to cover up how stymied they were. His father's name was never mentioned. There was a flimsy profile of the victim, which contained yearbook-type material and the utterly predictable observations of her school classmates that she was a quiet, not well-known girl who seemed friendly enough and didn't have an enemy in the world—as if, Jeffrey thought, the man who sought her was filled with a specific hatred, when the truth was far more general.

He then tried to find a news story about the auto accident. Jeffrey thought the Trenton *Times* a hybrid sort of newspaper: just big enough to make a serious stab at covering some of the ways of the world, certainly important enough to focus on the state's business being concocted a block away in the capitol offices, but not so big that it would ignore an auto accident that claimed a local life, especially if the spectacular aspect of a fire were added to it.

He searched the news pages diligently, unable to find a word. Finally, on the obituary pages three days after the New Year, he found a single, small entry:

Jeffrey Mitchell, 37, a former history teacher at St. Thomas More Academy in Lawrenceville, passed away suddenly on January 1.

Mr. Mitchell was driving a vehicle that crashed in Havre de Grace,
Maryland, killing him instantly, according to police there. Funeral
arrangements are private at the O'Malley Brothers Funeral Home, in
Aberdeen, Maryland.

He read through the obit several times. He had absolutely no idea what
his father was doing on a New Year's night in a small, rural Maryland town.
Havre de Grace. Harbor of Safety. This made him pause. He tried to think
like an overburdened editor, half of whose staff wanted to spend the holidays with their families. Ordinarily, one might expect an editor to see the
obit and think there might be some story there. But would he be willing to
spend manpower to head a hundred miles south on the mere possibility?
Maybe not. Maybe it would just slide.

Jeffrey flipped through the successive issues of the paper, searching
for a follow-up, but could find none. He pushed back in his seat, letting
the machine idle and hum in front of him. He was discouraged, thinking
he would probably have to visit Maryland in search of a funeral home
that likely had long since disappeared, trying to find a police report that
probably had also been absorbed by the years. *Harbor of Safety.* He doubted
the town had a newspaper of its own, which might help him with information. Aberdeen was larger, and probably did, but how much help, he couldn't
begin to guess. He ran his tongue over his lips and thought about the person
located a few blocks away, in his well-appointed legal offices, who could
answer his questions.

He was about to close down the machine when he glanced one last time
at the page on the screen in front of him. There was a small story in the
lower right-hand corner of the State page that caught his attention. The headline read: LOTTO JACKPOT CLAIMED BY ATTORNEY.

He twisted the dial on the focus knob to bring the story into sharper contrast and read the precious few paragraphs:

The anonymous winner of the state's third largest ever Lotto jackpot
has surfaced, sending Trenton attorney H. Kenneth Smith to Lotto
headquarters to collect her $32.4 million award.

Smith presented officials with a signed and notarized winning
ticket—the first winner in the six-week string of contests that built up
the prize—and told reporters that the winner was eager to remain
anonymous. Lotto officials are precluded by law from releasing information about a jackpot winner without the individual's permission.

The lucky winner's prize will be an annual check for the next
twenty years totaling over $1.3 million, after state and federal taxes.

Attorney Smith declined comment on the winner, except to say that she was a young person who treasured her privacy, and that she was afraid of being besieged by unscrupulous suitors and con artists.

Lotto officials estimated next week's award at slightly more than two million dollars.

Jeffrey leaned over in his chair, bending his head toward the microfilm screen, thinking, There it is. He smiled as he considered what an easy lie it must have been for the lawyer to use the feminine pronoun when refusing to identify the prizewinner. A small, harmless deception that gave a false credibility to much. What other lies were there? The out-of-town auto accident. A funeral home that probably never existed. Jeffrey was certain he could find some truths in the melee of fictions, but that the totality was simple: to create an exit to the life of Jeffrey Mitchell, and to provide an entry to the life of someone not different, but equipped with a new name and identity, and more than enough funds to support an old and evil desire in any fashion he might want. Jeffrey remembered what the history teacher had told him. *He said he inherited some money. . . .* This was an inheritance of a different sort.

Jeffrey did not know how many people had died at his father's hands, but it struck him as ironic that every death had been fully subsidized by the state of New Jersey.

The murderer's son laughed out loud at this thought, which made the pockmarked clerk look over in his direction. The clerk said, "Hey!" as Jeffrey stood up and walked out of the library, leaving the machine running. He thought he would try yet another conversation with the lawyer, only this time, he suspected, it might be wise to be more forceful.

There were a few neglected elm trees on the street where the attorney's office was located, and darkness was beginning to fill their bare branches. A yellow sodium-vapor street lamp buzzed briefly as its timing system turned it on, insinuating diffuse light into a circle in the middle of the block. The row of brownstone houses converted into offices began to darken as knots of office workers emerged. On more than one occasion Jeffrey watched security personnel march their charges down the street, automatic weapons held cross-arms. It was not unlike watching some sheep dog guarding the flock.

He sat in his rented car, fingering the trigger guard on the nine-millimeter pistol. He didn't think he'd have to wait long for the attorney to emerge. He hoped the man, in his arrogance, would exit alone, but did not place too much trust in this possibility. H. Kenneth Smith, Esq., had not managed to succeed to the degree he appeared to have risen without being cautious.

Anticipation and fear arose in Jeffrey as he realized that the step he was taking would bring him to some point closer to his father.

It had not taken him long to guess the attorney's evening routine. A quick walking tour of the neighborhood between the capitol and the office an hour earlier had produced a single parking lot mainly filled with late-model luxury cars and a large sign proclaiming: MONTHLY ACCOUNTS ONLY. NO DAILY RATES. The lot did not have a guard; instead, it was secured by a twelve-foot-high, chain-link fence topped with razor wire. Entry to and exit from the lot was controlled by a single-lane sliding gate operated by a remote electronic eye. There was a narrow doorway cut into the fence as well. This was opened by an infrared key; point, click, and the door lock would buzz open.

Jeffrey had little doubt that the lawyer kept his vehicle in the lot. The trick was to intercept the man where he would be vulnerable, and that was a difficult place to identify. The husky security guard was likely to include in his duties seeing his employer safely behind the wheel. Jeffrey thought the guard would very likely not hesitate to shoot anyone who seemed a threat—especially in the distance between the office and the lot. Once inside the parking area, they were protected by the fence and beyond his reach. Jeffrey pulled back the action on the pistol, chambering a round, and decided he'd have to make his move on the street, just before the lawyer reached the lot. At that point they would be concentrating on what lay ahead of them, and perhaps unaware of someone moving swiftly from behind. He recognized that this was not a good plan, but it was the only one he could come up with on short notice.

If it came to it, he would treat the security man the same way Agent Martin would have: as an expendable obstacle in the path of the information he wanted. He was not completely sure he could actually shoot the man, but he needed the lawyer's cooperation, and he believed that cooperation would have a price.

Other than making an intellectual commitment to using his weapon—a commitment, he recognized, that was far different from actually pulling a trigger—he had no plan other than surprise. This bothered him, adding to the unsettling blend of excitement and anger mingling within him.

He shook his head and began to hum tunelessly and nervously as he watched the front door to the lawyer's office.

Dusk closed around the car, and the first of the evening's distant police sirens had swept past, barely a block away, when he saw the security guard step through the sally port and cast a wary eye up and down the street. As soon as the man turned away, Jeffrey stepped out of his car and backed into the shadows collecting on the edge of the walkway. As he watched, his position concealed by parked cars, a tree, and darkness, the pistol in his right hand held tightly by his leg, he saw the attorney, the bodyguard, and the secretary emerge from the building. The night was chilly, and the three of them, hunched inside their overcoats, walked quickly against the wind, which was picking up and swirling paper debris about the sidewalk. Jeffrey said a small thank-you to the cold; it made them less attentive to what was happening behind them, and kept their focus on where they were heading.

He was right about the parking lot. The trio quick-marched through the darkening evening, unaware of his parallel trip on the opposite sidewalk. He tried to move patiently, allowing them enough distance so he wouldn't be the first thing they saw if they made a sudden turn. He picked up his pace slightly, thinking that perhaps he'd left too much distance. He had the fleeting thought that Agent Martin would probably have known precisely how far away to remain—just distant enough not to be noticed, just close enough so that at the critical moment he could close quickly and efficiently.

He thought that his father, too, probably would have known the correct technique.

As the lawyer and his small entourage approached the lot, Jeffrey spotted their destination; the last three vehicles in the lot, parked together in a row. The first was a four-wheel-drive truck, with fat tires and a highly polished chrome rollover bar that glistened in the lot's spotlights. Next to that was a more modest sedan, and in the final space, a large, black, European luxury car.

Jeffrey cut across the street behind them, along the edge of the shadow thrown by a streetlight. He'd thumbed back the hammer of the pistol and clicked off the safety mechanism. He could hear his own breathing coming in short, raspy gasps and see bursts of vapor like smoke coming from his mouth. He gripped his weapon tightly and could feel the muscles in his body taut with a combination of excitement and fear he might have found delicious were his focus not so intent on the three people a half block ahead. He picked up his pace again to close the distance.

The voice to his side took him by surprise. "Hey, man. What's the rush?"

Jeffrey pivoted, almost stumbling. In the same motion, he raised the pistol into a firing position.

"Who are you?" he blurted at a shape blending into a shadow.

There was hesitation, then a reply: "I'm nobody, man. Nobody."

"What do you want?"

"Nothing, man."

"Step out where I can see you."

A black man, wearing dark slacks and a black leather jacket that seemed to cloak him like a second skin, stepped from a space hidden from the street-lights. He held his hands wide. "Meant no harm," the man said.

"Like hell," Jeffrey replied, training his weapon on the man's chest. "Where's your gun? Or knife? What were you going to use?"

The man stepped away from him. "Don't know what you're talking about, man." But he grinned, as if appreciating the lie. Jeffrey locked his eyes onto the man's as he continued to keep his hands up but increased the distance between them, sliding down the street. "This be your lucky night, boss," the man said with a small lilt, like the emphasis on the punch line of a joke. "Not gonna get taken down tonight. Best watch your step tomorrow and the next day, boss. But tonight, you be lucky man. Gonna get to live to see the morning." The man laughed, slowly reached into the pocket of the leather coat, and removed a large switchblade knife that flashed as it flicked open. He smiled again, carved a slice from the night air with a single slashing motion, then rapidly turned and walked away with the air of some-one who knows that an opportunity has been lost but that the world is filled with second chances.

Jeffrey kept the pistol aimed at his back, but noticed a quiver in his own hand. He recalled that he'd hesitated, and so indeed was lucky, because hesi-tation could mean death. He breathed out slowly, and when he saw that the man had been swallowed by the night gloom, turned back toward the lawyer, the secretary, and the security guard.

He could no longer see them, and raced forward, cursing the seconds that had been lost. He was perhaps thirty yards away from the parking lot when he suddenly saw the headlights of the three vehicles all switch on, almost in unison.

He slowed, drifting into a shadow but still walking forward. Lowering his weapon, he breathed out slowly, calming his heart. He hunched his shoulders up and dropped his chin to his chest. He did not want to be recog-nized, nor draw attention to himself by hiding. He decided to keep walking past the lot, and reassured himself that he would have another opportunity in the morning—like the mugger who'd cost him precious seconds.

As he watched, the security guard's truck throttled forward, engine rum-bling. It hesitated as it bumped the electronic eye that swung the gate open. The truck moved forward, paused on the lip of the sidewalk, then acceler-ated, tires squealing into the street. Jeffrey expected the other two vehicles to follow in short order, but they did not.

Abruptly, the lights in the secretary's car went out. A moment later she stepped from the vehicle. Her eyes traveled up and down the street then, searching, before she swiftly moved to the passenger side of the lawyer's car. The door opened and she dipped in.

In the same instant, Jeffrey, spurred by an urge he'd never trusted before, jumped past the sliding gate, into the lot. He pressed himself back against a redbrick building wall, unsure whether he'd been seen.

He let out his breath in a slow whistle.

He could see only the meager outlines of the two figures in the lawyer's car, wrapped together in a long embrace.

Seeing his chance, he sprinted ahead, his runner's muscles responding to the sudden need for speed. He closed the yards rapidly, arms pumping, and made it to the side of the car before the lawyer and the secretary had disengaged. There was a microsecond when they became aware of his presence, pulling apart in shock, and then he took the butt end of the pistol and smashed it against the driver's window, shattering glass about the two lovers.

The woman screamed and the lawyer shouted out something incomprehensible, reaching, in the same moment, for the gear shift.

"Don't touch that," Jeffrey said.

The lawyer's hand hovered over the gear knob, then stopped. His voice was high-pitched, shaky with surprise. "What do you want?" he asked. The secretary had shrunk back, away from the barrel of Jeffrey's pistol, as if each inch she retreated might prove critical to her survival. "What do you want?" the attorney asked again, a plea, not a demand.

"What I want?" Jeffrey replied slowly. "What I want?" He could feel adrenaline coursing through his ears. The fear he saw on the attorney's once arrogant face, the prim secretary's panic, were intoxicating. He thought, in that second, that he was more in control of his life than ever before. "What I want is what you could have given me with considerably less trouble, and far more politely, earlier today," he said coldly.

As he had partially suspected, there was a second, concealed alarm system installed in the woodworking of the entrance to the lawyer's office. He could feel the wire sensor just beneath a small ridge of paint. It would be a silent alarm, Jeffrey recognized, connected either to the Trenton police or, if they were not reliable, some security service.

He turned toward the secretary and the lawyer. "Disconnect it," he demanded.

"I'm not sure how," the secretary answered.

Jeffrey shook his head. He turned and looked idly at the pistol in his hand, as if checking to see if it were a mirage. "Are you crazy?" he asked. "Don't you think I'll use this?"

"No," the lawyer replied. "You seem like a reasonable man, Mr. Clayton. You work for a government agency. They would probably frown on the use of a weapon as the basis for a search warrant."

The attorney and the secretary were standing with their hands clasped behind their heads. The professor saw a quick glance between the two of them. The initial shock of his approach had worn off. They were recovering their equanimity, and along with it, a sense of control. Jeffrey thought for a moment.

"Remove your clothes, please," he said.

"What?"

"Just what I said. Remove your clothes, now."

For emphasis, he sighted the pistol at the secretary.

"Under no circumstances will—"

Jeffrey held up his hand to silence the man. "Hell, Mr. Smith, it's more or less what you were intending to do when I so inconveniently interrupted you. We're just altering the circumstances and the locale, perhaps. And maybe disrupting some of the pleasure involved."

"I won't."

"You will, and so will she, or for starters I will blow a hole in your secretary's foot. It will cripple her and be incredibly painful. But it won't kill her."

"You won't do it."

"Ah, a doubter." He stepped forward. "I hate to have my sincerity questioned." He aimed the weapon, then stopped, and looked up into the secretary's frightened eyes. "Or perhaps you would prefer I do *his* foot? It really makes little difference to me. . . ."

"Do his," she said swiftly.

"I could do both?"

"No, his."

"Wait a second!" The attorney looked wildly at the barrel of the gun. "All right," he said. He began to loosen his tie. After a moment's hesitation, the secretary started to undo her shirt. Both paused when they reached their underwear.

"This should be sufficient," the lawyer said. "If you truly just need information, then we shouldn't be forced to lose our dignity."

"Dignity? You're concerned about losing your dignity? You must be joking. Completely," Jeffrey replied. "Being naked, I think, creates an interesting vulnerability, no? One is far less likely to produce obstacles when one has no clothes on. Or take chances. This is fairly rudimentary psychology, Mr. Smith. And I have already told you who my father is, so I would suspect that you would understand that even if I only know half of what he does about the psychology of dominance, it's still a considerable amount."

Jeffrey paused while the attorney and the secretary dropped the remainder of their clothes to the floor.

"Good," he said. "Now, how do I disarm the alarm?"

The secretary had inadvertently dropped one hand to cover her crotch, while keeping the other behind her head. "There's a switch behind the painting on the wall," she said grimly, glaring first at Jeffrey, then at her lover.

"Progress," Jeffrey said with a grin.

It took the secretary only a few minutes to find the right file from a hand-carved oaken cabinet in a corner of the lawyer's office. She carried it across the room, her feet padding against the soft carpet, tossed it on the desk in front of the lawyer, and removed herself to a chair against the wall, where she did her best to scrunch herself into a ball, trying to conceal her nakedness. The attorney reached for the file, his skin making a squeaking sound against the leather of his armchair. He seemed less uncomfortable than the young woman, as if he was resigned to nakedness. He flipped open the file, and Jeffrey could see, to his disappointment, that it was extremely thin.

"I did not know him well," Smith said. "We met only once or twice. After that, perhaps a phone call or two over the years, but that was it. Nothing in the last five years. But that's understandable. . . ."

"Why?"

"Because five years ago the state stopped paying off the lottery debt. He had exhausted his winnings. Well, not exactly exhausted. I have no knowledge of how he invested his money. But wisely, I would suspect. Your father struck me as a very careful, very composed man. He had a plan and he carried it out to exacting detail."

"The plan?"

"I collected the winnings. I then took the money, minus my fee, of course, put it through my client's account—which is covered by the attorney-client privilege from any prying eyes—then shipped it to a series of offshore Caribbean banks. What happened to it then, I don't know. Probably, as in most ordinary laundering schemes, after paying an extremely modest transaction fee, it was reshipped to another account belonging to some fictitious individual or corporation. Eventually, it landed back in the U.S., but by that time its connection to the original source would be thoroughly obscured. All I did was start the ball rolling. Where it stopped, I cannot tell you."

"You were well paid for this?"

"When you're young, without much in the way of resources, and a man tells you that he'll pay you a hundred thousand dollars each year merely for an hour's worth of banking transactions . . ." The attorney shrugged his bare shoulders. "Well, it was a good deal."

"There was something else, his death."

"His death was accomplished solely on paper."

"What do you mean?"

"There was no crash. There was, however, an accident report. There were insurance claims. There was a cremation purchased. Notices sent to newspapers, to his old school. As many items supporting a nonevent as could be obtained. Copies of those are in the file. But there was no death."

"And you did this for him?"

The attorney shrugged. "He said he intended to start over."

"Explain."

"He never came out and said outright that he intended to become someone different. And I was careful never to ask, although any damn fool could see that's what was going on. You know, I did a little bit of background checking, and he had no local police record, and certainly no national entry in any computer. At least, none that I could discern. So, tell me, Mr. Clayton, what was I to do? Turn down the money? A man with seemingly no reason for it, a man respected at his profession, without any obvious criminal or social needs for it, wants to depart from one life and create a new one, somewhere else. Somewhere different. And he's willing to pay fabulously well for this privilege. Who am I to stand in the way?"

"Did you not ask him?"

"In my brief meeting with your father, I came away with the distinct impression that it was not my responsibility to question him as to his motives. When he mentioned an ex-wife, and left the letter for her, I raised the issue, but he bristled and requested I merely do what I was being paid for, a quality that I am most comfortable with."

The attorney gestured around the room. "The money from your father helped create all this. It was what got me started. I am in his debt."

"Can I trace who he became?"

"Impossible." The lawyer shook his head.

"Why?"

"Because the money wasn't dirty! He established a laundering system for *clean* funds! Because what he was trying to protect wasn't the money, it was himself! See the distinction?"

"But surely the IRS—"

"I paid the taxes. State and federal. There was nothing to pursue from their point of view. Not from this end. How it ended up, and how the money was used somewhere far from here, for what purpose, to achieve what end, this I cannot even speculate on. In fact, the last time I actually heard from your father was twenty years ago. Outside of what I've already described, that was the only occasion he requested something of me."

"What was that?"

"He asked me to travel to West Virginia, to the state prison there. I was to represent an individual in a parole hearing. This I did, successfully."

"This person? Did they have a name?"

"Elizabeth Wilson. But she won't be able to help you."

"Why not?"

"Because she's dead."

"How?"

"Six months after her release, in the little backwoods town she lived in, she got drunk in a bar and let herself get picked up by some degenerates. They found some of her clothes out in the woods. Streaked with blood. Panties, I believe. I don't know why your father wanted to help her, but whatever reason he might have had, it came to nothing."

The lawyer seemed to have forgotten his nakedness. He stood up and walked around the desk, jabbing his finger in the air for emphasis.

"I envied him sometimes," Smith said. "He was the only truly free man I have ever known. He could do anything. Build anything. Be anyone. I sometimes thought the world was his for the asking."

"Do you have any idea what that world consisted of?"

The attorney stopped, standing in the center of the room. "No," he said.

"Nightmares," Jeffrey replied.

The lawyer hesitated. He glanced down at the pistol in Jeffrey's hand.

"And," he asked slowly, "like father, like son?"

THE FIRST
UNLOCKED DOOR

Diana and Susan Clayton descended the airline walkway carrying their hand luggage, a significant number of medications, some weapons that they were surprised to have been given clearance to bring, and an undetermined amount of anxiety. Diana looked around at the flow of well-dressed business travelers, confused momentarily by the high-tech, glistening lights of the airport, and realized this was her first trip outside the state of Florida in more than two dozen years. She had never gone to visit her son at his home in Massachusetts—had never actually been invited. And because she'd so effectively exiled herself from the rest of her family, there had been no one else to visit.

Susan, too, was an inexperienced traveler. Her excuse in recent years had been to not leave her mother alone. But the reality was that her own voyages took place either in the intellectual satisfaction of the games she created or in the solitude of her trips in her flats skiff. She thought of each fishing expedition as a unique adventure. Even when she traveled familiar waters, there was always something different and unusual each time. She thought much the same of the inventions of her alter ego, Mata Hari.

They boarded the flight in Miami filled with a sense that they were approaching the conclusion of a story that they had never been told included them, but that dominated their lives in an unspoken fashion. Susan Clayton, in particular, since learning that the man stalking her was her father, was gripped with the odd orphan's excitement that had supplanted much of her fears: *Now I will find out why I am who I am.*

But as the airline engines droned them closer to the unfamiliar new world of the Fifty-first State, the confidence that excitement brings had eroded, and by the time they circled and started their final turn for the airport just outside New Washington, they were both enmired in a silence riven with doubts.

Knowledge is a dangerous thing, Susan thought. Self-knowledge can be as hurtful as it is helpful.

Although they did not articulate these fears to each other, both were aware of the tension that had built within them. Diana especially, with a mother's inchoate anxiety about anything beyond her immediate understanding, felt that their lives were now unsteady, adrift on the edge of a storm with a stalled motor as they desperately turned an ignition key, listening to the grinding of the starter as winds mockingly picked up around them. She closed her eyes as the landing gear thumped down, wishing she could remember a single moment when Jeffrey and Susan were young and it had just been the three of them, poor but safe, hidden away in their small house in the Keys, from the nightmare they'd escaped. She wanted to think of an ordinary, routine, normal day, when nothing happened of any note. A day filled with nothing except the passing of hours, unnoticed and unspecial. But such a memory seemed elusive, and suddenly impossible to obtain.

As the two of them hesitated in the walkway, Agent Martin peeled himself off the opposite wall of the corridor, where he'd been leaning against a large sign that cheerily said: WELCOME TO THE BEST PLACE ON EARTH. Below the sign were arrows pointing toward IMMIGRATION, PASSPORT CONTROL, and SECURITY. He took the distance between them in three large strides, hid his frustration over doing what he considered to be a chauffeur's job with a wide and probably transparent smile, and greeted the mother and daughter.

"Hello," he said. "The professor sent me to get you."

Susan eyed him warily. She inspected his credentials for what the detective thought was a second or two too long.

"Where is Jeffrey?" Diana asked.

Agent Martin smiled, with a phoniness Susan spotted this time. "Well, actually, I was hoping you might be able to tell me. He would only tell me that he was going home."

"Then he went to New Jersey," Diana said. "I wonder what he was looking for."

"Are you sure you don't know?" Martin asked.

"That's where we were both born," Susan informed the detective. "It's where we got started. It's where a lot of things got started. What he went looking for is some sign on the trail that points to where these things are going to finish up. I'd think that observation would be pretty obvious, especially to a policeman."

Agent Martin frowned. "You're the one who invents games, right?"

"You've done some homework. Yes."

"This isn't a game."

Susan grinned humorlessly. "Of course it is," she said. "It's just not a very nice game," she added sardonically.

There was a moment of silence between them, as the detective didn't respond, and into that, Susan asked, "And now, you're going to take us somewhere?"

"Yes." He pointed at the business travelers dutifully lining up at immigration checkpoints. "I've made some arrangements and we can bypass all the usual paperwork. I'm going to take you someplace safe."

Susan laughed cynically. "Excellent. I've always wanted to see that place. If it exists."

The detective shrugged and picked up one of the bags Diana had dropped on the floor. He reached for Susan's as well, but she waved his offer away. "I carry my own things," she said. "Always have."

Agent Martin sighed, smiled, said with yet more false cheeriness, "Well, suit yourself," and decided that upon first impression, he did not much like Susan Clayton. He already knew he didn't like her brother, and he suspected he simply wouldn't have an opinion one way or the other about Diana Clayton, although he was curious about what sort of woman married a killer. A murderer's wife. A murderer's children. On the one hand, he had little use for all of them, but on the other, he knew they were crucial to what he needed to accomplish. He swept his arm forward, pointing in the direction of the exit, reminding himself that when all was said and done, he would not care one bit if the Clayton family all died in solving the problem plaguing the Fifty-first State.

Agent Martin gave the Claytons the quick version of the Cook's tour of New Washington. He showed them the state offices, but did not take them inside, especially to the space he was sharing with Jeffrey. He kept up a cheery travelogue as they drove through the city streets, down the office park boulevards. He swung them through some of the nearer housing developments, sticking to green areas, and finally ended up at a somewhat isolated row of town homes on the edge of some pricier suburbs and a fair distance from the downtown businesses.

The town homes—a design intended to mimic row houses in parts of San Francisco, with some baroque flourishes and flowery vines—were on a dead-end street on the edge of some rough foothills, a few miles from where mountains rose up in the west. There was a community swimming pool and a half-dozen tennis courts across the street, as well as a small playground area dotted with jungle gyms and swing sets designed for toddlers. Behind the town homes there were modest grassy plots—just enough space for a table, some chairs, a barbecue pit, and a hammock. A nine-foot-high solid wooden fence demarcated the rear of each plot. The fence was less for security than to prevent small children from tumbling down into a steep ravine that dropped away from the property lines. Beyond the ravine was a tract of undeveloped space, mostly scrub brush, weed, and gnarled sage trees.

The last of the houses was owned by the state.

Agent Martin swung his car into a small parking area. "This is it," he said. "You'll be comfortable here." He went around the back and grabbed the bags that belonged to Diana, leaving the trunk open for Susan. He began to walk up the short sidewalk to the house when he heard Susan ask:

"Don't you want to lock up?"

He turned, shook his head. "I told your brother the same thing. Don't *need* to lock your car here. Don't *need* to lock your front entrance. Don't *need* to put electronic homing devices on your kids. Don't *need* to set the alarm system every time you go in and out of the house. Not here. That's the whole point. That's the beauty of this place. You don't need to lock your doors."

Susan paused, letting her eyes sweep down the dead-end street, surveying the area cautiously.

"We do," she replied. Her words seemed out of place amidst the constant plunking sound of tennis balls coming from the courts and the removed but unmistakable noise of children at play.

It did not take long for the detective to show the two women around the house. There was a kitchen with a connected dining area that flowed into a small living room. Adjacent to that was an audiovisual room, with computer, stereo, and television. There were other computers in the kitchen area, and a third in one of the three upstairs bedrooms. The entire house had been furnished in an undistinguished style, a cut above a good hotel but a step below what a real family would invest in. Agent Martin explained that the town house was used by the state to accommodate business people who preferred not to stay in any of the hotels.

"You can get whatever you need through the computer," he told Susan. "Order your groceries. A movie. A pizza. Whatever. Don't worry about the cost, I'll put it all on one of the State Security accounts."

Martin flicked on one of the computers. "Here's your password," he said as he typed in 2BETA. "Now you can get whatever you want delivered directly to the front door." There was a cheeriness to his voice that masked a lie.

He stepped back, watching Susan to see if she noted the play on words, but her face remained impassive.

"All right," he said after a moment. "I'll be leaving you now to get settled. You can contact me directly through the computer. Your brother, too, when he returns, but I suspect he'll be in touch before that. At that point we can all get together and figure out the next step."

Agent Martin stepped back. Diana was standing beside the computer, and with a flourish pulled up a grocery store menu. The screen blinked: WEL-COME TO THE A&P! and an electronic shopping cart started to move down Aisle One/Fresh Vegetables and Fruits. Susan was continuing to eye Martin with some caution, and the detective thought: Don't trust that one.

"We'll be fine," Susan said.

As Martin exited he heard the unfamiliar sound of the door being dead-bolted behind him.

Susan walked through the town house as her mother used the computer to order some foodstuffs and arrange delivery with the local grocery service. She was pleased to hear her request some items they would ordinarily have considered indulgences; some Brie, imported beer, an expensive char-donnay, a shell steak. Susan surveyed the small house as a general would a piece of land where he might do battle. It was important to her to note just where she would fight, if she had to. Locate the high ground; identify where she might be able to spring an ambush.

Diana, meanwhile, noted what Susan was doing, and decided to prepare herself as well. As she completed her grocery order on the computer, she queried the delivery service for a description of the person who would be sent with the food items. She also asked for a description of the delivery vehicle. But as she disconnected the line, she was struck with a residual fatigue, left over from the flight and from the tension surrounding why they were there. So, instead, she sat down heavily and watched her daughter move slowly through the house.

Susan saw that the only locks on the downstairs windows were old-fashioned and probably ineffective. The front door had a single bolt, but no chain to back it up. There was no alarm system. The rear door was a sliding patio style, with only a latch-type lock that wasn't actually designed to prevent anything. She found a broom in a storage closet, propped it up against a wall, and then, with a swift kick, broke the handle away from the head. She wedged the handle between the slider's frame and the door, crudely but effectively locking it tight. Anyone entering in that fashion would be forced to break the glass.

The upstairs was probably secure, she thought. She hadn't spotted an easy way for anyone to reach the upstairs windows without a ladder. In the rear of the town house there was a small trellis, with flowers, that climbed to a balcony off the master bedroom, but she doubted it would support an adult's weight, and the rose vines entwined in the wooden framework had sharp thorns. She was a little wary of the adjoining homes; she thought it possible that someone might come across the roofline, but realized there was no precaution they could take against that. Fortunately, the pitch of the roof was steep, and she suspected anyone attempting to break in would first try the more obvious downstairs locations.

She unzipped her small duffel bag and removed three different weapons. There were two handguns—a short-barreled Colt .357 Magnum pistol loaded with wad cutters, which she thought a remarkably effective tool at close range, and a lightweight Ruger .380 semiautomatic pistol, which carried nine shots in the clip and a tenth in the chamber. She also had a fully automatic Uzi machine pistol, which she'd obtained illegally from a retired drug dealer in the Keys who liked to share fishing information with her and was never dismayed when she routinely turned down his requests for a date. The would-be suitor had given her the Uzi in much the same way others in an earlier era might have presented her with flowers, or a box of chocolates. She hung the machine pistol from its strap around a clothes hanger in the upstairs bedroom closet, covering it with a sweatshirt.

In the upstairs hallway there was a linen closet; she placed the automatic, cocked and ready to fire, between two towels on the middle shelf. The Magnum was concealed in the kitchen, behind a row of cookbooks. She showed her mother where the weapons were located.

"Did you notice," Diana said, in a small, whimsical tone, "that there weren't any armed guards around? At home it seems everywhere you go there are guards. Not here."

She didn't get a response.

The two women went to the living room and plopped down across from each other, the exhaustion of traveling and tension now coming over Susan, too. Diana Clayton, of course, felt the pain of her disease gnawing away within her. It had been quiet for a while, almost as if waiting to see what these strange developments meant to it. And now, abruptly, satisfied that this change of scenery was no threat, it took it upon itself to remind her of its presence. A streak of hurt ran through her stomach, and she gasped out loud.

Her daughter looked up. "Are you okay?"

"Yes. No problem," Diana lied.

"You should rest. Take a pill. Are you sure you're okay?"

"I'll be fine. But I will take a pill or two."

Susan slid from her chair and perched at her mother's knees, stroking the older woman's hand. "It hurts, doesn't it? What can I do?"

"We're doing what we can."

"Maybe we shouldn't have come?"

Diana laughed. "Where else should we be? Waiting at home for him now that he's found us? This is precisely where I want to be. Pain or no pain. Whatever happens. And anyway, Jeffrey said he needs us. We all need each other. And we need to see this thing to a conclusion. Whatever it is."

Diana shook her head.

"You know, dear, in some ways I've been waiting twenty-five years for this time to arrive. I wouldn't want to cheat myself now."

Susan hesitated. "You never talked about our father. I can't remember ever talking about him."

"Ah, but we did," her mother replied with a smile. "A thousand times. Everytime we talked about ourselves. Everytime we talked about each other. Whenever you had a problem or a hurt or even just a question, we were talking about your father. You just weren't aware of it."

Susan hesitated, then asked: "Why? I mean, what made you leave him, back then?"

Her mother shrugged. "I wish I could tell you. I wish there was some specific moment. But there wasn't. It was in the way he sounded, the way he spoke. The way he looked at me in the morning. The way he disappeared, and then I would find him at the sink, washing his hands obsessively. Or find him at the stove, boiling a hunting knife in a cooking pot. Was it the edge to his eyes? The harshness in his words? I once found some awful, violent pornography, and he screamed at me to never, ever, intrude on his things. Was it his smell? Can you smell evil? Did you know that the man who identified the Nazi Eichmann was blind—but remembered the death architect's cologne? In a way, it was the same for me. There was nothing, yet everything. Running away was the hardest and the easiest thing I've ever done, all at once."

"Why didn't he stop you?"

"I don't think he believed I would succeed. I don't think he truly imagined I would actually take you and your brother away. I think he believed we would turn around at the end of the block. Or maybe at the edge of town. Certainly before we reached the bank and I was able to get some money. He never imagined that I would keep driving and not ever look back. He was far too arrogant to think that I would do that."

"But you did."

"I did. The stakes were high."

"The stakes?"

"You and your brother."

Diana smiled wryly, as if this was the most obvious observation in the entire world, then reached into her pocket and removed a small vial of pills. She shook two into her hand and popped them into her mouth, swallowing hard, without water.

"I think I'll lie down for a while," she said. Making a conscious effort to walk without hesitation, to remove any stagger or limp the disease might be giving her, she crossed the room and headed up the stairs.

Susan stayed in her chair. She listened for the sound of the bathroom door and then the bedroom door closing. She leaned her head back then, closed her eyes, and tried to picture the man who was closing in on them.

Gray hair, instead of brown? She remembered a smile, a loose, mocking grin that frightened her. What did he do to us? Something. But what? She cursed the imprecision of her own memory because she knew something had happened but it was concealed by years of denial. She envisioned herself as a young girl, a tomboy with a ponytail, dirty fingernails, and wearing jeans, running through a big house. There was a study, she reminded herself. That's where he would be. In her mind's eye she was small, just a little bit older than a toddler, standing outside the door to the study. In this reverie, she tried to force the image of herself to open the door and stare at the man inside the room, but she could not bring herself to do it. She opened her eyes suddenly, gasping, as if she'd been holding her breath underwater. She gulped for air and felt her heart racing. She didn't move until it slowed.

Susan remained sitting like that for a few minutes, until the telephone rang. She rose quickly, crossed the room in a single stride, and grabbed the receiver.

"Susan?" It was her brother's voice.

"Jeffrey! Where are you?"

"I've been in New Jersey. I'm heading back. I just have one more person to see and he's in Texas. But that's only if he'll see me, which I'm not at all sure he will. Are you and Mom all right? Was the flight okay?"

Susan jabbed on the computer linkup, and Jeffrey's face jumped into focus on the screen. He had an air of enthusiasm around him, which she thought surprising.

"Flight was fine," she said. "I'm more interested in what you've found out."

"What I've found out is that I suspect it will be impossible to find our father through any conventional means. I'll explain in greater detail when I see you. But this leaves unconventional methods. Which is, I would guess, pretty much what the authorities there had figured when they first called me in. They may not have known it exactly, but that's the effect."

He paused, then asked: "So, what do you think of the future?"

Susan shrugged. "It's going to take some getting used to. This state is so squeaky clean and correct, you sort of wonder what would happen if you belched in a public place. Probably get a ticket. Or arrested. It kinda gives me the creeps. People like it?"

"Oh yes. You'd be surprised what people are willing to give up for something more than the illusion of safety. You'll also be surprised how quickly you can get used to it. Has Martin been helpful?"

"The Incredible Hulk? Where'd you find him?"

"Actually, he found me."

"Well, he showed us around, and then stuffed us in this house to wait for you. How'd he get those scars on his throat?"

"I don't know."

"Probably a story there."

"I'm not sure I want to ask him to tell it."

Susan laughed. Jeffrey thought it was the first time in years he'd heard his sister laugh.

"He does seem like some super-tough guy."

"He's dangerous, Susie. And don't trust him. He's probably the second most dangerous person we're going to have to deal with. No, correct that. The third. I'm going to go see the second before I return there."

"Who's that?"

"Someone who might help me. But he might not. I don't know."

"Jeffrey . . ." She hesitated. "I need to know something. What did you find out about . . ." She stopped once before continuing. ". . . our dad? That doesn't sound right. Our pop? Father dearest? Jesus, Jeffrey, how do we think of him?"

"Don't think of him as a person who shares blood. Just think of him as an entity that we are uniquely qualified to deal with."

Susan coughed. "That's a trick. But what did you find out?"

"I found out that he's educated, street-smart, extremely rich, and totally heartless. Most killers don't fit into any of those categories except for the last one. A few might fit two, which makes them pretty much immune from apprehension. I've never heard of a killer who fits three, much less all four."

This statement stopped Susan cold. She felt her throat go dry, and thought she should be asking something clever, or saying something profound, but she couldn't find any words. She was relieved when Jeffrey asked:

"How's Mom?"

Susan looked back over her shoulder, up the stairs toward where their mother was resting and hopefully sleeping.

"Holding up pretty good so far. In pain, but she seems less crippled, which is an odd contradiction. I think she's being made oddly stronger by all this. Jeffrey, do you know how sick she is?"

Now it was the brother's turn to fall silent. He thought of several responses, but came up only with: "Very."

"That's right. Very. Terminal."

They were both silent then, trying to absorb the word.

Jeffrey thought of his father's past as a tableau of wet cement that had been expertly smoothed over and set hard over the years. And he thought of his mother's past as a canvas, scorched with bright colors. And that, he concluded, was the difference between the two of them.

Susan was shaking her head. "But she wants to be here. In fact, like I said, she seems almost energized by all this. She was fairly spry all day, traveling."

Jeffrey paused, then was struck with an idea. "Do you think Mother could spend some time by herself?" he asked. "Not long. Just a long day."

Susan didn't answer right away. "What do you have in mind?"

"Maybe you'd like to accompany me on an interview. It'll give you a little better idea what we're up against. Also give you a little better idea what I do for a living."

Susan, intrigued, shot an eyebrow upward. "Sounds interesting. But I don't know about leaving Mother. . . ." Behind her she heard a noise, and she turned and saw her mother, standing at the base of the stairs, watching her and Jeffrey's image on the screen. But Diana answered the question for them both.

"Hello, Jeffrey," she said, smiling. "I thought I heard your voice and believed it was a dream, and then I realized it wasn't, so I came downstairs. I can hardly wait until the three of us are together again."

Diana turned to her daughter and thought of all the difficult words Susan and Jeffrey had shared in the past years, and found it almost amusing that they might have their relationship restored by the man they had so long ago fled. "Go," she said. "I'll be fine for a day. I'm just going to take it easy. Get some rest. Maybe take a walk. Perhaps I'll get someone to show me a little more of the state. And anyway, I think I like it here. It's very clean. And quiet. It reminds me a little bit of what it was like when I was a child."

This surprised Susan. "Really?" Then she nodded. "All right. If you're sure . . ." Her mother waved a hand dismissively. "What do I do?" she asked her brother.

"Go back to the airport in the morning and take the first flight to Dallas, Texas. Then take a commuter flight to Huntsville. They leave hourly. I'll meet you when you get there. The computer code that Agent Martin gave you should take care of all the flights and payment and anything else. Don't pack much. Especially no weapons."

"Okay. What's in Huntsville, Texas?"

"A man I once helped to arrest."

"He's in prison?"

"On Death Row."

"Well," she said after a small pause, "I guess his future is clear."

In his office at security headquarters, Agent Robert Martin replayed a tape of the telephone conversation just concluded between brother and sister. On his video monitor he inspected Jeffrey's face, searching for signs that the professor had acquired some information that would lead them to their quarry. Listening to the younger man speak with his sister, Martin concluded that Jeffrey had indeed gained some knowledge he needed. But he resisted the urge to seek it aggressively. What he needed to know would come to him, he thought, as long as he watched and listened carefully.

He terminated the tape of the conversation and cued up the computer to duplicate anything that was typed on the house computers by either mother or daughter. In a few minutes, as he suspected, he saw the airplane reservations being made. A few moments later he saw that a car service had scheduled an early morning pickup. There was also a tape recording of the conversations in the house, but he decided he didn't need to eavesdrop on that.

Martin rocked back in his seat. Incredible Hulk, he thought with irritation. He found himself fingering the scars on his neck.

They still hurt. They had always hurt.

A psychologist once explained phantom pain to him, describing how an amputee could still feel hurt from his missing leg. A physician suggested that the burning sensation he felt from his scars was in the same category. The injury was no longer physical, but mental. But the pain was the same. He'd thought it might disappear when the brother that had put them there—a pan of boiling bacon grease flung across a table at him at the end of an argument—had died, but that hadn't happened. His brother had been killed in a prison yard stabbing more than a decade earlier, and the scars still hurt. Over the years, he'd become resigned to the sensation and the pain and to the thought that he wore a memory on his skin that filled him with equal parts hatred and hurt.

He stared at the computer, envisioning Jeffrey Clayton's face.

You are almost right, Professor. I am the most dangerous man you'll ever meet, he thought to himself. Not second and not third, and certainly not someplace in a row behind your old man. But the top of the list. And the day is fast approaching when I'll prove that to you, and to your father as well.

Robert Martin smiled. The only difference between his own dead brother and himself was that he owned a badge. And that put his propensity for violence into a different realm altogether.

Martin pushed himself back from the computer. He took note of the time the car service was slated to arrive at the house, and thought he should be there to watch Susan Clayton's departure.

The screen wavered in front of him, like the filmy air above the highway on a hot day. He'd already typed in a single entry, authorizing the state to pay for all requests submitted by 2BETA.

He had underscored this by identifying 2BETA as Diana and Susan Clayton of Tavernier, Florida, on an internal memo. A copy of this memo had been shipped electronically to his bosses in Security as well as Immigration and Passport Control. This would allow the two women to travel freely in and out and throughout the Fifty-first State.

He smiled. The memo, of course, was precisely what Jeffrey had told him not to do.

Agent Martin did not know how long it would take for the man he was hunting to discover that his wife and daughter were living in a state-owned town house. He might already know, Martin thought, but he doubted that even a killer as proficient as Jeffrey's father would be that alert. Somewhere in the twenty-four to forty-eight hour range, he guessed. After he learns this, Martin thought, and reads some of their computer traffic, he'll still be cautious, cautious but curious. And the curiosity will slowly but certainly take over. But simply reading the computer messages won't be enough, will it? No, he'll need to see them. So he'll go to the town house and spy on them. But still, that won't be enough, either, will it? No. He'll need to talk to them. Face-to-face. And then, after that, maybe he'll even need to touch them.

And when he does that, I will be there. Waiting.

Agent Martin rose: 2BETA. Two-bait-a.

Not a good pun, he thought. But a pun nevertheless.

He wondered, then, whether the goat, staked out in the forest, started to bleat out of fear as the tiger approached, or frustration, because it knew its small life was going to be sacrificed just so the hunter concealed amidst the jungle trees could get a single clear shot.

Agent Martin exited the office, feeling, for the first time in weeks, as if he'd gained an advantage.

It was still pitch-dark when the detective left his own home and headed toward the town house where the mother and daughter were sleeping. There was little traffic in the predawn hours—life in the Fifty-first State had less urgency to it than other places, and banker's hours seemed more suitable to the residents—and so he made good time as he swept past developments still quiet. He barely glanced at the occasional vehicle that cruised past him, or whose lights crept into his rearview mirror. He guessed there was a good ninety minutes before first light, as he slowly made his way past the turnoff onto the dead-end street where the Claytons were located.

He had chosen the town house with care. The state owned a number of houses in different areas, but not all were bugged to the same extent as this one. And not all provided the same advantages of terrain. The steep drop-off in the rear of the development, the high fence at the edge of the ravine, effectively prevented anyone from approaching in that direction. He especially doubted that the man he was seeking would try that route; it would require an athleticism that he did not think the older man still had. That also did not seem to be the killer's style; Jeffrey's father wasn't the sort of murderer who overpowered his victims; he seemed to be the sort who outthought and seduced them, so that when they finally realized that the man whose eyes they were staring into meant them the greatest of harm, it was already far too late to struggle and fight.

Martin drove for another minute or so, rising into some foothills. He almost missed the dirt road he was searching for, and had to slam the brakes and twist the wheel sharply to make the turn. The unmarked car bumped as the tires hit the loose rock and gravel, and a plume of brown dust billowed behind him, until it seemed to be absorbed by the night.

The road was filled with potholes and small gullies carved by rain, and he slowed and cursed and saw his headlights pitch wildly. A jackrabbit spooked in front of him, disappearing into the bush. A pair of deer were momentarily frozen by his lights, the eyes gleaming red for an instant, before the animals abruptly bounded into the scrub.

He doubted there were many other people who knew about the road, and he guessed that few people had been down it in recent years. Bird-watchers and hikers, maybe. Dirt bikers and four-wheelers on the weekends. Not much other reason to come up that way. The road had been cut by a survey crew examining the area for potential housing; but it had proven to be low priority. Difficult to get water and building materials up the hills, and the view wasn't spectacular enough to warrant the effort.

The tires scrunched in the sandy dirt as he stopped. He shut the engine off and sat for a moment or two, letting his eyes adjust to the dark. On the passenger seat, Martin had two pairs of binoculars: a regular set, for after the sun rose, and a larger, unwieldy, military-issue, olive-drab-colored night-vision pair. He looped the straps for both around his neck. Then he grabbed a small flashlight that emitted a red-shaded night beam, a satchel holding a fruit Danish and a thermos of black coffee, and headed off.

He swept the flashlight beam across his path, scared mostly that he might run into a sleeping rattlesnake. The place he was pointing toward was only a hundred yards from where he'd parked the car, but the topography was rough, strewn with boulders and loose-packed shales of sand as slippery as ice on a frozen lake. He stumbled more than once, fought for his balance, then pressed on.

It took Martin almost fifteen minutes to scramble and slide the distance. But his reward was obvious when he reached the end of the narrow trail. He stood on the edge of a substantial bluff, overlooking the community swimming pool and tennis courts. From where he was situated, his view commanded the entire row of town homes. But, more critically, he had a clear sight line of the last of the row. And, with the height of the bluff, he was even able to see a portion of the rear patio area.

Martin leaned up against the edge of a large, flat boulder and lifted the night-vision glasses to his eyes. He swept the area quickly, searching for any movement in the street below, but saw none. He lowered the glasses, opened the thermos, and poured himself a cup of coffee. The liquid blended with the night; it was as if he were drinking a portion of the air, save for the scalding sensation as it coursed down his throat. The air was cool, and he cupped his hands around the thermos, seeking warmth.

Between gulps, he hummed. First show tunes from Broadway musicals he'd never seen. Then, as the minutes slid, anonymous sounds, flowing into musical riffs of indeterminate origin that disappeared into the blackness around him, ineffectively beating back the solitude of his wait.

The cold and the hour conspired to make him lose his focus, but he fought off distraction. The night seemed to be making sounds; a rustle in the weeds and brush, a sudden rattling of stones. Occasionally he would swing the night-vision glasses around him and search the area immediately behind him. He spotted a raccoon, and then an opossum, nocturnal animals busily making use of the last of the night.

Martin breathed out slowly, reached his right hand up under his jacket, and felt the reassuring presence of his semiautomatic pistol in a shoulder harness. He cursed once or twice out loud, letting the expletives burst like match light into the darkness around him. He railed against the time, the loneliness, and the unsettled feeling of being perched like a bird of prey on the bluff. He was uncomfortable and slightly nervous. He did not like the rural areas of the state. In an urban area, there was no darkness that he feared. But he had stepped just a few hundred yards past developed land, into a space more primitive, and this made him jerk around at any rattle or creak.

Agent Martin looked toward the east. "Come on, goddamn it, morning. About time."

He was not so optimistic to think that his quarry would show the first night. That would be too lucky, he told himself. But he did not expect to wait long before Jeffrey's father arrived. Martin had reviewed all the other cases, searching for a time element that might lead him to pick one hour over another, but he'd been frustrated. Abductions had taken place in both daytime and nighttime, early and late. The weather had ranged from hot and steamy to cold and rainy. Although he knew there were patterns in the crimes, those patterns were in the deaths, not the acquisition of victims—and so he found nothing to guide him. He'd relied on his best judgment. He planned to be back on the bluff the next night, from midnight to dawn.

Of course, he did not intend to let Jeffrey know where he would be.

The detective hunched his shoulders forward and reminded himself to bring a warmer coat and a sleeping bag tomorrow night. And more to eat. And something less sticky than the Danish, which left his fingers coated with an unpleasant jelly, which he licked at like an animal. He dried his hands on a wad of tissue paper, then tossed the paper aside. He shifted around uncomfortably, since the hard rock he was leaning against cut into his backside.

Looking at his watch, he saw that it was almost five-thirty. The car service was scheduled for ten minutes before six. Susan Clayton's flight was set to depart at seven-thirty. As he expected, he saw a hallway light blink on in the town house.

At almost the same time, he noticed the faintest of dawn light creeping over the hill. He held his hand out in front of his face, and for the first time was able to see the scars on the back side. Martin put the night-vision glasses away and pulled up the regular pair of binoculars. He peered down through them and swore at the indistinct, gray world that they showed him. He realized he was caught in that slippery moment before the dawn, when neither the night vision nor the day vision were entirely appropriate.

It was an indecisive time, and he didn't care for it.

The edge of morning and the car service seemed to arrive simultaneously, as he strained his eyes to watch.

He saw Susan Clayton, carrying only a small bag, still running a hand through half-dry hair, emerge from the town house just as the car rolled down the street. He looked at his watch and saw that the car was five minutes early. She waited on the sidewalk as it approached slowly.

Robert Martin twitched, abruptly sitting up straight.

He exhaled sharply, his body suddenly charged.

Five minutes early.

He slapped the binoculars to his eyes.

"No!" he half shouted. Then he whispered with a sudden, terrifying certainty, "It's him."

He was too far away to shout a warning, and he wasn't sure he would do that anyway. He tried to organize his thinking, and imposed an iron coldness to his actions, steeling himself. He hadn't expected his opportunity to come so quickly, but it seemingly had, and when he thought about it, it appeared obvious. An arrangement made with a car service, on the computer. This was the easiest of substitutions. She would enter whatever car showed up without paying attention, without thinking about what she was doing.

And especially without noticing the driver.

As he watched, he saw the car slow and stop. Susan Clayton reached for the door just as the driver half emerged from behind the wheel. He kept the glasses trained on the man, who wore a baseball-style hat that was pulled down low, obscuring his face. Martin swore again, cursing the deep gray air around him, which made everything in his vision blurry. He pulled the glasses away from his eyes, rubbed them hard for a second, then resumed his inspection. The man seemed thick through the shoulders, strong, and more important, had what seemed to the detective to be a sheet of gray hair sticking out from beneath the cap. The driver hesitated by the side of the car, as if seeing whether Susan Clayton needed help with her bag or if he should come around and open the door for her—neither of which she required. Then the driver ducked back inside the vehicle, out of sight behind the wheel, providing Martin with only that momentary glimpse; but just enough, he thought. Right age. Right size. Right time.

Right person.

Martin took one last look, marking the color and make of the vehicle. He watched as it turned around in the parking area, and he noted the license plate number.

Then, as the car slowly headed back down the dead-end street, he turned and raced for his own car.

The detective crashed through the brush and shrubs like a linebacker seeking the ball carrier. He vaulted one rock and scrambled through loose shale, fighting anything that was in his way. He did not care about the racket he made, nor did he notice the small animals that spooked and fled as he thrashed ahead.

Twenty yards from his car the path leveled slightly, and he picked up his pace, now flat-out, arms pumping, face red with strain. He was already envisioning the car service's route, trying to anticipate which direction the man behind the wheel would turn and when the moment would arrive when he would no longer head toward the airport, but set off, in surprise, in his own direction. *He'll tell her that it's a shortcut, and she won't know enough to realize the truth.* Martin, breathing hard with the exertion of his sprint, knew he had to catch up to them before the killer made that move. He had to be there, on his tail, right at the second when Jeffrey's father turned toward death.

The detective's lungs screamed, and he gulped down thin dawn air. He could feel his chest surging, heart pumping. The car loomed ahead of him, a dim shape in the faded light, and he sprinted forward, only to be tripped by a loose rock, which sent him sprawling into the dirt.

"Jesus fucking Christ!" Martin filled the air with an explosion of obscenities. He pushed himself to his feet, tasting sandy dirt in his mouth. Pain coursed through his ankle; it was twisted and throbbing with the insult of the fall. His pants were ripped and he could feel blood starting to trickle down his leg from a long, burning scrape in his knee. He ignored the hurt and pushed ahead. He did not bother to even dust himself off, but leapt forward, trying not to lose another second.

He grabbed the door handle, jerked it open, and threw himself into the car, tossing the binoculars onto the passenger seat with one motion, fumbling with his car keys.

"Goddamn it!" he swore as he jammed the keys at the ignition.

"What is the hurry, Detective?" a voice demanded in a low whisper from behind his right ear.

Robert Martin shouted, almost a scream, incomprehensible, not a word, just a noise of sudden and complete fear. His body jerked tight, like a rope tethering a boat to a dock when a large wind and surge of waves abruptly pulls at the hull. He could not see the shape of the person who had risen from behind him, but in the surge of panic that crushed him in that second, he knew who it was, and he dropped the car keys and reached for his automatic.

His hand had traveled half the distance to the holster when the man spoke again: "You'll be dead as soon as you touch your weapon."

There was a cold, matter-of-fact tone to the voice that stopped the detective's hand in midflight. It hovered in the air in front of him. He became aware then of the blade at his throat.

The man spoke again, as if to answer a question that had not been spoken. "It's an old-fashioned straight-edge razor, with a genuine carved-ivory handle, Detective, which I purchased at some expense not too long ago in an antiques store, although I doubt that the dealer suspected what use I had in mind for it. Remarkable weapon, you know. Small, comfortable to grip. And sharp. Ah, very sharp. It will open your jugular with a flick of my wrist, which they say is an unpleasant way to die. It is the sort of weapon that creates interesting possibilities. And there is a sophistication to it that has lasted over the centuries. Unimproved in decades. Nothing modern about it, except the slice it will make in your throat. So, you have to ask yourself: Is this how I want to die, right now, right this instant, after coming so far in my pursuit? Without getting any of my questions answered?"

The man paused.

"So, is it, Detective?"

Robert Martin's lips were suddenly dry and pursed. His voice was cracked as he responded. "No."

"Good," the man said. "Now, do not move, while I remove your weapon."

Martin felt the man's free hand snake around him, reaching for the automatic. The razor did not move from its position edged up coldly against his neck. The man struggled for a second, then removed the pistol from Martin's holster. The detective looked at the rearview mirror, trying to see the man behind him, but the mirror had been twisted out of position. He tried to sense the size of the person behind him, but could see nothing. There was merely the man's voice, calm, unruffled, unexcited, penetrating the gloom of early morning.

"Who are you?" Martin asked.

The man laughed briefly. "This is like the old children's game of twenty questions. Are you animal, vegetable, or mineral? Are you bigger than a bread box? Smaller than a station wagon? Detective, you should try to ask questions that you don't already know the answer to. Regardless, I'm the man you have been hunting for all these months. And now you've found me. But not, I think, exactly the way you had in mind."

Martin tried to relax. He desperately wanted to see the face of the man behind him, but even the slightest shift in his position tightened the razor against his throat. He dropped his hands into his lap, but the distance between his fingers and the backup revolver in its holster around his ankle seemed a marathon, unreachable and unobtainable.

"How did you know I was here?" Martin croaked out.

"Do you think I have managed to reach this point by being stupid, Detective?" The voice answered the question with a question.

"No," Martin replied.

"All right. How did I know you were here? There are two answers to that question. The first is simple: because I was not far when you met my daughter and my wife at the airport, and I followed you on your leisurely trip through our fair city, and I knew that you would not actually leave them alone to wait for me. And, knowing this, did it not make more sense to anticipate your moves than it did theirs? Of course, I never thought I would actually be as fortunate as I have been. I never thought that you would bring *yourself* to precisely the sort of location I would have selected for us to meet, had it been my choice. A nice, deserted, quiet, forgotten spot. Lucky for me. But then, isn't luck the stepchild of good planning? I believe so. Anyway, Detective, that is one answer to your question. The more complex answer, of course, is slightly deeper. And that answer is: I have spent my entire adult life setting traps for people to walk into without warning. Did you think I would not recognize the same set so enticingly for me?"

The blade twitched against the detective's throat. He coughed a response. "Yes."

"But you have been proven wrong, Detective."

Martin grunted. He shifted in his seat again.

"You would like to see my face, wouldn't you?"

Martin's shoulders were rigid.

"Did you dream about our first and only meeting, back so many years ago? Have you tried to picture how I've changed since we had that little conversation back then?"

"Yes."

"Don't turn around, Detective. Think of yourself. You were thinner then, more youthful and athletic. Would I not have the same signs of age? Less hair, perhaps. More flesh around the jowls. Thicker around the middle. These changes would be expected, no?"

"Yes."

"And did you search for some old photograph at my old employer, or maybe through motor vehicle licenses, that you could apply some computer imaging techniques to? Did you not think that maybe a machine could help you to learn how I look?"

"There were no pictures. At least none that I could find."

"Ah, tough luck. But still, your curiosity is different, is it not? You think: there has been surgery involved. Correct?"

"Yes."

"And right you are about that. Of course, the real test lies ahead. There are three people who should know me. They should know me the instant they see me. The second they smell me. The moment they hear me. But will they? Will they be able to see through the years that have passed and the finest in surgical attentions? Will they spot the alterations in the chin, the cheekbones, the nose, whatever? What is the same? What is different? Will they be able to see that which hasn't been changed instead of that which has? Now, that is an interesting question. And that is a game that remains to be played out."

Martin was having trouble breathing. His throat was dry, his muscles tense, and his hands twitching. The sensation of the blade at his throat was like being tied by unbreakable, invisible line. The killer's voice had a rhythmic softness to it; he could hear the education in his words, but far worse, he could feel the murderer in the tones, as they covered him, oppressive like unrelenting heat on a summer day. He knew that the softness, the fluidity of the killer's words, had all been used before, to quietly reassure some victim at the precipice of terror. The quiet certainty of his language was disorienting; it didn't connect with the violence that was to follow, but invoked something different, something far less terrible than what was truly going to happen. Like the crocodile's tears, the killer's calmness was a mask, obscuring what was designed to take place. Martin struggled hard, inwardly, with fear; he thought that he was a man of action himself, and a man of violence. He insisted that he was a match for the man with the blade tickling away at his throat. It was what he knew and what he was comfortable with. He reminded himself of his own dangerousness. *You are as much a killer as he.* He told himself that he would not die without a fight.

He will give you an opportunity. Don't miss it.

Martin steeled himself, waiting.

But what move he would make, and when, seemed distant and impossible to guess.

"Are you scared of dying, Detective?" the man asked.

"No," Martin replied.

"Really? I'm not, either. Most curious. Odd that, don't you think? A man as intimate with death as myself still has questions. It's strange, don't you think? Everyone fights the aging process in their own way, Detective. Some people seek the attentions of surgeons. I would see them when I had my own operations. Of course, my agenda was different. Others invest in trips to expensive spas for mud baths and painful massages. Some people exercise, or go on diets or eat nothing except sea anemones and coffee grounds or some such silliness. Some people grow their hair ponytail-long and buy a motorcycle. We hate what is happening to us, we hate the inevitability of it all, don't we?"

"Yes," Martin answered.

"Do you know how I manage to stay young, Detective?"

"No."

"I kill."

The voice was cold, yet animated. Harsh, yet seductive.

The man paused, as if considering his words. Then he added: "The urge has lessened, perhaps, as the years have passed, but the skills have improved. The need is less, but the task is easier. . . ."

Again he hesitated, before saying: "The world is a curious place, Detective. Filled with all sorts of oddities and contradictions."

Martin moved his hand out of his lap, toward his hip, a few inches closer to the weapon just above his right foot. He remembered the configuration of the holster. A single strap held the revolver in place. There was a snap that sometimes jammed when he hadn't bothered to oil it. He'd have to flip that snap loose before he seized the pistol grip. He tried to remember if the safety was on, and in that second was unable to recall. He squinted his eyes shut for an instant, trying, but this important detail remained just beyond his consciousness, and inwardly he cursed himself. The razor continued to pressure his neck, and he realized that unless it changed position, when he jerked forward, reaching for the backup revolver, he would in all likelihood slice his own throat.

"You would like to kill me, would you not, Detective?"

Martin paused and made a small shrug before answering. "Absolutely."

The killer laughed. "That was the whole plan, wasn't it, Detective? Jeffrey would find me, but he would be ambivalent. He would hesitate. He would have doubts, because after all, I am his father. So he would not act— at least not right away. Not right at the crucial moment. But you would be there, to step into that slack second. And you would put an end to me without hesitation, without doubts, and without the slightest feelings of remorse. . . ."

The voice hesitated, then added: "There was never to be an arrest, was there? No charges, lawyers, and trials, right? And especially no publicity. You were just going to remove the state's problem instantly and effectively, correct?"

Robert Martin didn't want to answer. He licked his lips, but it was as if all the moisture within him had been sucked out by the cold pressure of the killer's words.

The razor twitched beneath his chin, and he felt a small slice of pain.

"Correct?" the killer asked.

"Yes," Martin said, croaking his answer.

There was another moment of silence before the killer continued.

"That was a predictable response. But tell me, you've spoken with him. I daresay you've gotten to know him a little bit. Do you think Jeffrey will be willing to kill me as well?"

"I don't know. I never expected to give him that decision."

The man with the razor considered this.

"That was an honest response, Detective. I appreciate it. You were always meant to be the assassin here, right? Jeffrey's role was limited. Unique but limited. Am I not right?"

Martin thought lying would be a mistake. "Obviously."

"You're not really a policeman, are you, Detective? I mean, you might have been once, but no more. Now you are merely a killer paid by the state. A cleaner of messes, right? A sort of specialized janitorial service."

Agent Martin didn't reply.

"I've read your personnel file, Detective."

"Then you shouldn't need to ask me that question."

The voice cracked a single, dry laugh. "Touché," he said. He paused for an instant, before continuing: "But my wife and daughter, how is it that they fit into this equation? Their departure from Florida took me by surprise. That was where I intended to make their reacquaintance."

"They were your son's idea. I'm not sure exactly what he wants them to do."

"Do you know how much I have missed them, in recent years? How much I have wanted us to be together? Even in old age, an evil fellow such as myself needs the comfort of his family."

Martin shook his head slightly. "Don't give me any sentimental bullshit. I don't believe that."

The killer laughed again. "Well, Detective, at least you're not stupid. I mean, a little stupid, of course, to come up here and not pay attention to the car following you. And certainly stupid for not locking the door to your car. Why didn't you do that, Detective?"

"I never do. Not here. This world is safe."

"Not anymore, is it?"

Martin didn't respond, and suddenly the razor pressed a little tighter to his neck. He could feel a thin rivulet of blood dripping down, staining his shirt collar.

"You don't get it, do you, Detective? You never have."

"Get what?"

"It is one thing to kill. Many people do that. It is a constancy of life today. Even to kill with impunity and total freedom and frequency. Getting away with murder isn't hard. It isn't even all that notable, is it?"

"No. Your son said much the same thing to me, once."

"He did? Clever boy. But tell me, Detective, put yourself in my shoes— that shouldn't be so hard. After all, that's what good policemen do, isn't it? Rule number one: Learn to think like a killer. Duplicate those thought patterns. Anticipate those emotional surges. A oneness of understanding. Learn to understand what makes the murderer kill, and you should be able to find him. Right? Isn't that what they teach? Isn't that in every course? And isn't that a lesson passed from every old, retiring detective to every hotshot newcomer who comes up through the ranks?"

"Yes."

"You know, did it never occur to you that the reverse is equally true? All a really proficient and efficient killer has to do, in response, is learn to think like a policeman. Did you ever think of that, Detective?"

"No."

"That's all right. You're not alone in that particular blindness. But it did occur to me. Many years ago."

The man with the razor hesitated.

"And you were right. Way back then. I did boil that first pair of handcuffs after using them on that young woman."

Robert Martin's hands tensed. The car was filling with the light of morning, but he still could not see that man's face. He could feel the killer's breath on the back of his neck but that was all.

"Do you regret not pursuing me a little more diligently twenty-five years ago?"

"Yes. I knew it was you. But there was nothing to hold you on."

"And I knew you knew it was I. The difference, of course, between myself and others like me, is that I had no fear. Never. I always had too much going against the grain of murder, Detective. I'm white. Educated. Articulate. Intelligent. A professional academic. Married, with a lovely family. They, of course, were the critical piece, you know. The ultimate in camouflage. They provided the veneer of normalcy. People can be made to believe anything about a single male—even the truth. But a man with an apparently loving and devoted family? Ah, such a man can get away with murder. He can get away with a dozen murders . . ."

He coughed, once.

". . . as, of course, I did."

The killer paused again. Martin realized that the man was enjoying himself. The irony of the situation almost made him smile. Jeffrey's father was like any academic: in love, entranced by his chosen field of expertise. He would rather discuss nothing else. The problem, of course, was that his field was death.

Abruptly, bitterness penetrated the tone of the killer's words. Martin could hear the anger coalesce in the stale air just behind his right ear:

"Damn her eyes. Damn her to hell forever! When she stole them, she stole my cover. Stole what I had created! Stole the perfection from my life! It was the only time I was scared, you know. Having to explain their departure to you. I thought, for a few minutes, that you might see it for what it was. But you didn't. You weren't smart enough."

The detective felt suddenly cold. He shivered involuntarily before answering. "I should have been," he said. "I knew it. I just didn't act."

"Hamstrung by the system, right, Detective? Laws. Rules. Conventions of society, correct?"

"Yes."

"But here, it's not exactly the same, is it?"

"No."

"And that's the point of this world, right?"

"Yes."

"And my point as well."

"I don't follow."

"Let me explain, Detective. It's not that complicated, really. The world is filled with killers. Killers of all shapes, sizes, and styles. Thrill killers, sex killers, contract killers—you name it. The busywork of death on a daily basis—no, hourly basis—no, minute by minute. Second by second. Violent death is ordinary and routine. We are no longer shocked, are we? Depravity? Ho-hum. Sadism? Nothing new. Indeed, we use violence and death to entertain us. To excite us. It's in our cinema, our literature, our art, our history, our souls . . .

". . . it is," the killer said, taking a breath, "our one real contribution to the world."

Martin squirmed slightly in his seat. He wondered whether the lecturing tones would give him an opportunity to pitch forward, reaching for the backup pistol. But, almost in answer to this, the razor blade once again tightened on his neck, and the killer leaned forward, so that his words were hot on the detective's neck.

"You see, Agent Martin, when I go to Hell, I want there to be applause and cheers. I want an honor guard of killers—all the rippers and butchers and maniacs—to stand in respect. I want to take a place in history, beside them. . . .

"I will not," the killer whispered coldly, "be forgotten!"

"How do you mean to do that?" Martin asked.

The killer snorted. "This state," he answered slowly. "This proposed Fifty-first State of the greatest union that history has ever known. What is it? It is a geographical location, but its real boundaries are philosophical, are they not?"

"Yes."

"The proof of that statement, Detective, is right here. Us. You and I and the unfortunately unlocked door that allowed me to crawl back here and wait for you. Would you not agree?"

"Yes."

"So, detective, tell me. Who will be more remembered by history—the gaggle of politicians and businessmen who conceived of this throwback world, this place that purports to hold all of our futures by reinvoking our pasts—or . . ."

Martin could sense the man grinning.

". . . the man who destroys it?"

Martin coughed out a protest. "You won't succeed," he said. He thought his words sounded pathetic.

"Oh, yes, I will, Detective. Because the concept of personal safety is so fragile. In fact, I would have succeeded already, but your efforts to cover up the extent of my actions have been so extraordinarily complete—if a tad ridiculous. I mean, wild dogs? Really, now. But that, of course, made me think of another way of playing out this game. Which required, of course, the presence of my son. My almost famous son. My well-known and respected son. As for our personal battle—with the political fate of this state in the balance, do you really think that's a story the news media in the remaining fifty states would ignore? Is this not a contest that invokes something primal, something ancient, and something of overwhelming commonality? Father against son. And that is why I had you bring him here, Detective."

Jeffrey's father took a deep breath.

"You were always expected to find him and bring him to me, Detective. And for doing precisely what I predicted you would, I thank you."

Martin felt it was impossible to breathe. He stared out the front window and saw that morning had gripped the world before him. Every rock, every bush, every little cut and scrape in the earth that had seemed so treacherous in the dark and gloom when he'd arrived, was now clear, sunlit, benign.

"What do you want from me?" he asked. He moved his hand as close to his leg and the backup revolver as possible. He raised his knee slightly, trying to close the space between hand and weapon. He thought when he made his move, he would reach up with his left, grabbing for the razor. He expected he would be cut, but if he moved fast enough, and suddenly enough, he might prevent a fatal slice. He moved his fingers and tensed his muscles, readying himself for the explosion.

"What I want from you, Detective? I want you to carry a message."

Martin hesitated. "What?"

"I want you to take a message to my son. And to my daughter. And to my ex-wife. Think you can do that, Detective?"

Martin was astonished. His heart soared. *He's going to let me live!*

"You want me to take a message. . . ."

"You're the only one I can trust with this task, Detective. Are you capable?"

"Take a message? Of course."

"Good. Excellent. Hold up your left hand, Detective."

Martin did as instructed. A large, white, letter-sized envelope was thrust toward him.

"Take that," the killer said. "Good. Grip it very tightly."

Martin again did as instructed. He seized the envelope in his hand and waited for another instruction. A second or two passed, and from behind him in the backseat he heard the familiar clicking noise of his own weapon as a round was thrust into the firing chamber of the semiautomatic.

"Is this the message you want me to take?" he asked.

"Part of it," the killer replied. "There is a second element."

THE MORNING
CONSTITUTIONAL

Diana had been awakened by the meager noises her daughter made when she rose in the predawn hours; the shower running, a kitchen cabinet door clacking shut, the front door being closed with authority. For a few seconds she'd considered rising and seeing Susan off, but sleep was seductive, and she'd sighed and rolled over and hadn't awakened again for several hours. She happily dreamed of being a child again.

The older woman had taken the master bedroom in the town house, and after swinging her legs out of bed, wriggling her toes and stretching once, she wrapped a spare blanket around her shoulders and padded out onto the small balcony in her bare feet. She stood for a moment, simply breathing in the morning air. There was a cold sharpness to it, a sense of inhaling the edge of a blade. The air was still, but the cool cut through her thin nightdress and raised goose bumps on her skin. The early winter sun gave the world before her a clarity and distinction she'd missed in the humid world of South Florida. She could smell the mountains in the distance, and see great white cumulus clouds, high against the blue sky, traveling east on the jet stream, as if idly searching for some snow-covered peak on which to rest.

She shivered once, and thought: I could belong here.

Diana gulped at the air as if it were medicinal. She let her eyes swing over the terrain. The house did not have enough elevation to look back toward the city. Instead, she saw the scrubland of the ravine behind the townhouse fence, dirt brown with occasional streaks of green shrubbery. She listened, heard the sound of voices and the rhythmic plop of tennis balls being struck with more delicacy than devotion, and guessed that the women of the development were out on the courts getting their regular morning exercise.

Just breathing in clear air and listening, Diana reflected how strange it seemed that there was so little noise. Even in the Keys there was always noise; trucks on Highway 1, the swordlike branches of the palm trees battling the breeze with futility. She'd assumed that the rest of the world was always noisy. Certainly Miami, and the other great cities, were always filled with sound. Traffic, sirens, gunshots, anger, and frustration turning to rage. In the modern world, she thought, sound was violence.

But she could hear nothing that morning other than the noise of normalcy, which she recognized as the powerful vision of the Fifty-first State. She'd thought she would find this normalcy trite, or irritating, but she didn't. It was comforting. Had she accompanied her daughter a few days earlier on Susan's accidental visit to the hospice, Diana would have discovered that the selective silences of that place were much the same as those she listened for on this morning.

She went back into the bedroom, but left the sliding door to the balcony open behind her, welcoming the fresh air to join her inside. This was not something she would have done at her own home. She dressed rapidly and descended to the kitchen.

Susan had left enough coffee in the machine for her to fill a cup, which she did, stirring in milk and sugar to steal the bitterness from the brew. She wasn't hungry, and though she knew she should eat, decided to put it off.

Carrying her coffee cup into the living room, Diana saw an envelope thrust halfway through the mail slot in the front door. She thought this odd, and reached for the letter.

The envelope was blank white paper, without an address.

Diana hesitated. For the first time that morning, she reminded herself why she was there in the Fifty-first State. And, also for the first time that day, she reminded herself that she would be alone, probably until evening.

Then, because caution was something she thought accompanied weakness, she tore open the envelope.

There was a single sheet of white paper inside. She unfolded it, and read:

Good Morning, Mrs. Clayton:

I'm sorry that I cannot personally give you an additional tour of New Washington today, but our mutual task requires my presence elsewhere.

Your time, of course, is your own, but I would strongly recommend you at least enjoy our western air with a brief, brisk walk. The best route is as follows:

Exit your town house and bear to the left, keeping the pool and tennis facility on your right. Proceed to the end of the street. Take a right turn onto Donner Boulevard. Isn't it unusual how many things in the West are named after that unfortunate party? Continue in that direction for one-half mile. You will see that the paved road on which you are traveling ends approximately one-quarter mile ahead. But fifty yards from the dead end you will discover a dirt road leading off to your right. Take this road.

Continue traveling on the dirt road for another half mile. The grade will steepen, but you will be rewarded by persistence. The view from the rise—only another two hundred yards ahead—is unique. And, once there, you will see a sight which your son Jeffrey will find especially intriguing.

> Sincerely,
> Robert Martin,
> Special Agent, State Security

The letter was typed, as was the signature.

Diana stared at the directions and thought that a morning walk would be nice, and that she could use the exercise; and also that the letter she held in her hands wasn't a suggestion, or a recommendation, but a command.

But what the order implied, she wasn't certain. She was also confused by the last sentence, and tried to guess what sight she could see from the elevation above the town homes that Jeffrey would be interested in. On this question, she drew a blank.

She read through the letter again, then glanced at the telephone, thinking of contacting Agent Martin and asking him precisely what he meant. Once again she reminded herself why she was there inside the Fifty-first State, and reminded herself, too, who else was there.

Diana returned to the kitchen and put the coffee cup in the sink. Without hesitation, she went to the cupboard where Susan had concealed the revolver. She took it from its hiding place, hefted it in her hand, cracked open the cylinder to make certain that the gun was fully loaded, then went to find her walking shoes.

It had been close to two years since she'd actually been able to touch her brother. His voice, accompanied by the image on a video-telephone, had made this time seem unimportant right up to the moment when the small commuter flight banked sharply and lowered flaps and wheels and she realized he would be there, waiting for her.

Susan descended into a world of misgivings.

She wished she could remember precisely what it was that had caused the two of them to drift apart, but she was unable to recall a single moment or event. There had never been a fight or an argument, shouts, tears, whatever, that produced the distance between them. Instead, she recognized that it had been a process, insidious, built like a brick wall, slowly, with the mortar of doubt and the bricks of solitude. When she tried to analyze her feelings, she was unable to come up with much that was firm, other than the quicksand of belief that he'd left her alone to fend for herself, and to tend to their mother.

As the small plane bumped against the tarmac, Susan told herself that what would take place over the next days had nothing to do with her relationship with her brother, and so she shunted whatever feelings she had into a separate place within her, thinking they would be secure there and wouldn't affect anything until afterward. For a woman able to recognize the subtleties of the most complicated of puzzles, this was an oddly blind conclusion.

Jeffrey was waiting by the ramp. He was accompanied by a lanky Texas Ranger, who perfectly fit the caricature of the role. He wore mirrored sunglasses, a wide-brimmed cowboy hat, and ornately tooled pointy-toed boots. The ranger also carried an automatic weapon over his shoulder, and had an unlit cigarette in the corner of his mouth.

Brother and sister embraced tentatively. Then, holding each other at arm's length, they took a moment to assess each other.

"You've changed," Susan said. "Do I detect a gray hair?"

"Not a one," Jeffrey replied. He grinned. "Have you lost weight?"

It was Susan's turn to smile. "Not a pound, damn it."

"Then, have you gained weight?" he asked.

"Not a pound, thank God," Susan replied.

He released her arms. "We have to go," he said. "There's not much time if we expect to get back this afternoon."

The ranger gestured toward the exit.

In response to the unasked question, Jeffrey said: "I am owed some favors by the authorities in this state. Hence security and a fast driver."

Susan looked at the man's weapon. "That's an Ingram, isn't it? Clip holds twenty-two, forty-five-caliber high-impact rounds. Fires the entire clip in less than two seconds, right?"

"Yes, ma'am," the ranger answered, startled.

"Prefer an Uzi myself," she said.

"Except they jam sometimes, ma'am," he said.

"Not for me," she replied. "How come that cigarette isn't lit?" she asked.

"Why, ma'am, don't you know smoking is dangerous?"

Susan laughed and punched Jeffrey on the shoulder. "The ranger has a sense of humor," she said. "Let's get going."

They ducked into the ranger's vehicle and within minutes were traveling through the low, flat dust of South Texas at far in excess of a hundred miles per hour.

For a moment or two Susan stared out the window, watching the world stretch away from them, then turned to her brother. "The man we're going to see?"

"His name is Hart. Eighteen deaths I was able to attribute to him directly. Probably others that I don't know about and that he's never bothered to tell anyone else about. Probably forgot about some of them, anyway. I helped arrest him. He was in the process of eviscerating a victim when we arrived, an intrusion he did not take kindly to. He managed to put a major-league slice in my leg with a rather large hunting knife before he passed out from his own loss of blood. He took two rounds from one of the detectives he killed. Teflon-coated, high-velocity, nine-millimeter shells. I would have thought they'd have stopped a rhino in its tracks, but they didn't. Anyway, he got some real quick attention in the emergency room and managed to pull through in order to take up residence on Death Row."

"Not too much longer, Professor," the ranger interrupted. "Governor's signing some death warrants day after tomorrow, and word out of Austin is that old boy Hart is number one on the hit parade. He ain't got no legal bull-shit, excuse me, miss, left to try, anyways."

"Texas, like a lot of states, has expedited death penalty appeals," Jeffrey told his sister.

"Makes things move along a bit quicker," the ranger said, his voice drawling some sarcasm. "Not like the old days when you could hang on a decade or longer. Even after killing a cop."

"On the other hand, quick isn't so good if maybe you've got the wrong man," Susan said.

"Hell, miss, that hardly ever happens."

"And if it does?"

The ranger shrugged and grinned. "Ain't nobody perfect," he said.

Susan turned to her brother, who was enjoying the turns in the conversation. "Why do you think this guy will help us?" she asked.

"I'm not sure he will. About a year ago he gave an interview to a reporter at the *Dallas Morning News* where he said he wanted to kill me.

The reporter sent me a copy of the videotape of the interview. It made my day. As you can imagine."

"And because he wants to kill you, you think he'll help us?"

"Yes."

"Interesting logic."

"It will make perfectly reasonable sense to him."

"We'll see. And what is it you expect to find out from this man?"

"Mr. Hart has a quality that I think . . ." Jeffrey hesitated, searching once again for the right word. ". . . our subject shares."

"What's that?"

"He built himself a special place. A killing place. And I think the man we're hunting has constructed the same somewhere. This is an unusual but not unheard of phenomena. There's not much in the forensic literature of murder about these sorts of places. I just want to know what to look for, and how to look for it—and this man can tell us. Maybe."

"If he will."

"That's right. If he will."

Diana wore a light windbreaker against what she thought would be the morning chill, but soon discovered that the high sun was erasing the leftover cold of the night. She'd traveled barely halfway down the block before she stripped the jacket off and wrapped it around her waist, tying the arms in front of her. She carried a small pack on her back, which contained her identification, a painkiller, a bottle of springwater, and the .357 Magnum. In her hand, she carried the letter with its directions.

To her right she saw some children playing in the toddler's area. She paused to watch them for a few moments, then continued down the road. Her feet kicked up small puffs of light brown dust as she walked. To her left, in one of the town homes, a young woman emerged carrying a tennis racquet. Diana guessed she was the same age as her own daughter. The woman saw her and gave a wave, almost as if she knew her. A moment of familiarity between strangers. Diana waved back and continued walking.

At the end of the street she bore to the right, following the directions. She saw a single, brown street sign, which told her she was indeed on Donner Boulevard. Within a few yards she recognized that the row of town homes was the last development in the area, and that the boulevard she was on went nowhere. It had also seen less maintenance than other streets. There were some potholes, and the sidewalk that she walked down was cracked, chipped, and scarred by weeds growing between ill-fitted slabs of concrete.

Diana continued her sortie through the morning until she reached the dirt road leading off to her right. As the letter had informed her, she could see ahead to the end of Donner Boulevard. The street ended in a pile of dirt shoved up against a rise. There was a single barrier with flashing yellow lights and a large red sign that read ROAD ENDS, which was a redundancy.

She paused, opened the bottle of springwater, and took a modest swig, starting up the dirt road. She performed a quick internal inventory. She was a little short of breath, but not seriously so. She wasn't tired; indeed, she felt strong. There was a thin line of sweat on her forehead, but nothing that suggested a sudden exhaustion was lurking somewhere, unannounced. The pain in her stomach had recessed, as if permitting her the pleasure of the morning walk. She smiled and thought: It does like to bide its time.

For a moment she turned about, luxuriating in the isolation and quiet.

Then she stepped forward into the loose, sandy dirt and started to slowly climb up the abandoned road.

Death Row in Texas, like most states, wasn't a row at all. The name had survived, but the location had changed. The state had built a prison dedicated to the sole concept of killing violent offenders. It was situated on a flat stretch of ranch land, isolated from cities or towns, with a single double-lane black macadam highway running through the plains. The prison itself was one large ultramodern building plunked down behind three separate chain-link and razor-wire fences. In a way, the prison resembled a large dormitory, or a small hotel, except that all the windows were little more than slices barely six inches wide, cut into the concrete walls of the building. There was an exercise area and a library, several high-security meeting rooms, and a dozen different tiers of cells, twenty in each block. All were occupied. All were adjacent to a central chamber that upon first appearance seemed to be a hospital room but was not. There was a gurney with shackles and a killing machine. The man to be executed would be hog-tied onto the gurney, an intravenous line run from the artery in his left arm across the floor to a box on the wall. Inside there were three small containers, all of which fed into the line. Only one contained the lethal substance. Three different state employees, upon a signal from the warden, would press buttons releasing the concoctions simultaneously. The theory was the same as the firing squad where one man was issued a blank. No one knew for sure that it was their trigger that had released the poison.

The killing agent also had been improved. Streamlined. Close the eyes, count backward from one hundred. Dead, usually by ninety-six. Occasionally, a large prisoner would make it to ninety-four. No one had lasted longer than ninety-two.

The interior of the prison was equally modern, every corner monitored by closed-circuit cameras. It had a highly polished, antiseptic air to it; it was like entering a world that mimicked the strands of razor wire in the fences; efficient, steel clean, shining, and deadly.

Jeffrey and Susan Clayton were escorted by a prison guard into one of the interview rooms. There were two chairs on either side of a single metal table. Nothing else. Everything was bolted to the floor. On one side of the table, bolted to the surface, there was a steel ring.

Jeffrey made one comment while they waited: "He's bright. Very bright. Closer to exceptional than normal. He quit school in eighth grade because the other kids mocked him, because he has deformed genitalia. For ten years he did nothing except read. Then, for another ten, he did nothing except kill. Don't underestimate him, not at any point."

A side door opened with an electronic thunk as a lock was switched off, and another guard, accompanied by a wiry, ferretlike man, arms littered with tattoos and a sheet of white hair above red eyes, an albino, entered the room. Wordlessly, the guard attached the prisoner's handcuff chain to the table ring. Then he straightened up and said: "All yours, Professor." The guard nodded to Susan Clayton, then exited.

The prisoner was dressed in a white one-piece jump suit. He was thin, with a sunken chest and contradictory large, clawlike hands that shook slightly as he bent over and lit a cigarette. Susan saw that he had one eye that drooped, while the other looked alert, the eyebrow shooting up as he measured her.

For several seconds he eyed Susan. Then he turned to Jeffrey.

"Hello, Professor. Never expected to see you again. How's the leg?" The man's voice was oddly high-pitched, almost like a child's. She thought it concealed all his anger successfully.

"It healed quickly. You missed the artery. And the ligaments."

"That's what they told me. Too bad. I was rushed. I needed a little more time."

The man smiled quirkily, lifting the edge of his mouth like a twitch, and turned again to Susan.

"Who are you?"

"My assistant," Jeffrey answered rapidly.

The killer hesitated, hearing the lie in the speed of the response. "I don't think so, Jeffrey. She has your eyes. Cold eyes. A little like my own, I daresay. Make me fair want to shudder and shiver and curl up in a little ball of fear myself. A little bit of your chin as well, but the chin only says something about stubbornness and perserverance, unlike the eyes, which tell me about what's in your souls. Oh, I can see a definite resemblance. Clear to anyone with even the most modest powers of observation. And mine, as you are undoubtedly aware, Professor, are significantly sharper."

"This is my sister, Susan."

The killer smiled. "Hello, Susan. I'm David Hart. We're not allowed to shake hands, that would be a violation of the rules, but you may call me David. Your brother, on the other hand, lying scum-sucking pig that he is, must call me Mr. Hart."

"Hello, David," Susan said calmly.

"Glad to meet you, Susan," the killer replied, adding a small lilt to her name that filled the room. "Susan, Susie, Susie-Q. What a pretty name. Tell me, Susan, are you a whore?"

"I'm sorry?"

"Oh, you know," the killer continued, his voice rising with each word, "a prostitute. A streetwalker, a woman of the night or of easy virtue. A harlot, a hooker, a trollop, a hustler. You know what I mean: a woman paid to suck the purity from men. Who steals their essences. A disease-carrying, filthy piece of trash, infectious and disgusting. A parasite. A cockroach. Tell me, Susan, is that what you are?"

"No."

"Then what are you?"

"I invent games."

"What sort of games?"

"Word games. Puzzles. Anagrams. Crosswords."

The killer thought for an instant. "That's interesting," he said. "So, you're not a whore?"

"No."

"I liked to kill whores, you know. Slice them from . . ." He paused and smiled. "But your brother has probably told you that."

"Yes."

David Hart's eyebrow rose again and his face twitched into the distinctive, twisted smile. "He's a whore, and I would like to slice him in half as well. I would get much satisfaction from that."

The killer paused, coughed once, then added: "Ah, hell, Susie. I'd probably like to slice you from crotch to chin, too. No use lying about it. Cutting you would be a joy. A pleasure. Doing your brother, there, well, that would be more like business. An obligation. Paying back a debt."

He turned to Jeffrey. "So, Professor, why are you here?"

"I would like your assistance. We both would."

The killer shook his head. "Fuck you, Professor. Interview finished. End of talk."

Hart half rose in his seat, simultaneously gesturing with his cuffed hand to a mirror on one wall. It was obviously a two-way mirror, behind which the interview was being watched by prison officials.

Jeffrey didn't move. "You told one reporter not too long ago that you wanted to kill me because I was the one who found you. What you told him was that if it hadn't been for me, there wouldn't be a prostitute left in the city. And because of me, there remain dozens and dozens, plying their trade with impunity, and so your work was never completed . . . and for that, for stepping between you and your desire, I deserved to die." Jeffrey paused, watching the effect his words had on the killer. "Well, Mr. Hart, this is your one and only chance."

The killer hovered above the seat for an instant. "My chance to kill you?" He held out his manacled hands and rattled the chains. "A lovely idea. But pray, how so, Professor?"

"Because this is an opportunity."

The killer paused. Smiled. Sat down. "I will listen," he said. "For a few seconds. In deference to your lovely sister. Are you sure you're not a whore, Susan?"

She didn't reply, and Hart smiled and shrugged.

"All right, Professor. Tell me how it is that I can manage to kill you by helping you."

"That's simple, Mr. Hart. If I am able to find the man I'm searching for, with your help, he'll want to do to me what you want to do, Mr. Hart. He is as intelligent as you and every bit as deadly. The risk is: I'll get him before he gets me. Either is a possibility. But there's your chance, Mr. Hart. It will be the best one you'll get in the little time you've got left. Take it or leave it."

The killer rocked back and forth in the metal chair, considering. "A most unusual proposal, Professor. Most intriguing."

He stared at the end of his cigarette. "Very clever. I can help you, and therefore put you at risk. Bring you a little closer to the flame, no? The challenge for me, if I may be so bold, is to just give enough information so that you both succeed and fail at the same time."

Hart took a deep, wheezy breath. He smiled again. "All right. The interview continues. Perhaps. What is it that I know about that you now want to know?"

"All your crimes were committed in a single location. I believe the man I'm searching for does the same. We want to know about the killing place. How you chose it. What is important about it. What are the critical elements. What are the essential features. And why did you need a single location? That's what we need to know."

The killer considered this. "You believe that if I tell you why I created my special place, you'll be able to extrapolate this information into a scheme for finding your man's hole in the wall?"

"That is correct."

Hart nodded. "Ah, so the man you seek is a man after my own heart." He giggled.

"That's a pun, Susan the game maker, is it not?"

Diana Clayton had walked barely fifty yards, stumbled once, catching herself just before she pitched forward into the dirt and small rocks of the road. She stopped, slightly out of breath, and kicked at the sandy surface of the world beneath her feet, streaking the white toe of her walking shoes with a dusty, gray-brown color. She breathed in sharply once or twice, then glanced up into the wide sky above her, as if searching the expanse of blue for the answer to some question she had not yet asked. The sun's glare tricked her eyes, and she could feel that the band of sweat on her forehead had doubled. She wiped away the moisture, then saw it glisten momentarily on the back of her hand.

She reminded herself that she was old. That she was sick.

Then she asked herself why she was continuing. If exercise was her goal, she'd already accomplished that. A part of her suggested that turning around and forgetting about the view, regardless of how unique it was, as Agent Martin had insisted in his note, would certainly be within the realm of reason.

And, just as swiftly, another part of her refused.

She reached for the folded letter in her pocket, as if her fatigue would be negated by reading it again, but stopped her hand short of the paper. The handgun in her satchel weighed far more than she'd expected, and she wondered why she'd brought it along. She was of half a mind to leave it on some rock, pick it up on her way back, but decided against this.

Diana did not exactly know why she was compelled to reach the location Agent Martin had told her about. Nor did she know why it was so important to see the view he'd mentioned. But she recognized a certain stubbornness and willfulness rooting within her, and thought there was nothing wrong with this, and so she walked on, after treating herself to another lukewarm swig from the water bottle.

She told herself that the world of the Fifty-first State was new, and that on her first full day inside this world she would not allow herself to be frustrated and defeated by exhaustion, illness, or faintness of heart.

It was difficult to walk in the loose sand, and she allowed herself a series of long, loud curses, filling the clear air around her with some obscenities that helped her keep pace. "Fucking dirt," she said. "Goddamn rocks. Stupid cocksucking road."

She smiled as she struggled forward, still climbing. Diana Clayton rarely used these words, so letting them fly from her lips had an exotic, forbidden feel. She stumbled again, though not as severely as earlier. "Fucking goddamn!" She giggled to herself. She stretched out each word, taking a step forward with each syllable of each obscenity.

The road bent around to the left, ducking like a wayward child out of sight.

"Can't be a helluva lot further," she said out loud. "He said a half mile. Can't be much more."

She walked on, following the path, sensing that she'd risen high above the quiet suburban street that she started from. For an instant she was reminded of her home in the Keys, and thought that it was not unlike there, where one instant everything was all pink-painted, garish roadside development, strip malls, and T-shirt shops, and the next the ocean thrust its presence forward and reminded her that nature and the wild, despite all man's hasty and determined efforts to the contrary, was just seconds away. There was a similar quality here. She could feel a sense of solitude. This comforted her. She liked being alone, and thought it one of the few really effective qualities that she'd passed on to her daughter.

She took a deep breath and sang a few bars of an old song. "We are marching to Pretoria, Pretoria. . . ."

The sound of her voice, ragged with exertion, but still hitting the notes more or less squarely, echoed slightly off some of the rocks, rebounding into the high air above her.

"When Johnny comes marching home again, hoorah, hoorah. When Johnny comes marching home again, hoorah, hoorah. When Johnny comes marching home again, we'll give him a mighty cheer again, and we'll all feel glad when Johnny comes marching home. . . ."

She picked up her pace and started swinging her arms.

"Off we go, into the wild blue yonder. Climbing high, into the sky . . ."

She pushed her head back and squared her shoulders.

"Quick march," she barked. "Count off: one-two-three-four. One-two. Three-four—"

She rounded the turn and stopped.

"One-two . . ." she whispered.

The car was pulled just to the side of the road some fifty yards ahead.

It was a white four-door government sedan, the same as the one Agent Martin had used to pick Susan and her up at the airport. She saw the red all-access sticker.

Why would he have driven his car up this road to meet her? She remained standing where she was, filling with other questions. Then, realizing she could not provide answers without stepping forward, the questions were replaced with fear.

Slowly, she reached inside her satchel and removed the pistol.

She thumbed back the safety mechanism.

Then, after swinging her eyes around her and searching the area as best she could from the spot where she was rooted, sharpening her ears to listen for the sound of any other person, but being answered only by the short rasps of her own breath, she stepped forward very slowly and carefully, as if she were suddenly walking along the very narrow edge of a very slippery precipice.

"All right," Hart said, "first tell me a little bit about the man you're seeking. What do you know?"

"He's older than you," Jeffrey replied, "in his sixties, and he's been doing this for years."

The killer nodded. "Right away that's interesting."

Susan looked up. She was taking notes, trying to not only catch the killer's words, but the inflections and the emphases, which, she thought, might ultimately tell her more. There was a video camera mounted on one of the walls, recording the session, but she did not trust technology to capture what she might hear, sitting only a few feet from the man.

"Why is that interesting?" she asked.

Hart grinned his lopsided smile. "Your brother knows. He knows that the basic serial killer profile, the one that scientists like him have been modifying for decades, doesn't really like older men. It prefers younger men, such as myself. We're strong. Filled with dedication. Men of action. Older men tend toward the more contemplative, Susan. They'd rather think about killing. *Fantasize* about killing. They have less energy for the actual *doing*. So, from the start, your man out there must be driven by mighty forces. Immense desires. Because otherwise, he would probably have retired from the field ten years, maybe fifteen, earlier. He would have been caught and killed by the greatest serial killers of them all . . ." Hart swung a quick glare at the two-way window. ". . . or he might have killed himself, or simply given up and gone into retirement. To stay active when other men are collecting pensions, ah, now that is a man of substance."

The killer reached out with his handcuffed hands and removed another cigarette from the package on the table in front of him. "But you know this, Professor. . . ." Hart bent forward, stuck the cigarette between his lips and struck a match.

"Nasty habit," he said. "I like nasty habits."

Jeffrey maintained a cold, clear voice. He had the distinct sensation of being in a zoo, and staring through a plate of glass into the eyes of an

African mamba snake. Being so close to something so deadly had given him a strange sense of peace within. "His victims have been young."

"Fresh," the killer said.

"Abducted without witnesses . . ."

"A man of great care and great control."

"Found in isolated locations, but not hidden. Arranged."

"Ah, a man of messages. He wants his work to be seen."

"With no link to any crime scene."

The killer snorted. "Of course not. It is a game, is it not, Susan? Death is always a game. If we're sick, do we not take medications to outwit the reaper? Do we not put air bags in our cars and wear our seat belts, trying to anticipate how he might sneak up on us and seize us when we're unawares?"

Susan nodded.

"I am death," Hart said quietly. "Your subject is death. Play the game. That's why your brother has brought you here, I suspect. You must see the game, and play it."

The killer turned back to Jeffrey.

"You were clever with me. I take my hat off to you, Professor. I had anticipated so much—stakeouts, decoys—all the usual police entrapments. It never occurred to me that you would simply use all those women carrying all those electronic homing devices as bait. It was such a stroke of genius, Professor. And so cruel, why, near as cruel as I. You couldn't have expected the first to successfully trigger the device. Maybe not even the third. Or the fifth. It has always bothered me, Professor. Just how many women were you willing to sacrifice before springing the trap?"

Jeffrey hesitated, then replied: "As many as it took."

The killer grinned. "A hundred?"

"If it needed to be."

"I left you no other option, did I?"

"None that I could determine."

David Hart giggled again. "You liked killing them as much as I, didn't you, Professor?"

"No."

Hart shook his head. "Okay, Professor. Sure you didn't."

There was a small silence in the room. Susan wanted to turn and look at her brother, to try to figure out precisely what was going through his mind, but she was afraid to turn away from the killer in front of them, fearing that somehow the rush of words would crack and split, like a rock exposed to too much heat. He's going to tell us what we want to know, she thought.

The killer lifted his head. "First, you must understand, there is a vehicle."

"What sort?" Susan asked.

"A transportation vehicle. It must be large enough to handle the victim. It must be ordinary enough to avoid any attention. It should be reliable. These out-of-the-way places? Four-wheel drive?"

"Yes. Very likely," Jeffrey answered.

"It will be customized, for special purposes. Tinted windows."

Jeffrey nodded. Not a truck, he surmised, because that would be notice-able in a suburban area. Not a fancy four-wheel-drive utility vehicle, because he would have to shove the body into the backseat, or lift it high into a trunk. What would fit? He knew the answer to his own internal ques-tion. There were several types of minivans manufactured with four-wheel drive. Perfect suburban vehicles, they would be common in communities where parents were always driving squads of kids to Little League games.

"Go on," Jeffrey said.

"Did the police ever find tire tracks?"

"Tracks were identified. But never a consistent pair."

"Ah, that tells me something."

"What?"

"Did it not occur to you, Professor, that perhaps the man changes the tires on his vehicle with every adventure, because he knows tread marks can be traced?"

"It has."

The killer grinned. "That is the first problem. Transportation. The next is isolation. Your subject, is he wealthy?"

"Yes."

"Ah, that helps. Immensely." Hart once again turned toward Susan. "I did not have the luxury of unlimited sums of money. So I was forced to choose a place that was abandoned."

"Tell me about that choice," Jeffrey asked.

"One must be careful. One must be confident that one cannot be seen. Cannot be heard. Cannot be noticed. That his comings and goings will not draw attention. There are many criteria. I searched for weeks before I found my place."

"And then?"

"A careful man knows his own ground. I measured and memorized. I studied every centimeter of the warehouse before I moved in, ah . . . my materials."

"What about security?"

"The place itself should be by nature secure. But I set up small pitfalls and noisemakers—a trip wire here and there, cans with nails, that sort of thing. Of course, I knew how to avoid all this. But a clumsy professor and two stumbling detectives, why, they made a complete racket coming in. All that noise cost them dearly, Susan."

"So I gathered."

Hart laughed again. "I like you, Susan. You know, even though I'd like to slice you in half, it doesn't mean I want someone else to have that unique and very sweet pleasure. So, Susan, here is a bit of warning from your admirer. When you find your man, be quiet. Be very quiet. Be very cautious. And assume, always assume, Susie-Q, that he is waiting in the very next little shadow for you."

The killer let his voice drop, just slightly, so that the whiny, childlike quality was suddenly replaced by a coldness that surprised her. "And your brother can tell you from his own experience: Do not hesitate. Not even for one second. If you have the opportunity, take it, Susan, because we are all of us very quick when it comes to delivering death. You will remember that, won't you?"

"Yes," she replied, a small crack in her voice.

Hart nodded. "Good. Now I've given you a little chance." He turned back to Jeffrey.

"But you, Professor, even though you know these things, I am confident that you will hesitate and that it will cost you your life. You are too interested in the seeing. That is what drives you, no? You want to watch. You want to see it all happening, in all its uniqueness and glory. You are a man of observation, not action, and when the moment arrives, you will be trapped in your own hesitancy and that will mean your death. I will save a place in Hell for you, Professor."

"I caught you."

"Ah, no, Professor. You *found* me. And had it not been for that dying detective's two shots and the unfortunate loss of blood I experienced, that scar on your thigh would be somewhere else."

The killer gestured toward his chest, drawing a slow, long line in the air with his talonlike index finger.

Jeffrey found his right hand dropping inadvertently to his leg, to the spot where Hart's knife had carved him.

He remembered being frozen, rooted to a single spot, as the killer had passed out at his feet, after swinging the hunting knife once, slicing him badly.

Jeffrey wanted to rise and leave right at that moment. He found himself already imagining the excuse he would concoct for his sister. But in the same instant he knew that he had not yet learned what he needed to know.

He thought this knowledge might be close, and so he shifted about uncomfortably and remained in his seat. It took a great force of will for him not to rise and flee the small room.

The killer hadn't noticed Jeffrey's short breaths, but his sister did, though she didn't turn his way for she knew that would draw Hart's attention in that direction. Instead, she blurted out: "So, you needed security and isolation. What else?"

Hart eyed her. "Privacy, Susan. Complete privacy." He smiled. "You need to be able to focus without even the mildest threat of distraction. All your attention, all your strengths, all your being, is directed in that single location. Isn't that true, Professor?"

"Yes."

"You see, Susan, the moment you want is special. It is unique. It is powerful. Overwhelming. It fuses everything within your being into that one glorious moment. It belongs to you and her and no one else. But, at the same time, you know that like every great achievement that's ever been accomplished throughout the long and tedious history of our world, this one is fraught with danger: fluids, fingerprints, hair fibers, DNA results—all these details that the authorities are so mundane and expert at collecting. So, your place must accommodate your control of all these things. But at the same time, you cannot make the adventure, ah . . . antiseptic. Then the excitement would be lost."

Again Hart paused, raising a single eyebrow. "You understand all this, Susan? Do you understand what I'm saying?"

"I'm beginning to."

"The tunes you play are your own," the killer said.

Susan nodded, but Jeffrey sat bolt upright.

"Say that again," he said.

Hart turned to him. "What?"

But by this time Jeffrey was waving his hand. "No, no, it's all right." He stood, gesturing toward the two-way mirror. "We're finished. Thank you, Mr. Hart."

"I'm not finished," Hart said slowly. "We're finished when I say so."

"No," Jeffrey said. "I know what I need. End of interview."

The killer's eyes bulged wide for an instant, and Susan almost recoiled from the strength of his sudden hatred. The handcuffs rattled in the metal restraint. Two burly prison guards entered the room. They both took a single look at the twisted man, sitting at the table, seething, and one of them went to a small intercom system mounted on the wall and matter-of-factly called for a "special escort team." Then he turned to the Claytons and said: "He seems to have become agitated. It might be a good idea if the both of you left first."

Susan could see a vein bulging on the killer's forehead. He'd slumped over, but his neck muscles were rigid with tension.

"What did I say, Professor?" Hart asked. "I thought I was being cautious."

"You gave me an idea."

"An idea? Professor," Hart said, barely raising his head, "I will see you in Hell."

Jeffrey put his hand on his sister's back, half pushing her through the door. She saw a squad of a half-dozen prison guards coming down an adjacent corridor, armed with riot batons, wearing protective helmets, face shields, and flak jackets. The steel toes of their boots clacked against the polished linoleum floor.

"Perhaps," Jeffrey replied, pausing in the exit. "But you'll get there faster than me."

Hart giggled again, but this time without amusement. Susan guessed it was the same last sound that a number of young women had heard on this earth.

"I wouldn't count on that," he said. "I might guess you're fast on your way there. Hurry, Professor. Be quick."

The prison guards pushed past them, into the room.

"Let's get out of here," Jeffrey said, grabbing Susan's elbow and steering her down the hallway. Behind them, they heard a massive bellow of rage, and several voices in near cry. A smattering of shouted obscenities slid through the air. There was a shuffling of feet and a sudden thwack of bodies coming together hard.

They heard another roar, half outrage, half pain.

"They maced him," Jeffrey said.

The sound abruptly disappeared as they stepped through an electronic sally port. The tall Texas Ranger who'd driven them to the prison was waiting.

He was shaking his head. "Man, that's one sick puppy," the ranger said. "I watched through the observation window. Miss, I thought you kept mighty cool at a couple of real tricky moments. Y'all ever want to quit being what you are and be a Texas Ranger, why, you'd get my vote, sure enough."

"Thank you," Susan said. She took a deep breath, then stopped short. She turned and faced her brother.

"You knew, didn't you?"

"Knew what?"

"You knew he wouldn't even see you, except maybe to spit in your eye. But you also knew that he couldn't resist boasting to me. That's why you wanted me here, right? My presence would loosen his tongue." Her voice had a small quiver to it.

He nodded. "It seemed an appropriate gamble."

Susan let out a long, slow sigh. Then she whispered to her brother: "All right. What the hell did he say?"

" 'The tunes you play are your own.' "

Susan nodded. "Okay. I heard that. But what did you get from it?"

They were quick-stepping through the prison, as if each second was both dangerous and important. "Do you remember, when we were young, the rule? Never disturb him when he was practicing. Down in the basement."

"Yes. Why there? Why not in his study? Or the living room? But he took that violin into the basement to play." Susan's voice was suddenly quick with recognition. "So, what we're looking for is—"

"His music room."

The Professor of Death gritted his teeth.

"Except it isn't music that he plays there."

Diana Clayton had covered half the distance to the car when she saw the figure slumped forward behind the steering wheel. She stopped, once again listening for any sound. Then she gingerly stepped ahead. It seemed the sun's heat had suddenly increased, and she shielded her eyes from the glare reflected off the metal sheen of the vehicle.

Adrenaline was pumping in her ears and her heart was racing. She wiped sweat from her eyes and felt she should hold her breath. She had to force herself to remain alert for anyone else, yet could not help but fix on the figure in the car. She tried to remember when she'd seen other dead bodies, but realized that all the victims of random violence, or highway accidents, that she'd come across in her life had all only provided fleeting visions—a form beneath a sheet, a glimpse of flaccid skin as it was zipped into a body bag. She had never approached a dead person before, and certainly never alone, and never been the first—save one—to confront the facts of violent death.

She tried to imagine what her son would do.

He would be cautious, she told herself. He would not want to disturb the scene of death, because there might be clues to what had happened lying about. He would be alert for every nuance and disturbance surrounding the death, because these things would all tell him something. He would read the area like a monk reading a manuscript.

She stepped forward slowly, feeling utterly inadequate for the task at hand.

She was about ten feet away when she saw that the driver's side window glass was shattered and scattered outside the car. The few shards that remained in place were streaked with crimson and flecks of gray bone and brain matter.

She still could not see the man's face. It was pitched forward against the steering column, jammed down. She wished she could tell who it was by the shape of the shoulders or the cut and color of the clothes, but she could not. She realized she'd have to move much closer.

Her grip on the revolver tightened. She swung around slowly, once again searching the area.

Moving like a parent entering a sleeping child's room, Diana moved to the side of the car. A quick glance in the rear seat showed her it was empty. Then she forced her eyes to focus on the body.

Dangling from the man's right hand was a large-caliber semiautomatic pistol. Gripped in his left was an envelope spattered with blood.

She moved a little closer. The man's eyes were open, and she gasped out loud.

Diana stepped back abruptly as she recognized him.

She backed away from the car unsteadily, a little like a partygoer who realizes she's had one too many, and slumped up against a nearby boulder, still staring at the dead man. She didn't need to remove the note in her pocket to recall what it said. Nor did she think any longer that it was the dead man who'd written the letter, recommending a nice brisk morning walk.

She knew who the author was, just as she knew who the author of the view in front of her was. The thought left an acid, bitter taste in her mouth, and she reached for the water bottle. She took a quick pull, swishing the warm liquid around her tongue. He'd said that what she'd see would be *unique*, she reminded herself. And she supposed that, in a way, death was the only thing that's both commonplace and unique at the exact same time.

UNDERSTANDING THE
ARCHITECTURE OF DEATH

There was an edgy dryness to the afternoon air, which promised a chill that would drop through the darkness of night in the next few hours. It greeted Jeffrey and Susan Clayton when they were escorted to the location where their mother had discovered Agent Martin's body earlier that day. They hadn't been given any details of the death when they landed at the airport and were met by another State Security agent, only informed that "an accident" had taken place.

Susan spotted the turn to their town house, and whispered this information to her brother. There were a pair of State Security cruisers parked at the spot farther up the road, where their mother had turned off Donner Boulevard that morning on her walk. Two uniformed officers guarded access, but had little to do. There was no crowd of excited or curious onlookers. The agent escorting the brother and sister was rapidly waved through. He remained glum and silent, as he had throughout the entire drive from the airport, refusing all conversation. His own vehicle bounced along the rough road surface for a few hundred yards, then skidded to a stop.

A half-dozen vehicles were pulled up short, scattered haphazardly up the old construction trail. Jeffrey could see the same crime scene vehicles that were at the location where the last victim's body had been found. He recognized many of the same faces milling about, as if unsure precisely what to do—which was an unusual response to a crime scene.

"I stop here," the agent said. "They'll want you up there." He gestured toward the activity ahead.

"Where's my mother?" Susan asked, her voice just touching the corner of demand.

"She's up there. Supposed to give a statement, but I heard she said she'd only talk when you got here. Shit," the agent said. "Bob Martin was a friend of mine. Son of a bitch."

Jeffrey and Susan emerged from the car. Jeffrey paused, kneeled down and felt the loose, sandy earth surface, letting a handful slide through his fingers, like some Depression-era Dust Bowl farmer letting his own ruin pass through his hand.

"This is a bad spot," he said. "Dry, windy. Hard on evidence. Bad for clues."

"Someplace else would be better?"

"Someplace moist. There are places where the earth simply holds the details of everything that happens on it. Tells the entire story. You learn how to read those areas, just like a bunch of words on a page. This isn't one of those spots. This is one of the places where much that's written is erased almost as soon as it happens. Damn. Let's go find Mother."

He spotted Diana leaning against the side of a state truck, drinking warm coffee from a thermos. At the same moment, Diana Clayton turned, saw the two of them approaching, and waved with an excitement that seemed to mingle the pleasure of spotting her son and daughter with the sobriety of the situation. Jeffrey was surprised at her appearance. It seemed to him that a pale quality ran right through her entire body. Seeing her on the telephone video screen had not conveyed the wasting effect of the disease. She appeared thin, fragile, as if her muscles and tendons were all that were holding her together. He tried to hide his surprise, but Diana saw it instantly.

"Oh, Jeffrey," she said in mocking reproach. "I don't look all that bad, now, do I?"

He smiled, shaking his head, stepping toward her embrace. "No, no, not at all. You look beautiful."

They hugged, and Diana whispered the truth in her son's ear. "It's like I have death inside of me."

Still holding him by the arms, she leaned back and looked at him closely. Then she lifted one hand from his elbow and stroked it alongside his cheek. "My beautiful boy," she said softly. "You have always been my beautiful boy. It will probably be wise to remember that in the days ahead."

Then Diana half turned and waved to Susan, who'd held back, and gestured her into the embrace. "And my perfect girl," she said. A tear had formed in the corner of her right eye.

"Oh, Mother," Susan said, her voice almost like a teenager's, as if she were embarrassed by the affection but secretly delighting in it.

Diana stepped back, forcing a smile onto her face and shaking away any other display of emotion. "I hate what's brought us all together," she said, "but I love the three of us being together."

The three of them lingered for a moment, then Jeffrey looked up.

"I have work to do," he said. "How did—"

Diana pressed the letter she'd received, with the directions for her walk, into his hand. Susan read over his shoulder.

"I followed the instructions. It all seemed innocent enough until I started climbing up here and found poor Agent Martin over there, in his car. He'd shot himself. Or so it appeared. I didn't get too close. . . ."

"You didn't see anyone else?"

"If you mean *him*, no . . ." Diana hesitated, then added, "but I could feel him. Sense his presence. Smell him, maybe. I thought he was watching me the entire time I was up here, but of course there wasn't anyone here. Anyway, there was nothing I could do, so I called the authorities and then waited for you two to return. Everyone, I must say, has been very polite. Especially the gentleman in charge . . ."

Jeffrey turned, the letter still open in his hand, and saw the official he called Manson standing by the agent's car, staring in at the body.

Susan was still reading. "Agent Martin never wrote that," she said quietly. "That would never be his style. Nor his wording. Too arcane, too generous with words." She paused. "We know who wrote that."

Jeffrey nodded.

"I wonder why he wanted me to come up here," Diana said.

"Maybe to see what he's capable of," Susan replied.

Jeffrey nodded. "Stay close, Susie, Mom. I may need your help." Then he walked toward Agent Martin's car.

Manson was staring hard at the blood-spattered glass strewn next to the driver's side window as Jeffrey approached. He turned and a wan politician's smile slipped across his face. Then he reached into the pocket of a sport coat, removing a pair of latex gloves, which he flipped through the air toward Jeffrey. "Here. Now I can watch the famous Professor of Death performing his real job."

Jeffrey wordlessly snapped the gloves on.

"Of course, publicly, there's no story. At least, not much of one," Manson continued. "Despondent over recent job difficulties, no family to support him, a trusted and dedicated state employee unfortunately chose to take his own life. Even here, where so much is right, there's little we can do about the occasional depression. It only serves to remind the rest of us how fortunate we truly are. . . ."

"He didn't kill himself. You know that."

Manson shook his head. "Sometimes, Professor, our world requires two separate interpretations of events. There is, of course, the obvious—which I've just stated. And then there's the less obvious. This interpretation remains, shall I say, more private? Between us." He looked toward the crime scene technicians. "Their job here is merely to process anything that you determine might be of help in your inquiries. Otherwise, this is a suicide, and will be treated as such by State Security. Tragic."

Manson stepped away from the side of the car. With a slight bow and a sweep of his arm, he motioned for Jeffrey to join him. "Tell me what happened, Professor. Tell me exactly what you see. And tell only me."

Jeffrey moved to the passenger side of the car and opened the door. His eyes swept over the interior swiftly but carefully. He noted the two sets of binoculars tossed on the seat. Then he turned his attention to Agent Martin's body. He felt a coldness within him, almost as if he were inspecting a painting in a gallery by a second-rate artist. The longer he paused, searching the canvas in front of him, the more apparent the flaws in the portrait. The agent's body had slumped sharply to the left, driven by the force of impact from the shot. His eyes and mouth were open, macabre, as if astonished by death. The wound itself was massive, destroying much of the skull, which only served to make the expression on the blood-streaked face even more eerie, gargoylelike.

Still leaning across the seat, he saw that the left hand held an envelope that was also coated with blood trails and flecked with viscous, clear brain matter. The right hand, loosely gripping the huge nine-millimeter pistol, was flopped on the seat. He continued to search the body with his eyes, and spotted the rip in Martin's pants, just at the knee, and saw that his leg was scraped and had been bleeding prior to death. He bent in farther and lifted the detective's pants leg from the ankle. The flat throwing knife that he'd worn the afternoon they'd first met at the university lecture hall had been replaced by a short-barreled .38-caliber pistol strapped into a leather ankle holster.

He dropped the pants leg.

Not too many people carry two separate weapons to their own suicides, he thought.

He looked again at Martin's eyes.

Was that your last thought? he wondered. How to get to that pistol? How to fight back? He shook his head: You didn't have a chance.

Through the window, Jeffrey glanced out at Manson, who had stepped back from the death scene. He didn't say anything, but thought: *So, now the assassin who was supposed to solve your problem after I delivered my father to him has been ambushed and killed himself. Not quite sharp enough. Not quite smart enough. Not quite deadly enough.*

He saw Manson grimace, as if the same thought had struck him simultaneously.

And now you must place all your hopes for a solution in someone you can't control. And you probably find that considerably less pleasant, don't you? Not as unpleasant as what will happen if I don't find my father. But unpleasant nevertheless.

He smiled briefly, envisioning the answer to that question.

Jeffrey half stood and made a quick search of the backseat, but found nothing obvious, although he knew that's where his father, the killer, had been sitting. He allowed himself the small hope that there might be some microscopic clothing fiber or hair residue left behind. Maybe even a fingerprint. But he doubted it. He doubted further that, despite what Manson had said, he'd be permitted to order a complete processing of the car.

Jeffrey stood up and reached inside a jacket pocket, removing a small leather case, which contained a few metal instruments. He took a set of gleaming steel tweezers and leaned back inside the car, across the passenger seat. Gently, but firmly, he removed the envelope from Martin's dead fingers. Taking care not to touch it, he saw, printed on the exterior in thick black pencil marks, the initials *J.C.*

He started to open the envelope, then stopped.

He turned and beckoned to his sister, twenty yards away. She saw him, nodded, and left Diana, who was still sipping coffee.

"What is it?" Susan asked as she approached.

Jeffrey saw that she kept her eyes averted from the inside of the car. But then she bent down and stared inside.

After a moment, Susan straightened up. "Ugly," she said.

"He was an ugly man."

"And he met an ugly end. Still . . ."

"This was in his hand. You're the expert with words. I thought you should read it with me."

Susan carefully examined the envelope and its J.C. initials. "Well," she said, "I don't suppose there's any doubt as to whom it's addressed, unless perhaps Jesus Christ is on our dear old dad's mailing list. Open it up."

Using the tweezers delicately, not unlike a surgical resident who doesn't quite trust the steadiness in his hands yet, Jeffrey undid the envelope. It had been sealed with tape, not saliva, a detail he noted ruefully. Both brother and sister could see a single sheet of common white note paper folded inside. Grasping it by the edge, Jeffrey unfolded the paper on the hood of the car.

For a moment they both remained silent.

"Well, I'll be damned," Susan said, whistling the words between her teeth.

The paper was blank.

Jeffrey knitted his brows. "I don't get it," he said quietly.

He turned the page over and saw that the back side was blank as well. He held the paper up, toward the setting sun, searching the page for signs of writing, even in lemon juice, or some other material that would perhaps show up under fluoroscopic light.

"I'll have to take this back to some lab," he said. "There are techniques for bringing out hidden words. Black light, laser technology—a bunch. I wonder why he would hide what he's written. . . ."

Susan shook her head. "You don't get it, do you?"

"Get what?"

"The blank page. That *is* his message to you."

Jeffrey snatched a quick breath of air from the growing chill surrounding them. "Explain," he said softly.

"A blank page says as much as one that's filled with words. Says more, probably. It says you don't know anything. It says to you he's unknown, blank. It tells you to learn from what you see, not what you're told. What is a child to a father? You start with a blank, and then form a personality upon that baby. Many things. The white canvas waiting for the painter's first stroke. The author's first words on a blank page. It's all symbolic. The strength of what he *doesn't* say is far greater than what he might have said. Symbolism. Symbolism. Symbolism."

Slowly, her brother nodded. "The detective deals in concretes. . . ." he said.

"But the killer deals in images."

Again Jeffrey inhaled cool air from the still afternoon. "And the professor, the teacher . . ." he said.

"Should be able to bridge the two," Susan finished.

Jeffrey turned away from the car, taking a few brisk steps along the dirt path. Susan hesitated, letting him distance himself for an instant, then quickly jogged after him.

The two of them settled into a walking pace, quiet with their thoughts. Susan felt a sense of fear creeping through her as she watched her brother struggle with his own unsettled feelings.

"We should just get the hell out of here," he said, stopping abruptly.

"No," she replied. "We've been found. No hiding again."

"And what are we supposed to do? Arrest him? Kill him? Ask him to leave us alone?"

"I don't know."

"He is evil."

"I know that."

"And he is a part of us. Or, maybe we're a part of him."

"And?"

"I don't know, Susie."

Again they were both quiet.

Jeffrey turned away from his sister, staring up the path. "What the hell were they doing up here?" he asked abruptly.

Then he spotted a small black shape in the loose, sandy dirt. It was not unlike a stone, but far too perfectly round to be made by nature. He picked it up and dusted it off. It was the lens cap from one of the sets of binoculars. He looked back at the car, then continued walking, his sister keeping pace beside him.

They walked stride for stride around the small bend, then down the pathway. "What was he up here looking for?" Jeffrey asked.

Susan stopped. She pointed ahead, and Jeffrey saw stretching below him the complex of town houses.

"Us," she said. "The good agent was spying on us. Why?"

Jeffrey thought for a moment. "Because he expected his quarry to show. That's why he was up here."

He scanned the scene, and near a rock saw the discarded and crumpled-up cellophane wrapper from Agent Martin's Danish roll. "He waited here, watching. Then, for some reason, he turned and headed fast back down the path. I'd say he was running hard, because there's a scrape mark on his leg that must have been caused by a stumble and fall. Probably where I found the lens cap."

"A man in a hurry for his own suicide?"

"No. A man who thinks he saw something, only to discover something else."

"A trap?"

"A man who sets a trap is usually filled with a false confidence, which in most cases prevents him from seeing the trap he's walking into. Anyway, that's a reasonable guess. He came up here alone to spy, only he wasn't alone. I can think of a couple of scenarios. He tried to run. Maybe. He gets into the car, but by this time he's already got a gun to his head. Maybe. Or maybe his killer was waiting for him in the car. Maybe. Anyway, then he dies. Actually, he's killed. One bang and the killer shoves the pistol—the detective's own pistol—into his hand. Simple enough. There's just enough contrived phoniness for the state to say he killed himself. . . ."

Jeffrey caught himself thinking of young women who disappeared and were said to have been attacked by wild dogs. He did not say this out loud. He thought inwardly that to kill in a place so actively dedicated to obscuring the truth must be a fabulous luxury for the killer. He looked up and off into the distance, measuring the ridges of mountains just catching the last of the day's light, glowing with a fertile green and red, spectacular, pristine. An expanse of world waiting for a new history to be written on it. The safest place in the nation to live was also the safest place in the nation to kill.

He doubted that Manson would as readily appreciate that irony.

"We don't need to know precisely. . . ." Susan was speaking slowly, and Jeffrey turned to listen. "Sometimes a message rests in the juxtaposition of events. Of ideas. What he wants us to know is how he controls the details of death."

Jeffrey nodded.

"He sets elaborate snares. He wants you to think one thing, right up to the moment you realize that something completely different, that he controls, is happening."

"Exactly. The best puzzles are always mazes. There are always clues and evidence that point the wrong way."

Susan hesitated, letting a grimace slide around the corners of her mouth. There was a hardness to her eyes that Jeffrey hadn't seen before. "There's one other thing that occurs to me," she said.

"Which is?"

"Don't you see how he communicates with us?"

Jeffrey shook his head. "I'm not sure I follow."

Susan's voice seemed to grow small in the air around them, as if each word was swept up and pummeled by the breeze. "To me, he has written games. Played with words. In other words, he's spoken to me in the language I know. *Mata Hari.* The queen of puzzles. To you, something different. His messages for you are in your language: violence and murder. *The Professor of Death.* They're puzzles of a different sort, but puzzles nonetheless. Isn't that just like a parent? Tailoring the means of communication to the unique abilities of each child?"

Jeffrey suddenly felt sick inside. "Damn," he whispered.

"What?"

"Seven years ago, shortly after my appointment to the university, one of my students disappeared. A student I didn't really know, just another face in a large lecture hall. She was found in a posture similar to the girl who was killed when we left New Jersey, when we were children. And the same way as the first victim here in the Fifty-first State. It was this connection that Agent Martin used to bring me here. . . ."

"But it wasn't really Agent Martin who was calling you here," Susan said slowly. "It was him."

"And did he know I'd bring you? And Mother?"

Susan paused again. "I think we'd best assume he did. Maybe that was the point of all the messages to me."

They both remained quiet for a moment.

"The question remains: Why?" Susan said.

"I don't know that answer. Not yet," Jeffrey said slowly. "But I do know one thing."

"Which is?"

"We damn well better find him before he answers that question for us."

Diana retired to the small room with the cot in order to rest, which was difficult for her. Not merely the pain that had taken this moment to remind her of its presence, but the unsettling nature of the policeman's death, mingling with her fears about what the next hours or days held for her children and herself—all conspired to keep her fidgeting on the bed. She knew that in the adjacent room her two children were trying to figure out how to find the threat to the three of them, and she felt a twinge of frustration, being left out of the process.

Brother and sister sat at the computer terminals in the main office, isolating the factors they would search for.

"On the plans," Jeffrey said, "it will be identified as a music room."

"Or den? Audiovisual theater?"

"No. Music room. Because he will have wanted to insulate it with soundproofing material."

"A theater would require the same."

"All right. That's true. We'll look for that as well."

"But the location inside the house should be critical," Susan added. "If someone were a piano player, for example, or even a cellist, they would want something centrally located. Main floor, perhaps adjacent to the living room or family room. That sort of thing. Because, you know, they wouldn't want to hide what they were doing—it should only have the capacity for privacy. We're looking for a different sort of separateness."

Jeffrey nodded. "Isolation. Removed from the mainstream of the house. Not buried—there should be some easy access. But close to it. And perhaps some sort of hidden exit as well."

"Do you think he would build a guest house? And devote it to his music?" she wondered.

"No. Not necessarily. A guest house seems to me to be more vulnerable. Remember what your friend Mr. Hart said about controlling the environment. And back in Hopewell, he did that in the basement, removed but not separate. There's another element which contributes to this. . . ."

"What's that?"

"The psychology of killing. The deaths he's created are a part of him. A part of his essential being. They're close to his core. He'll want them to be near him at all times."

"But the bodies, they were spread around the state. . . ."

"The bodies are merely detritus. Waste product. They have nothing more to do with who he is and what he does. What happens in that room . . ."

"That's what makes him who he is," Susan said, completing his thought. "I can see that. That's what, more or less, *your* friend Mr. Hart was saying." She sighed, staring at her brother. "It must hurt you," she said quietly.

"What?"

"That you can think of these things so readily."

He did not reply at first, which she took to be a difficult answer. Finally, he nodded. "I'm scared, Susie. Terrified."

"Of him?"

Jeffrey shook his head. "No. Of being like him."

She was quick to rush a denial through her lips, but forced herself to stop short, making a small gasping sound as she did.

Jeffrey reached into a drawer and slowly removed a large semiautomatic handgun. He clicked the release, dropping the loaded clip to the floor, then pulled back on the action, popping the chambered cartridge out, where it, too, clattered against the desktop before tumbling silently to the carpet. "I own several weapons," he said.

"Everyone does," his sister responded.

"No. I'm different. I won't allow myself to shoot," he said. "I've never pulled a trigger."

"But you've been part of so many arrests. . . ."

"I've never fired. Sure, I've pointed. And made threats. But actually pulled the trigger? Never. Not even in practice."

"Why not?"

"I'm afraid I'll like it."

He was quiet for a while. He set the weapon down on the edge of the desk in front of him.

"I never screw around with knives," he said. "They're too obvious a temptation. It's never bothered you?"

"Never."

"And you would have no doubts? No hesitation?"

"No . . ." she replied, less forcefully. "But then, I've never seen it in the same context before."

Jeffrey nodded. "Makes you think, no?"

"A little."

"Susie, if it comes to it, don't hesitate. Shoot. Don't wait for me. Don't expect me to act. Don't expect me to be decisive. You've always been the impetuous one. . . ."

"Sure," she replied cynically. "The one who stayed at home with Mom while you went out and made something of yourself. . . ."

"But you have been. Always. The one who took the risks. I was Mr. Study Drone. Mr. No Life Except Work and Books. Don't count on me when it all comes down to needing action. You take charge. Do you understand what I'm saying?"

Susan nodded. "Of course."

But inwardly she had her own doubts.

The two remained silent until Jeffrey swung around at his seat, abruptly facing the computer screen. "All right," he said, with a sharpness in his words that spoke of determination. "Let's see if all these rules and regulations and agreements and restrictions that they've got in this brand-new world of tomorrow can actually help us find him."

He punched some keys, and in moments the screen filled with the words: APPROVED ARCHITECTURE PLANS/51ST STATE.

Checking through the housing plans was drudgery. They were limiting themselves only to houses constructed in blue areas, because they didn't think that homes built in lesser economic strata would have the same element of privacy. This was a close call, however, because Jeffrey recognized there was a certain satisfaction for the killer to place his work dangerously close to neighbors. The literature of murder, he reminded his sister, was filled with tales of dull neighbors who'd heard heartrending cries coming from some adjacent home, only to ignore them, or to attribute them to some benign if farfetched source, like dogs or cats. Isolation, he pointed out, could often be psychological, not necessarily physical. Still, they knew from Jeffrey's trip to New Jersey that their father had plenty of money, so they stuck with the custom-designed, highest-priced homes.

The computer had records and plans for every house, condo, town home, shopping mall, church, school, gymnasium, and security station built in the state. It also had plans for any older houses that had been redone according to state-mandated specifics, as the various territories were incorporated in the state. Jeffrey did not spend much time with this category; he suspected that his father had arrived in the Fifty-first State with an agenda, and sought out a blank slate on which to start writing. It will be a new house, he told himself, dating from the first year or two of the proposed state as it took form, driven by the forces of money and security.

The problem was, there were just under four thousand top-of-the-line homes in the state. By cutting away all the homes built after the first confirmed disappearance of a young victim, they managed to reduce that number into the seven hundreds.

Jeffrey thought this ironic. He is a man of planning, he thought, and a man of spontaneity. He is adaptable, yet rigid.

He will not have killed here before he was completely ready. Until he had all the securities of design in place and correct. He would want his knowledge of the state, and how it functioned, to be complete. The preparation for a murder would be almost as intriguing and as exciting as the killing itself. And when it happened, with smoothness and precision, it must have been thrilling for him.

He thought of the violin at his father's fingertips: practice runs, practice scales, practice movements, practice finger positions, practice each note until it was correct—and then and only then would he play the entire symphony from start to finish.

Jeffrey moved another set of plans to the screen in front of him. He tried to recall the offspring of any great musician—any musician whose work had lasted through the centuries—whose child's efforts had equaled the father's genius. He could not think of any. He imagined artists, writers, poets, filmmakers—and still could not think of any case where the child had gone beyond the parent.

Am I the same? he wondered.

He looked at the set of plans hovering on the screen in front of him. It was a beautiful home, he thought. Airy, filled with graceful shapes and spaces, rooms that spoke optimistically of the future, not the past, like so many of the homes in the Fifty-first State.

He punched a key and sent the plans back into computer storage oblivion. Not that one. He stole a glance at his sister. She, too, was shaking her head and moving to another set.

Brother and sister sat, working together, for hours.

Whenever either pulled up a set of architect's floor plans that had a space that conceivably could fit their hypothesis, they isolated the house. They then checked the site plan, to see its relationship to other homes in the housing areas. Then the computer would provide a three-dimensional rendering of the home. If the room in question still seemed to fit the necessary

criteria of location, isolation, and access, they found the contractor's specifications and searched through these for the materials that would deaden the
sound in the room.

This processing eliminated most of the homes. The few with rooms that
conceivably could be used for the music of murder were set aside.

It was several hours after midnight when they managed to reduce the
operative list to forty-six houses.

Susan stretched her arms. "Now," she said, "the issue is how do we
figure out—short of knocking on each and every damn door—which,
assuming we're right, belongs to our father. What's the next eliminating
criteria?"

Before Jeffrey could reply to his sister's question, he heard a noise
behind him. He swiveled in his seat and saw his mother standing in the
doorway. "You should be resting," he said.

"Something occurred to me. Two somethings, actually," Diana responded.
She strode across the room, pausing and looking down at the last schematic
drawing on the computer screen in front of Susan.

"What is it?" Susan asked.

"First of all, we're here because he wants us to find him. Because he has
three different agendas. He's shown that already."

"Go on," Jeffrey said slowly. "How do you mean?"

"Well, he's tried to kill me once. His bitterness toward me should be
simply a single, cold rage. I stole you away. And now, in effect, the two
of you have brought me back to him. He will kill me, and he'll enjoy my
death."

Diana hesitated as an image assaulted her. He will consider killing me
the same way a thirsty man views a quenching glass of water on a hot day,
she thought.

"Then you must leave," Susan said. "We were stupid to bring you here
in the first place. . . ."

Diana shook her head. "This is where I belong," she insisted. "But what
he has in mind for the two of you is different. Susan, I think he poses the
least threat to you."

"To me? Why?"

"Because he was the one who saved you in that bar. And there may be
other moments that we don't even know about. There's something special
about a daughter to most fathers, no matter how awful that father may
be. They're protective. They're in love, in their own way. I think, twisted
as it is, he wants you to love him, too. So I don't think he wants to kill
you. I think he wants to enlist you. That was the thrust of the games he's
played."

Susan snorted a denial, but did not voice it. It would have been a weak-kneed protest.

"That leaves me," Jeffrey said. "What do you think he has in mind?"

"I'm not precisely certain. Fathers and sons struggle. Many fathers speak of how they want their sons to do better than they, but I think most men lie when they say that. Not all, but most. They'd rather prove that they're superior, just as the son wants to supplant his father."

"Sounds like a lot of Freudian garbage to me," Susan interjected.

"But should we ignore it?" Diana replied.

Again Susan didn't respond.

Diana sighed. "I think you're here for the most elemental of contests," she said. "To prove who is better. The father or the son. The killer or the detective. That's the game we've been caught up in. We just didn't know it." She reached out her hand and touched Jeffrey on the shoulder. "I just don't know how exactly one wins this contest."

Jeffrey felt like a child, growing smaller, more insignificant, less powerful, with each word. He thought his own voice might crack and quaver, and he was thankful when it did not. But in the same moment, he became aware of a rage within him, an anger that he'd shunted away, hidden and ignored for the entirety of his life. This fury started to boil within him, and he could feel the muscles on his arms and across his stomach tighten.

She's right, he thought. There's just one fight that I'll have in my entire life, and this is it, and I must win it. "There was something else, you said, Mother? Another idea?" Jeffrey asked.

Diana frowned. She turned to the remaining house plan on the computer screen, gesturing with a bony finger at the dimensions. "Big, right?"

"Yes," Susan said.

"And there are rules here, are there not?"

"Yes," Jeffrey said.

"House is too big for a man alone, and the state doesn't allow single men except under exigent circumstances. And, after all, what were we, twenty-five years ago? Camouflage. The buffer that created the illusion of normalcy. The fiction of the happy suburban home. Don't you see what he's got here?"

Both Susan and Jeffrey remained silent.

"He's got a family. Like us." Diana's voice was low, almost conspiratorial. "But this family will be different from us in one critical way." Diana turned toward Jeffrey, fixing him with a solid, dark look. "He will have found a family that *helps*," she said.

She stopped, a look of astonishment crossing her face, as if surprised by her own words. "Jeffrey, is such a thing possible?"

The Professor of Death quickly inventoried his internal history of killers.

Names leapt out at him: the Philadelphia shoemaker Kallinger, who took his thirteen-year-old son along on his gruesome sex and killing sprees; Ian Brady and Myra Hindley and the Moors murders in England; Douglas Clark and his lover, Carol Bundy, in California; Raymond Fernandez and the immense sexual sadist, Martha Beck, in Hawaii. Studies and statistics jumped into his head.

"Yes," he said slowly. "It is not only possible. It is probably likely."

THE NINETEENTH
NAME

It was midmorning when Jeffrey was summoned to Manson's office. He, his mother, and his sister had spent what little remained of the night in his office, occasionally sleeping fitfully, but primarily trying to identify the factors that would narrow the field of possibilities in discovering where his father lived. His mother's recognition that her husband would have acquired a second family had placed all three of them in a state of confusion tinged with despair. Jeffrey, in particular, knew the dangers inherent in the idea that the man stalking them had accomplices; but it also seemed to him to be an opportunity. He found himself reviewing cases mentally, from the volume of knowledge he'd acquired about repetitive killers. And he wondered whether these adjuncts to his father's world, these lieutenants, however many there were, would be as clever and as capable as he was. He doubted his father had made any mistakes; he was less certain the same would be true of his new wife. Or new children, for that matter.

His shoes slapped against the polished floor as he approached the security director's office. What are they providing? he asked himself. The answer: safety. Obedience to the rules of the Fifty-first State. The illusion of normalcy, just as we did once. What else? He felt certain that his father was determined not to be betrayed again—as his mother had betrayed him. So Jeffrey was drawn to the idea that whoever his father had enlisted would be taking an active role in the creation and execution of his perversions.

A woman of defect, he thought. But a woman of capability.

A sadist, like him. A killer, like him.

But not someone independent. Not someone creative. Not someone who would question his desires for an instant.

A woman of loyalty and devotion.

That's who he found and brought with him here to establish their new life together, he decided. Like some hellish pair of pilgrims arriving on the shores of his own state four hundred years earlier.

But where did he find her?

This last question froze in Jeffrey's imagination. His father, he knew, like so many other repetitive criminals, would have a sixth sense about picking his victims from a crowd, drawn with an evil accuracy to the weak, the indecisive, and the vulnerable. But selecting a partner—that was a different issue. And one that bore examining.

Jeffrey paused, wondering: *And what have they produced?*

He opened the door to the large Security Department warren of office cubicles and took in the steady blur of activity. Then he smiled, as an idea struck him.

He walked swiftly through the room, cheerily greeting the occasional secretary or computer technician who looked up and acknowledged his passing.

He paused outside the director's office, and the secretary-receptionist motioned for him to enter, saying, "He's been expecting you for the past hour. Go right in."

Jeffrey nodded, took a single step, then, as if in an afterthought, turned back to the secretary. "Say," he said casually, "I wonder if you could do me a small favor. There's a document I need for this meeting with the director, but I haven't had time to get it. Could you get one printed out on your computer there?"

The secretary smiled. "Of course, Professor Clayton. What is it?"

"I'd like a listing of everyone who works for State Security, with their home address."

The secretary looked daunted. "Mr. Clayton, that's nearly ten thousand people across the state. Do you mean at every substation and every State Security office? And what about the security people who work for Immigration? Do you mean them, too, because that will be more—"

"Oh," Jeffrey said, still smiling, "I'm sorry. Just the women, please. And only those who have access to computer codes. That should cut the figure down some."

"Over forty percent of State Security employees are women," the secretary pointed out. "And almost all of those know at least some of the computer locks and keys."

"Still need the list."

"Even on the high-speed printer it'll take some time. . . ."

Jeffrey stopped, still thinking. "How many different levels are there in security locks? I mean, as you go up the information ladder in State Security, how many different controls are there?"

"There are twelve, ranging from the entry level codes, which just allow you to access routine information on the security network, right up to the top, which puts you into everyone's computer, including my boss. But at the highest couple of levels, there are individual locks and passwords, so that documents can be kept confidential."

"All right, then. Just print out the names of women with the top three clearances. No, make that four. Presumably anyone that high would be pretty skilled with computer information?"

"Yes. Absolutely."

"Good. Those are the names I'd like."

"It will still take some time. And a request like that—well, it's likely to draw some attention. People whose names are on the list are likely to know that a computer in this office has requested their names and addresses. Is this a secret? Does it have anything to do with what you're here for?"

"The answer to that is maybe. Try to make the inquiry appear as routine as possible, can you?"

The secretary nodded, wide-eyed, as the impact of what he was suggesting with his request sank in. "You think someone in State Security—" she began, but he cut her off.

"I *know* nothing. I just get suspicions. And this is one of them."

"I'll have to tell my boss."

"Wait for our meeting to be finished. And don't get his hopes up."

"Suppose I request all male and female names?" she asked. "Maybe that would draw less attention? And I can add a notation to the request that State Security, specifically the director's office, is considering upgrading a computer level. We do that from time to time. . . ."

"That would be good. As normal, everyday business as possible. Otherwise—well, don't even think about the otherwise. I'd appreciate it. And keep this to this office, too."

The secretary regarded him as if he were crazy to imagine that she'd ever share information about her job or her boss's job with anyone, including a husband, lover, or family pet. She shook her head, then motioned toward the director's door. "He's been waiting," she said briskly.

Inside the office, Manson was once again swiveled about in his seat, staring out his wide picture window.

"You know, it's odd, Professor Clayton," the director said without turning around, "but poets love dawn and dusk. Painters like late afternoon. Lovers like the nighttime. The romantic times of the day. But me? I like midday. Bright sunlight. When the world is at work. When you can see it being built. Brick by brick . . ." He turned away from the window. ". . . or idea by idea."

He reached across his desktop, plucked a water glass from a tray, and filled it from a glistening metal pitcher. He did not offer any to Jeffrey. "What about you, Professor? What time of the day do you like best?"

Jeffrey thought hard for a moment. "I like the deepest night. Shortly before dawn."

The director smiled. "An odd choice. Why is that?"

"It is the quietest time. A secret time. The time that anticipates all things starting to take on the clarity of morning."

"Ah." The director nodded. "I should have guessed. A truth seeker's response."

Manson looked down for a moment at a paper sitting square in the middle of the desk pad in front of him. He fingered the corner of the page but did not share its contents with Jeffrey. "Tell me, Mr. Truth Seeker, what was the truth of Agent Martin's death?"

"The truth? The truth is that he was either tricked or followed into a trap set behind the trap he had created and which he thought would work out the state's dilemma. He was up there on that bluff watching the town house where he'd placed my mother and sister, like a fisherman watching the bobber on his line. I presume he violated the order I gave him, to keep their presence and location secret. . . ."

"A correct assumption. He posted their arrival with Immigration and with State Security."

"On the computer network?"

"That's the way these things are done."

"With your approval, I also presume . . ."

The director hesitated, saying much in the small pause. "It would be easy for me to lie," he said. "I could say that Agent Martin was on his own, which, for the most part, is an accurate statement. I could also say that his actions were all of his own design. That, too, would be true."

"But you would never expect me to completely believe that."

"I can be persuasive. Perhaps sow just enough doubt."

"Agent Martin was never intended to help me in any inquiry. His capabilities as a detective were limited. He was always meant to be the man who would pull the trigger when the moment came. I've known this for some time."

"Ah, I thought his behavior might be too obvious. But his performance as, shall we say, an eradicator of state problems, was exceptional. He was the very best we had, although I suppose one could argue the word *best*."

"But now your killer has been killed."

"Yes." The director hesitated again, smiling. "Now, I suppose you will truly have to earn your money, because I do not have an inexhaustible supply of Agent Martins. . . ."

"No more killers?"

"I would not say that."

Jeffrey stared at the director. "I see," he said. "What you're saying is that Agent Martin's replacement won't be quite as prominent. I hunt while someone I don't know watches me."

"That would be a reasonable assumption. But I have confidence," Manson said coldly, "that you will deal with my problem, just as you deal with your problem, because they remain one and the same."

The director took another sip from the water glass, still staring at Clayton. "It has a nice medieval quality to it, doesn't it? Either bring me his head or tell me where I go to take it myself. You understand? We are speaking of a justice that functions with even more swiftness than is ordinary. This is what happens, Professor. Find him. Kill him. And if you cannot bring yourself to do that, then merely find him, and we will kill him for you."

Again the director's eyes shifted downward momentarily. He sighed, then looked up at Jeffrey with a harsh, narrow gaze. "There is no more time."

"I have some ideas. A few avenues that might provide leads."

"There is no more time."

"Well, I think—"

Manson slammed his palm down on the desk like a shot. "No! No more time! Find him now! Kill him now!"

Jeffrey paused. "I warned you," he said with frustrating coolness, "these sorts of investigations are lengthy. . . ."

Manson's upper lip seemed to curl, like an animal baring its teeth. But the force of his rage was contained in the slow, deliberate way he spoke: "In approximately two weeks' time the Congress of the United States will vote on granting statehood to us. We expect this vote to be substantially in our favor. We have massive corporate backing. Large sums of money have changed hands. But this support, despite all the lobbying, the bribery, and the influence we can muster, is still fragile. After all, these Congress people are being asked to grant statehood to an area which in a de facto manner restricts certain important rights. *Inalienable* rights, our forefathers called them. We deny these rights because they lead to the anarchy of crime that is infecting the entire nation. This creates a sticky situation for these congressional idiots. You can see that, surely, Professor?"

"Yes. I can see the situation is tenuous."

"We are not a new land, Professor. We are a new idea contained within a part of the old land."

"Yes."

"And with the arrival of statehood—official, enfranchised, take-your-place-at-the-table statehood—the entire nation takes a step forward. An irretrievable step in a distinct and important direction. It is the start of them becoming like us. Not us becoming like them. I cannot emphasize that enough, Professor!"

"Yes, I can understand. . . ."

"So, imagine the impact on that vote *this* will have!"

With that, Manson thrust the single sheet of paper in the center of his desk across the surface at Jeffrey. The edge fluttered briefly as if caught in the still air, but Jeffrey snatched it before it floated away.

The paper was a letter, addressed to the director.

My Dear Director:

In October 1888, Jack the Ripper sent George Lusk, head of the Whitechapel Vigilante Committee, a small present, to wit: a piece of human kidney. I suspect this made his point, whatever it was, rather dramatically. As part of his overall amusement, the Ripper also sent a letter to one of Fleet Street's finest outlets, promising them an ear from his next victim. He did not keep this promise, although one has little doubt that he could have, if he'd been of the inclination.

His letter to the paper, his gift to Mr. Lusk, both had the effect one would suspect they'd have. The city of London was thrown into a frenzy and panic. There was but one story those days on everyone's lips: the Ripper and what he might do next.

Interesting, don't you think?

So imagine for yourself what the effect of the following names and dates would be, were I to send them to the real *Washington Post*—not the phony one we have in New Washington—or the *New York Times* and perhaps a television network or two.

That is what I intend to do, in the very near future.

The intriguing thing about this letter is that it is not a threat. Nor is it some crude attempt at extortion or blackmail. You have nothing I want. At least, nothing I can be purchased with. It is merely my way of demonstrating how powerless you truly are.

You might recall, as well, they never caught the Ripper. But everyone remembers who he is.

Beneath this final statement were nineteen names of young women, followed by a month and a day and a place. A quick glance told Jeffrey these cor-
responded to the month and day they disappeared and the location where they
were last seen alive by someone other than their killer. But before he could
examine every name on the list, his eyes were drawn to the final entry. At the
end of the list there was a twentieth name, written in boldface: PROFESSOR JEF-
FREY CLAYTON OF THE UNIVERSITY OF MASSACHUSETTS. It was noted with an
asterisk, and the sarcastic addendum: DATE AND LOCATION TO BE DETERMINED.

Manson was watching Jeffrey's face carefully. "I would think that last
entry might be an added incentive," he said briskly.

Jeffrey did not reply.

"It would seem to me that we both face a considerable threat," Manson
continued. "Though yours has a personal element that renders it somewhat
more provocative."

Jeffrey started to respond, but the security director cut him off.

"Oh, I know what you're going to say. Once again you're going to
threaten to flee. Say that it's not worth it. Run away. Take your mother and
sister and try to hide again. But one must admire your old man just as one
hates him—like the Ripper, I guess. Because by adding you to that list,
whatever he really has in mind, he places such an intriguing doubt in your
mind. And he places it there forever, doesn't he? I mean, regardless of where
you try to hide, you'll always wonder, every time the mail arrives, or the
phone rings, or there's a knock on the door, won't you?"

The director shook his head, and continued. "It's crude, you know, but
effective. If he mails that letter—and you do not find him—well, your professional career is pretty much over, isn't it?"

"Yes," Jeffrey finally replied. "I would guess so."

"There's one other thing I notice as well," the director went on. "Your
father likes to play a major psychological chord, doesn't he? I mean, when he
puts you on that list and makes it public, he pretty much defines the rest of your
life. Wherever you go. Whatever you do. Do you think anyone will ever think
of you as Professor Clayton the expert? The academic? Or will they only
think of you as the murderer's son? And wonder, as I do right now, what
impact those genes flowing through your bloodstream will really have?"

Manson rocked in his chair, watching the agony twist around inside
Clayton.

"You know, Professor," he said slowly, "were the stakes not so high for
all of us—billions of dollars, an entire way of life, a philosophy for the
future—I would find this altogether fascinating. Can the son erase a half of
himself by killing the father?" He shrugged. "Ought to be some really gory
Greek tragedy that tells us the answer. Or some biblical tale."

The director of security smiled humorlessly. "I'm not really up to date on my Greek tragedies. And my Bible studies, shall we say, have suffered in recent months. How about you, Professor?"

"I will do what I have to do."

"I'm sure. And quickly, too. Isn't it interesting that he says he hasn't yet mailed the letter? I can think of only one reason for that."

"Which is?"

"He wants to give you a chance. This provides us with both an opportunity and a curse."

"How?"

"Can't you see, Professor? If you find him and we succeed, why, then we'll have saved everything that so many people have worked so hard for. If we do not—if the date and location of your demise are added to the bottom of that list—why, that is a story that will hit every front page. And, I think, will elevate your father right up there, next to the Ripper. Don't you think?"

Jeffrey thought hard. His own imagination was racing, like a calculator working hard on a problem, grabbing at numbers and factors and searching through the intricacies of a mathematical formula for a conclusion.

"Yes," he said. "And that's the game being played. By ruining you and by ruining me, he sets himself apart. He gives himself a place in history."

Manson nodded. "That's quite an ambitious game. Does your ambition equal it?"

Jeffrey folded the list and placed it in his shirt pocket. "We'll find out, won't we?" he answered.

The director's secretary was waiting with a computer printout, which she thrust at Jeffrey as he emerged from the inner office. He hefted the bulky list in his hand and said, "There must be a thousand names here."

"Actually, eleven hundred and twenty-two. Top four clearance levels." She handed him a second printout, equal in size. "Thirteen hundred forty-seven. All men."

"One quick question," Jeffrey said. "The director's electronic mail. Who would know how to send him a memo or letter?"

"He has two different electronic mailboxes. One is a general comments and suggestions box. Then there is a second, more selective box."

"The letter he received—"

"From your subject?" the secretary interrupted. "Actually, I retrieved it and made certain it went straight to him, without anyone else taking note."

"Which box did it come in?"

The secretary smiled. "It would have been helpful if it came in the private mailbox, wouldn't it? Only the top two security levels have that address. It would have made your job a bit easier. Unfortunately, it came in the general box. This morning. It was time-stamped at 6:59 A.M. Actually, that's sort of interesting. . . ."

"Why?"

"Well, seven A.M. is when I routinely arrive at my desk, and one of my first jobs is always clearing the overnight electronic mail. Usually this only takes a few minutes; I just redirect the comments and suggestions to the appropriate subdirector, or to the security ombudsperson. I can do that by punching a couple of keys. Anyway, there the letter was, number one in the queue, ahead of the usual 'we need a raise' and 'why can't Security change the paint scheme in this substation or another. . . .' "

"So," Jeffrey said slowly, "whoever sent it knew what your first job of the morning is, and when you do it."

"I'm an early riser," the secretary said.

"So is he," Jeffrey replied.

Susan was poring over the case files of abducted and murdered young women when her brother returned from his meeting with the security director. She had spread crime scene photographs and location reports on the floor around her desk, creating a macabre enclosure. Diana stood outside the circle of the dead, her arms folded in front of her, as if trying to hold something within her. They both looked up as Jeffrey entered.

"Progress?" Susan asked immediately.

"Perhaps," her brother replied. "But trouble as well."

He glanced quickly at Diana, who read his eyes, his voice, and the way he held his body, all in a second, and said: "Don't think of excluding me! There's something bothering you, Jeffrey, and your first damn thought is to somehow protect me. Not a chance."

"This is hard," Jeffrey said.

"For all of us," his sister added.

"Maybe. But look at this. . . ."

He handed the two women the copy of the electronic letter the security director had received that morning. "It's my name at the bottom, not yours, Mother," Jeffrey said. "I suppose that's at least fortunate. You aren't on the list."

Susan continued to stare at the letter. "There's something wrong here," she said. "Can I keep this?"

Jeffrey nodded. "On a brighter note, I had an idea. A possibility, I suppose. . . ."

"What?" Susan asked, looking up.

"I was thinking about what Mother said. About a new wife for our dear old dad. And I asked myself: What would he be looking for, in a woman?"

"Jesus. Someone like him?" Susan asked.

Diana didn't say anything.

Jeffrey nodded. "In the literature of repetitive killers there are a few, a noticeable percentage of murderers, who work in pairs. Usually these are a pair of sicko men who've managed, through some undefinable and awful process, to find each other. The confluence of their personalities buttresses and supports the indulgence of their shared murderous perversions—"

"Stop talking like a damn teacher," Susan interrupted. "Get to it."

"But there have been numerous cases of men and women."

"You said that. Last night. The point?"

"The point is, in almost every case, it is the man's perversion that drives the relationship. The woman's is an adjunct. But as the relationship deepens, so does her enjoyment of the torture and the killing, so that ultimately the two become partners in the most real, deepest sense."

"Yes?"

Diana interrupted. "I know what he's driving at," she said softly. "The woman is helping him. . . ."

"Correct. And how does he need help?" Jeffrey gestured widely, around him. "This is where he needs help. This is where he needed to break in, both physically and electronically. This is where he's been watching me. Right from the start. I think the new wife works for the state. For State Security."

He tossed the computer printout on the desktop, where it made a small paper thud. "It's as good a guess as any. And our time is limited."

Susan nodded. "Triangulation," she whispered.

"I'm sorry?"

"It's how one used to find their position on the ocean with radio beacons. If one knew the direction of three different lines, they could determine their position, anywhere on the face of the earth. The key, of course, is knowing the three signals. In a way, that's what we're doing."

Diana joined in. "We know what sort of house to look for, with what sort of space he needs for what he does. . . ."

"And we add to that a name from this list . . ." Jeffrey said.

Susan hesitated, then blurted: "And remember what Hart said, in the prison? A vehicle! The right kind of vehicle for transporting a kidnap victim. A minivan. Tinted windows. Four-wheel drive. Can we get that list as well?"

Jeffrey started working on the computer. "That won't be a problem," he said.

Susan reached for the printout of State Security employees. She started to read from the top of the first page, then stopped. She set the printout down and picked up the letter that had come that morning. Her eyes scanned the pictures of dead women. "Something's wrong," she said. "I can feel it."

She looked over at her mother, then her brother. "I'm never wrong," she said. "It's like those old 'what's wrong with this picture' games that used to come in kids' magazines. You know, where the clown had two left feet, or the football player was holding a baseball."

Again she scanned the pictures of the dead. "I'm never wrong," she repeated.

Jeffrey hit a few computer keys, and on another desk a computer started to print out another list, this time of cars. Then he turned to his sister. "What do you see?" he asked.

"It's all a puzzle, isn't it?" she repeated.

"Every crime is. Serial crimes even more so."

"The positions of the bodies," Susan said, "why are they important?"

"I don't know. Snow angels. When killers are that careful about the way their crimes will be seen and interpreted, it almost always has some psychological reflection. In other words, it *means* something. . . ."

"Snow angels. It was the positioning that brought you here, right?"

"Yes."

"And it created speculation, right? Didn't it make you spend time trying to decipher what was meant by the positioning?"

"Yes. My first weeks here. It fed into my refusal to believe—"

"And then one body . . ."

"It was, in effect, the opposite. Like a little test."

Susan rocked back in her chair, eyeing the dead women. "It means nothing. It means everything." She abruptly swung toward her mother. "You knew him," she said bitterly. "As well as anyone. Snow angels? Young women stretched out as if crucified? Did he ever . . ." She couldn't bring herself to finish the question.

But Diana knew what she was being asked. "No. Nothing that comes to mind. And when we were together, it was always cold and passionless. And quick. As if a duty. Maybe a job of work. There was no pleasure."

Jeffrey opened his mouth as if to respond, then stopped. He looked again at the pictures, stepping to his sister's side. "Maybe you're right. It could be just a deception."

He took a deep breath and shook his head, as if trying to deny what he was thinking, but unable to. "That would be very clever," he said slowly. "There's not a detective in the world—or a psychologist, for that matter—who wouldn't be obsessed with the distinctive arrangement of the victims' bodies. It's the sort of thing we're trained to analyze. It would dominate our thinking precisely because it *is* a puzzle, and we would be compelled to solve it. . . ."

Susan nodded. "But suppose the solution is that what seems to be so critical, really means nothing?"

Jeffrey inhaled sharply. "I hate it all," he said slowly. He closed his eyes. "The index fingers, that's all he really wanted. That was enough to remind him. It's the *doing* that's important to him. The rest is just part of the overall concealment and deception."

Jeffrey let loose a long whistle of air, reached out, and placed his hand on his sister's arm. "We can, you see?"

"Can what?" Susan asked. Her voice was suddenly unsteady, because she saw the exact same thing in the same moment that her brother had.

"Think like him," Jeffrey replied.

Diana gasped. She shook her head hard. "You are mine," she said. "Not his. Remember that."

Both Jeffrey and Susan turned to their mother, smiling, trying to reassure her. But there was a weakness in their eyes that showed only fear about what they were learning about themselves.

Diana saw this, almost panicking. "Susan!" she said sharply. "Put those pictures away! And no more talk about—" She stopped. She realized that the only thing they *could* talk about was precisely what was frightening her.

Susan reached out for the photographs and for the files of the dead women and slowly started to collect them, placing the pictures into manila envelopes, matching documents with pictures. She kept quiet, troubled, still concerned, but of what, she wasn't sure.

She reached for the last picture and stuck it into its proper folder. "There we go, Mother, that's all." Then she turned to her brother, wild-eyed, suddenly crippled by fear.

He saw her, and without knowing why, was struck with the same sudden anxiety.

For an instant Susan held her position, and Jeffrey could almost see her mind working hard. Then Susan pivoted and began counting. "Something wrong, something wrong, oh Jeffrey, Jesus . . ." She moaned.

"What?"

"Twenty-two case files. Twenty-two young women dead or disappeared."

"Right. And?"

"Nineteen names on the letter."

"Yes. Statistically, I was always figuring on ten to twenty percent of the victims' deaths or disappearances being attributable to some other, legitimate cause—"

"Jeffrey!"

"I'm sorry. Don't talk like a teacher. I understand. What do you see?"

Susan grabbed the letter off of the desktop. She groaned. "Number nineteen," she whispered, doubling over as if someone had punched her in the stomach. "The name right above yours."

Jeffrey looked at the name and the numerical entry beside it. "Oh, no," he said. He abruptly reached across and grabbed at the dead files, rifling through them.

"What is it?" Diana asked, her own voice finding the same fear that the others were already enmeshed within.

Jeffrey turned to his mother. His voice was overcome with a cold, harsh bitterness.

"The nineteenth name is not in this pile. And the date is eleven slash thirteen. No year. That's today. The location given is simply *Adobe Street*. I didn't see it," he said, his lip trembling slightly, "because all I could see was my *own* name following it."

MISSING

Jeffrey and Susan stood on the corner of Adobe Street, which was located in a modest community called Sierra, approximately an hour and thirty minutes north of New Washington. A driver from State Security leaned up against a car a half block away, watching the two of them as they slowly surveyed the street. For a moment or two Jeffrey had wondered whether this agent was also the new assassin assigned to shadow their steps, waiting for the moment they uncovered their father. But he doubted it. The replacement killer will be concealed, he thought. Concealed, and anonymous. Following them, waiting for the right moment to emerge. He thought these were capabilities that were probably in short supply in the Fifty-first State, although not so difficult to find in the other fifty. The policemen inside the new world were mostly paper pushers and bureaucrats, closer to accountants and clerks. That was why he guessed the loss of Agent Martin was so problematical.

He spun around abruptly, as if he could catch a glimpse of Agent Martin's double lurking in some hidden spot. He saw no one, which, upon reflection, is what he expected. Manson was not the sort of politician who made the same error twice.

Standing a few feet away from the brother and sister were a middle-aged man and woman. They shuffled their feet nervously, keeping their eyes on the Claytons, not speaking to each other. They were the principal and the assistant principal for student affairs at Sierra High School. The principal was a caricature of the species: small, round-shouldered, and balding, with a nervous habit of rubbing his hands together as if they were cold. He kept clearing his throat, trying to get their attention, but he didn't say anything, although he occasionally glanced at the State Security man, as if expecting the policeman to explain why the two of them had been abruptly pulled from the daily routine of the high school and transported to this small side street a quarter mile away.

The street itself was little more than a dust-strewn swatch of black macadam, barely two blocks long. That it had a name at all seemed a stretch. Midway down the second block was a corrugated steel garage painted a glossy white and deep green, which Susan guessed were the Sierra High School colors. Part of the roof was dedicated to a huge cartoon of a tree replete with arms, legs, face, and snarling teeth, with the logo FIGHTING FIRS OF SIERRA HIGH beneath it.

Jeffrey and Susan walked down the street slowly, their eyes scanning back and forth, searching for anything that might tell them what had taken place that morning. The street dead-ended at a yellow metal gate that guarded a small, dirt access road. There was no other fence, or any other device, simply some mounds of loose gravel and the gate. Jeffrey noticed a touch of color jammed next to one of the concrete pillars that held the gate posts. He walked over and found a red plastic essay holder. Picking it up by the corner, he saw there were a half-dozen printed pages inside. He wordlessly showed the folder to his sister.

The two of them turned back and inspected the garage. It was about the size of a basketball court, and about one and a half stories high. There were no windows, and the large, swing-open double doors in front were padlocked. They walked around the building. Jeffrey kept his eyes on the ground, thinking perhaps there would be tire tracks, but the area was dusty, and swept clean by the wind.

When they emerged from behind the building, the school principal stepped forward.

"That's the shed where we keep our heavy equipment," he said. "A couple of tractors, mowing attachments, a snowplow which we never use, hoses, and sprinkler systems. All the stuff for maintaining the football and soccer fields. Like the line machines for putting down the yard markers. Some of the coaches keep stuff like soccer goals and a baseball hitting cage in there as well."

"The lock?"

"A bunch of people know the combination, especially just about everybody in maintenance. The lock is really just to prevent any overexuberant student from deciding to borrow a tractor on a wild Saturday night."

Jeffrey turned and looked. The dirt road guarded by the gate led through a thick stand of trees. "Through there?" he asked, pointing.

"The road leads to the playing fields behind the school," the principal said, rubbing his hands together vigorously. "The gate is there to keep any student vehicles out. That's all. Actually, we've never had a problem, but you know, with teenagers, it's wiser to anticipate than react."

"I'm sure," Jeffrey said.

The assistant principal, a woman wearing khaki slacks and a blue blazer, with eyeglasses that hung from a gold chain holder draped around her neck, stepped forward. She was perhaps a half foot taller than the principal, and had an officiousness in her voice that spoke of discipline.

"They're not supposed to come to school this way. There's not exactly a rule against it, but . . ."

"It's a shortcut, isn't it?"

"Some of the kids who live in the brown development a short ways away cut through, instead of walking all the way around like they're supposed to. Especially if they're late. I mean, we'd rather have them get to school on time. . . ."

Susan looked down at a notepad. "Kimberly Lewis? What time did she need to be at school today?"

The assistant principal opened a cheap leather briefcase and pulled out a yellow file. She opened it, read quickly, then said, "The morning bell rings at seven-twenty. She had a study hall for her first-period class. That would be from seven-twenty to eight-fifteen. At eight-twenty she was supposed to be in Honors American History. She did not arrive."

Susan nodded. "She had a paper due today, didn't she?"

The assistant principal looked surprised. "Why, yes."

Before she continued, Susan regarded the folder Jeffrey had retrieved from next to the gate. "A paper on 'The Compromise of 1850.' Now, the study hall. She's a senior, right? Was she required to be there?"

"No. She was Dean's List. Mandatory study hall is waived for Dean's List students. . . ."

"So she would have been traveling to school sometime later than the rest of the student body?"

"Today, yes. Just about everyone else would already be in class."

"The maintenance men? Who would be here?"

"Actually, today they're in the boy's locker room, painting. That's been scheduled for some time. We had to send out a notice saying the locker room would be closed today. While the paint dries. So nobody would be here. The painting supplies are kept in the maintenance room at the school."

Susan looked over at her brother and saw that each detail was jabbing at him like a stiletto, each a new and unique pain. A confluence of little details that added up inexorably into an opportunity for a killer. She, on the other hand, felt a distinct and total cold inside, as if each bit of understanding merely fed an anger that was growing within her. It was no different from the sensation she'd felt staring at the pictures of the murdered young women.

"So," Jeffrey said, stepping into the conversation, "after she doesn't show, what happens?" His voice had a hard edge to it.

"Well, it was midmorning before I got to all the absentee reports," the assistant principal replied. "The established procedure then is to call home for any student who hasn't checked in with us already. Shortly before noontime, I called the Lewis household. . . ."

"No answer, right?"

"Well, her parents both work, and I didn't want to bother them at their offices. I thought I'd get Kim on the phone. I figured she was sick. We've had a flu going around and it really knocks the kids for a loop. They mainly sleep it off. . . ."

"No answer, right?" Jeffrey asked again, harder.

The assistant principal looked angrily at him. "Correct," she said.

"And then what did you do?"

"Well, I figured I'd call back later. After she woke up."

"Did you call State Security, to tell them you had a student missing and unaccounted for?"

The principal lurched forward. "Now see here, Mr. Clayton, why would we do that? Absenteeism isn't a security matter. It's a school discipline matter. To be handled internally."

Jeffrey hesitated, but his sister answered for him.

"It depends on precisely what sort of absenteeism we're talking about," she said bitterly.

"Well," the assistant principal snorted, "Kimberly Lewis isn't the sort of student who gets into trouble. She's a top student and very popular—"

"Does she have friends? How about a boyfriend?" Susan asked.

The assistant principal hesitated at first. "No. No boyfriend, not this year. She's an all-around good kid. Probably heading to a top college."

"Not anymore," Susan said beneath her voice, so that only her brother could hear her.

"She had a boyfriend last year?" Jeffrey asked, suddenly curious.

The assistant principal again hesitated. "Yes. Last year. She was in an intense relationship of the sort we try to discourage. Fortunately, the young man in question was a class ahead of her. He left for college and the relationship self-destructed, I suppose."

"You did not like the boy?" Jeffrey asked.

Susan turned and looked at him. Quietly, she asked him: "What difference does it make? We know what happened here, don't we?"

Jeffrey held up his hand, stopping the assistant principal's response, then took his sister's elbow and walked a few feet away. "Yes," he said softly, "we do know what happened here. But when did he pick this girl out? What was the route of the information that he needed? Maybe the ex-boyfriend will know something. Maybe the relationship that the assistant principal thinks self-destructed wasn't quite so broken up. Anyway, it's something we might need to check out down the road a bit."

Susan nodded. "I'm impatient," she said.

"No," her brother replied, "you're focused."

They returned to the two school officials.

"You didn't like the boy?" Jeffrey repeated.

"A difficult but extremely bright young man. Went East for college."

"How difficult?"

"Cruel," the assistant principal said. "Manipulative. Always felt as if he were mocking us. Not sad to see him graduate. High grades and top test scores and the chief suspect in a suspicious laboratory fire we had last spring. Never proven, of course. Awful. More than a dozen lab animals, guinea pigs and white rats, burned alive. Anyway, at least he's out of the picture now. Probably will be wildly successful out in the other fifty. I don't think this state's for him."

"You have his student file, still?"

The assistant principal nodded.

"I'll want to see it. I may need to speak with him."

The principal again interjected himself. "I'll need a State Security authorization to release it," he said pompously.

Jeffrey smiled nastily. "Why don't I just send a squad of agents over to pick it up? They could march right into your office. That will give the entire student body something to talk about for days to come."

The principal glared at the professor. He shot a quick glance toward the State Security driver, who merely nodded.

"You'll get it," the principal said. "I'll ship it to you electronically."

"The entire file," Jeffrey reminded him.

The principal nodded, his lips tight, as if withholding an obscenity or two. "All right, we've answered your questions. Now it's time for you to tell us what's going on here."

Susan stepped forward, speaking with a harshness that was unfamiliar, but which she thought she might need in the near future. "That's simple," she said. She gestured around her. "See? Take a real good look around you."

"Yes," the principal said, in an exasperated tone he'd perfected on way-ward students, but which had no impact on Susan. "What precisely is it that I'm supposed to be seeing?"

"Your worst nightmare," she replied briskly.

They were both quiet for the first few minutes of the drive back to New Washington, sitting in the backseat of the state car as the agent accelerated for the highway. Susan flipped open the missing teenager's term paper and read a few paragraphs, trying to get a sense of the girl herself through the writing, but she could not. What she read told her bleakly about slave states and free states and the compromise that allowed them into the Union. She wondered if there was something ironic in this.

She spoke first: "All right, Jeffrey, you're the expert. Is Kimberly Lewis still alive?"

"Probably not," her brother replied glumly.

"I didn't think so," Susan said quietly. She exhaled with frustration. "Now what? Wait for the body to turn up somewhere?"

"Yes. Hard as it seems. We just go back to doing what we were doing. Although there's one scenario I can think of that might mean she has a chance."

"What's that?"

"I guess there's a small possibility that she's part of the game. Maybe she's the prize."

He blew out slowly. "Winner take all."

Jeffrey spoke in a low, defeated voice. "It is painful," he said slowly. "Seventeen years old, and either she's already dead simply because he wants to mock me, to show that even with the famous Professor of Death on his trail, he still has the power to snatch someone right from beneath our noses—after even telling us what he was going to do before he did it, only I was too stupid and self-centered to see it."

He shook his head and continued, "Or else there's this girl sitting chained in a room somewhere, wondering when she's going to die, hoping someone will come save her. And the only someones out there are us, and I'm sitting here saying, 'We need to move cautiously. Take our time.' "

Jeffrey snarled. "Real brave of me," he said cynically.

"Jesus," Susan said slowly, drawing the name out, as she appreciated the dilemma. "What are we going to do?"

"What can we do other than what we were doing?" Jeffrey spoke between clenched teeth. "We take the list of houses, compare it with every name on the security list, then double-check it against every vehicle capable of transporting victims. And then see what we come up with."

"And suppose while we're doing all that, young Miss Kimberly Lewis is still alive?"

"She's dead," Jeffrey said abruptly. "She was dead just as soon as she set off out the door this morning, late and alone, and leaving herself just enough time to take the shortcut on a deserted street. She just didn't know it, but she was dead already."

At first Susan didn't reply, although she allowed herself the smallest hope that her brother might be wrong. Then she quietly added: "No, I think we should act. As fast as we can. As soon as we've identified a potential house. Act then. Because if we wait just one minute too long, we might be one minute too late, and we could never forgive ourselves. Not ever."

Jeffrey shrugged his shoulders. "You're right, of course. We'll act as fast as we can. That's probably what he wants. That's probably why poor Kimberly Lewis got caught up in all this. Not really out of any perversion or desire. But merely as an incentive to make me act headstrong and fool-hardy." Jeffrey sounded resigned. "He's succeeded, I guess, on that score."

Susan had a sudden thought, which nearly stopped her short. "Jeffrey," she whispered. "If he stole her to make you act—which sounds right, although we don't know it for sure, because we don't know anything for sure—but if he did, then isn't it logical to think that there's something in her abduction that will tell you where to look for her?"

Jeffrey opened his mouth to respond, then hesitated. He smiled. "Susie, Susie, the puzzle queen. Mata Hari. If I survive this, you must come up and teach one of my honors classes with me. That ranger back in Texas was right. You'd make a helluva detective. I think you're absolutely right."

He reached out and patted his sister's knee affectionately. "The hard thing about this is that every observation we make that takes us closer, the worse it is." He smiled again, but this time it was a sad smile.

The two remained silent the remainder of the drive back to the State Security offices. Susan made up her mind to retrieve all her weaponry from the town house, where it was hidden, and ruefully decided that for the remainder of her stay in the Fifty-first State, she was going to carry enough firepower to solve once and for all all the moral and psychological puzzles dogging her and her family.

Diana Clayton watched as her son painstakingly went through the printed list of State Security employees. She could see the frustration within him grow as he scanned name after name. The women with security clearances were mostly secretaries and lower-level executives. There were some dispatchers and a number of agents mingled into the list.

Part of Jeffrey's problem was that the boundaries for computer clearances weren't precise; it seemed obvious to him that someone with a Level Eight clearance would probably have some Level Nine access—it was the way most bureaucracies worked. And, Jeffrey thought, if his father's new wife were truly clever, she would remain at a lower level, while learning how to access the upper levels. This would help her maintain her secrecy.

As her son worked, Diana said little. She had insisted that he and Susan fill her in on what had happened at the school, and this they'd done, in a sketchy, perfunctory manner. She hadn't pushed them. She recognized that they were afraid for her, and probably thought her the weak link. She realized as well that her presence, and the belief she had that she was a primary target of the man she'd once married, made them all vulnerable. Still, she clung inwardly to the idea that she would be needed. She reminded herself that twenty-five years earlier, when they were children, they'd needed her to act, and she had. And, she thought, the time was fast approaching when they might have to call on her once again.

So she kept her counsel, and kept quiet, and stayed out of the way, which was not an easy thing for her at all. She hadn't even objected when Susan announced she was taking the car and driver and heading over to the town house to pick up some clothes, some medicines that had been left behind, and a few other items, which she hadn't specified but her mother knew about.

Jeffrey had worked up through F in the alphabet, highlighting in yellow any name that had an address in a green development. He would then check the highlighted name against the list of forty-six houses they'd identified as possible locations. So far, he'd produced thirteen different matches, which he set aside for closer examination after he'd completed the drudge work of processing the list. To be thorough, and because he had doubts about the list of forty-six, he sometimes took a name and went back to the computer's master list of plans for thousands of custom-built homes and found the original floor design for the woman's home, just to be certain he hadn't overlooked some possibility. This added time to the process, time he would not allow himself to think was being stolen away from a terrified seventeen-year-old girl.

As he worked, the adjacent computer beeped three times.

"That must be electronic mail," he said to his mother. "Check it for me, would you?" He barely looked up.

Diana went to the computer keyboard and punched in a password. She read for an instant, then turned to her son. "You requested a file from Sierra High School?"

"Yes. The boyfriend. Is that it?"

"Yes. There's a note from a Mr. Williams, who must be the principal, which isn't very friendly. . . ."

"What's it say?"

"It reminds you that it's a yellow-level misdemeanor punishable by a significant fine and community service for you to use confidential student files in an unauthorized fashion, or distribute them in an unauthorized manner. . . ."

"What a jerk," Jeffrey said, smiling. "Anything else?"

"No . . ."

"Well, print it out, I'll get to it in a little while."

Diana did what she was told. She read a little from the top of the file, and remarked, as the printer started to hum, "Young Mr. Curtin here seems a most remarkable child. . . ."

Jeffrey continued searching through the printout of names. "Why?" he asked idly.

"Well, he seems to have been a troubled kid. Straight A's and just as many disciplinary problems. Disruptive in class. Practical jokes. Accused of writing racist graffiti, but not proven. Believed to have orchestrated sexual harassment of another student, who is gay, but again, not proven. Chief suspect in a lab fire. No action taken. Suspended for bringing a knife to school . . . I thought that wasn't supposed to happen here in this state. Told a classmate that he had a handgun in his locker, but a subsequent search was negative. The list goes on and on. . . ."

"What is his name again?"

"Curtin."

"What's his first name?"

"That's odd," Diana said. "The same as yours, just spelled the other way: G-E-O—"

"Geoffrey Curtin," Jeffrey said slowly. "I wonder . . ."

"There's a school psychologist's report here that suggests he get counseling and recommends that he be given a battery of psychological tests. There's also a note that his parents refused to allow any testing whatsoever. . . ."

Jeffrey swiveled in his seat and leaned toward his mother. "How do they spell the last name?"

"C-U-R-T-I-N."

"Are the parents' names listed?"

Diana nodded. "Yes. The father is . . . let me see, it's here somewhere. Yes: Peter. The mother is Caril Ann. But she spells it with an I-L. That's an unusual spelling for her first name."

Jeffrey stood and walked to his mother's side. He stared down at the file, blinking on the screen as it was printed out nearby. He nodded slowly. "That's correct," he said carefully. "I've only seen that spelling once before, that I can recall."

"Where?"

"On Caril Ann Fugate. The young woman who accompanied Charles Starkweather through Nebraska in 1958 on his killing spree. Eleven dead."

Diana looked at her son wildly.

"And Curtin," he said, still cautiously, like an animal just sniffing a dangerous smell on a wayward wind, "well, that's an Americanized version of the German, Kurten."

"That means something?"

Jeffrey nodded again. "In Dusseldorf, Germany. Around the turn of the century. Peter Kurten. The Butcher of Dusseldorf. Child-killer. Pervert. Rapist. Remorseless. That famous movie *M* was made about him."

Jeffrey exhaled slowly. "Hello, Father," he said. "Hello, stepmother and half brother."

RECKLESSNESS

Jeffrey worked hard, worked fast.

The Curtin family home was located at 135 Buena Vista Drive, which was in the blue suburb outside of the town of Sierra. Despite its name, Buena Vista Drive didn't appear on any map to have any view of significance; it was set back in a heavily forested area, a small promontory of development in a landscape left mainly wild. The house was also number thirty-nine on Jeffrey's list of custom homes. In short order he also discovered that Caril Ann Curtin was the executive secretary for the assistant director of Passport Control, which was a division of State Security. It was her third job within the state's governmental apparatus; each time, she'd been elevated with glowing recommendations about her work ethic and dedication to her duties. She had acquired an eleventh-level security clearance. That clearance listed her husband as a retired investor, specializing in real estate. It also showed that he had contributed significantly to the Fifty-first State Fund, which was the financial arm of the state lobbying organization.

In the Fifty-first State government directory he found Caril Ann Curtin's telephone extension. It rang three times before it was answered.

"Mrs. Curtin, please," he said.

"This is her assistant. I'm afraid she's not in today. Can I take a message?"

"No, thank you. I'll call back."

He hung up. Far too busy this day to go to work. She probably took a personal day, he thought with a smirk.

Jeffrey then requested her confidential personnel file from the State Security computer.

At the same time, he went to Motor Vehicle Registration and discovered the Curtin family owned three vehicles: two expensive late-model European sedans, and the older four-wheel-drive minivan that Jeffrey expected. This made him pause; he'd expected four different vehicles, one each for father, mother, and teenage son, like any well-to-do, suburban upper-class family. And then the fourth with its highly specialized purpose. He made a mental note about this.

From a different branch of State Security he requested a listing of weapons owned by the Curtin family. Under the state's gun control laws, the family was designated both as *collectors* and as *recreational hunters*—a designation that Jeffrey found ironic, if astonishingly truthful—and their arsenal of both antique and modern weapons was extensive.

Finally, from Passport Control, he requested photographs of each member of the family. This demand required processing and was not immediately answered. He was told that authorization would be forthcoming. So, he waited.

He did not know which of the numerous computer requests he made would have the trap on it, but he knew one did, and he strongly suspected it would be this last computer query. It was not a complicated program to write, especially if one were connected to the upper levels of the hierarchy of the state, as Caril Ann Curtin was. But he knew that, somewhere, she had placed a computer order that would let her know if anyone came searching for information about her or any member of her family. This was a routine precaution that someone would take, especially someone who had much to hide in a society where nothing was supposed to be hidden. He realized that he'd probably triggered the warning, but he didn't see a way around this. He tried to conceal his requests by obscuring who precisely was demanding the information, but doubted that these efforts would have anything more than a momentary delaying impact.

He understood. There was not much time.

He knew as well that this was a day that his father had not only prepared for, but may have induced. He could see no other explanation for the abduction of his other son's onetime girlfriend. Kimberly Lewis's selection was designed to be provocative; it forced recognition and demanded a response. The more he thought about it, the more uneasy Jeffrey became, because a part of him envisioned this particular kidnapping as the sort of crime the criminal doesn't expect to get away with. It lacked the anonymity and

obscurity of his other selections. His father's crimes were like sudden lightning strikes on a humid summer evening, instant, unique. But this crime had
an agenda far different.

Jeffrey rocked in his seat at the computer and thought that probably
never in the history of crime had a pursuer known more about his quarry
than he did about his father, the killer. Even the famous FBI profile of the
Unabomber in the mid-1990s, which seemed to have anticipated virtually
every detail of the bomber's personality, did not have the intimacy of knowledge that he'd both acquired and recalled from deep within his instinctual
base. But all that information and understanding was useless, he thought,
because his father, the killer, had managed to obscure one critical element:
his purpose.

He had provided evidence to suggest that his killings were political—
designed to ruin the new state. Or perhaps they were personal—messages designed to speak to his son, the professor. Perhaps they were part of a contest,
perhaps part of a plan. Of course, they could be both or neither of those
things. There was evidence that supported the idea that the killings were perversions. Or ritualistic. They could be a product of evil or a product of desire.
They were solitary acts that he'd enlisted aid in achieving. They were novel,
yet as old as recorded criminal history.

They were like a modern musician's symphonic score, Jeffrey thought.
They invoke the past with sound, while touching the future. They are at the
same time antique and futuristic.

What is he going to do? he wondered.

Then he berated himself. You should know. You know him and yet you
do not. His imagination filled with possibilities: He will prepare his own
ambush. They will execute the young woman. They will disappear.

It was this last possibility that frightened him the most.

Jeffrey did not say it out loud, but he'd steeled himself to a single,
critical decision. Whatever terror came out of the relationship between
the new family and the old, it ended that day. Close it all down. He reached
out and seized the automatic pistol from the desktop. He slowly fingered
the trigger guard and tried to imagine the sensation of the weapon as it
fired. Bring it to an end, he told himself. Last chapter. Final stanza. The ultimate note.

The problem, he realized, was that his father might wish the same.

He set the gun down and began fiddling with the computer again. Within
seconds he'd brought up the three-dimensional plans for the Curtin family
residence. He began to study them, with the focus and devotion of a student
cramming for an exam.

What he saw was that the "music" room was windowless, and located next to a space designated as the "family" room, in a finished basement. It showed only a single door, with an inside-the-house entry, which surprised him. He checked more closely. It makes no sense, he thought. Not for what he's used that room for. Once he'd completed his tasks, he wouldn't want to bring a body, no matter how carefully wrapped, right through his house. That would be the very definition of losing control. He knew his father was far too clever for that.

The contractor's name was on the plans. Jeffrey picked up the telephone and called the company's office. It took him a few minutes to penetrate the telephone receptionists, who finally transferred his call to the head of the firm, who was at the site of a newly designed elementary school.

"What is it?" the contractor demanded. He had the tone of a man who'd spent the day dealing with numerous modest screw-ups and mistakes, and who had little tolerance or patience for anyone else.

Jeffrey identified himself as a special agent with State Security, which only served to stifle the man's gruffness mildly. "I'm interested in a house you built more than a half-dozen years ago, on Buena Vista Drive outside of Sierra. . . ."

"You expect me to remember one house? From that long ago? Look, fella, we do lots of projects, not just houses, but buildings and offices and schools and—"

Jeffrey interrupted. "You'll remember this house. Family's name was Curtin. It was a custom job. High-priced."

"Can't say I do. Look, sorry not to be able to help, but I'm busy here—"

"Try harder," Jeffrey said.

As he spoke, the door to his office opened and his sister entered, carrying a satchel. The satchel made a metallic clanking sound as she set it down.

Diana turned to her daughter and said cryptically, quietly: "We've found them."

Susan gasped, and was about to respond when Jeffrey pointed animatedly to the pile of documents coming across the computer printers.

"What the hell is it you want to know, anyway?" the contractor asked sharply.

"I want to know what changes you made."

"What?"

"What I want to know is how the house is different from the official plans you submitted to the state, for their architectural review and approval."

"Look, fella, I don't know what you're talking about. That's against state statutes. I could lose my license to build here—"

Jeffrey was abrupt and cold. "You'll lose it anyway, if you don't tell me now what I want to know. What changes aren't on the plans? And don't tell me you don't remember, because you do. Because I know the man building that house came to you and wanted to make some changes that don't show anywhere on any architect's drawing. And he probably paid you very well simply to make the changes without putting them in the official documents. You have a choice. Tell me now, and I'll consider it a favor and not make any mention of this conversation to the licensing boards. Or stonewall me, and your license to build at these artificially inflated Fifty-first State rates that are making you richer than you ever imagined will evaporate by midday tomorrow."

Jeffrey hesitated, then added: "There. That's just as goddamn clear as I can make this threat. Now think about it for thirty seconds and then answer my fucking question."

The contractor contemplated before answering. "I don't need the thirty seconds. Screw it. You want to know what's different? Okay. There's a concealed exit door from the basement studio room. Leads to the outside. My guy did a helluva job on it; it's hard as hell to see. There's also an unauthorized security setup disguised as an air-conditioning system. All the hardware is in the ceiling, and there are video monitors in the upstairs study, behind a fake bookcase. There are sensors placed throughout the external grounds with infrared heat detection devices. Had to go all the way to Los Angeles to pick that sucker up. Against the law here. And don't need it, like I told the guy. I guess he thought this place was actually gonna turn into Dodge City. Crazy. Don't need anything more than a dead-bolt lock on the door, but he wouldn't hear of it. I mean, that's the whole point, right? But he was willing to pay. And pay good, and hell, no one at the start really knew for sure whether this state was gonna work out or not, so I went along with it. I'll bet I'm not the only guy who did that sort of thing, back at the beginning. What else? Oh, it's also not on the plans, but there's a small garage-sized shed or guest house, two hundred yards away from the house. The house is on a small rise, and this is down the hill, right next to a couple zillion square miles of dedicated conservation land that can't be developed. I don't know what it's used for. We poured the flooring, put up the framing, the insulation, and the walls. All he wanted was for us to include the finishing materials in the house specs, which I did. He said he'd do it up the way he wanted."

"Anything else?"

"No. And this is the only time I've ever made these sorts of changes. Now the state sends an inspector out, walks you through before occupancy, plans in his hands. But this was back when things were first getting started, and things were a lot looser then. Maybe he paid off some inspector, too. You're not *supposed* to be able to do that, but there are tales. So, there you have it, fella. I'll hold you to your promise."

Jeffrey hung up, idly wondering whether the contractor was pouring substandard cement in the school he was building. But he'd found out what he needed.

Behind him, he heard his mother quietly say: "Jeffrey. Susan. The photographs are coming in now."

The three of them stood in front of the printer as the machine whirred and finally pushed out the identification picture of Geoffrey Curtin. He was an average-sized teenager, with deep brown, recessed eyes, and a shock of dark hair barely combed. His face was flat, his cheeks and chin prominent, and his mouth was turned down in the affected smile he'd adopted for the camera. He wore a scraggly goatee as well. The state listed his home address and his out-of-state residence as Cornell University, in Ithaca, New York.

Susan took the photograph and stared at it. But before she could say anything, the second photo emerged. This was of Caril Ann Curtin.

She was slight, cadaverously thin, with a pinched face and high cheekbones, which she'd given to her child. She wore her blond hair in a childlike ponytail, pulled back from her face, and had old-fashioned, wire-rimmed eyeglasses. She was not pretty, nor was she the opposite; she was intense, in an unsettling manner. She wasn't smiling, which gave her a secretarial officiousness.

"Who are you, really?" Diana asked as she looked at the photo.

Jeffrey took it out of her hands. He shook his head. "I know who she is," he said. "The lawyer in Trenton told me, but I didn't follow it up. She's a woman who died in West Virginia twenty years ago, shortly after being released from prison there. Stupid, stupid, stupid. I am stupid."

He was about to continue when the printer began to eject the third picture, of Peter Curtin.

It was Diana who spoke first. "Hello, Jeff," she said quietly. "My, how you've changed."

In the first seconds, all three saw something different, something the same. Whether it was the eyes that stared out penetratingly or the forehead that sloped upward into a bald pate or the chin or the cheeks or the ears hugging the oval face or the lips spread just slightly in a mocking smile, they all saw a memory, saw a shape that they shared, or just an image that had been shunted away deep within them.

He was a man who appeared younger and more vigorous than his sixty-odd years would suggest, which sliced at Diana Clayton's heart, making her think suddenly how old and close to death she must seem.

Jeffrey looked down at the photo, afraid of seeing himself.

Susan stared at the face on the glossy white page and found herself filling with a rage that defied easy description, for rolled together inside this anger was not only a hatred of all that the man had done, but all the loneliness and despair that she'd felt throughout her own life. It would have been hard for her to access which of these furies was deeper.

Jeffrey turned to his mother: "Has he really changed?"

She nodded. "Yes," she said slowly. "Almost every feature has been altered, just enough to create a whole that seems different. Except for the eyes, of course. Those are the same."

"Would you have recognized him?"

"Yes." She took a deep breath. "No. Maybe." Diana sighed. "I guess the answer is: I don't know. I hope so. But maybe not."

"He doesn't look like much," Susan said harshly.

"They never do," Jeffrey replied. "It would be nice if the worst of men wore all that evil on their faces, but they don't. They are nondescript and ordinary, mild and unnoticeable, right up to the second that they take charge of your life and deliver your death. And then they do become something special and different. Sometimes you can see little flashes—like we did with David Hart down in Texas. But usually, no. They blend. Maybe that's what's so awful. That they seem so much the same."

"Well," Susan said with a small, humorless laugh, "thanks for the education, brother of mine. Now let's go get him."

"We don't have to," Jeffrey said curtly. "I can make a single phone call to the director of State Security and he'll take a SWAT team out and blow the place to Hell. And everyone in it. We can sit and watch from a safe distance."

Diana looked at her son and shook her head. "There has never been a safe distance," she said.

Susan nodded in agreement. "What makes you think that the state will solve our problem to our satisfaction?" she asked. "When has the government of anything ever performed to that level?"

"This is our problem. We should seek our own solution," Diana said. "I'm surprised you would consider anything else."

Jeffrey looked bewildered, especially toward his sister. "You underestimate the danger involved," he said. "Hell, you're not underestimating it, you're ignoring it. Do you think he'll hesitate to kill us?"

"No," she answered. "Well, maybe. After all, we are his children."

The three of them were silent for an instant before Susan continued. "He's played a game with each of us, designed to bring us to his doorstep. We've found each clue, interpreted each act, risen to every lure, and now, piecing it all together, we know who he is, and where he lives, and who his family is. And, having come this far, you think we should turn it over to the state? Don't be ridiculous. The game has been for us all. We should all play it to its conclusion."

Diana nodded. "I wonder if he anticipated this conversation?" she asked.

"Probably," Jeffrey answered glumly. "I see your point. I admire your determination. But what do we gain by taking him on ourselves?"

"Freedom," Diana replied briskly.

Jeffrey thought his mother romantic, his sister impetuous. In a way, he admired these qualities. But their understanding of the capabilities of the onetime Jeffrey Mitchell and the current Peter Curtin was abstract, idealized. His own knowledge was far more precise, and therefore more terrible. His sister and his mother had looked at photographs, and shuddered, but this was not the same as actually staring down at the tattered body of some victim and implicitly understanding the rage and desire that stoked the force behind every slice and slash in the flesh. That he had acquired a female companion to second him in these acts further complicated the situation. And that the two of them had created a son, added yet another potential evil to the mix. He could see nothing but danger in the situation they were rushing headlong toward. He could see, as well, that there might be no alternative.

He dropped his head into his hands, filled with a sudden fatigue. He thought: This was always how it was meant to play out.

"Don't forget the other factor," Susan said abruptly. "Kimberly Lewis. Honor student. Pride and joy of a couple of confused parents who are right now wondering what the hell is going on and where the hell their daughter is."

"She's dead. And even if she isn't, assume she is."

"Jeffrey!" Diana objected.

"I'm sorry, Mother, but as far as that young lady is concerned, well, is she lucky? I mean, is she really, really lucky? Is the God of Good Fortune going to smile down on her and rain the wildest and most improbable good luck down on her head? Because if he does, then maybe she'll escape from this with only enough scars to ruin what remains of her life. But for our purposes, assume she's dead. Even if you hear her crying for help, assume she's dead. If you hear her begging and screaming and it breaks your heart, assume she's dead. Otherwise, we give him an advantage that we cannot afford."

"I don't know if I can be that cynical," his mother replied.

"If you can't, we'll have no chance."

"I understand that," she said. "But—"

Jeffrey cut her off with an upraised hand. He looked at his mother hard, then at his sister. "All right," he whispered. "If you want to deal with the reality instead of the abstract, then you must understand. We leave behind all humanity. Leave behind everything that makes you who you are. All we take with us are some weapons and a singleness of purpose. We're going to go and kill this man. And understand as well, the new wife, the new child, they're nothing more than extensions of him, created by him, to be like him. They are just as dangerous. Can you do that, Mother? Can you forget who you are and employ only the most hidden parts of yourself? The anger and hatred? That's what we need to use, nothing else. Can you do this without hesitation and without the slightest remorse or doubt or second thoughts? Because we'll have only this one opportunity. Never again, understand. So, if we enter his world, we must be prepared to play by his rules and meet his standards. Can you do that?"

He looked at his mother, who did not reply. "Can you be like him?" He suddenly swung and eyed his sister, demanding the same answer. "Can you?"

Susan did not want to answer his question. She thought her brother correct in every word. He understands how reckless we are, she told herself. But sometimes recklessness is the only alternative life gives you.

"Well," she said, grinning falsely. She licked her lips. Her throat felt suddenly parched, as if she needed a drink of water. She moved close to the computer screen, hoping her mother and her brother would not see how nervous she was, and began studying the layout of the house on Buena Vista Drive, simultaneously filling the room with a completely undeserved bravado. "We'll see, won't we? And we'll see tonight."

THE SECOND
UNLOCKED DOOR

It was well after dark when Jeffrey led his mother and sister out of the huge, stolid State Office Building on what he fully expected to be his last night inside the Fifty-first State. Over his shoulder he carried a midsized dark blue duffel bag, as did his sister. Diana held a canvas briefcase in her right hand. She surreptitiously swallowed several painkillers as they stepped into the black air, hoping that neither of her children would notice. She breathed in sharply, tasting the cool ridge of a near frost on the edge of the night, and she thought this a strange and wonderful flavor. She looked briefly off into the distance, away from the hills and mountains that rose up to the north, instead turning toward the south. A world of desert, she thought. Sand, blown dust, tumbleweed, and scrub grasses. And heat. Penetrating heat and dry air. But not this night; this night was different, a contradiction of image and expectation. Chill instead of warmth.

The parking lots were mostly empty, only the stragglers' vehicles left behind. There were very few office lights still on in the building behind them. For the most part, the state's work force had packed up and headed home for the evening. Dinner with the family, some talk, followed by a movie or a sitcom on television, or maybe helping the kids with their homework. Then bed. Sleep and the promise of the same routine tomorrow. It was seductively quiet outside the office building; they could hear the scraping noise their shoes made against the cement sidewalk.

It did not take more than a few seconds for Jeffrey to spot their car and the security agent assigned to drive them. It was the same man who'd accompanied them to the spot on Adobe Street where Kimberly Lewis had disappeared. He was a sullen, thickset man, with closely cropped hair and a flat, bored look that told Jeffrey he wished he was elsewhere, doing something different. Jeffrey guessed that the agent had been given minimal information about who he was and about his actual purpose in the Fifty-first State. As always, he assumed that somewhere behind them, out of sight, was Agent Martin's replacement, trailing from an appropriate distance, waiting for them to tip their hand and point at the man to be killed. For an instant Jeffrey swung his eyes upward, as if expecting to see a helicopter lurking above them, rotors turning with a dull throb, in a silent mode. He paused, trying to anticipate how they were being tracked. The car would have an electronic homing device, he knew. There were ways of painting clothing with undetectable infrared material that could be read from a safe distance. There were other secret military techniques as well, lasers and high-tech, but he doubted that the authorities in the Fifty-first State had access to these. They might, in a couple of weeks, when they sewed a new star onto the U.S. flag, but probably not now, before that vote was taken.

Jeffrey eyed the driver. A nobody. He assumed the man's orders were simple: to accompany them everywhere and to inform the director of their every action. At least, it's what he was counting on.

They had a plan, but it was minimal. Trying to outmaneuver the spider when he invites you into his web was probably a foolish endeavor anyway. Instead, one went, and hoped that one's strength would prove too great for the strands that would entangle and trap.

The driver stepped forward. "They told me you were in for the night. Nobody authorized another trip."

"If that's what they told you, why are you still here?" Susan asked quickly. "Open the trunk, will you?"

The driver opened the trunk. "It's procedure," he said. "Got to wait for final clearance before I can leave. We going someplace?"

"Back to Sierra," Jeffrey said as he threw his duffel bag on top of his sister's.

"I got to call it in," the agent said. "Give them a destination and time frame. Orders."

"I don't think so," Jeffrey said. He removed his unused nine millimeter from his shoulder holster in a single, smooth movement, punching the barrel at the agent, who recoiled, putting his hands in the air. "Tonight, we're improvising."

Susan laughed, but it had a hollow ring. She gave the agent a small push on the back. "Jump in," she said. "You drive, Mr. Agent Man. Mother, up front. Reunion time."

Jeffrey placed the pistol on the seat between his sister and himself. He balanced the briefcase that his mother had been carrying on his lap. From an inside jacket pocket he removed a small pen-sized flashlight that emitted a red, nighttime beam. He switched this on and removed two different files from the case. There were perhaps a half-dozen sheets in each.

The first was the confidential State Security dossier for Caril Ann Curtin. He scanned this quickly, searching for anything that might give him some insight into how she would act when confronted with the truth. But this was an elusive question; the dossier revealed a dedicated, if private, state employee. She did extremely well on advancement tests and performance reviews, was said to work efficiently and effectively with coworkers, received high marks of praise from supervisors. There was little data about her social life, other than an entry that worried Jeffrey, that Caril Ann Curtin belonged to a women's shooting club, where she had obtained several handgun proficiency awards. The dossier also showed that she was active in church and civic organizations, had several health club memberships, and had run a sub-four-hour marathon time the previous year in the annual New Washington Road Race.

As for her life before arriving in the Fifty-first State, the dossier was even shallower. She was said to have obtained an associate's degree in business administration from a community college in Georgia. She had a limited employment history—but just enough to make her secretarial skills considerable. There were two letters in the file from previous employers, who recommended her highly. One came from the attorney in Trenton—a detail the man had left out of the forced conversation he'd had with Jeffrey Clayton. The other, Jeffrey assumed, was forged or purchased, but no doubt adequate enough when the state was first taking form, back at its beginning. She was outwardly qualified, seemingly perfect. Her husband had money and was generous with it. Once into the bureaucracy, she'd swum upward with the determination of a salmon returning home.

Jeffrey set this file aside and opened the second.

This was even shorter. It was a computer printout from the National Crime Information Center. At the top it read: *Elizabeth Wilson. Subject Deceased.*

Jeffrey shook his head.

Not deceased, he thought. Just reborn.

The entry in the national computer bank described a young woman who'd grown up in rural West Virginia. She had an extensive juvenile record of break-ins, arson, assault and battery, and prostitution. There was a short Probation Department report from authorities in Lincoln County, saying there was unconfirmed evidence that she'd been repeatedly molested as a child by her stepfather.

Elizabeth Wilson had gone to prison for manslaughter at age nineteen. She'd taken a straight-edge razor to a drunken customer reluctant to pay her after sex. The customer had punched her several times before realizing that she'd sliced him from belly to hip. She was paroled after serving three years in the state penitentiary in Morgantown. Within six months of her release, the report stated, she gained employment at a biker's bar in a rural area of the state, some seventy miles from the city. Her first night working, she'd accompanied a man out the door and never been seen again. Ripped, bloodied clothing was discovered by police in a tangled hollow, but no body was ever found. It had been late in the winter, and the terrain was formidable. Even a dog team was unable to penetrate the territory. Police subsequently questioned several men at the bar that night who'd been seen talking with her, and arrested one man whose pickup truck had bloodstains on the seat. The bloodstains matched Elizabeth Wilson's type, and eventually, DNA testing showed it was hers. A search of the truck also turned up a large hunting knife, shoved beneath a broken floorboard, which also contained trace amounts of blood on the blade. Despite claiming he'd been drunk that night and couldn't remember anything, much less a murder, the man was tried and convicted, and sentenced to life imprisonment.

Jeffrey thought this must have given his father some amusement. Planting some blood in a stranger's car. The knife, too, he thought, was a clever detail. He wondered if his father had coached Elizabeth Wilson as he'd drawn blood from her earlier that evening: draw attention to yourself; flirt, get into an argument, then leave with the drunkest man barely able to stand. The man who won't remember a single detail.

Then, his father had taken the young woman whose death he'd invented and re-created her, just as he had reinvented himself earlier. She must have been like a baby that night, naked, her clothing ripped and streaked with her own blood, shivering in the cold, afraid.

Jeffrey closed the file and thought: She will owe him everything.

He swung a quick look at his sister, then his mother.

They don't know how dangerous this woman can be, he thought. There's nothing in her life that hasn't been invented by my father. She'll be as devoted to him as a vicious guard dog. Perhaps even more so.

There was an old photograph that had been transmitted with the file. It showed a young, angry face with a lopsided, gap-toothed scowl, and a broken nose that had been improperly set, all surrounded by stringy, un-kempt blond hair.

He mentally compared this picture with Caril Ann Curtin's passport photo. It would have been difficult to believe that the young woman holding the police station identification numbers beneath her face was the same confident adult who had proven to be so invaluable in so many official capacities. The teeth had been fixed, the chin softened. The broken nose repaired, reshaped. She'd been carved by an expert, Jeffrey thought. Physically, emotionally, and psychologically. Eliza Doolittle and Henry Higgins. But the Henry Higgins of death.

Jeffrey put the two files back in the canvas briefcase, tucking them up against the school's report on Geoffrey Curtin and the picture of Peter Curtin. There had been no information in the computers on him, other than the secondary references contained in the wife's and son's reports.

There was a State Security telephone in the car, and Jeffrey picked it up and started to punch in numbers. It took him three frustrating tries before he reached Campus Security at Cornell University. He identified himself and asked to speak with the officer in charge. It took a few seconds to locate the man, but when he picked up the telephone, his voice seemed far closer than the hundreds of miles separating them.

"Security captain here, what's the problem?"

"Captain, I need to know whether a student at Cornell is currently in residence."

"I have that information. Why do you need it?"

"There's been an auto accident out here," Jeffrey lied, "and we're still sorting through a lot of burning wreckage. This could be a next-of-kin situation. But we have unidentified bodies as well. It would help us if we could eliminate at least one person. . . ."

"What's the name of the student?"

"Geoffrey, with a G, Curtin, spelled C-U-R-T-I-N. . . ."

"Let me check on that for you. . . ."

"Clayton. Special Agent Clayton."

"You know we're getting more and more applications from kids in the Fifty-first State. Good kids. Good students. But man, do they have a rough first couple of weeks when they hit campus. Things are different here than there. . . ."

The campus security officer paused, then added: "Hey, you sure you got the name right?"

"Yes. Geoffrey Curtin. From Sierra in the Fifty-first State."

"Well, I don't show anyone by that name."

"Double-check for me."

"I have. No one here. I've got the master list, you know. All students, faculty, campus workers—anyone connected with the university. He's not there. You might want to try Ithaca College. Sometimes people get confused, you know, they're right down the road from us."

When Jeffrey hung up, he reached inside the school report. Attached to the file was a copy of the acceptance letter from Cornell, which had a guidance counselor's handwritten note on top: *Deposit Mailed.*

Jeffrey realized both his mother and sister were watching him. "He's not there," he said. "Which is where he's supposed to be. That could mean he's here. . . ."

The sullen agent in the front seat muttered, "Try Passport Control. They'll know if he's in-state or not."

Jeffrey nodded.

The agent continued, beneath his breath: "I'm supposed to help, for Christ's sake, but you gotta pull a gun. . . ."

Jeffrey made the call. His security clearance got him a quick answer: Geoffrey Curtin, eighteen, 135 Buena Vista Drive, Sierra, had exited the state on September fourth, listing Ithaca, New York, as his destination, and had not as yet returned.

"So," Susan said, "what do you think? Here? Or not?"

"I think not. But we'll be cautious."

"My middle name," Susan joked.

"No it isn't," Diana said darkly. "It never has been."

The main street in Sierra was jammed with cars honking horns, flashing lights, and weaving down the two-lane roadway. Teenagers were shoehorned into the vehicles, hanging from the backs of pickup trucks or waving from open windows; all noise, all racket. In the center of the town common there was a bonfire, lifting a streak of orange-red flame perhaps thirty feet into the night blue-black sky. A fire truck was parked a discreet fifty yards distant, and a half-dozen firemen, an uncharged hose at their feet, stood with arms folded, grinning, watching, as a line of kids snaked around the fire, their gyrations outlined against the glowing core. Two State Security cruisers, their red and blue strobe lights beating time, also hung on the periphery of the crowd. It was not only teenagers; the crowd was filled with both the very young staying up past their bedtimes and adults who, while perhaps not quite as vigorous, and considerably more ridiculous, were equally committed to the dance. From a half-dozen, souped-up car stereos deep thumping music thudded through the air. They were finally drowned out by a marching band that came sweeping around one corner, the brass instruments gleaming in the mingled lights of the cars and the fire.

"High school football playoffs," the agent in the front said as he steered their car gingerly through the milling crowds. "Sierra must have won tonight. That would put them in the state schoolboy super bowl. Not bad. Not bad at all."

The agent honked his horn at a convertible filled with teenagers that had come to a halt in front of them. The kids turned, laughing, gesturing wildly but not aggressively. With a jerk and squeal of tires, the girl behind the wheel managed to swing her car out of the way.

"We'll be out of this in a minute. Looks like just about everybody who's anybody in this town is here tonight."

"How long will it go on?" Susan asked.

The agent shrugged. "That fire looks pretty new. And I don't see the team here yet. Gotta wait for them. And the coach. And probably the mayor and town council and who knows who else will have to get a bullhorn in their hands and say a few words. I'd say this is a party that's just getting started." The agent rolled his window down and shouted at a small covey of teenage girls, "Hey, ladies! What was the final score?"

All of the girls turned, looking at the agent as if he'd just descended from Mars. One shouted out: "Twenty-four, twenty-two. Never in doubt," and the group all laughed.

The agent smiled. "Who's next?"

"Next victim?" the girls screamed in unison. "New Washington!"

The agent rolled the window back up. "See?" he said. "Some things never change. High school football, for one."

Jeffrey eyed the crowd and thought it a fortunate thing. If they were being trailed, it would be exceedingly difficult for anyone following them to make their way through.

The agent turned the cruiser off the main street, passing under a banner that read RALLY ON THE COMMON FOR STATEHOOD NOV. 24.

Jeffrey turned in his seat, watching the street behind them to see if they were being followed. The lights and noise started to fade behind them. They passed a few groups of people hurrying toward the center of town, then swung out of Sierra, sliding quickly into the darkness of a narrow road. Stands of trees crept up to the macadam, and the car's headlights seemed blocked by their black trunks. Within minutes the world around them appeared closer, tighter, tangled, and knotted. They passed a few driveways, with lights just visible, deep in the forested world they were penetrating, and then Jeffrey broke the silence: "Pull over. Now."

The agent did as he was told. The tires crunched against some gravel on the lip of the road surface.

Jeffrey had the pistol in his hand. "Let's get out," he said.

The agent hesitated, then fixed his eyes on the pistol. He undid his seat belt and exited the car.

Jeffrey did the same. He took a deep breath, looked up the roadway, as if trying to see just beyond the limits of the headlights, then turned back.

"All right," he said. "Thanks for your help. Sorry to be so rude. Tell me right now: How are we being trailed?"

The agent shrugged. "I'm supposed to call your whereabouts into a special team. Around the clock."

"What kind of team?"

"A team of cleaners. Like Bob Martin."

Jeffrey nodded. "And when they don't hear from you?"

"That's just not supposed to happen."

"All right. So, now it's time for you to make that call."

"Out here in the middle of fucking nowhere?" the agent said. "I don't get it."

"No." Jeffrey shook his head. "Not from here. Can you run?"

"What?"

"What sort of shape are you in? Can you run?"

"Yeah," the man said. "I can run."

"Good. It's not more than four, five miles back to town. Shouldn't take you longer than, oh, maybe a half hour or forty-five minutes in those shoes. Maybe an hour, because you'll be carrying this . . ."

He handed the agent the briefcase.

The man continued to look at Jeffrey—more in frustration than in anger. "I'm not supposed to leave you," he complained. "Those were my orders. I'll get in trouble."

"Tell them I forced you to. Actually, that's true." Jeffrey waved the pistol. "And anyway, they'll be too busy to get too pissed at you."

"What am I supposed to do with this?" The agent shook the briefcase.

"Don't lose it," Jeffrey said. He smiled briefly, then continued: "This is what you do when you get to town. No matter how hard you're breathing and how many blisters you've raised on your feet, you go directly to the local substation of State Security. Ignore the bonfire and the party. Just head for Security. When you get there, make your call to your hit squad. Then place a call to the director. Don't call your supervisor, don't call the watch commander, don't call your wife, and don't call anyone else. Call the director of State Security. No matter where he is or what he's doing, he'll want to talk to you. Trust me. By doing this, you're going to save your career. Because in the next few minutes you're going to become the *only* person in this world he'll want to hear from. Got that? Okay, when you get him on the phone—and nobody else, not secretary, not assistant, nobody else—you tell him exactly what happened tonight. And tell the director that I gave you a briefcase that contains the identity of the man he wanted me to find, as well as his address, and a few details about his family. He'll probably want to know where we've gone, and you tell him the address is there in those dossiers, but that we went ahead because it's at this point that his problem and our problem diverge. Can you remember to tell him that, exactly as I said it?"

Even in the oblique light by the side of the car, illuminated only by the headlights facing away from them, Jeffrey could see that the agent's eyes had widened. "*Diverge.* Right? This is important, right? This must have something to do with why you were brought in here in the first place, right?"

"Yes, to both your questions. And maybe by the end of the night, we'll all have found some answers," Jeffrey said. He glanced into the darkness surrounding them. "But it's possible, as well, that the answers will find us."

He pointed with the pistol barrel down the road, back toward town. The agent hesitated, Jeffrey gestured again, and then the agent took off, running slowly, clutching the briefcase to his chest.

Susan had emerged from the car, and now stood by the open door. "Well," she said. "Well-y, well, well." Then she ducked back inside.

The entrance to Buena Vista Drive was barely a half mile farther up the road. The map had showed only three houses widely situated off a dead-end street. The house they sought was the last of the three, and the most isolated. Jeffrey would have preferred to fly over the location in a small plane or helicopter, but that had been impossible. Instead, he'd relied on State Security's topographical maps, which he assumed were only as accurate as the owner and the contractor wanted them to be, and in this particular case, he understood, that was probably not very accurate. He was concerned about the approach, about the hidden alarm sensors, and, in particular, about the small off-house that wasn't on any map or any plan but which the contractor had told him about. He'd wracked his imagination for the purpose of this structure, and continually come up blank. He knew it had some critical importance to his father, but precisely what, he was unable to deduce.

It bothered him immensely.

Jeffrey pulled the State Security vehicle to the side of the road and killed the headlights just outside the single lane entrance to number 135. The only sign that there was a house hidden deep within the dark forest was a single small number on a wooden plaque by the side of the dead-end street. There was no fence or gate, just a solitary black drive that disappeared into the trees.

For a moment or two the three of them sat silently in the darkness. Their plan was simple, perhaps too simple, for it left many things unsaid.

Jeffrey was to arm himself, walk down the driveway to the house and head in through the front as best he could—even if it meant knocking on the front door. He had assumed that shortly after he started his advance, he would trigger the alarms, and that he would be first monitored, then confronted. That was the point of his approach, to draw the complete attention of the occupants of 135 Buena Vista Drive. If he could do this without being disarmed, all the better. Once he was inside, Susan and Diana were to follow, as surreptitiously as possible. It was Jeffrey's belief that as soon as he'd drawn the attention of the occupants, they would not be as alert for a second wave. Susan and Diana were to make their way around to the rear, trying for surprise. The contractor had told him that the video monitors were upstairs, so Jeffrey knew he had to keep the occupants of the house downstairs. Simple as that.

The assault on the house rested on the shakiest of psychological factors: Jeffrey believed that by appearing alone, his father would think he was trying to protect his mother and sister, by leaving them in some distant and seductively safe location. Selfless. Confronting the father—and whatever danger he represented—by himself.

This was a lie he thought he could sell.

The truth, of course, was the opposite. Mother and sister were the bar on the trap. He was merely the spring.

The three of them exited the car quietly and gathered by the rear trunk. All wore dark clothing, jeans, sweatshirts, and running shoes. Jeffrey opened the trunk and from the first of the two duffel bags removed three Kevlar-reinforced bulletproof vests, which they quickly fastened onto their torsos. Susan had to help her mother, who was unfamiliar with how the vest fit.

"This works?" Diana asked. "Because it sure as hell is uncomfortable."

"Against conventional weapons and ammunition, but—"

"There's always a but," Diana said briskly. "And what about your father suggests he will be in the slightest bit conventional?"

This question made Jeffrey smile nervously. "I think it will be wise to wear them anyway. Think of all this stuff as dear departed Agent Martin's going-away present. It came from his locker in the office." The gallows humor made them all grin. He reached for the second duffel bag, unzipped it, and started removing weapons.

Jeffrey helped his sister adjust her handgun in its shoulder holster, then checked his own. The two of them then slung submachine guns over their arms, and pulled black navy watch caps onto their heads. From the bottom of the duffel bag Jeffrey removed a pair of night-vision binoculars, one set which he draped around his own neck, the other over his sister's. He then reached in and grabbed two small crowbars, sticking one in his belt, handing the other to his sister.

Diana was reminded for a moment of the two of them as children, playing together, as if this was some sort of especially evil make-believe game of cops and robbers. But as this benign thought moved through her heart, her son abruptly turned, handed her a similar cap, and helped her strap a pistol to her chest. She was given the revolver that Susan had brought from Florida.

Jeffrey lingered for a moment with his arms halfway around his mother. She seemed small and frail to him then, older than he ever thought she would be, weakened by disease and by all that had happened. There was not much light, but in what there was, he could see lines of concern on her forehead.

Diana, on the other hand, felt none of these things.

She breathed in sharply, gulping at the cool air, thinking that there was nowhere in the world she would rather be. For the first time in weeks and perhaps months, she was able to summon strength from within her and forcefully stuff her illness into some recess, like slamming a door upon disease. She had spent her entire adult life frightened that she and her children would be cornered and consumed by the man she'd once called husband, and it gave her an immense quiet hope and satisfaction to think that it was she who stalked him this night, instead of the other way around, and that she was armed and dangerous, and for the first time ever, possibly even more dangerous than he was.

Susan checked the action on the machine pistol. She turned to her brother. "What about the wife and son?"

"Caril Ann Curtin is a viper. Do not hesitate."

Diana shook her head. "She's as much a victim as we are. Worse. Why should we—"

Jeffrey interrupted. "Maybe once. Maybe if once upon a time she had fled, the way you did with us. Maybe if she'd run away when she first realized why he wanted her and why he was teaching her and why she was there to support him. Maybe she could have saved herself then. The woman she's named after, Caril Ann Fugate, cried out a warning to the Nebraska State policeman who came up pretty much accidentally upon her and Charles Starkweather. Saving that policeman from her lover probably saved her from a trip to the gallows herself. So, maybe, maybe. Maybe when we arrive on the scene she'll decide to save herself . . ."

He looked at his mother sharply.

". . . but don't count on it." His voice was as cold as the night air.

"And Geoffrey?" Diana persisted. "Your namesake? He's just a teenager. What do we really know about him?"

"Really know? Nothing. Nothing for certain. Actually, I hope he's not here tonight. The odds are better three against two. Three on three might be tough. Anyway, my guess is that he's not, because I think Passport Control here in this state is pretty efficient."

"But . . ." Susan started. She paused, then finished: "Suppose he is? Is he dangerous? Is he like *him* or is he like *us*?"

"Well," Jeffrey said, "that's a distinction we're all going to learn tonight, aren't we?"

He didn't wait for his sister's reply before continuing: "Look, it's a process. A growth. It doesn't just happen. It needs to be nurtured. It's like a scientific experiment that takes years to bring to fruition. You add the right elements—cruelty, torture, perversity, abuse—at the right times, as a child grows up and older, and you get something evil and misshapen. Mother stole us away just as that process was starting. This child? I don't know. He's been there from the beginning. Let's just hope he's off at school."

"Yeah, at school. But not at the school where he's supposed to be," Susan said with a hard edge.

"Nothing is what it's supposed to be," Jeffrey said. "Not me or you or him or this entire state. I figure we have between sixty and ninety minutes before State Security arrives. It will be helicopters and SWAT units, automatic weapons and tear gas. Their orders will be to eradicate the problem. It would be wise not to be in the way. Whatever we're going to do, we're going to do it in the next hour. Understood?"

Mother and daughter nodded.

Diana reminded them of the other factor. "What about Kimberly Lewis. Suppose she's alive?"

"Rescue her. If possible. But we must deal with our own problem first."

This was unsettling to Diana. Susan seemed to understand it better. She greeted this order from her brother with a shrug.

"We'll do what we can," she said.

Jeffrey smiled wanly, put his arm around his sister, and squeezed her. Then he turned and hugged his mother briefly, not the sort of show of affection that was anything other than momentary, routine, as if the trip he was about to take was as predictably normal as the world around them claimed to be.

"I'll see you up ahead," he said, trying to infect his voice with a calm and a determination. "Make certain you give me enough time to draw his attention."

And with that Jeffrey turned and started jogging up the driveway, holding his weapons at port arms, the blackness of the night immediately swallowing him.

It took a few seconds for his eyes to adjust to the dark, but when they did, he was able to make out the winding driveway, trickling through a cavern of trees that stretched over the narrow space, almost shutting out the moon and stars above. He listened to the night around him, the occasional rattle of branches rubbing together as a slice of wind blew by, mingling with the raspy sound of his own breathing. He could feel a wintry dryness in his throat and a contradictory summer stickiness beneath his arms from nervous sweat. He paced forward, feeling like a man being asked to inspect his own crypt.

He suspected that he'd already triggered an alarm inside the house; these would be heat-and-size sensitive, set to ignore the opossum or raccoon that passed through the woods, more likely triggered by the mule deer that ventured too close to the house. But tonight, he knew, no alarm would be dismissed as just another deer. Mounted in the trees somewhere were night-vision cameras capturing his progress down the drive. Still, he moved cautiously, with deliberateness, as if he believed that his approach were unseen. This was important, he thought. Maintain the illusion. Make him think I'm alone and that I haven't the sense or the knowledge to avoid walking into his trap.

The driveway curved ninety degrees to the right, and Jeffrey found himself lingering in the last trees that might conceal him, at the edge of a cleared, manicured green lawn at the foot of a small rise. The house stood perhaps fifty yards away, directly in the center of the gentle upward slope. There were no shrubs, no obstacles, no shapes that would hide his approach over the last stretch of terrain. Moonlight gave the grass a silvery sheen, almost as if it were a placid pool of water.

The house was a two-story, neo-western design—modern, sweeping, a gracious, inviting exterior that spoke of money spent on details. It was completely dark, not a light showing anywhere.

Jeffrey exhaled slowly and paused on the edge of the lawn, narrowing his gaze and staring straight ahead.

He tried to imagine the house as a fortress, to regard it as a military objective. He lifted the night-vision glasses and began to search the exterior. There were bushes beneath every ground-floor window. These would not be ordinary bushes, he thought; they would be filled with spiked, razor-sharp thorns, impenetrable. They would be set in smooth gravel rock as well, the sort that made an unmistakable rattling sound when stepped upon. Around one side he saw a windowed sun room, but even this glassy space was surrounded by thick tangles of shrubs.

Jeffrey shook his head. One way in through the front door. Another way through a back door. A third through the hidden door that led to the room where Kimberly Lewis had learned that the world was not quite the safe and perfect place she'd been told it was. He could not see the back door, but remembered its location in the plans—off the kitchen. But that wouldn't be its most salient factor, he thought. It would have a clear field of fire, both inside and out.

Jeffrey lowered the glasses, continuing to search the house for some access point other than the two doors, front and rear, knowing he would not find one. He shrugged and thought that this was not terrible: When one is going to confront something evil, perhaps it's psychologically better to walk through the front, rather than try sneaking around the rear. Of course, he hoped that his sister would have the good sense to break in from the back, as she'd been told. He worried about this detail; Susan had a quality of unpredictability about her, and she might decide something different. In an odd way, he was counting on this.

He stared again at the dark house.

That he could see no light meant nothing. He did not think that his father had fled, or that he'd retired for the night. What he knew was that his father was a man comfortable in the dark, and never impatient as he waited for his quarry to come to him.

Jeffrey gripped the automatic weapon to his chest. It was mainly for show. He did not expect to use it. But arriving at the house armed was part of the illusion.

Once again he breathed out slowly. He'd lingered long enough on the periphery of the lawn, and on the periphery of much of his life itself, and now it was time for him to step forward. Exhaling slowly, crouching at the waist, he broke from the trees and ran fast and hard toward the front of the house. He had one quick thought: that all his adult life he'd been a teacher and a scientist, worlds of planning and results, of study and expectations; and in this moment, he'd launched himself into a world far different, a world of complete uncertainty. He remembered heading into such a place once before, in an abandoned warehouse in Galveston, searching for David Hart. But he'd been accompanied then by a pair of stone-cold detectives, and the urgency he'd felt was merely a shadow of the pressure built around him this night. And this time, despite the presence of his sister and mother moving slowly somewhere in the wide dark behind him, he was traveling utterly alone. He remembered what he'd said to his sister a few days earlier: "If you want to defeat the monster, you must be willing to descend all the way into

Grendel's lair." He could feel his fingers clutching the metal of his weapon. They seemed slippery with anxiety.

Breath came hard as he sprinted forward.

The distance appeared to expand. He could hear his feet slapping against the slick grass, which seemed icy and unstable. He gulped at the night, then suddenly, as if by surprise, the distance abruptly tightened and the main door loomed up in front of him. He raced on, finally throwing himself up against the thick wood, his back to the house, trying to squeeze himself into some smaller shape, gasping for air.

For an instant, he hesitated.

He started to reach for the small crowbar, to force the door open, but something made him stop. He remembered his own apartment door, back at his home in Massachusetts, charged with a shot of electricity. Anyone seeking to break in, he thought, is bound to at least try the door handle first. So instead of forcing the lock with the crowbar, he extended his hand and placed it on the door handle.

It turned in his hand.

Unlocked.

He bit down hard on his lip, holding the handle. He could just make out the small sliding noise of the door hardware mechanism. He slowly pushed against the solid wood.

An invitation, he thought.

I am expected.

He hesitated, letting this last thought fill him with a mingled fascination and terror. He realized that he was opening more than simply the door to a home, but perhaps the door to every question he'd ever had about himself. Still crouched over, he slid through the open space into the house. For a second he wanted to leave the door open behind him, but he knew that made no sense. Using two hands to steady himself, he quietly closed it, shutting away the moonlight outside, darkening the world around him further.

He crept a few paces forward, keeping his back to the door, lifting the machine pistol in his hands. He took another deep breath and started to move slowly, crablike, through the vestibule. He tried hard to keep the house floor plan in his head, mentally going through each space. Entranceway leads to the living room, then to the dining area and kitchen. There are stairs leading up to the right, with bedrooms at the top, sandwiching a small office—that's where he's got the alarm-system monitors. Behind the stairs is a doorway that leads to the basement. It was pitch-black inside the house; he was abruptly terrified that he would stumble and smash into some table or chair, knock a lamp to the floor or crash into a vase and announce his presence in some clumsy, awkward fashion.

He stopped, reaching with his hand for the wall, trying to let his eyes adjust again. He searched his pocket for the red-light, pen-sized flashlight he'd used earlier that evening in the car. He desperately wanted to flick it on, just to give him a chance to see where he was and orient himself. But he knew that he'd expose his position even with the smallest, most insignificant of lights.

Where will he be? he asked himself.

Upstairs? Downstairs?

He took a single step forward, slowly, listening for any sound that might help him in the hunt, concentrating hard. He stopped abruptly, craning forward, when he heard a low, harsh sound, a cry or moan, from somewhere deep and withdrawn. His first thought was that it was the young girl, down in the music room. He took another step forward, putting his hand out in front of him, searching for the opposite wall.

Then he heard a second sound. It sent a jab of cold night through his stomach; it was a small clicking noise behind his right ear, immediately followed by the sudden, horrific sensation of a gun barrel at the top of his neck, like a sliver of ice.

Then a voice, half hiss, half whisper: "If you move, you die."

He froze in his spot.

There was a scratching sound as a hidden closet door pushed open from the wall he'd pressed against seconds earlier, and a small black-clothed shape slid out into the vestibule. The shape, the voice, the pressure of the gun barrel against his neck, all seemed part of the night. Again he heard the voice behind him order: "Place your hands up on your head."

He did as he was told.

"Good," came the voice. Then slightly louder: "I have him."

A second, deeper voice came from the adjacent room.

"Excellent. Take off the glasses."

Like an explosion, the house lights suddenly all flooded on, blistering his eyes, like heat from a furnace door thrown open. Jeffrey blinked hard as dozens of images poured into his vision. Furniture, artwork, designs, carpets. The white walls of the house seemed to glow around him. He felt dizzy, almost as if he'd been slapped hard across the face. He squeezed his eyes shut for a second, as if the light were painful. When he opened them, he found himself staring into eyes that seemed for a second to be his own, as if he were staring into a mirror. He inhaled sharply.

"Hello, Jeffrey," his father said quietly. "We've been waiting for you all evening."

THE LAST FREE MAN

The sudden explosion of light from within the house made Diana Clayton gasp and Susan curse sharply, "Jesus!" almost as if the dark space in front of them had abruptly burst into flames. Both women shrank back from the edge of brightness that raced across the lawn, threatening to expose them at the lip of the forest, not far from where Jeffrey had paused just a few minutes earlier. Susan slowly removed the night-vision glasses from around her neck and tossed them aside. "No sense in carrying these any further," she muttered.

Diana crawled forward, picking up the glasses and hanging them around her neck. The two women lay prone amidst the damp, musty dirt smell of dead leaves and untended wild bushes. The house in the center of the clearing continued to glow with otherworldly intensity, bright, as if mocking the night.

"What's happening?" the older woman asked, still whispering.

Susan shook her head. "Either Jeffrey triggered some sort of internal alarm, which switches on every light in the place, or else they switched on every light in the place and Jeffrey was caught. One way or the other, he's inside, and we haven't heard any gunfire, so I think it's safe to assume that whatever's going to happen has started happening. . . ."

"We need to get around to the back, then," Diana said.

Susan nodded. "Stay low. Stay as quiet as possible. Let's move."

She started to make her way quickly amidst the snarls of bushes and trees, their shadowy path illuminated by the artificial light filtering through the trees, emanating from the house. For a second, Susan found it unsettling; the glow from the house had obliterated the moonlight. It made her feel as if they were no longer alone, and in constant danger of being spotted. She moved swiftly, crouched over, darting from tree to tree like a nocturnal animal fearful of the dawn, working hard to remain concealed. Her mother struggled behind her, pushing aside bushes, an occasional expletive marking the moments when she caught her clothing on a thorn or when a branch snapped back into her face. Susan slowed her pace, in deference to her mother's difficulties, but only slightly; she didn't know if she had lots of time or none at all, but her heart told her to hurry, but not to rush, which was a tricky distinction, she thought, when lives were at stake.

She paused, breathing hard, but not from any exertion, her back up against a tree. As she waited for Diana to catch up, she noticed an infrared eye invisibly piercing the air in front of her. The device was small, barely six inches long, like a miniature telescope. But she knew it was evil, knew why it was there. That she'd spotted it was only luck. She'd probably creased the beam of a half-dozen other devices as they traveled through the forest, she thought. Indeed, the three of them had anticipated as much. It was her brother's job to keep the people inside the house occupied, and prevent them from paying attention to the second wave of the assault.

Diana slumped next to her, and Susan pointed at the device.

"Do you think they've seen us?" Diana asked.

"No. I think they're more interested in Jeffrey." She didn't reveal what she was thinking: If her brother was wrong about this, they might all die that night.

Diana Clayton nodded and whispered, "Let me just catch my breath. . . ."

"Are you all right, Mother? Can you go on?"

Diana reached out and squeezed her daughter's hand. "Just getting a little older, you know. Not quite as ready for a hike through the woods in the middle of the night as you seem to be. All right, let's go now."

Susan considered several responses, all of which immediately seemed foolish, but no more foolish, she realized, than the idea of her desperately sick mother fighting her way through a maze of forest with few thoughts other than murder on her mind. She stole a single quick glance toward Diana, as if trying to measure the older woman's strength and endurance. But she knew she could never accurately assess these qualities with a glance, that it's in the nature of children, no matter how grown, to think their parents either stronger or weaker, more ideal or more flawed, than they truly are. Assuming her mother was filled with resources that she did not even know about, Susan decided she would simply rely on them, whatever they were.

She turned away and took another look in the direction of her father's house. She was struck by the thought that a few weeks earlier she'd felt nothing but confusion toward her brother, and now she was slipping through the damp moss and scraggly bushes, a weapon in her arms, while he exposed himself to the worst of all dangers, relying on her to tip the scales in his favor. She bit down hard on her lip and kept moving.

Diana followed as her daughter moved on, sliding through the obstacles. She had the oddest of thoughts then: Susan was as beautiful as she'd ever seen her. Then a branch snapped back at her and she ducked, and muttering an obscenity, labored forward.

Clutching their weapons, they continued to fight their way through the trees, working steadily and inexorably around to the rear of the target, hoping their progress went unobserved by the occupants of the house.

Jeffrey sat on the edge of an rich dark leather sofa in the large living room of his father's home, surrounded by expensive paintings on the walls, a mixture of modernist vibrant colors splashed across white canvases along with traditional western art, Frederic Remington–styled visions of the Old West—cowboys, Indians, settlers, and Conestoga wagons, in romanticized and noble poses. There were numerous small objets d'art spread throughout the high-ceilinged room: Indian vases and bowls; a hand-hammered copper lamp with a burnished shade; authentic, antique Navajo carpets on the floor. On a glass coffee table, next to a large book about Georgia O'Keeffe, there was a coiled, mummified rattlesnake, mouth agape, fangs exposed. It was a rich man's room, and even if something of a hodgepodge of design and style, it was still furnished with education and exquisite taste. Jeffrey doubted there were any reproductions in the house.

His father sat in a wood and leather armchair across from him. Jeffrey's bulletproof vest, machine pistol, and semiautomatic were collected at his feet. Caril Ann Curtin stood directly behind her husband, one hand resting on his shoulder, the other still gripping a small semiautomatic pistol, either a .22 or .25 caliber, he guessed, and fitted with a cylindrical silencing device. An assassin's weapon, he thought. A weapon that delivers death with stealth and a small, barely noticeable popping sound. Both were dressed in black; his father in jeans and a cashmere turtleneck, Caril Ann in stirruped pants and a hand-knit, woolen sweater. In appearance and atmosphere, he seemed younger than his years. He was extremely trim, still athletic; his skin smooth, stretched

tightly over knotted muscles. There was a feline sense about him, a languid-
ness of motion that undoubtedly hid speed and strength. He toed the weapons
gathered on the floor, a small look of disgust creeping across his face.

"Did you come to kill me, Jeffrey? After all these years?"

Jeffrey listened to the sounds of his father's speech, remembering the
tones from a time long ago, like suddenly being struck, years later, with a
memory of a bad moment behind the wheel of a car, a slick highway, a skid,
a swerve barely survived.

"No, not necessarily. But I did come *prepared* to kill you," he replied
slowly.

His father smiled. "You mean to suggest there was a chance you would
not have shot me down, had your rather bumbling approach actually gone
unnoticed?"

"I hadn't made up my mind." Jeffrey paused, then added: "I still
haven't."

The man now known as Peter Curtin, and once as Jeffrey Mitchell, and
probably other names as well, shook his head, tossing a glance toward his
wife, who acknowledged nothing, but continued to eye the evening's inter-
loper with a wraith's unbridled hatred.

"Really, now? You truly believed that this night could come and go
without one of us dying? I find that hard to imagine."

Jeffrey shrugged. "You will believe what you want," he said briskly.

"That is absolutely true," Peter Curtin answered. "I have always believed what I wanted. And done what I wanted as well." He looked across at
his son with iron eyes. "I am, perhaps, the last truly free man. Certainly the
last free man you will ever encounter."

"That depends on how you define freedom," Jeffrey replied.

"Does it really? Tell me, Jeffrey, you've seen this world of ours. Do we
not lose some of our freedoms every minute of every day? So much so, that
to try to hang on to the few we have, we live behind walls and security, or
move here, to this new state, which wants to create walls with rules and
regulations and laws. None of which can touch me. No, their freedoms are
illusions. Mine are realities."

This was said with a coldness that filled the room. Jeffrey thought he
should answer, perhaps debate, but instead kept mute. He waited while the
small, slightly lopsided, sardonic grin that had occupied the corners of his
father's mouth slowly settled back into neutrality.

"We are missing your mother and sister," Peter Curtin said after a
moment. Jeffrey thought his voice had a slight singsong quality to it, filled
partly with sarcasm, partly with mocking smugness. "I had been looking forward to all of us being here. They would make this reunion complete."

"You didn't really expect me to allow them to come with me, did you?" Jeffrey replied quickly.

"I wasn't certain."

"Expose them to danger? Let you kill us all with just three bullets? You don't think I would believe it smarter to make each of our deaths a little more difficult for you to achieve?"

Peter Curtin reached down, picking up Jeffrey's large nine millimeter and slowly removing it from the harness. He examined the weapon for a moment, as if he found it curious, or strange, then casually chambered a round, flicked off the safety, and took aim directly at Jeffrey's chest.

"Shoot him now," Caril Ann Curtin hissed. She squeezed her husband's shoulder in encouragement, her knuckles white against his black sweater. "Kill him now."

"You didn't make it particularly difficult to achieve your death, did you?" his father asked.

Jeffrey fixed his eyes on the barrel of the gun. He was filled with two raging, contradictory thoughts. *He won't. Not yet. He has not yet got from me what he wants.* And then, just as abruptly: *Yes, he has. This is where I die.*

He took a deep breath, and replied in as dispassionate a tone as he could push past his parched throat and dry lips. "Don't you think that if I'd taken as much time to plan my approach to this house as you do to plan your assassinations, it would be me holding the gun and not you?" He spoke carefully, trying to keep his own words from trembling.

Peter Curtin lowered the weapon. His wife made a low, groaning sound, but did not move.

When Peter Curtin smiled, he revealed polished, perfectly even white teeth. He shrugged. "You ask questions like the academic that you are. With a nice little rhetorical flourish, I note. This tone must be effective in the lecture hall. I wonder, do the undergraduates hang on your every word? And the young women, perhaps their pulses quicken and they moisten between the legs when you come sauntering into the classroom. I'll bet they do." He laughed, reached up and touched the hand of his wife, resting on his shoulder. Then, colder and more calculating in his words, the older man continued: "You are making assumptions about my desires that may or may not be true. Perhaps I mean no harm to either Diana or Susan."

"Really?" Jeffrey asked, arching an eyebrow. "I don't think so."

"Well, that remains to be seen, doesn't it?" his father replied.

"You won't find them again," Jeffrey insisted, putting force into his lie.

His father shook his head slowly. "Of course I will, if and when I want to. I have been able to anticipate every other decision you made, Jeffrey, every other step you've taken. The only one I was uncertain about was whether it would be just you tonight or the three of you blundering ahead, triggering every alarm in the system. The problem was, I could not tell just how great a coward you are, Jeffrey."

"I came, didn't I?"

"You had no choice. Let me rephrase that. *I left you no choice. . . .*"

"I could have sent a SWAT team."

"And miss this confrontation? No, I don't think so. That was never a real option, not for you, your mother, or your sister."

"They're safe. Susan is guarding Mother. She's more than a match for you, anyway. And you won't find them. Not this time. Not ever again. I sent them someplace completely safe. . . ."

Peter Curtin laughed abruptly, a braying, cold sound. "And pray, where would that place be? *This* is supposed to be the 'last safe place.' And I've shown everyone just how great a lie that can be."

"You won't find them. They've gone far from your reach. You've taught me that much."

"I would think that I've shown you in the past few weeks that nothing is beyond my reach."

Peter Curtin smiled again. Jeffrey took a deep breath and decided to take a quick jab, a counterpunch.

"You think too highly of yourself—" He stumbled slightly, a small hesitation as he stopped himself from using the word *Father*. He hurried to fill the void he'd created, adding, "That's not an uncommon phenomenon for killers such as yourself. You enjoy a self-deluding belief that you're somehow special. Unique. Extraordinary. Of course, the truth is the exact opposite. You're just another one of many. Routine."

A flash of darkness slid across Peter Curtin's face, a small narrowing of the eyes, as if he were suddenly staring past Jeffrey's words, directly into his imagination. Then, almost as quickly as it arrived, the look disappeared, once again replaced by the grin and amused tones in his voice. "You tease me. You want to make me angry before I'm ready to be angry. Isn't that just like a child? To try to discover some weakness in their parent and exploit it? But I'm forgetting my manners. You've only met your stepmother, Caril Ann, by experiencing her efficiency. Caril Ann, dear, this is Jeffrey, whom I've told you so much about. . . ."

The woman did not make a motion, nor did she smile. She continued to stare at Jeffrey Clayton with unhidden fury.

"And my half brother?" Jeffrey asked. "Where might he be?"

"Ah, I think you will discover eventually."

"What do you mean?"

"He's not here. He's off . . . ah, studying."

The two men lapsed into a small silence, staring at each other. Jeffrey felt flushed, as if his temperature had risen. The man sitting across from him was both a stranger and an intimate, a man he knew everything and nothing about. As a student of killers, as a pursuer, as the Professor of Death, he knew much; as a child of the man, he knew only the mystery of his own emotions. He felt an odd dizziness, wondering what it was they shared and what they didn't. And, with every inflection of his father's voice, every gesture he made, every little mannerism that emerged, Jeffrey felt a stab of fear, wondering whether that was the way *he* spoke, the way *he* looked, the way *he* acted. It was like staring into a carnival funhouse mirror and trying to measure where the distortion started and where it quit. Jeffrey felt as if he'd breathed the same air, or drunk from the same glass, as a man suffering from some highly virulent, deeply infectious disease. And all that remained was the incubation period—to find out whether or not the virus had taken root within him.

He sucked in air sharply. "You will not kill me," he said bluntly.

His father grinned again, a man enjoying himself immensely. "I may," he replied, "and then again, I may not. But this time you ask the wrong question, son."

"And what is the right question?" Jeffrey demanded.

The older man arched a single eyebrow, as if astonished either by the tone of Jeffrey's response or because his son did not know the answer. "The question is: Do I have to?"

Jeffrey thought the heat in the room had increased suddenly. His lips were dry. It was his own voice he was listening to, but the words seemed to be alien, as if spoken by someone else, someone foreign and far away. "Yes," he replied. "I think you must."

Again his father looked amused. "Why is that?"

"Because you could never be certain again. Never be sure I wasn't out there, hunting you. And never be certain that I would not find you another time. You cannot function unless you feel safe. Completely safe and secure. It is an integral part of your makeup. And, knowing I still lived, you could never be absolutely free from doubt."

Peter Curtin shook his head. "Oh yes," he said. "I can guarantee those things."

"How?" Jeffrey demanded sharply.

His father did not respond. Instead, he reached out to an adjacent reading table and removed from it a small, handheld electronic device. He lifted it so Jeffrey could see. "Usually," his father said, "these things are for young parents, with newborn children. I think your mother used one when both you and your sister were born, but I can't recall with precision. It's been a long time. Anyway, they are remarkably effective."

Peter Curtin pushed a switch and then spoke into the electronic intercom. "Kimberly? Are you there? Can you hear me? Kimberly, I just want you to know: your only chance has finally arrived."

Curtin pushed another switch, and Jeffrey heard a tinny, frightened voice push beyond some static:

"Please, somebody, please, somebody help me—"

His father clicked the switch, severing the voice in midplea.

"I wonder if she'll live," he said with a laugh. "Can you save her, Jeffrey? Can you save her and your sister and your mother and yourself? Are you that strong and that smart?"

He grinned again. "I don't think that's possible. Not to save everyone."

Jeffrey didn't answer. His father continued to stare at him.

"Have I raised you right?"

"You had nothing to do with raising me."

Peter Curtin shook his head. "I had everything to do with raising you." He held up the intercom again.

"What has she to do with—" Jeffrey began.

"Everything."

Again both men were quiet.

Into this silence, Caril Ann Curtin whispered once again: "Peter, let me kill them both now. Please. I beg of you. We still have time."

But Peter Curtin merely dismissed this request with a wave of his hand. "We are going to play a game, Jeffrey. A most dangerous game. And she is the sole piece."

Jeffrey sat mute.

"The stakes are large. Your life against mine. The lives of your mother and sister against mine. Your future and their future against my past."

"What are the rules?"

"Rules? There are no rules."

"Then what is the game?"

"Why, Jeffrey, I'm surprised you don't recognize it. It is the most basic game of all. The game of death."

"I don't understand."

Peter Curtin smiled wryly. "But of course you do, Professor. It's the game they play in the lifeboat, or on the side of the mountain when the rescue helicopter arrives. It's played in foxholes and in burning buildings. It's who lives, who dies? It's making a choice knowing just how cataclysmic for someone else your choice will be."

He waited, as if expecting to hear a response, but received none, and continued: "Here is the game for this night. You kill her and you win. She dies, and you win your life and your sister's and mother's and my own, for you will be free to take it. Or, if you so choose, turn me in to the authorities. Or you could simply exact a promise from me to never again kill, and I will honor that pledge. That way you could let me live and not stain your hands with that most Oedipal of bloods. But the selection will be yours. Whatever you wish. I will be at your disposal. And all you have to do to win is to kill her . . ."

The air in the room seemed stifling.

". . . kill her for me, Jeffrey."

The older man paused, watching the impact of his words on his son's face. He held up the intercom, clicked the receiver button, and for a few seconds let the room fill with the harrowing sound of a terrified young woman sobbing.

The distance between the edge of the forest and the rear of the house was shorter than in the front, but still a substantial pond of light to cross. Susan Clayton eyed the space with wariness; it was about the same length she could throw a fly with accuracy toward a cruising fish. She could almost hear the swishing sound of the line above her head as she grunted and released it forward, zipping across the blue choppy waters of her home. This was something she knew she was good at, measuring just how much effort it took to deliver a small illusion of feathers, steel, and glue directly to the path of her quarry. She was less certain of her ability to measure how quickly she herself could cross the open space.

Diana Clayton, as well, was assessing their position.

It did not fully make sense to her. She breathed slowly, trying to organize her thoughts. Both she and her daughter were lying prone on the damp earth, staring ahead, but her mind was elsewhere, trying to remember every detail of a life a quarter century earlier, and, more important, every feature of the man she'd lived beside.

"I can get across," Susan whispered. "But only if no one is watching." Then she shook her head. "If someone is, I won't make it five feet before they see me." She paused. "I don't suppose I have much choice."

Diana reached out her hand and grasped her daughter's forearm. "Something is not quite right, Susie. Help me out for a minute."

"What?"

"Well, first, we know there are two doors back here. The routine back door, which we can see, that heads into the kitchen. It's just like any rear door. Or at least, it appears that way. And then there's a concealed door that leads from the music room outside. We need to find that. It should be over there, to the left, next to the garage."

"Okay," Susan said, "we'll work in that direction."

"No, something else is bothering me. We should come across the off-house. You know, the one the builder said wasn't on the plans. That should be located back here somewhere. I think we should find it."

"Why? Jeffrey's in the house. So is he. . . ."

"Because," Diana said carefully, "what precisely is the point of having an alarm system? Why make certain that if someone approaches through the woods, or down the driveway, you can monitor their progress? Why install this fancy, illegal system, here in this state?" She shook her head. "I can think of only one reason. To give yourself some time. To warn you. It's not to protect him from anything, especially the police. It's simply a warning system that will allow him a few minutes' head start, right? Give him a slight edge of time. Why would he need that?"

The answer to this question was obvious. Susan replied in a low voice filled with understanding. "Only one reason. Because if someone came looking for him, someone who knew who he was and what he's been doing, he wanted time to be able to exit. To run."

Diana nodded. "That's how I see it," she said.

"An escape route," Susan went on, thinking aloud. "David Hart, the man in Texas whom Jeffrey took me to see—he said to expect that. A way in. A way out."

Diana rolled over, peering into the darkness behind her. "What was it the contractor said was back there?"

Susan smiled. "Wild. Empty. Undeveloped. Badlands and mountains. Conservation land. State forest. Goes for miles and miles . . ."

Diana stared into the blackness of the night that seemed to have creeped along behind the two of them, sliding on their heels as they had worked their way through the woods. "Or perhaps," she said quietly, "that's the back way out of the Fifty-first State."

The two started to move backward, away from the rim of light, angling obliquely away from the house, searching the tangle of trees behind them. The underbrush seemed thicker, like so many bony hands grabbing at their clothes, scratching at their faces. Despite the coolness of the night, they were sweaty, both with exertion and tension, and probably fear as well. Susan felt as if she were trying to swim in some fetid mire. She pushed forward aggressively, fighting the forest as if it were some enemy. The light from the house was diffuse, difficult, and their progress seemed marred by shadows and pits of black. Susan swore under her breath, took a step, found her sweater gripped by a thorn bush, pulled at it and lost her balance, tumbling forward with a small cry. Her mother, struggling just as hard behind her, called out in a stage whisper: "Susan! Are you okay?"

Susan did not at first respond. She was sorting through several things—the surprise of the fall, a gash from a thorn on her cheek, a blow to her knee from a rock, but most important, a sensation of cold metal beneath her hand. The darkness made it extremely difficult to see, but she groped forward, ignoring all other sensations, and abruptly felt a sharp point, which cut her palm. She gasped in sudden pain.

"What is it?" Diana asked.

Susan did not answer her for a moment. Instead, she felt about the sharp point carefully, finding a second, then a third, all concealed beneath scrub brush and weeds.

"I'll be damned," she said. "Mother, check this out."

Diana moved to her hands and knees, taking up a stance next to Susan's. She let her daughter guide her hand forward until she, too, felt the row of stakes in the ground.

"What do you suppose—"

"We're on the right track," Susan said. "So, imagine you were heading this way, but you didn't want anyone in any vehicle to be able to follow you. These would do the trick nicely on a set of tires, wouldn't they? Move carefully, there may be other traps."

Ten feet farther, Susan came across a low axle-breaking trench dug into the earth. She turned back toward the house. It glowed, perhaps a hundred yards away, throwing light into the sky. She could just make out the narrowest of channels through the forest, leading to the light. It was a path, she thought, but one littered with enough shrubs and bushes so that if you didn't precisely know the direction, you would end up, as they had, ensnared by the undergrowth. But if you did know the proper route, you'd be able to move with quickness through exceedingly difficult terrain.

"There it is," her mother said suddenly.

Susan turned, letting her eyes adjust once again to the night, and saw where Diana was pointing. Another twenty feet in front of them was a small building, almost invisible amidst trees and growth. It was slung low, a single story, and weeds and ferns had been planted to grow up the sides and over the roofline. They approached the building slowly. There was a garage-type door in front. Susan reached for it, then stopped.

"There might be an alarm," she said. "Or maybe a booby trap."

She didn't know if she was right about this, but the possibility was strong. And if she was clever enough to think there might be a device on the door, she told herself she ought to honor that suspicion.

Diana had worked her way around the side. "There's a window," she said.

Susan hurried to join her. "Can you see inside?"

"Yes. Barely."

Susan pushed her nose to the cold glass and stared into the building. She sighed slowly. "You called it, Mother. You were right."

The two women could just make out the square form of an expensive, modern four-wheel-drive vehicle, painted in camouflage colors. From what they could see, it was loaded with bags, packed and ready to depart.

Diana stepped back from the window. "There'll be a road. Not much of one, probably, but a road. It'll head back through the trees. He'll have a path mapped out, an escape route. . . ."

"But what about planes, or maybe choppers?"

Diana shrugged. "Mountains, canyons, forests—who knows? He'll have thought about how he would be pursued, and anticipated it. You know, there's probably another garage, somewhere miles from here, with another vehicle. And maybe a third, up near the Oregon border. Or over toward California. Probably there, if you think about it. An easy state to get swallowed up inside. And not that long a run down to Mexico, and there are even fewer questions asked down there, especially for a rich man."

Susan nodded.

"It doesn't have to be perfect. It just has to be unanticipated. That's all he would need. Just a crack, and he'll slide through."

Susan turned back toward the house, taking a deep breath. "I have to get inside," she said. "This has taken too long, and Jeffrey may be in real trouble." She turned to her mother, who was sucking wind from the cold night. "You stay here," she said. "Wait for something to happen."

Diana shook her head. "I should stick with you."

"No," Susan replied. "What we don't want is for him to escape. No matter what happens, he can't get away. And also, I think I can move faster and make decisions easier if I know you're at least safe down here."

Diana could see the logic in this, even if she didn't like it.

Susan pointed at the obscure path through the underbrush toward the house. "That's the route. Keep an eye on it."

For an instant she wanted to embrace her mother, utter something maudlin and affectionate, but she fought off the urge. "See you in a little bit," she said with phony enthusiasm. Then she turned and started to make her way as swiftly as possible back to where she thought her brother was surely hanging on by the barest of psychological threads.

Jeffrey's throat was parched, as if he'd run a fast race on a hot, dry day. He licked at his lips, trying to find some moisture, discovering none. His voice sounded brittle. "Suppose I refuse?" he asked.

His father shook his head. "I don't think you will. Not when you really examine the offer I'm making."

"I won't do it."

Peter Curtin shifted about in his seat, as if his son's response was inadequate, unfinished. "That's a knee-jerk, uninformed decision, Jeffrey. Review the offer more carefully."

"I don't need to."

His father frowned. "Of course you do," he said, with a half mocking, half exasperated tone, as if he was unsure which was more appropriate. "The alternative, for me, of course, is to simply turn to my beloved wife here and take the advice she's been so insistent about. How hard would that be, do you think, Jeffrey, for me to say to Caril Ann: 'You solve this dilemma for me'? And you know what she would do."

Jeffrey shot a glance toward the hard-eyed woman, who remained rigid, her finger moving ever so slightly on the trigger to her pistol. She continued to glare at him, holding back her anger with the barest of restraints. He thought that just as his father had anticipated this meeting, so had she. He wondered what it was that he'd said to her over the years, and over all the murderous events they'd shared, to prepare her for this last act. Like blooding a dog, slowly, surely. Her eyes remained fixed on him, her muscles taut beneath her sweater. And like that dog, whose whole essence is wrapped up in the single command from its master, she was waiting for the right word. He thought: This is a woman who has put aside every thought or feeling, leaving only rage within her. And all that rage is directed at me. The force of Caril Ann's gaze was like standing in the face of a strong, evil wind.

"Still reluctant?" his father asked. "Still hesitant?"

"I cannot do it," the son replied.

Peter Curtin shook his head from side to side, in exaggerated disappointment.

"Cannot do it? Ludicrous. Anyone can kill, given the proper incentive. Hell, Jeffrey, soldiers kill on the flimsiest of orders from officers they've learned to hate. And their reward is considerably less than what I'm offering you this night. Anyway, Jeffrey, what do you really know of this girl?"

"Not much. A senior in high school. She had a relationship with your other son, I believe. . . ."

"Yes. That's why I chose her. That plus the utter convenience of her schedule and her habit of taking a shortcut through a delightfully abandoned section of our new little town. Actually, I've always liked her. She's personable, a little confused about life, but then, so are most teenagers. She's attractive, in a fresh, untouched way. She seems bright—not overly, you know, not exceptional, but intelligent nonetheless. Certainly heading to a good school. It's hard to tell precisely what sort of future, though. Now, others are brighter, more accomplished, but Kimberly has a quality about her, an adventuresome quality. A little bit of rebelliousness—I suppose that's what attracted your half brother to her—that makes her more interesting than the majority of the cookie-cutter kids this state produces."

"Why are you telling me this?"

"Ah, you're right. I shouldn't. Who she is shouldn't be a part of the equation. That she has a life, dreams, hopes, desires—whatever, well, that's not really important, is it? What is it about this young woman that makes you think for one instant that her life is more valuable that your own? Than your sister's, and your mother's? And the lives of how many other young women whom I might select in future days to come? It seems to me that this is the simplest of decisions. If you kill her, you save yourself. And then, as an added incentive, you save all these other people. You can bring an end to my career, even my life, as I said. Killing her makes sense financially, economically, aesthetically, and emotionally. One life lost. Many lives saved. Justice obtained. The cost seems extremely small."

Peter Curtin smiled at his son. "Hell, Jeffrey, you kill her and you'll become famous. You'll be a hero. A hero for this modern world we live in. Flawed, but decisive. You'll be celebrated from coast to coast by virtually everybody, with the possible exception of young Kimberly's next of kin. But their protests should be minimal. And that's even if they're heard at all, which is a question, considering how effective the folks who operate this state are at covering up unpleasantness. So, really, I can't imagine why you would hesitate for even a single split second."

Jeffrey didn't reply.

"Unless . . ." his father continued slowly, "you're scared of what it is you'll find out about yourself. That could be a problem. Is there some window deep within you, Jeffrey, that you don't want to open? Not even the smallest crack, because you're afraid what you might let in? Or out, perhaps . . ."

Peter Curtin was clearly enjoying himself. "Ah, I suppose that might make the price of this one eminently forgettable young lady's death slightly higher than we first envisioned. . . ."

This was a question Jeffrey was not willing to answer.

He stared across at the couple in front of him, measuring the glint in his father's eyes, contrasting it with the deep cold in the wife's. They seemed oddly matched at that moment. The woman was coiled, wound tight, eager to kill. His father, on the other hand, seemed to be loose, generous with words, unconcerned with time, enjoying every second of the dilemma he was delivering. For him, the killing was merely the dessert; the torture was the main course. It was not hard for Jeffrey to imagine from his father's mocking tones how harsh the last minutes of so many lives had been.

The brightness of the room, the heat building up around him, the steady lilting pressure of his father's words, all conspired to press on his chest like the force of deep water. He wanted to struggle to the surface, gasping for air. He realized in that second that he'd fallen into the most elemental trap of all, and one that the man sitting across from him had known his child would stumble directly into: that the distinction between his father and himself was the subtlest of lines; he cared for lives. His father did not.

He wanted to live.

His father, who had taken so many lives, did not care whether he lived or died that night. His agenda was far different.

Jeffrey remained quiet, trying to find composure within each difficult breath of stifling air.

Time, he thought abruptly. You need to steal time.

His mind started working rapidly. His sister had to be closing in, he thought, and her arrival might swing the balance just enough to extricate him from the noose his father had slipped around his heart. And then, beyond Susan's arrival, there would be the State Security forces.

The situation seemed viselike, tightening with every second.

He looked at his father. Fence with him, he thought. "How can I trust you?"

Peter Curtin smiled. "What? Not trust the word of honor from your very own father?"

"Not trust the word of honor from a killer. That's all you are. I may have come here with questions, but you've answered them for me. Now all I have to do is answer a few questions of my own."

"Isn't that life?" Curtin replied. "And who knows more about the game of life and death than I?"

"Perhaps I do," Jeffrey responded. "And perhaps I know that it's not a game."

"Not a game? Jeffrey, I'm surprised. It's the most intriguing game of all."

"Then why are you willing to give it up tonight? If, as you say, all I have to do is to put a bullet between the eyes of a complete stranger, will you then just bow your head and receive whatever it is I choose for you? I don't think so. I think you're lying. I think you're cheating. I think you have no intention of doing anything other than kill me tonight. And how am I to know that Kimberly Lewis actually lives? You could be triggering a tape recording with your little intercom there. Maybe she's like all the others, abandoned and thrown away, trashed and spread-eagled in the woods somewhere she won't be discovered—"

Curtin raised his hand rapidly, a flash of near anger crossing his face. "They were never abandoned! That was never the plan."

"The plan? Sure," Jeffrey said sarcastically. "The plan was to enjoy fucking them and killing them like every other twisted—"

Curtin made a sudden slashing gesture with his hand. Jeffrey expected to hear fury in his father's voice, but instead listened to the coldest of calculated tones.

"I'd expected more from you," Curtin said. "More intelligence. More education." He put the fingertips of his hands together in front of him, then peered over the bridge his hands made, staring deeply at his son. "What do you understand about me?" he asked abruptly.

"I know you're a killer—"

"You know nothing," Curtin interrupted. "You know nothing! You do not know how to behave in the presence of greatness. You show no respect. You understand nothing."

His father shook his head. "It has nothing to do with simply killing. Killing is the easiest thing of all. Killing for desire, killing for fun, killing for whatever reason. It is the simplest thing, Jeffrey. It is merely a diversion. If one puts his mind to the study of it all, it really presents little challenge. The challenge lies in creating out of death . . ." He paused, before adding: ". . . and that's why I'm special."

For a moment father stared at son, as if this was all something the child should have seen before.

"I've been prolific, but others have been as well. I've been savage, but that, too, is no great shakes. Did you know, Jeffrey, that there came a day, a number of years ago, when I stood over the body of a young woman *knowing* I could walk away from that spot and no one would ever have the slightest comprehension of the depth of feeling, the profound sense of accomplishment, that I had? And in that moment, Jeffrey, I realized that it was all too easily accomplished. I ran the risk of getting bored by that which I thought was my reason for living. In that second, I considered suicide. I considered other mad acts, terrorism, mass murder, political assassination, and discarded them all, for I knew that then I would be dismissed and forgotten. And never understood. But my desires were higher, Jeffrey. I wanted to be remembered. . . ."

He began to smile again. "And then I learned about the Fifty-first State. This new territory filled with so many hopes and dreams and this truly American vision of the future based on the oh so idealized vision of the past. And who fit into that vision more than I?"

Jeffrey said nothing.

"Who is remembered, Jeffrey? Especially out here, in the West. Who are the heroes? Do we honor Billy the Kid, with his twenty-one victims, or his disgraceful ex-friend, Pat Garrett, who shot him down? There are songs about Jesse James, a murderer of savage proportions, but none about Robert Ford, the coward who put a bullet in his back. It has always been that way in America. Melvin Purvis interests us very little. He seems dull and calculating. But John Dillinger's exploits live over the years. Doesn't it embarrass us when a drone like Eliot Ness puts away an Al Capone? On tax and jury-tampering charges! How pathetic. Do you remember who prosecuted Charlie Manson? Come on, Jeffrey: Aren't we more intrigued by proving that Bruno Richard Hauptmann didn't do it, than feeling sorry for Lindbergh's baby? Did you know that in Fall River they still celebrate Lizzie Borden—an axe murderess, for goodness' sakes? I could go on and on. But we are a nation that loves its criminals, Jeffrey. Romanticizes their bad deeds and ignores their horrors, replacing them with song and legend and the occasional festival, like D. B. Cooper Day up in the Pacific Northwest."

"Outlaws have always had a certain appeal. . . ."

"Precisely. And that is what I have been. An outlaw. Because I will steal from this state its most important feature: its safety. And that is why I will be remembered."

Peter Curtin sighed. "I've already achieved that. Regardless what happens to me tonight. You see, I can live or die. My history is assured. It is assured by your presence and by the attention this night will get before it's over."

Again there was a momentary silence in the room, before the killer spoke again.

"Now we have reached the moment for a decision, Jeffrey. You are a part of me, I know. Now you must reach down and seize hold of that part we share, and you must make the obvious choice. It is time, Jeffrey. Time for you to learn about the real nature of killing."

He looked at his son: "Killing, Jeffrey, will set you free."

Curtin stood up. He quickly reached over to the small reading table and opened a drawer with a short scratching noise. From inside he removed a large army-issue knife, which he slid from an olive-drab scabbard. The polished steel of the serrated blade reflected the room's light. Curtin admired the weapon, just stroking the dull edge for an instant, then flipping the knife over and placing his finger against the cutting edge. He lifted his hand and showed Jeffrey a thin rivulet of blood on his thumb.

He watched for his son's reactions. Jeffrey tried to maintain as blank a face as possible, while inwardly his emotions pulled at him like a sudden riptide off the beach in summer.

"What?" Curtin said, once again grinning. "Did you think I would let you undergo this experience with something as antiseptic as a gun? Where all you had to do was close your eyes, say a prayer, and pull a trigger? As removed and clean as a firing squad? That would not help you find the road to real understanding."

Curtin abruptly tossed the knife across the room. It flashed in the air for an instant, before it thudded on the carpet at Jeffrey's feet, still glistening, almost as if it were alive.

"It is time," his father said. "I have no more patience for delay."

THE MUSIC ROOM

Susan once again paused at the edge of light, surveying the rear of the house. She let her gaze work slowly from a far corner, all the way past the obvious rear door, slowly absorbing everything she could see, until she reached the end of the house. As her brother had, she noted the gravel beneath the windows, and spotted the thorn bushes surrounding the perimeter. These were tangled together in an impenetrable mass save for a single, three-foot-wide break just across from where she was poised. She realized instantly that the break in the barrier would lead directly to the alleyway through the forest, and then down toward the hidden garage where Diana was waiting patiently for something to happen.

For an instant Susan stared at this small gap. It had the appearance of a landscaping oversight, as if a single plant had died and been removed, and then she realized what it was: the other door.

From where she was poised, she was unable to make out the shape or size of the door. The wall of the house appeared to be seamless. Had the contractor not told them of the door, she would not have believed it was there. She could not tell where the handle was hidden, or how it opened, and she realized, as well, that it was actually possible there was no way to open the door from outside. But she thought it far more likely that there was some concealed latching system. The problem would be finding it.

And finding it unlocked.

There's no more time, she thought.

Susan took a final glance at the windows, trying to spot her brother or any kind of motion within, hoping for some indication of what was happening, but she saw no activity. She tightened the muscles of her arms, squeezed her leg muscles, spoke to her body as if it were a friend, saying, "Move quickly, please. Don't hesitate. Don't stop. Just keep going, no matter what happens." She took a deep breath, gripped her machine pistol tightly, and suddenly, without being aware of rising and stepping forward, found herself racing in a half crouch across the expanse of light. She was aware, in that second, only of the awful brightness that appeared to surround her with heat and grab at her with a sharpness that seemed razored. The cool air of the forest abruptly dropped away, replaced by a steamy asthmatic wheezing wind. She thought her feet leaden, as if encased in stone, and each time her foot skidded down on the damp grass with the most meager of slapping sounds, she thought instead it was like a ringing bell. She believed she heard voices crying out in alarm. She believed she heard sirens starting to blare. A dozen times she heard the cracking sound of gunfire, and a dozen times anticipated bullets slamming into her as she ran on the blade edge between reality and hallucination. She reached out for the house like a swimmer, out of breath, straining for the wall at the end of a desperate race.

And then, just as quickly as her run started, she was there.

Susan tossed herself into a slight shadow, cowering close to the wide wooden clapboard siding, trying to make herself small and inconspicuous, after having been so large and clumsy and loud as she ran. Her chest heaved with exertion, her face was flushed, and she gulped away at the night, trying to calm herself.

She waited for a moment, letting the drums of adrenaline in her ears start to fade, and then, when she felt, if not in complete control, at least tethered to it, she twisted about and, kneeling in the dirt, started to run her hands over the house, trying to find the door she knew was there.

Susan felt the rough texture of the wood beneath her fingers, thought it cold, and then found the smallest of ridges, hidden by the clapboard panels. She continued to search, and discovered a pair of metal hinges concealed by wood. Encouraged, she began testing each panel, expecting one to lift up and reveal a handle that could turn. She had not yet begun to consider what she would do if the door were locked; the small crowbar was still stuck in her belt, but its value was questionable.

She tested each piece of wood but found no knob.

"Damn it," she hissed. "I know you're here somewhere."

She continued pulling at each piece, without success.

"Please," she said. She bent down farther and ran her hands along the space where the wooden framing of the house was joined to the concrete of the foundation. There, beneath the lip of the wood, she felt a metal shape, not unlike a trigger. She fingered it for a second, then closed her eyes, as if she expected the device to explode when she pushed it, but knowing she had no choice.

"Open sesame," she whispered.

The latch mechanism made a small thunking sound, and the door slid free.

She hesitated again, just long enough to take a single, deep breath of what she thought might be the last safe air she'd ever taste, and then slowly, gingerly, began to slide the door open. It moved with a nasty, creaking sound, as if small pieces of wood were being splintered. She tugged it open perhaps eight inches, then peered around the edge, into the house.

She was looking down into a black space. The only light in the room was the single diffuse slice from the illumination in the yard that penetrated back through the crack she'd made by opening the door. There was a small wooden landing, and then a modest flight of steps leading down toward a shiny, reflective flooring that seemed almost plastic in its glow. She guessed it was some slick, nonporous material. Easily cleaned. The walls of the room were a stark, glistening white.

Susan pulled the door open slightly farther, enough to allow herself to creep in, and the extra light scooted into the far corners of the room. She heard the voice only an instant before she saw the figure, crouched against a wall.

"Please," Susan heard. "Don't kill me."

"Kimberly?" Susan answered. "Kimberly Lewis?"

The face that had been hiding turned toward her, filled with sudden hope. "Yes, yes! Help me, please, help me!"

Susan saw that the young woman's wrists and ankles were handcuffed, and that a steel chain held her to a ring embedded in the wall. There were two other, as yet unused rings at shoulder height, spread apart. Kimberly was naked. As she bent toward the floor, like a dog cowering, afraid it would be hit, her ribs showed, as if she were emaciated.

Susan stepped through the door, blocking the weak light for an instant, then moving away from the entrance, allowing the little light to guide her down the steps and to the young woman's side.

"Are you all right?" she asked, which she thought a remarkably stupid question. "I mean," she amended, "are you injured?"

The teenager tried to grab at Susan's knees, but the chain prevented her from moving more than a foot or two in any direction. She was streaked with dried blood and feces around her legs. She smelled of diarrhea and fear.

"Save me, please, save me," the panicked teenager repeated.

Susan stayed beyond the reach of her hands. Sometimes, she realized, you should reach out for the drowning person. Other times, keep your distance because they might drag you down into the water with them.

"Are you hurt?" she demanded sharply.

The teenager sobbed and shook her head negatively.

"I'll try to save you," Susan said, surprised at the coldness in her own voice. "Is there a light in here?"

"Yes, but no. The switch is in the other room, outside," the girl replied, gesturing with her head toward a door at the far side of the room. Susan nodded, and swept her eyes over the space she could see. There was a large roll of what appeared to be plastic sheeting propped up against one wall. The ceiling was thickly soundproofed. Ten feet from where Kimberly was chained, in the center of the room, Susan saw a single stiff-backed wooden chair and a gleaming, tubular, steel music stand with several booklets of music open on it.

Susan walked across the room slowly. She carefully put her hand on the door leading to the main part of the house. The handle would not turn. The door was locked. She saw a single dead bolt, but there was no key to open it from the interior of the room.

The key is on the other side, she thought. This is not a room that anyone is expected to leave. She was unsure, in that second, why her father had not locked the hidden door leading to the outside world. The thought chilled her suddenly that he *wanted* her to arrive from that direction.

She snatched a breath in near panic.

He knows I'm here. He saw me run across the field. And now I'm cornered, right where he expects me.

She pivoted sharply, looking longingly toward the exit, a voice within her telling her to escape, to seize the moment and flee while she still had just the smallest of chances.

She struggled to maintain control over her emotions. She shook her head, inwardly insisting: *No. It's okay. You ran and you weren't spotted. It's still safe.*

Susan looked over at Kimberly, and realized in the same instant that flight was not an option. For a moment she wondered if this was the last game her father designed for her. A simple, deadly game, with a simple, deadly choice. Save yourself, leave her to her death. Stay, and face whatever will come through that locked door.

Susan felt her lower lip quiver with doubt.

Once again she looked at the girl. Kimberly was watching her with wide-eyed piteousness. "Don't worry," Susan said, surprising herself with a confidence she thought was ill-deserved. "We'll be okay." As she spoke, she saw a small, black shape a few feet away from the teenager's legs, just outside her reach, lying on the floor by the wall.

"What's that?" she asked.

The girl swiveled with difficulty, restrained by the cuffs, locked into position. "An intercom," she whispered. "He likes to listen to me."

Susan's eyes widened in abrupt fear. "Say nothing!" she whispered frantically. "Don't let him know I'm here!"

The girl was about to reply, but Susan leapt across the room and clasped a hand over her mouth. She bent down, nearly nauseated by the smell, and hissed into Kimberly's ear: "All I have is surprise."

If that, she thought.

She held her hand in that position until the teenager nodded in comprehension. Susan lifted her hand and leaned back toward the girl's ear. "How many upstairs?" she whispered.

Kimberly held up two fingers.

Susan thought: two plus Jeffrey.

She hoped he was still alive. She hoped that her father hadn't been listening on the intercom system when she came through the door. She hoped he would need to show her brother his prize, because she could think of nothing else to do except wait.

Standing up next to the teenager, she marked with her eyes where the door leading to the rest of the house was. Then she moved to the stairs, counting the steps it took her to reach the base. There were six risers up to the landing. Placing her hand on the wall, she climbed toward the exit.

This was too much for the panicked teenager.

"Don't leave me!" she cried.

Susan pivoted, anger creasing the air between them. The look in her eyes silenced the girl. Then she reached out and, with another deep breath, pushed the outside door closed, dropping the room into complete and utter black. She turned carefully on the landing, once again placing a free hand on the wall. She counted the steps as she descended into the darkness, then counted again as she paced across the room. The smell from the teenager helped her find the girl. Kimberly Lewis gave a small cry, a half sob of both terror and relief when she realized that Susan had returned to her side.

Susan slumped down next to the chained girl.

She placed her back against the wall, facing across the music room. Hefting the machine pistol in her hand, she realized it would not serve her purpose that night. It was designed to spray fire indiscriminately, killing everything within the parameters of its swing. This was useless, she realized, unless she was willing to risk killing her brother as well as her father and the woman he now called his wife. For a half second she thought it a reasonable risk, but then understood it was not one that she'd expect her brother to take were their positions reversed. So she placed this most efficient of killing devices on the floor next to her, close enough where she could find it if she had to, and close enough to Kimberly's hands so that maybe it would save her. Instead, Susan reached for the nine-millimeter pistol in the shoulder harness beneath her vest. It was hot in the room, and she tugged off her cap and shook her own hair free. Kimberly, cringing, pushed herself as close to Susan as her restraints would allow. The teenager breathed sharply, terrified for an instant, then relaxed slightly, as if reassured by Susan's presence. Susan touched the girl on the arm, trying to settle both their nerves. Then she clicked off the safety on the pistol, chambered a round, and took aim at the black space in front of her where she believed the entranceway to be. The gun felt heavy in her hands, as if she were suddenly exhausted. She rested her elbows on her knees, keeping the weapon pointed straight ahead, and waited that way, like a hunter in a blind, for the quarry to arrive, telling herself to be patient, to be steady, to be prepared. She hoped she was doing the right thing. She didn't see any alternative.

Jeffrey walked with a condemned man's pace.

Caril Ann Curtin was directly behind him, the silenced muzzle of her automatic pistol pressed into the small hollow behind his right ear, a pressure that effectively prevented him from any foolishness, such as wheeling about and trying to fight. Then, marching in the rear, his father followed, like a priest in a procession, except that instead of a Bible, he carried the hunting knife. Caril Ann would tap the gun against his skull when he was expected to change direction.

The house and its furnishings seemed out of focus. He could feel his faculties of control sliding away in fear at what was happening, and he struggled inwardly to keep a grip on rational thought.

Nothing had happened as he'd expected.

He had anticipated a single confrontation between himself and his father, but that hadn't materialized. Everything was muddied. Indistinct. He could see no feeling, no emotion, no direction with any sort of clarity. He felt like a small child on the first terrifying day of school, being pushed out the door away from safety, security, and everything he'd taken for granted. He breathed in sharply, searching for the adult within him, battling against the child.

They reached the doorway leading to the basement area.

"Down we go, son," Curtin said.

Descending into Hell, Jeffrey thought.

Caril Ann tapped the pistol against his head firmly.

"There's a famous story, Jeffrey," Curtin continued as they went down the stairs. " 'The Lady or the Tiger.' What is it behind the door? Instant death or instant delight? And did you know there was a sequel to that tale? It was called 'The Discourager of Hesitancy.' That is what you should consider my lovely wife here. The discourager of hesitancy. Because indecision is punished sharply in this world. People who do not seize their opportunities are abandoned quickly."

They reached the basement. It was a finished rec room, furnished in a modern design. There was a large-screen television on one wall, with a comfortable leather couch a few feet away, arranged for viewing. His father paused, picking up an electronic channel changer from a coffee table. He pointed this at the screen, clicked it, and a huge picture of static jumped onto the television, streaking it with gray and white lines of interference.

"Home movies," his father said.

He clicked the device a second time, and a washed-out video leapt into focus. His father must have pushed the mute button, for there was no accompanying sound, which made the images all the more horrific. On the screen, Jeffrey saw a naked young woman, hanging by her wrists from rings on a wall. She was pleading with whoever held the camera, tears and panic creasing her face. The camera zoomed in on her eyes, in the last stages of exhaustion, fear, and despair. Jeffrey choked as he recognized the living face of the last victim, a face he'd known only in death. His father pushed another button, and the picture froze on the wall-sized screen.

"It still seems distant, doesn't it?" his father asked, his voice picking up some quickness of enjoyment. "Faraway and impossible. Unreal, although we both know it was once very real and very intense. Super real, maybe."

His father punched the clicker again, and the image disappeared.

Caril Ann pressed the gun barrel against his head sharply, pushing him across the rec room toward the door to what Jeffrey knew was the music room.

Curtin smiled. "All the decisions from here on in are yours. All the choices are yours. You have all the information. You have had all the lessons. You know everything you need to know about murder except one thing: What it is to take a life yourself."

Curtin stepped to the side of the door, reaching out and flicking a light switch. Then he turned the dead-bolt key in its lock. Like a surgeon's assistant, he reached out, seized Jeffrey's right hand, and slapped the handle of the hunting knife into it. Now that he was modestly armed, Caril Ann dug her gun's muzzle into his flesh. Curtin looked back at Jeffrey, grinning, taking a total and absolute delight in the agony he was delivering. The passion for this moment seemed to glow in his face, and Jeffrey realized that years earlier he'd been saved by his mother, but like a foolish child who will not believe in what to the world seems right, he had never completely understood that he'd been free, that he'd been safe, but through obstinacy, bad luck, and indecision had brought himself right back to the moment when he was nine years old, looking back over his shoulder at the man standing next to him now. He should never have looked back. Not once in twenty-five years. And instead, all he'd done with his entire life was look back, and finally, what had been behind him all along had caught up with him, and was now designing a ruin to his future.

He wanted to fight back, but didn't know how.

"Caril Ann," Curtin said briskly, "will discourage any act of hesitancy." Once again father's and son's eyes met across the gap of time and despair. "Welcome home, Jeffrey," he said as he opened the door to the music room.

The soundproofing was effective; neither Susan nor the whimpering, panicked teenager huddling beside her had been able to hear the people approaching the room, so that when the overhead ceiling light burst on, both young women gasped sharply. Susan managed to stifle a scream only by biting down hard on her lip. Sweat crept into her eyes, stinging them, but she did not move, save to adjust her aim, narrowing her gaze down the barrel of her pistol.

Her finger tightened on the trigger as the door abruptly swung open, and she held her breath. She heard a single word in a voice that carried through decades of memory, but the only figure she saw was her brother's, half stumbling, half pushed, through the doorway.

He looked across the room and their eyes met.

In her vision she was abruptly aware that there were other figures, directly behind him, and in that second she cried out:

"Jeffrey, dive right!"

And then she started firing her weapon.

Hesitation can be measured in the smallest of time frames. Microseconds. Jeffrey heard his sister's command and acted upon it, throwing himself toward the floor, out of the line of fire, but not quite quickly enough, for the first shot from the nine millimeter came crashing in his direction, tearing into the flesh above his hip, creasing his waist.

As he rolled to the floor, red pain filling his eyes, he was aware that Caril Ann had instantly stepped forward and dropped to a kneeling position, her own weapon barking out with small popping sounds, shots muffled by the silencer. But each of her replies was answered by the deeper roar of the nine millimeter as Susan tugged desperately at the trigger. Bullets spattered the door frame, splintering wood, sending up plumes of dust as they hit the wall.

There was a scream as a shot struck home. He couldn't tell where it came from. Then a second. He was deafened by the noise of the firing. He spun about, half rising, slashing with the knife at the woman beside him, the blade finding the forearm and wrist that held the automatic pistol. Caril Ann howled in sudden pain and swung her weapon toward Jeffrey, the barrel only inches away, when there was a single, last booming sound in the small room, coming from Susan's weapon, which rose above the noise of screams and his own voice bellowing in terror. This shot struck the woman directly in the forehead, her face seeming to explode in front of him, a shower of scarlet spitting at him, pitching her backward.

The room echoed with noise and death.

Jeffrey slumped back, aware that he was shouting something incomprehensible, staring at the destroyed face of the woman he'd never known. Then he spun toward his sister. She was white-faced, frozen in her compact shooting position, still gripping the nine millimeter, propped up on her knees. The action had thrust back, the clip emptied, but she continued to pull uselessly on the trigger. He could see blood on the wall behind her, and more blood dripping onto her sweatshirt.

"Susan!"

She didn't reply. He scrambled across the floor toward her, reaching out for her. His hands hesitated above her, trying to determine where she was hit, almost as if he was afraid to touch her, as if she were suddenly fragile and too much pressure might cause her to shatter and break. It seemed to him that one shot had creased her ear, slicing the lobe before crashing into the wall behind her. Another seemed to have clipped her leg—her jeans were rapidly staining with deep maroon—and a third had struck her shoulder but been deflected by Agent Martin's bulletproof vest. He tried to put reassurance in his voice.

"You're wounded," he said. "You'll be all right. I'll get help." The pain in his own side seemed electric, red-hot.

She looked pale, terrified.

"Where is he?" she asked.

"But I'm right here," came the voice behind them.

The teenager started to wail then, a single, pent-up shriek of complete panic as Jeffrey spun about and saw that his father was crouched down in the doorway, just above the twisted body of Caril Ann Curtin. He had picked up his wife's automatic, which he now pointed at the three of them.

Diana heard the volley of gunfire and felt a great shaft of fear plunge directly through her body. The silence that followed the spasm of shots was

equally terrible, equally frightening. She jumped forward, found herself running as best she could through the darkness of the forest, heading toward the
light of the house. Every twig, every blade, every vine that littered the path
threatened her progress. She stumbled, righted herself, pushed ahead, trying
to make her mind nothing more than a blank, pushing away from the rim of
her consciousness the horrifying visions of what might have happened. As
she ran, she seized the pistol that her daughter had given her, thumbing off
the safety mechanism, readying herself to use it.

She reached the edge of darkness and stopped.

The silence that faced her was like a wall. She breathed in broken shards
of cold air.

Peter Curtin stared across the room at his two children and the lost
teenager, who shuddered and sobbed. His eyes met Susan's and he shook
his head.

"I was wrong," he said slowly. "So, Jeffrey, it turns out that it's your
sister who is the killer."

Susan, suddenly exhausted by her wounds and tension, lifted her pistol
again, tugging at the trigger.

"You would kill me?" her father asked.

She dropped the nine millimeter to the floor, where it made a metallic
crack.

"In chess," she said, speaking slowly, as if exhausted, "it's the queen
who has the power and makes all the crucial moves."

Curtin nodded. "Touché," he said blithely. "You probably could have
handled that fellow in the men's room without my assistance," he added. "I
sold your capabilities short."

The killer lifted the gun, starting to take aim.

Into that small moment, Jeffrey realized he had to fight hard with something other than a gun or knife. With a single, deep burst of understanding he
saw how to stymie the man across the room from him.

He smiled. Right through the wounds and pain.

It was sudden. Unexpected. A look that made his father pause.

"You've lost," the son said.

"Lost?" the father said after a moment. "How?"

"Did you count?" Jeffrey demanded sharply. "Did you?"

"Count?"

"Tell me, father, are there three rounds left in that pistol? Because if
there aren't, well, then this is where you'll die. Right here, in this room you
made. I'm surprised. Did you design it with your own death in mind, as well
as all those others? That doesn't seem like you."

Curtin hesitated again.

Jeffrey barreled on, almost laughing.

"Just precisely how many times did your beloved wife and helpmate fire that weapon? Let's see, the clip holds what? Seven shots? Nine? I think seven. Now, it was her weapon, so are you really familiar with it? And was she in the habit of putting an eighth round in the chamber? Look around, you can see holes in the wall. Susan is bleeding as well, from how many different spots? How many shots did your wife squeeze off before Susan blew her forehead off?"

Curtin shrugged. "It makes no difference," he said.

"Oh, yes, it does," Jeffrey replied. "Because the rules of the game seem to have changed, haven't they?"

His father did not immediately reply, and Jeffrey gestured toward the Uzi, cocked and ready, near his sister's feet. He would have had to reach across her to seize the weapon. Kimberly Lewis was closer, and Jeffrey saw that her eyes, panicked though they were, had found the weapon. He knew that if either grabbed for it, his father would fire.

"I'm sure you're familiar with a weapon such as that," Jeffrey continued, keeping his voice level, cold, and confident. "It's the stupidest of weapons, really. Just blows the hell out of everything. Sort of a nonspecific killer, unlike you. Don't even have to aim the damn thing, just pick it up, start swinging it back and forth and pull the trigger. Kills to the right, kills to the left. Makes an unholy mess of things." He hoped that the teenager understood his directions.

"I'm aware of that," Curtin replied, a touch of anger creeping into his voice. "I still don't see how—"

"So, here's your choice," Jeffrey said, interrupting, mocking his father's own words. "Your first question is: Can I kill everyone? Because if I do not have three bullets left, then I die right here. And who will it be who kills you, Father? Shoot me, and that leaves Susan, whose proficiency has already been demonstrated. Shoot the two of us, and it will be little Kimberly there who grabs the Uzi from the floor and blows you straight to oblivion. And won't that be an ignominious end to all your greatness? Shot to shreds by a scared teenager. That will probably cause some amusement amongst the other killers in Hell when you join their ranks. Why, I can fairly well hear them laughing in your face already. So, Father, it's your decision now. What will work? Who will you kill? You know, there was a lot of gunfire in a very quick minute. I wonder if there are any shots left at all? But maybe there's one. Perhaps you should just use that on yourself."

Jeffrey, Susan, and the teenager all held still, frozen in a tableau.

"You want to bluff me," Curtin said.

"One way to find out. You're the historian. Who's holding the aces and eights?"

Curtin smiled. "Dead man's hand. A very interesting stalemate, Jeffrey. I'm impressed."

The killer looked down at the weapon in his hand, seemingly trying to tell what the clip contained by hefting it like a piece of fruit. Jeffrey inched his fingers toward the Uzi on the floor. So did Susan.

Curtin looked at his son. "Green River killer," he said slowly. "You recall him? And then there's my old friend, Jack, of course. Let me see, ah, yes, the Zodiac killer from San Francisco. And then the Houston headhunter. Los Angeles gave us the Southside Slayer. . . . You know what I'm saying?"

Jeffrey breathed in deeply. He knew exactly what his father was saying. These were all killers who'd disappeared, leaving police baffled as to who they were and where they'd gone.

"You're wrong," he replied. "I'll find you."

"I don't think so," Curtin answered. Then, moving steadily, surely, keeping the small automatic trained on the three of them, the killer made his way across the room. He climbed up the stairs to the exit door, paused, grinned, and without saying another word, threw the door open and jumped through, just as his son and daughter simultaneously grabbed at the machine pistol. Jeffrey's hand was faster, but by the time he'd lifted the gun and pointed it at the spot where his father had been standing, the killer was gone, the door slamming shut behind him.

Susan coughed once. She tried to say the word *Mother* before she lost consciousness, but was unable. Jeffrey, too, riveted with pain, felt a dizziness that threatened to tumble him out of consciousness. His bluff had taken even more energy than he thought he had. Gripping the wound in his side, he struggled forward, trying to lift himself back to his feet, worried mainly about his sister, and only then remembering that his mother, as well, was somewhere close by. He pushed himself toward the steps, nearly passing out, like a drunkard on the deck of a tossing ship. He did not think he could make it up the stairs, but knew he had to try. His ears suddenly started ringing with exertion and his eyes spun. In some foreign spot within him, he hoped they would all live through that night, and then he, too, slipped backward, slumping to the killing floor and into a total black exhaustion.

Diana saw a man's form emerge from the hidden door and recognized it immediately, simply by the predatory way he moved. The force of recognition after so many years drove her back a lucky step, for it removed her from any residual light, sliding her into a deep shadow by a tall, thick tree. She saw her onetime husband pause in the middle of the lawn and examine the weapon he held in his hand. She saw him remove the clip and heard him bray out a single fierce laugh before throwing aside the emptied gun. Then, like an animal searching for a scent on the wind, he lifted his head. She craned forward also, and at that second heard the distant noise of a police siren approaching fast and knew that their driver had accomplished the task Jeffrey had set him to.

She pushed herself closer to the tree and the solid darkness of the forest. She saw Peter Curtin turn and lope toward her, moving quickly, but not in panic, as efficient as an athlete who had practiced a single play over and over, and now, finally, had been called upon to run that sole play amidst the tension of the game's last second.

He seemed to know precisely where he was going.

She put both hands on the revolver and readied herself. Suddenly, she could hear his footsteps against the ground, the swishing of branches as they tugged at his clothes, and then the raspiness of his breathing as he hurried toward the garage and the hidden vehicle.

Curtin was only a few feet away, parallel to the tree where she was concealed, when Diana stepped from the shadow, just behind him, simultaneously lifting the revolver with both hands as Susan had taught her, and whispering: "Do you want to die now, Jeff?"

The force of her voice, as low as it was, was like a blow in the back, nearly knocking him over. Curtin stumbled, then righted himself, stopping abruptly. Keeping his back to his ex-wife, he lifted his empty hands up in the air. Then he slowly pivoted to face her.

"Hello, Diana," he said. "No one has called me Jeff in such a long time. I suppose I should have guessed you'd be here, but I assumed they'd want to keep you someplace significantly safer."

"I am someplace safer," Diana replied. She cocked the hammer of the pistol back. "I heard the shots. Tell me what happened. Do not lie to me, Jeff, because I will kill you now if you do."

Curtin hesitated, as if trying to assess if he should run or make a leap at her. He eyed the pistol in her hands and realized that either choice was fatal.

"They're alive," he said. "They won."

She remained silent.

"They'll be okay," he said, repeating himself, as if that would be convincing. "Susan killed my other wife. She's a helluva shot. I was most surprised. Very calm under rather difficult circumstances. Jeffrey, too, kept his wits about him. You should be proud. *We* should be proud. Anyway, they're both wounded, but they'll survive. Back to teaching and writing puzzles, I suppose, before too long. Oh, and my little guest for the evening, Kimberly, she's okay, too, although precisely what the future holds for her remains to be seen. Tonight, I think, has been singularly difficult for her."

Diana did not reply, and he stared hard at the weapon in her hand.

"It's the truth," he said, shrugging. He smiled. "Of course, I could be lying. But then, if I am, what difference would it make, one way or the other?"

Diana realized there was a perverse logic in this.

The noise of the sirens grew closer.

"What are you going to do, Diana?" Curtin asked. "Turn me in? Shoot me here?"

"No," Diana said quietly. "I think we'll take a trip together."

With the gun barrel, she gestured toward the garage.

Diana sat in the backseat of the four-wheel-drive vehicle, keeping the barrel of the revolver pressed up against her ex-husband's neck as he drove through the narrow darkness of the forest. The lights and sirens rushing toward Buena Vista Drive rapidly disappeared behind them; they headed deep into a blacker, older world than the one they'd left behind. The headlights carved out weird, twisting shafts of light as Curtin steered a path between stands of trees, thumping over rocks and pushing through bushes. They were on the wildest of trails, something that resembled a road only in the smallest sense, but still, a path that Diana was absolutely certain the man in front of her had mapped out beforehand and traveled at least once, testing his escape route.

He'd nervously asked her to uncock the weapon, afraid that a sudden sharp bounce through the undercarriage might make her finger just pressure the trigger enough to fire the Magnum, but she'd replied to this request with a single statement: "You should drive cautiously. It would be sad to lose your life to a bump on the road."

Curtin had opened his mouth, but then stopped. He concentrated on the ground that loomed up in the lights before them.

They continued to drive, the car pitching on the rough terrain like a boat broken loose from its mooring in the rough waters of a squall. Time seemed to slip through the darkness. Diana listened to her former husband breathe, remembering the sound from years before, when she would lay in their bed at night struggling with indecision and fears while he slept. She thought him completely familiar to her, that even with the changes of the years and the surgeries and the weight of all the evil he'd performed upon the world, she still totally understood him.

"Where are we going?" he asked after several hours had passed.

"North," she replied.

"Badlands," he said. "That's what's to the north. The road gets worse."

"Where were you intending to go?"

"South," he replied, and she believed him.

"Is there another garage? Another vehicle stashed somewhere?"

Curtin nodded, with a small, nervous grin. "Of course. You were always clever," he said. "We could have made a really effective team."

"No," she said. "That's not true."

"Yes, you're right. You always had a weakness about you that would have ruined everything."

Diana snorted. "And that's what I've done. I've ruined everything. It just took twenty-five years."

Curtin nodded again. "I should have killed you when I had the chance."

Diana smiled in reply. "Now, isn't that the statement of a weak and cowardly soul. Bemoaning lost opportunities."

She pushed the pistol up hard against his neck.

"Drive," she said.

She stole a quick glance through the window. The forest had thinned, turned rocky, dustier, filled with more scrub brush. To the east there was the barest insinuation of light creeping over the ridge of hills. They seemed to have risen in altitude, climbing through the rough terrain. The car struck some shale rock, skidding, and her finger almost pulled the trigger.

"I think this is far enough," Diana said. "Stop the car."

Curtin did as he was told.

They got out and began to walk through the first gray tones of dawn, single file, husband in front, the wife with the gun a few paces behind. Diana saw that there was a reddish yellow streak of the distant sky, and their trail was slowly coming into the focus brought on by the first weak strands of morning light.

The two of them marched wordlessly up a small hump of rock, rising above a small canyon. It seemed a deserted place, empty of life and far from any memory of the modern world. Diana could sense the mustiness of ancient time in the air, battling with the freshness of the day that was taking grip around them.

"Far enough," she said. "I think we've come far enough. Do you remember what was said when we were married? You put it in a letter once."

The man she'd known as Jeffrey Mitchell, and now as Peter Curtin, stopped and turned to face his ex-wife. He didn't reply to her question directly, instead saying: "Twenty-five years." He smiled. A skeleton's grin.

He moved closer to her, his arms spread wide, but coiled as well. "A long time has passed. We've been through a great deal. There's much to talk about, isn't there?"

"No, there isn't," she replied.

And then she shot him in the chest.

The gun's report seemed to tumble into the empty air of the canyon, rebounding off the walls, echoing up into the fading dark of the sky. The man she'd once married staggered back, eyes wide, astonished, his black shirt marred with a sudden burst of red. His mouth opened as if to say something, but the words choked him. Then he stumbled, like a marionette whose strings have been suddenly sliced, before finally pitching backward, sliding down the face of the rock. He fell free of the earth for just a single second, disappearing from her sight. She listened until she heard the sound of his body thudding against the hard ground somewhere distant and far away.

Diana sat down on a boulder, dropping the pistol. It clattered and fell away from her. She was suddenly exhausted. Old and tired, she thought. Old, tired, and dying. She reached into a pocket and removed a vial of pills. She stared at these for a moment, thinking it odd that not since hours earlier, when the night had begun, had she felt even the slightest twinge of pain from the disease within her. But she knew it to be coy, and every bit as treacherous as the man she'd just killed. And so, with a single, sharp gesture, she defiantly poured the entire contents of the vial into her palm, gripped the pills tightly for a single moment, then threw them all deep into her mouth, tossing her head back and swallowing hard.

She thought then of her children, and knew that of all the lies her one-time husband had told her, the only truth was that they lived, and now they were free. Both of him and of her and of her disease. She believed herself free, finally, as well.

This made her feel warm. She leaned back against the rock, finding it surprisingly comfortable, like the softest bed, surrounded by the deepest pillows. She took a long breath of air. She thought it as cool and refreshing as any drink she could remember from the coldest, clearest mountain streams of her childhood. Then Diana slowly turned her face toward the light of the rising sun and patiently waited for her old companion Death to find her.

EPILOGUE:
THE PSYCH 101
MIDTERM EXAM

It took close to two weeks before Diana Clayton's body was spotted by a State Security helicopter flying a search grid above and deep beyond the boundaries of the state's northern conservation land. The discovery was made early on the morning that both Jeffrey and Susan were scheduled to be released from the hospital in New Washington and two days after the Congress of the United States overwhelmingly voted to permit the inclusion of the Fifty-first State into the Union.

Frustrated, even before he regained his strength, Jeffrey had fought hard with the surgeons, demanding to be released from the hospital, wanting to accompany the State Security search teams that fanned out from the house at 135 Buena Vista Drive, seeking the conclusion to that night, but he'd been prevented. Susan, recovering in her bed, felt less compelled, as if she'd inwardly known with precision every detail of what had happened that night in the hours after their father fled the music room, and after both of them passed out from tension, loss of blood, and shock.

Curiously, the helicopter team had been able to extract Diana's body from the canyon ridge, but the narrowness of the landscape prevented them from descending into the ravine in search of Peter Curtin's remains. They'd been able to spot them from the air, but it would have required a team of mountain-proficient climbers to recover the body. This was an expenditure Security Director Manson refused to authorize.

He'd shown up at the hospital on the day of their release brimming with enthusiasm over the vote in Congress, fresh from meetings where a state-wide celebration was being planned for that weekend: fireworks, fire engines with sirens wailing, brass bands marching, baton-twirling cheerleaders, Boy Scout–type parades down the main streets of all the new towns, grandiose speeches and back-thumping congratulations. An old-fashioned, red, white, and blue, hot dogs, lemonade, and sarsaparilla, glorious Fourth sort of party, the onset of winter notwithstanding.

"You are of course not welcome to attend," he cheerily explained to the brother and sister. "Your visas, alas, have expired."

Manson handed checks to both Jeffrey and Susan. He said to Susan: "We really didn't have an agreement, of course, the way we did with your brother. But it seemed only fair."

"Hush money," Susan replied. "Keep-my-mouth-shut money."

"Which," Manson answered glibly, "spends as effectively as any other sort. Perhaps even better."

"I suppose young Miss Lewis is also being compensated for her injuries and for her silence?"

"Four years of college paid for. Therapy paid for. And an upgrade from a brown development to a green one for her family, at the state's expense. A new position, with a raise, for her father. The same for her mother. Oh, and we threw in a couple of cars, too, so they could commute to their new jobs in better style. Actually, the cars belonged to your late father and oh so wicked stepmother. There were a few other perks to the package, but it was the most remarkably easy job to sell to her family and to the young woman herself. I mean, they like it here, and really did not wish to leave. Certainly didn't wish to say or do something that might upset this particular apple cart."

"People will still talk," Susan insisted.

"Will they?" Manson replied. "No, I don't think so. They don't want to talk about those sorts of things. They don't want to believe that they can happen. Especially not here. So, I think, instead, they will be quiet. Have a few nightmares, perhaps. But remain quiet."

Manson reached down and opened a briefcase. He removed a two-week-old copy of the *New Washington Post* and tossed it to Susan. She saw the headline: SHOOTING ACCIDENT CLAIMS LIFE OF STATE EMPLOYEE. Next to the story was a photograph of Caril Ann Curtin. She stared at this, then turned to her brother.

Jeffrey was shaking his head, eyeing the check Manson had handed him. "The cost has been high."

"Ah, you have my sympathies. But your mother, I believe, did not have much time anyway—"

"That is correct," Jeffrey said, cutting him off. His voice had an angry edge to it. "But what is the price of six months? Or a single month? A week? A day? Maybe a minute? Every second is precious to a child."

Manson smiled. "Professor, it seems to me that you've asked questions that your mother has already answered most bravely, and to question further only serves to diminish her accomplishment."

Jeffrey closed his eyes for a moment. Then he nodded in agreement. "You're a clever man, Mr. Manson," he said. "In your own way, every bit as clever as my father was."

Manson smiled. "I will assume that is a compliment. You will be leaving soon? Today would be fine."

"He never mailed that letter to the newspapers, did he? The one that had you so damn panicked. And the letter that brought us to his home. But you lucked out, right? The weight of all that negative publicity never arrived at your doorstep, did it?"

"No," Manson said, shaking his head. "He did not mail the letter. We were most fortunate on that score."

"I wonder why he didn't," Susan said.

"There's a reason," Jeffrey replied. "There was a reason for everything. We just don't know precisely what that particular reason is."

He turned toward the politician, who was sitting in an uncomfortable armchair, but whose delight over the way events had turned out made him impervious to any discomfort.

"You know that he would have won. He was absolutely, one hundred percent correct about the effect that letter would have had. You would have spent the next six months making excuses and lying to every media outlet in the nation. And the vote in Congress? I don't know."

"Oh," Manson replied, with a small wave of his hand, "I knew that. I knew that all along. Public opinion is fickle. Safety is fragile. One can only cover up and obscure so much before either the truth emerges or, worse, some mythology, some rumor or what they call an urban legend takes over. This, I think, is the only question that remains, as far as I'm concerned, Professor. Why, when he'd done so much to bring you, your sister, and your late mother here, and after doing so much to torpedo the creation of this state, did he hesitate at the final act? The act that would have guaranteed him success, whether he lived or died. I find that most intriguing, don't you?"

"It worries me," Jeffrey said.

Manson smiled. He rose from his seat, stretching as he did so. "Well," he said with finality, "that's a worry you can take with you." He nodded at Susan Clayton, did not offer to shake hands, and exited the room.

Not far from Lake Placid, deep in the core of the Adirondack Mountains, there's a place called Bear Pond, which is reached by canoeing across the larger water of Upper Saint Regis Lake, past the hand-hewed logs of the great, antique estates that dot the water's edge, until one finds a small landing between the sentinel lines of deep green pines and firs. From the landing there's a half-mile portage to a smaller, swampier body of water, filled with the twisted, graying skeleton trunks of fallen trees, littered and choked with expanses of lily pads and silence. This second body goes without a name. It is shallow, unsettling. A dark, murky spot that one passes through rapidly. Then there's a second portage, not more than two hundred yards through pine needles and the white dust of the first snows that arrive in that part of the world from the north, carrying cold, Arctic winds and the promise of a harsh winter, because all the winters there are hard. At the end of the second portage, Bear Pond begins. The shoreline is rocky, a gray granite leading to the deep, rich green world of the forest, surrounding water that is crystalline and clear, deep, and filled with the shimmering shapes of rainbow trout hanging suspended in an opaque world. It's a place with few compromises; a chilled beauty, absorbed by quiet and the occasional ethereal laugh of a loon. Osprey work the blue-cold air above the pond, hunting for the occasional foolhardy trout that rises too close to the surface.

It had been Susan's idea to take Diana's ashes there.

This the brother and sister had done, finding an old fishing guide willing to accompany them. The morning was clear, frost-filled. The lakes had not yet iced over, though that time was probably only days away. There was a small breeze, just an occasional gust of frigid wind that penetrated the bright sunshine, reminding them that the world around them was closing down. The rich men's camps, built a century earlier by Rockefellers and Roosevelts, were boarded up and silent. They were alone on the lake.

The guide handled the rear, while Jeffrey took the bow, paddling rapidly against the cold, the light, ashen color of his paddle dipping and disappearing into the frigid water. Susan sat in the middle of the canoe beneath a red plaid blanket, clutching a small metal case with their mother's ashes, listening to the rhythmic sound of the canoe swishing across the lake.

When they reached the shore of Bear Pond, the breeze seemed to die down. The canoe crunched in the rocky gravel, and Susan could see the first ridges of ice forming at the water's edge. The guide left them alone while he went to scrape away some of the wet snow in the center of a modest clearing and begin building a small fire.

"We should say something," Susan said.

"Why?" Jeffrey asked.

His sister nodded, and then, with a great swing of her arm, threw the gray ashes out over the pond.

They stood, watching the surface for a few minutes while the ashes spread, dispersed, and finally sank like so many puffs of smoke into the clear water.

"What are you going to do now?" Jeffrey asked.

"I think I'll go home where it's warm all the damn time, and as soon as I get there, I'm going to fire my skiff right up and zip out and get up on a flat where there's nobody else and hang there smelling the salt air until I spot some old permit cruising around, looking for something nice to eat and not paying a helluva lot of attention to me. And then I'm going to lay a little puff crab fly right on his stupid nose, and surprise the hell out of him when he feels that hook. That's what I think I'll do."

This made Jeffrey smile, and he hunched his shoulders against the growing cold. "That makes sense," he said.

"What about you?" Susan asked.

"Back to the salt mines. Get my teaching schedule set. Work on the spring semester courses. Get into long, incredibly boring, and ultimately useless arguments with the other members of my department. Watch another bunch of thankless, illiterate, and generally spoiled students arrive at the university. It doesn't sound nearly as much fun as what you have in mind."

Susan laughed. "There's the difference between you and me," she said. "I suppose."

She looked up into the wide expanse of blue sky. "It's clear," she said. "But I think it will snow hard soon enough."

"Tonight," Jeffrey agreed. "Tomorrow at the latest."

They turned together, away from the pond.

"I guess we're orphans now," she said.

There were 107 students signed up for his next quarter Psychology 101, Introduction to Aberrant Behavior lecture series. Killing for Fun, One-oh-one. He did his usual speeches on thrill killers and perverts, and spent a little additional time on mass murderers and explosive rages. He devoted almost one entire lecture to the subject of the Dusseldorf killer, Peter Kurten, who had provided his father with his new name out in the Fifty-first State. He wondered why his father had chosen that particular killer to honor.

Kurten had been a savage, himself the product of incest and sexual abuse, a pervert with a disarming manner, utterly no feelings toward any of his victims except, oddly, the last, a young woman whom he'd inexplicably released from torture after she'd begged for her life by promising him that she would not tell a soul of what he'd done to her. Why he decided to release this young woman—when undoubtedly a dozen others had pleaded similarly for their lives—remained a mystery. Of course, she'd gone directly to the police, who'd gone straight to Kurten, arresting him and the family he'd surrounded himself with. He hadn't bothered with any attempt to flee, or even to defend himself in his subsequent trial. Indeed, the lasting image of Peter Kurten that his executioners came away with was that the killer became actively aroused at the thought of his own blood spurting free in the split second that the guillotine sliced through his neck. Kurten walked to the scaffold with a grin on his face.

His father, Jeffrey thought, had honored evil.

The midterm exam in Psych 101 was a blue-book essay test, an hour long. The students filed silently into his lecture hall, sullen, as if inwardly enraged that they would be tested. They jammed the seats as he looked at his watch, checking the time. He had the ubiquitous blue-book folders handed out and watched the students write their names on the covers.

"All right," he said. "No talking. If you need a second booklet, hold up your hand and I'll bring you one. Questions?"

A girl whose hair was spiked into a porcupine-styled headdress held up her hand: "If we finish early, can we leave?"

"If you want," Jeffrey replied. He supposed the girl had some assignation, or else had not bothered to study and didn't want to waste her entire morning sitting around unable to answer test questions. He looked around the room, saw no more hands, then went to the blackboard at the front and started writing. He hated that moment, his back to more than a hundred students, all of them furious that they were being required to take a test. Vulnerable, he thought. At least none of the alarms had gone off that morning.

In a corner of the lecture hall a campus security officer sat on a steel folding chair. Jeffrey now requested a policeman for every test. The officer wore body armor, which had to be uncomfortably hot in the jam-packed room, and swung a long graphite truncheon between his legs. His machine pistol hung over his shoulder. The man looked bored, and as Jeffrey wrote on the blackboard, he nodded to the officer, trying to get him to pay closer attention to the students in the auditorium.

There were two parts to the test. In the first part, students were asked to identify and describe the people whose names he placed on the board. These were a variety of killers, all of whom he'd discussed in lectures. The second part was a choice of essays from two questions:

(1) Although Charles Manson did not accompany the killers to their destination, he was still convicted of the murders. Discuss why, and what his influence was on the actual perpetrators of the crimes. Explain why this made Manson different from other killers we have studied.

(2) Explain and contrast Ted Bundy's attack at the Chi Omega House with Richard Speck's murder of the eight nurses in Chicago. Why were they different? What similiarities were there in the crimes? What social impact did they have on each community?

He finished writing on the board and returned to the seat behind his desk. While the students settled into writing, he picked up the morning newspaper. There was a story he found discouraging stripped across the bottom of the front page. A professor of Romance languages at nearby Smith College had been shot and killed the night before while walking across the campus shortly after dark. The professor's assassin had apparently walked up behind the man, removed a small-caliber pistol, and fired a single shot into the base of the skull before disappearing, unseen and unidentified, into the shadows. Police were questioning many of the teacher's former and current students. Especially the ones who'd flunked his courses. He was a notoriously hard marker in an era when high grades were given out routinely for impoverished work.

He continued to read, moving to the sports pages—another bribery and point-shaving scandal on the basketball team—and then to the local section. As he read, students started finishing the exam. He had placed a small, plastic basket at the foot of the lecture podium. They tossed the blue books into this and filed out. Occasionally one would be slow at the door, and he'd hear a snatch of laughter or complaints from the exiting figures. By the time the bell signaling the end of class rang, the room had emptied.

He gathered the blue books, thanked the bored campus cop, and returned to his small office in the Psychology Department. As was his custom, before starting to correct the tests, he counted them, to make sure that each student had handed in his booklet.

He was surprised when his tally reached 108.

This made him look curiously at the pile of tests. One hundred seven students in the course. No one asked for a second booklet. But 108 results. His first thought was that this was part of some elaborate cheating scam. It wouldn't have been the first time students had tried some such invention. With some of the more creative efforts, he thought if the students had only spent the same time studying, they wouldn't have had to resort to cheating. But he understood, as well, that the nature of modern education sometimes made deception preferable to learning.

He counted again. The numbers were the same.

Jeffrey flipped through the stack, wondering what form the cheating was going to take, when he noticed that one of the blue books did not have a name on its jacket. He sighed, thinking he'd accidentally dropped a blank book in with the completed ones, and pulled it from the pile.

He idly flipped it open, just to be certain.

Inside the blue book was a handwritten note:

You see, if one really wanted to kill the professor who had stolen so much from them, it would not be that hard. One way would be to obscure the true motive for the murder. You could do this easily, say, by randomly executing faculty members at the other four universities and colleges in nearby communities. Kill two others, then kill the actual target, then two more. You'll probably recognize this scheme, Professor. Agatha Christie came up with it in *The ABC Murders*. Written in 1935, almost a century ago. In that book, it took a clever Frenchman, a speaker of a Romance language, to figure out the plot. I wonder if that novel is still in print. I wonder if any of our local police are as smart as Hercule Poirot. That's just one idea, though.

I have others.

Our father taught me much. He always said I would need to be well educated in order to successfully take on the Professor of Death. Destroying the new world where I was raised is probably less of a challenge, so I think that either tomorrow, or maybe next year, but sometime soon, I will head home to the Fifty-first State. On our last night together, our father and I shared some ideas about what sort of terror I could bring to all their smug securities.

I just wanted you to know that I will return for you when I'm ready.

The note was not signed, which didn't surprise him.

Jeffrey Clayton felt an emptiness inside him, but not one that was created by fear, or by anxiety in the face of a threat, or even sadness. He thought he had suddenly learned much, and that all his life, knowledge had been the only thing that separated him from his father and the other men like him.

He felt a small, wry smile form on his face, and he understood then why his father hadn't mailed his sensational letter to the newspapers. *Because he knew what he was leaving behind.* A different sort of legacy. And what he'd left had all the potential in the world to rise far above his own accomplishments. Fathers and sons.

Jeffrey set the blue book aside. He welcomed the acquisition of even this unsettling information with a cold, harsh enthusiasm. He stared at the note one last time and realized also that the dead professor on the front page of that morning's paper was as much a part of the note as the handwritten words in front of him. He suspected he should be frightened, but instead he was intrigued and energized.

He shook his head. *Not if I find you first*, he silently said to the ghostlike image of his brother.

ABOUT THE AUTHOR

JOHN KATZENBACH is the author of five previous novels: the Edgar Award–nominated *In the Heat of the Summer*, which was adapted for the screen as *The Mean Season*; the *New York Times* bestseller *The Traveler*; *Day of Reckoning*; *Just Cause*, which was also made into a movie; and *The Shadow Man*, another Edgar nominee. Mr. Katzenbach has been a criminal court reporter for *The Miami Herald* and *Miami News*, and a featured writer for the *Herald*'s *Tropic* magazine. He lives in western Massachusetts.